THE IRON
AND
THE LOOM

a novel of Italy

Flavia Idà

Cover design by Niki Lenhart
nikilen-designs.com

Published by Paper Angel Press
paperangelpress.com

ISBN 978-1-944412-08-1 (Trade Paperback)

10 9 8 7 6 5 4 3 2

For more information about the author and her work visit:
flaviasvoice.com

Dedication

For my sister Anna, who never stopped believing in me,
and for my father Salvatore, who taught me fairness before all things.

With thanks to
Adnan Aydin, Laureen Hudson, Daniel J. Langton,
Niki Lenhart, Steven Radecki and Rocco Sabatino
for their help and support.

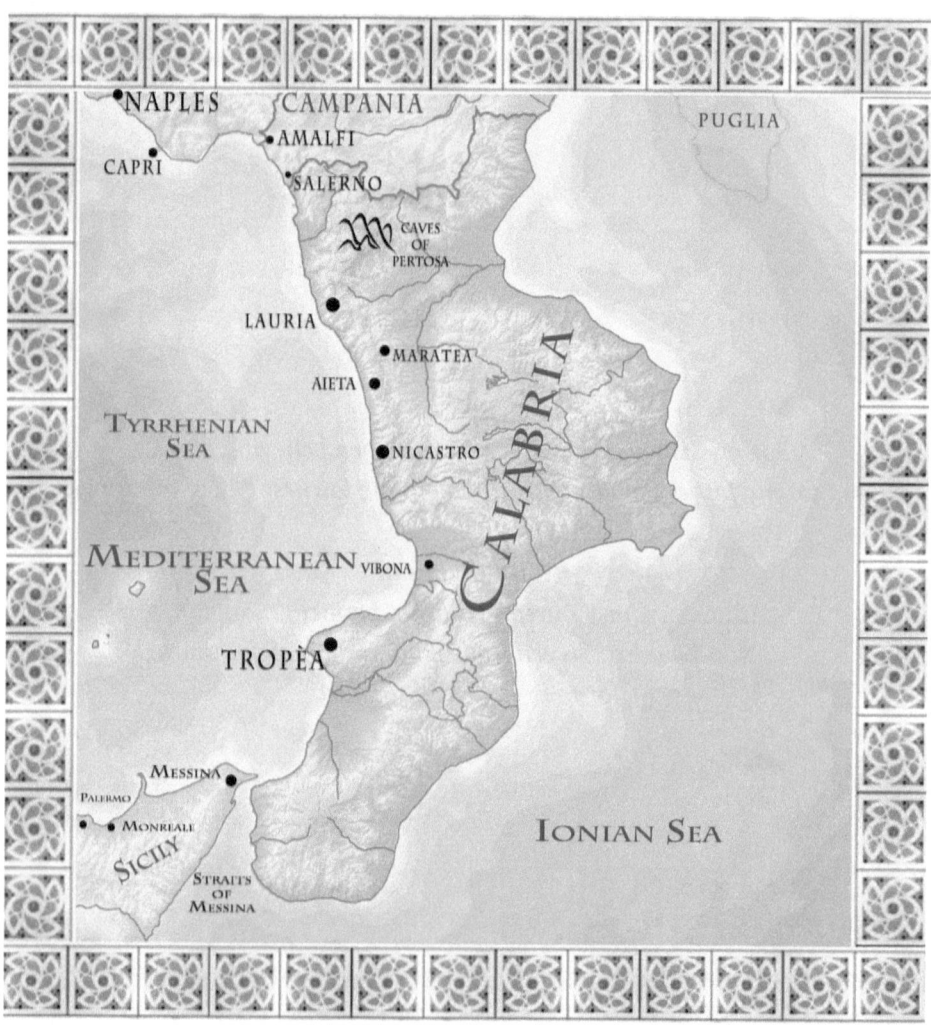

PART ONE

I

I N ROMAN TIMES, when heroes passed among men like comets, the town had been called Hercules' Harbor. In the year of Our Lord 1136 it was named Tropea, *"She who puts her enemies to flight."*

It rises high atop a spur of grey granite jutting into the Mediterranean along the rugged coast of Calabria, almost halfway between Palermo and Naples. Above the steep face of the cliff the walls came sheer out of the rock, rounding up in their hold a cluster of red tiled roofs that broke only at the two gates. From the Portammare, the Sea Gate, a long curving stairway cut into the stone led to the Marina, where the fishing boats were kept and ships cast anchor beyond two little islands of white sandstone molded by the wind; from the Porta Vaticana started the road toward the watchtowers of the coast and the farms of the inland.

To remind the people of Tropea that yet another foreign race had fallen in love with their land and was now their master, there was the tallest and newest building in town, the Castro. There the Norman governor sent from Palermo by King Roger d'Hauteville kept his soldiers and meted out justice.

Only the lords could look at that massive castle without fear, for they were the only ones who entered it or left it of their own will.

Safe in the shadow of the Castro and of the Norman Crown, Tropea gathered along its narrow streets its narrow houses, those of the local noblemen side by side with those of fishermen and artisans, yet kept solidly apart by invisible walls thicker than brick. The true heart of the town was Piazza Portèrcole, opening bright and unexpected between the marketplace on one side and the church of the Black Madonna on the other. From a house in Piazza Portèrcole one could watch the world unroll its endless tapestry woven of days and nights.

The house of Vasili d'Àrgira looked onto Piazza Portercole. Two stories high, it had been cut from a single block of granite. The two small round balconies with their black wrought-iron bars looked like two spiders that had stopped their climb to bask in the warmth of the stone. Each window had its fringe of swallows' nests under the sill, and each had its bunches of herbs hung to dry. Behind it was a garden bursting with fruit trees, while a lone palm shaded the roof; and by the steps of the front door rested two crossed oars, painted green and black.

If a fisherman's family could have a coat of arms, those two green-and-black oars would have been chosen for the d'Àrgiras of Tropea, to whom from time beyond memory the sea had been home, road, and often grave. Their name was Greek, meaning 'silver'. Not that any of them had ever been wealthy enough to deserve it; the pure sparkle it brought to mind spoke not of their pockets but of their souls.

In an age when a man could only accept injustice as he would have accepted drought and disease, Vasili d'Àrgira had been born with the hallmark of an undying hatred of everything unfair. He wouldn't just sigh and pray to God every time the armed servants of the Byzantine lords went down to the beach and took away in the span of a moment the best of an entire fishing season. First he had grumbled, then he had tugged at his basket of fish; finally one day he had openly refused. The scars left on his back by the whip had become his most precious possession.

For ten years since that day he had gathered around him the men whose trade was the lifeblood of Tropea. He had argued and he had fought, and the hangman's noose had often dangled closely before him. When the Norman rulers had replaced their Byzantine predecessors, with different titles but with the same arrogance, they had found him at the head of a guild of fishermen so strong that they had been forced to accept it along with every other long-established institution of the town.

Two generations of Falizza, the local breed of aristocrats, had wanted him dead. But to lay hands on the "most just man in Tropea" meant to face the anger of nearly every other man and woman in town; not to mention the frown of the Norman governor, who delegated to Vasili the task of peacemaker in litigations, and who that peace was very much interested in maintaining.

Yet no enemy Vasili d'Àrgira might have made ever afflicted him like a private nemesis all his own: his daughter Kallyna, whom he felt that God had given him as he would have given him a thorn in the side, to remind him day and night of his many other blessings.

Even the lack of a son had been remedied years before, when fate had sent to his house Michele and Arni, the two orphaned sons of his best friend. Michele had been pledged to Vasili's youngest daughter Sila since the two were children; to Michele he would hand over the leadership of the fishermen's guild, and both young men were as dear to him as true sons. But Kallyna seemed bent on defying Vasili's every plan for a peaceful old age. For years now she had refused to marry the man he had chosen for her, causing unending trouble within his home; until he had been forced to allow his youngest daughter to marry first, against every proper custom he knew.

It was now the middle of July. Summer dried up the hills and smoothed the sea into long days of blue sleep. For many months Vasili and his men had hunted the swordfish in the manner practiced along the coast of Calabria for thousands of years. Now it was time to end the hunting season and to think of the wedding, to celebrate with man's brief rituals the enduring ones of nature.

❄   ❄   ❄

"God willing, wife, this is the last day."

"God willing indeed. A supper table where only women sit is bad luck."

In the new light of dawn Vasili got up from bed, put on his shirt and his black vest, and reached for his cap.

He was one of those men who don't need to be tall to command respect. Everything in his spare frame had a quiet dignity about it. In his handsome face the eyes were of a strikingly clear blue, which stood out from his many wrinkles like the sea from beyond furrows of brown earth. His wife Neia only came up to his shoulders. She was a small, thin woman who even in her appearance knew how to keep her place, one step below her husband.

"Here is your lunch, eat it in good health," Neia said like every morning. That morning, however, she let a smile wander on her sunburned face. "Michele and Arni are down in the cellar grinding the spears," she added.

Vasili took from her hands the cloth bundle still warm with loaves of bread that had just come out of the oven. "Michele won't kill a single fish today," he grinned. "Not the day before his wedding." He stepped out on the landing, opened the door of the room next to his and glanced in.

The room was still almost in the dark; the thick shutters still held out against the first daylight. His gaze ran on the loom made of olive wood and tall enough to almost touch the ceiling, with the small icon of the Black Madonna nailed to the uppermost bar and the shuttle carved in the shape of a boat. The blanket Kallyna was weaving was almost finished. Bedsheets and linens were neatly piled on top of the walnut chest; Sila's wedding gown lay across a chair.

The embroideries seemed to gleam in the dimness, bursting into a rainbow of colors: baskets of fruit, ships and waves, birds, flowers and trees. Only Kallyna could turn the world into silk thread, Vasili thought with a pleased smile; and in what little space was left by the loom, the bed in which his daughters slept seemed to him only a little larger than their cradles of years before.

Sila slept peacefully, wise even in her rest; Kallyna lay instead wrapped in her long black hair, her hands gripping the sheets and a frown on her face. Suddenly she stirred in her sleep, shaking her head.

"No…no!" she whispered frantically.

Vasili eyed her for a moment, until she went back to sleep. Then he drew a long sigh and closed the door.

"Had you ever noticed that Kallyna talks in her sleep?" he asked Neia on his way downstairs.

"Yes," Neia nodded, "and it's not a good sign at all. Perhaps if we spoke to Padre Costantino, if he could finally give her some peace…."

Vasili went on down the creaking stairs. "She's young. Give her time. Once she'll have a little one crying for hunger at her breast she'll be all sweet," and his voice was sweet already at the thought.

Neia shrugged doubtfully, then followed him into the kitchen that gleamed dimly with the large copper pans hung above the hearth. "Let's hope so. Now that Sila is all settled down, Kallyna can marry Raimo Trani any day she wants."

Vasili turned around, looming over his wife's fragile figure. "You know she won't even hear Raimo's name anymore. By now I myself am not so sure I did the right thing when I promised her to him. Why, I think she spurns him even in her sleep!" he blurted out, remembering Kallyna's panicked whisper.

Neia approached him cautiously. "But she's been pledged to him for all these years," she reminded him softly. "You can't take back your promise now… or can you?"

Vasili didn't answer, annoyed. He slipped a slice of bread into his shirt, grabbed a chunk of cheese from a plate, and finally moved away from his wife's outstretched hands. "Michele, Arni, it's time to go!"

Neia's hands fell against her sides.

The two brothers stepped out of the cellar's door. Arni must have been teasing Michele, and was still smiling mischievously.

"Father," he said, "look how sharp the spear is this morning. Michele woke up to grind it earlier than he ever did in all his life."

Michele kept winding around his elbow the rope tied to the end of the double-pronged spear. Once more he pretended not to have heard anything. He pointed at the front door. "Go get the oars, huh?"

Arni kissed Neia goodbye and went out. In the hour before dawn the square was quiet and empty.

Resigned now to brooding alone over Kallyna's troubles, Neia stood patiently on the threshold to watch the three men leave. But first Michele cast a look at the window of Sila's room, and Vasili didn't miss that look. He grinned to himself, then spoke his gruff farewell to his wife.

"Come on, boys, come on. Like the proverb says, men do and women talk." Then under his breath he added, "And if women didn't talk, we'd all live like dumb beasts."

On the smooth cobblestones of Piazza Portercole their footsteps sounded so familiar, like drops of water from a fountain.

❋   ❋   ❋

Sila pushed the shutters open, letting in the early morning light to prance around all over the room. Kallyna screened her eyes, moaning, and Sila laughed.

"I wonder whether you'll be so sleepy the day before *your* wedding," Sila teased. She sounded light-headed with happiness; and she had every reason to be, Kallyna thought with envy. Sila had always belonged to the adults' circle, and of her own choice. She stood like a rock; Kallyna had no rest, like the tide.

Neia came in, always so quiet and always so worried, announcing the exhausting array of chores that awaited them.

"You certainly picked the right day for oversleeping, daughters. We have the trousseau to set, the water to draw, the bread to bake... and Aunt Tresa is going to be here any minute, God help us if the oven's still empty by the time she walks through that door."

Her eyes stubbornly shut against the light, Kallyna kicked away the sheets, grumbling.

"All this fuss... as if Sila were leaving for France or some other place at the end of the world."

She sat up, and as she shook her hair the sunlight made it look blue instead of black, like the wings of a crow.

Neia kept puttering around the room. "Sila *is* leaving, in a way," she said. "And you too have long been ripe for the same journey." Then she left, carrying an armful of tablecloths.

Kallyna didn't speak.

"Let's go now," Sila prodded her. A moment later she had already disappeared, leaving Kallyna behind. Kallyna always seemed to be left behind.

What a dreary night that had been, she thought. Always the same bad dreams... At last she left the bed. Through the open window came a scent of salty air and jasmine. She stretched out, making herself as tall as she could, as though she wanted to take flight and vanish; but all the supple strength of her body reminded her painfully that she was still on the ground.

She had never had a mirror; still Raimo kept telling her, in his own dark way, that she was lovely. Her sad, proud black eyes were large and lustrous under the shady mass of her hair that the braids had molded into light ripples. Her face had the shape of an almond, and her skin the soft glow of copper. Her very name, that Vasili had fashioned from the Greek word for 'beautiful,' reminded her constantly of a gift in which everybody seemed more interested than she was.

Voices rose from downstairs — excited, admiring women's voices. She imagined them, friends and neighbors, crowding around Sila's trousseau, feeling the fine linen cloth. And cries of wonder, laughter. All the things she could not share.

It was time to go. At least the preparations for the wedding would keep her away from Raimo. But all that sunlight made her eyes ache.

❋   ❋   ❋

It was daybreak again, and the fishing flotilla of Mastro Vasili d'Àrgira had already scattered to every corner of the sea. Five *ontri*, as the boats were called with the ancient word, were headed south. Their prows were decorated with painted eyes, to see the dangers of the deep, and with wooden figureheads of Saint Peter, protector of fishermen. A flock of gulls chased them, flying around like white banners.

Vasili's boat pointed the way. From its center rose the mast, three times as tall as the *ontre* was long, and scored by short pegs that led to the top. There, in a tiny cage at the top, Arni stood raking the water with his gaze.

It took the tireless attention of sharp young eyes to keep the long watch on that dizzying stand. Arni had been trained to be a lookout ever since he was barely ten. Now it was a joy to watch him climb the mast with all the nimbleness of his strong, slim body, every muscle taut under the brown skin. Fishermen's sons grow up fast, and indeed there was nothing childish left in Arni; yet one child-like smile could still dispel his many man-like sorrows. Arni had the deep and easy gentleness of a lamb, for which he was named.

Clutching the spear and following the wake of his brother's gaze, Michele stood poised on the long catwalk that thrust out from astern. The double tips of black iron bobbed up and down with the pitching of the boat. At his feet was the second spear that would be used if the first one was lost; but Michele had never lost a spear. He held the shaft with the powerful grace of the Archangel Michael battling the Evil One with his sword of fire. He was the living hope of the d'Àrgiras for the years to come. So many expectations rested on his broad shoulders; but carried confidently, lightly.

Vasili manned the rudder, riding or cutting the currents that he knew as he knew the lines in the palm of his hand. In his mind he thanked God for such a fine morning, and for so many others like this one.

Beneath the changing, oil-smooth water something stirred. Arni screened his eyes against the glare of the sun and leant over from his tall perch. Michele started to loosen the thick rope at the end of the spear, while the oarsmen rested, looking up in expectation.

Then Arni suddenly pointed ahead and uttered the sighting cry whose meaning had been eaten away by the sea wind in ten centuries of use.

"*Fa aleuu!*" There was the swordfish, its silvery back plowing the sea in long arching strokes.

The men bent on the oars and began to row toward their prey. Their breath merged on the same rhythm with the dip of the blades and the creaking of the wood against the rowlocks.

"*Eia,* come on, my friends!" Vasili urged them. But the fifteen-foot-long monster had seen the shadow of the boat above him. It turned sharply toward the open sea, his glassy eye staring in terror. The boat lurched after him. Michele's hand tightened around the polished ash wood of the spear's shaft.

Vasili's eyes narrowed with excitement. "Don't let him go. Lord, how fat he is!"

The fish knew he was doomed. He veered left, then right, then left again, wildly. Sweat glistened down the rowers' backs.

"We're on him… *Eia* now, *eia!*"

Leaping on the water, the ontre rushed so closely onto the swordfish that the hull resounded with the knock of his back. All eyes turned to Michele, leaning tensely from the catwalk. Frozen in the ancient stance of Grecian javelin-throwers, he weighed the spear in his hand once, twice, then tossed it with a master's thrust. The spear cut a deadly trail through air and water, then plunged into the sea and into the thick body below. The rope snapped taut between the boat and the fish, now tied inexorably together. Michele started tugging, helped by Gheorghe di Nico. At every tug the wound gaped larger under the water.

With a few last jerks the fish wriggled in the pale floating cloud of his own blood. Then Michele shouted, "Heave!" and the huge prey left forever the sea. Its long fearsome blade tossed crazily among the fishermen's bare feet. Then it finally rested on the bottom of the boat, lifeless.

Michele pressed his foot against the creature's side and pulled out the spear. "I tell you, this must have been the grandfather of all swordfish," he beamed.

Vasili grinned, rolling up the rope. "It will pay for the musicians at the wedding. And for the priest, and for the deacons, too."

The four oarsmen laughed, wiping their foreheads. Gheorghe di Nico slapped Michele on the shoulder. "But do leave the biggest portion for the groom, Mastro Vasili," he said. "He will need it, the morning after the wedding."

Michele shoved him down. "Fool."

Vasili hid his smile and handed Michele the rope. "Beautiful kill, son." Then he called Arni to come down the mast. It was almost noontime, they would row to the nearest beach and eat.

Arni had already his feet on the lower pegs when something glittered again underwater. He climbed back to the top, scanned the sea carefully.

"There's another one!" he shouted. "Right behind us!"

Hastily Michele took up the spear he had left on the bottom and bent down, searching the water. Then he looked at Vasili. "Father, it's the female... and she's full of eggs."

Vasili turned and observed for a while the smaller fish swimming around the *ontre*, utterly heedless of the danger in her frantic search. He smiled affectionately.

"She's looking for her mate. Look how close she comes, you could catch her with your bare hands."

Michele was waiting, the spear raised.

"Let her go," Vasili said.

❋   ❋   ❋

It was well past midday. The town had fallen asleep in the sultry afternoon. The thick dark shutters were closed like eyes closed against the sun, the houses hunched together to escape its might. Only the cicadas, the noisiest insects in God's creation, kept chanting their song from under the olive trees.

The oven was finally cooling off, a gaping mouth black with ashes and smelling of bread and cake. Aunt Tresa snored, with her head on her arm on the kitchen table. Neia and Sila were sewing, in the shade by the door.

Kallyna was sitting under the lemon tree. It was her favorite corner, the farthest one in the garden. Small green fruits were budding among the leaves of the tree; the hot motionless air was all scented with their bitter tang. On the trunk, endless lines of ants scurried up and down, always so busy. She watched them dully, thinking again and always about Raimo and about herself who hated Raimo and who would soon become his property for life.

There were lucky women who, like her mother, were given to a man they could learn to love in time; others, the Almighty's own pets, married someone they had chosen, like Sila. But Kallyna d'Àrgira was among the outcasts. Everything that was alive in her soul would forever be dead in Raimo's.

The cicadas stopped briefly, only to resume their tune with greater frenzy. It was all so quiet that she could almost hear her own blood running through her veins, carrying its swell of pain.

For two years Raimo had touched her like hot iron. All she knew about love were his thick hands searching her all over, and the taunts with which he tried to make her like it. He would not spare her one proud detail of his exploits in every whorehouse of the county; in utter good faith, to prove to her that he would make a good husband. And of course, like a good husband, he made a point of persecuting her with a jealousy bordering on obsession.

She nestled against the tree trunk. She wondered whether Michele had ever treated Sila that way; whether Arni would ever dream of making her feel what Raimo made her feel. Before Raimo she had been a happy, trusting girl. Now she had become "the moody one." She had gone through every one of the humiliating rituals of rebellious daughters: the endless arguments, the hysterical tantrums, the forced fastings. Nothing had helped, and in the process she had only bought a little time to ward off the inevitable. The worst thing was when she exasperated Vasili so much that he locked her up for days. Knowing that she alone could drive a man as mild as her father to such anger gave her the greatest pain and the greatest shame.

The grey cat must be skulking through the fuzzy leaves of the fig tree; wary, invisible. Neia's chair creaked.

Certainly after a while Raimo would grow tired of her and start chasing other women. Maybe then he would finally leave her alone. He would leave her alone and she would stay home to wait for him, with yet another brat of his growing in her belly. She hugged her knees and hid her face against them, as if to become a lump of stone that nothing could pierce.

Tonight again she would go talk to her father. By now she truly had nothing more to lose.

❋   ❋   ❋

In the last of the sunlight the town high on its rock looked like a crown of pink gold. Out on the far horizon the sun that night was setting directly behind the dark triangle of the Stròmboli volcano; the legend said it was a good omen.

The seven men in the *ontre* rowed slowly, tired. The catch had been good. Two swordfish rocked gently in the air, tied to the base of the mast as was the custom, so that those ashore could see right away that the day's work had been fruitful. The hunting season was over. Now the sea could finally grant rest.

The men's minds arrived home much faster than the boats. Michele sat by himself, his hands under his chin. He watched the wake left by the *ontre* and he thought that tomorrow night Sila would undo her long braids for him.

Arni pulled in the oars and jumped first onto the sand, while the others untied the heavy catch. The stairway from the Portammare became alive with the skirts of women and the bare feet of children coming down to welcome back the boats. It was also Arni who first noticed Kallyna in that crowd, and when Vasili ordered to pull the boat he missed his grip to look at her.

She smiled to all in a hurry, as though she had already something to be forgiven for.

"I'm happy to see you, Father. What a big one you caught! Supper's ready, are you hungry?"

From the way she sounded, so out of breath, everyone knew immediately why she had come. Arni wanted to say something; but he was not supposed to speak before Vasili, and Vasili delayed his answer. So Kallyna kept out of the men's way while they slid soapy planks under the prow, pulled the boat, tossed the planks again and pulled the boat again until it was on dry land.

"Of course we're hungry," Vasili said then quietly. "We've been working all day." He gathered up the planks and laid them on the bottom of the boat. Finally he looked up at her, but he didn't like what he saw: when Kallyna began twisting her hands together, it meant that she was hunting for words. "We're done with the preparations for tomorrow, Father," she began. "All we have left to do is set the tables in the kitchen."

Vasili drew himself up. "In the kitchen? No, no. We'll set the tables outside, in front of the main door. To my daughter's wedding all Tropea is invited," he said without haughtiness.

Michele looked at him in surprise. "Even the lords?" he asked.

Vasili unrolled the burlap sheet and spread it over the boat. "If they wish to come," he nodded. "All those who have nothing to hide can be my guests. I want the day to be remembered."

Michele's face lit up with admiration and joy. He shouldered boldly the oars and elbowed Arni to come along.

But Arni wanted to stay. If Kallyna had something to say, he wanted to take her side as he always did, with his silent and savage devotion. He turned to Vasili. "Father, do you want me to take a look at that crack in the hull? I can give you a hand with the caulking, too."

Vasili shook his head. "No, son, it's just a scratch. You go ahead."

Arni still wouldn't move; and while Vasili wasn't looking, Kallyna motioned him to go. Arni turned around. It hurt him so to imagine what was about to happen, and to see how impatient she was to try one more time, against all hope. He wrapped into his shirt the big shell he had found for her and then sadly followed Michele homeward.

After a while Kallyna gathered all her breath in. "Father, may I speak to you? About Raimo?"

Vasili tied the burlap sheet to the rowlocks and didn't look at her. "All I care to know is whether he's set the day and the month," he said simply.

Her hands clutched the gunwale. Perhaps it was better to end the conversation right there and then.

Gheorghe di Nico stopped by. "The catch is on its way, Mastro Vasili. We sold all of it already, and Manuele is minding your share, as always."

"Thank you, Gheorghe. Come to the wedding tomorrow, with your mother."

Gheorghe smiled. "We wouldn't miss it for the world, Mastro Vasili." Then he glanced at Kallyna; and Kallyna knew that Gheorghe had lived that day for nothing but that glance. The look of love in the young man's gentle eyes filled her with sorrow. Both knew she could not afford even to acknowledge it. She could only pretend, again, that she hadn't noticed it.

Gheorghe hung his head, with a smile of resignation. "Then good night, Mastro Vasili." "A good night to you, too," Vasili answered, and as Gheorghe walked away Kallyna had to bite her lips so she wouldn't start crying, not now.

Vasili pulled at the flaps of the burlap sheet to tighten it. "What's for supper?" he asked.

Kallyna couldn't remember. "I don't really know. Mother did the cooking today, I helped Sila with the trousseau."

Vasili hunkered down to look at the small crack in the keel of the boat.

"Father, please listen to me."

"I've been listening to you for two years. The neighbors, too, have been listening. What you want to tell me is as old as the rocks. You want to hear my answer again?"

Kallyna shut her eyes. He spoke with an even, patient voice, the voice of a man who knows in his heart that he's right.

"You were promised to Raimo Trani two years and three months ago. He would have married you then, had you not taken ill the week before the wedding and had you not opposed him ever since, God knows for what reason. That is all there is to the matter, and that is all there will ever be."

She looked away. Her words came out wooden, cracked. "I was not taken ill, Father. I had just found out that every night after he called on me he went to Bruna's house and…" She stopped abruptly, and couldn't go on.

Vasili rapped the keel of the boat, listening to the sound it made.

"Bruna is not the sort of girl a man would want for his wife," he said flatly. "She is what she is, and everybody knows it. As for Raimo, at his age he certainly cannot live like a monk." He searched the sand, looking for a sharp pebble. "What counts is that he loves you. He has said so and he has proven so, first of all with the bride price he paid for you, one that nobody else—"

Kallyna started to shout. "If he had seen a clay jar in the market that he happened to like more than the others, he would have done just the same, Father!"

14

Vasili stepped quickly in front of her, to hide her outburst from the eyes of the people crowding the beach. Startled, she raised her arm to protect her face from the slap. But he didn't hit her; Vasili had never hit anybody. He looked at her sternly, then let his hand drop. She breathed in hard, staring at the sand. Vasili squatted down again to scrape the edges of the crack with the sharp pebble. His voice sounded strangely hollow, like a sunken bell.

"I have held my own against the lords of Tropea for ten years, but I cannot get my own daughter to obey me." He glanced up at her; her face now wet with tears made him avert his eyes.

"I want nothing but that, to obey you," she whispered. "But you make it so hard! Anybody else... Gheorghe di Nico..."

"Put him out of your head," Vasili snapped. "Him *and* anybody else. Trani would drag me before the law for breach of promise, and Cosimo Falizza will not miss the smallest opportunity to have me hanged from the beam of my own front door. Is that what you want?"

She stooped toward him without shame. "Then I will not marry at all, ever. Tell Raimo that I want to become a nun, so he won't dare say that you cheated him or—"

Vasili's eyes sparkled with furious amazement. "In the name of all the saints! What could ever be so hateful about a man to make you say a thing like that?"

She backed away, shaking. She wondered how two people could live so close for so many years and still have to shout at one another as though they were standing on the opposite banks of a river.

Then Vasili quieted down. He threw away the pebble and headed for the stairway.

"Enough of this. We go home."

Kallyna wiped her eyes and started to walk after him, stumbling with her bare feet on the first stone step. She knew it was over for good, this time. Vasili would not talk about it anymore, or tolerate further arguments from her; and that same night, when Raimo would come as he did every night, he would set the date of the wedding himself.

A burst of outrage flared up inside her. At least she could speak out, the way prisoners did on the scaffold. She fixed her gaze upon the black figure climbing the stairs, turning his back to her.

"They call you the most just man in Tropea," she said slowly, each word sinking like a stone in the void between them. "How could you have become so deaf and blind? Raimo is not one of us, and you know it. His place is with the lords, because of his arrogance, of his love of money, of every other thing you've flung into the lords' faces for years. How can you be so unjust with *me*, with your own flesh and blood?"

On the step above, Vasili wheeled around, stunned. He stared at her as if she had just put a knife in his back. There was no anger of his that could put out the fire in her eyes. He looked frightened, defeated.

"Daughter," he said, "before God I swear that I have never done anything to harm you. Your mother broke her back on the hills for twenty years, picking broomflower for the weavers for five *scudi* a day. My daughters have been luckier. The Lord has seen fit that I should be able to give them a house, a craft, and good husbands who will spare them that life of humiliation and toil. No matter what you say to me, I have not a single regret to carry before my Maker when my time comes."

He looked all around him, sweeping with his clear eyes the setting sun, the coast and the sea, as if calling them all witnesses to his words. Then he shook his head.

"Still you're not happy. Still you keep flying about like a caged bird, with only one thought in mind — to escape, to bite the wind that nobody can bite. Ten more years of fighting all the Falizzas of the world will not wear me out like you did."

Inside Kallyna's throat words rolled like waves. She stepped up briskly, to lessen the terrible distance between herself and him, to wipe from his face that look of aching resignation. But Vasili had already resumed his climb, and now he walked bent, like an old man.

❁   ❁   ❁

Shortly before the curfew, when the soldiers sounded the horn from the turret and locked both gates, Vasili rose from his supper and went to sit on the front steps with Michele and Arni.

The sky peeked in from the half-opened door, already white with stars. Neia shook the crumbs off the tablecloth into the hearth. During the day she did that in the garden, but never at night, when the particles of food would draw the hungry souls of the dead to her door. Then she called Kallyna to help her make the bed in the room upstairs that up to a month ago had been empty and now was all done up, ready for the bride and groom.

Kallyna took the sheets and spread them with slow, heavy hands, lost in her own thoughts. Noises would drift from this room to hers, those sweet little noises she feared. Tomorrow night she would sleep alone, until the time would come when she would have to sleep with—

"Tuck the sheets in properly at the sides, Kallyna," Neia warned her.

She looked up with an air of sarcasm. "What for? They'll all be crumpled up anyway, the day after tomorrow."

Neia stopped, looking sternly at her from behind the pillow she was fluffing up. But Kallyna did tuck the sheets in as dutifully as if they were altar cloths.

The men's voices rose louder from below through the open balcony, together with a sound of steps approaching on the cobbled way.

"Have a good night, Mastro Vasili. Forgive me for coming so late tonight. I was up at the Castro."

Kallyna had waited in dread for that voice all night. Neia leaned out to see. "It's Raimo." Kallyna slipped another pillow into the pillowcase and said nothing.

He talked loudly, battering the quiet night like a hammer. Every word was mouthed heavily, to impress those who listened.

"And a good night to you, Mastro Raimo," Vasili was heard answering. "Please sit here with us."

He was the only person Vasili had ever addressed as "Mastro," that is as his own peer. Kallyna never missed the bitter irony of that word. In his clever way of courting Vasili, of flattering him and ingratiating himself, Raimo was truly her father's only master.

"May I go to bed now, Mother?" she asked, closing the shutters.

After a long and hard day finally left behind, Neia was too exhausted to start an argument. She would excuse Kallyna with Raimo for not showing up.

"All right," she surrendered. She kissed her daughter's forehead. "Sleep well, and say your prayers so you won't have bad dreams," she added with a sad smile.

Kallyna smiled back wanly; then she took shelter in her room. The room was dark except for the window's square full of sky. But she wasn't safe from the voices of the men below.

"Today I was given the plans for the new cathedral," Raimo was saying. "The bishop has finally gotten through his head that it must be build in a different spot, like I told him so many times, or else at the next earthquake it will end up just like the old one. I'm sure he's good at other things, but when it comes to building he ought to leave it to those who know how, am I right? Now I'll start looking for masons and stonecutters all over the county. We'll begin in September at the latest."

Vasili must be really impressed by Raimo's words not to notice that Raimo was talking about nothing except himself. "This is good news, Mastro Trani. Before that time, though, we must settle a family matter that you know well. With the help of the Lord, what do you say about the last day of August?"

Up in her room, Kallyna could just see the grin spreading on Raimo's face.

"I am your servant, Mastro Vasili. If you say the last day of August, the last day of August it will be."

That would be all, she thought. They had disposed of her life as they would have done with the purchase and sale of a head of cattle.

She buried her face in her pillow. So be it then. Now it would only be quicker, like the last stroke of a Norman sword.

II

CÒSIMO FALIZZA TOSSED HIS PURPLE CLOAK onto a chair and puffed out loudly, wiping his bald forehead with a scented handkerchief.

"I tell you, dear Corrado, the years do start to weigh on my poor shoulders. Coming up here on foot every night in this summer heat is going to kill me before my time... And for what? Protocol and formalities, the Italians' favorite pastimes."

Corrado Altamura leaned back and laughed hard, while Falizza slumped into the chair.

"It's those extra pounds of yours, my most esteemed friend. You bought yourself an Arab cook, and now the treacherous infidel is trying to dispose of his master in the way he knows best, with his delicious roast meats and his *cannoli à la mode du Roi Rogier.*"

The council room of the Castro was empty except for the two men. From the tall barred windows came a grating, monotonous sound of iron-shod feet pacing up and down the catwalk. The light of a single pine torch cast long shadows on the grey vaults and revealed creases in the battle banners hung on the walls.

Altamura, sitting at a huge sculptured table, had been poring over a pile of scrolls heaped like wood shavings on a carpenter's bench. Falizza grabbed a handful of them and made them rustle with a gesture of contempt.

"More poor fools pleading to 'Our Most Gracious and Compassionate Lord Roger' for the boundary wall of a farmhouse or a stray cow... Were it December, we would have already lit the fireplace with all this garbage."

Altamura put his quill down and looked at him, amused. "I would dare say, my dear marquis, that you grow more tired of your office by the day. Well, of course our little town must seem quite dull to someone who's had the good fortune of tasting the splendors of the court in Palermo."

It was Falizza's favorite subject, the one that always sent him daydreaming.

"Ah, you said it, Corrado, you said it. If you'd only seen the riches, the display! Roger's coronation robe alone must have cost your house and mine put together...." Altamura shrugged, believing not a word.

"And the women, my friend, the women!" Falizza went on rapturously, spreading his arms around his portly figure.

Altamura shook his head, grinning. Then he rolled up another parchment sheet and sighed.

"That was the last one, praise the Lord."

Falizza leaned over the table, peering at him. "Am I mistaken, or do I find you in a bad mood tonight, my dearest baron? Don't tell me you're still worried about those soldiers... I'm sure they will be here any day now."

Altamura scratched his forehead. "In thirty years of office I've never seen Tropea so empty of men. They are all off to Naples, dying like flies in that endless war."

He looked up. "We need that squadron, Cosimo. The sooner it gets here the better. Thank God at least the swordfish hunt is over and all able-bodied men are in town, still.... Do you know how many soldiers we're left with? Two hundred! You can't even cover the round of the walls with two hundred soldiers."

"But the watchtowers along the coast are full," Falizza said. "Which damned fool of a Saracen would think of attacking us in these clear summer nights?"

Altamura rubbed his eyes with his hand, tired. "So I reason myself. What more can I tell you? We're all in the hands of God. According to the latest messengers, the Normans were supposed to leave two weeks ago, but what I fear is that they're still in Sicily waiting to cross the Straits of Messina." He shook his head. "Not even they who are the sons of Vikings dare to brave those waters!"

For a moment each man followed his own thoughts, while the torch dwindled in a cloud of resin-scented smoke. Then Altamura stood up and reached for the bunch of keys that hung from his belt.

"Here. Like every night as prescribed, 'two good and trusted men shall lock the Council Hall'. I don't even know who the king is sending us this time. Let's hope it's not one of those snooty Norman greenhorns he has afflicted us with in the past."

The guard posted by the door was almost asleep on his lance. Altamura locked the door and yawned. "I hear Sila d'Àrgira got married to Michele d'Orta today," he said.

"Ah, yes," Falizza replied with a sneer. "For all I care about the d'Àrgiras and their stubborn breed."

"And in nine months, if not sooner, we'll have one more troublemaker on our hands," the baron added.

The two men crossed the corridor down to the main door, where two soldiers lifted the double grid for them. Faint echoes of music wafted through the narrow streets wrapped in darkness. The sky was milky with all the southern constellations shining high above the black earth. Followed by a guard who carried in one hand a torch and in the other a naked sword, the two men walked hurriedly toward home.

"Never did I see a night as clear as this," Altamura said softly. "It makes you wish you were a boy of seventeen, and in love for the first time."

❋ ❋ ❋

The music came from Piazza Portercole. On the deep beat of a drum and the tinkling of a tambourine, the notes of two wooden flutes and a clay ocarina chased one another like birds flying over the sand. In the middle of a sea of darkness the square was alive with torches, voices and dancing. None of the neighbors would dare complain about being kept awake by the sounds of joy.

Two long tables were set at both sides of the d'Àrgiras' front door. The doors were open to guests going in to admire the bride's trousseau and to leave wedding gifts. Above the window of the newlyweds' room was hung the horn of an ox, to keep away the evil eye. At one table sat Vasili with all the men, at the other the bridal couple with all the women.

People came and went from all over the neighborhood, just as Vasili wanted. The children made a noisy game of scrambling for the small copper coins that once in a while one of the guests tossed in the air, or else ran laughing around the musicians who kept piping and pounding tirelessly in their corner. Two young men were dancing a fast *cacciattacci* jig, others were coaxing the women into joining them. The women fended off the invitation, but not for long.

The tables shone with pink cowry shells arranged as centerpieces around tall candles. Inside a small cage cooed two snow-white turtledoves, a present from Neia's sister and her husband Gheorghe. The carved wooden platters were heaped with food. There were thick swordfish steaks surrounded by arugula; thorny black garlands of sea urchins slit open to show the bright orange roe; white ricotta cheese still warm in its wicker molds wrapped in fern leaves; wide ribbons of pasta-like *laganum* thickly laced with honey; bowls full of *confetti,* almonds covered in a hard sugar shell; and peaches, melons, figs, and the first grapes. That night Vasili d'Àrgira was celebrating also his defeat of poverty; and if some of the food would go to waste the following day, he could boast now that it was just like in the houses of the lords.

Never had Sila been more beautiful than on her wedding day and never would she be again, like all brides. On her head she wore a small garland of orange blossoms, the fragrant flowers of weddings. The veil had been removed by the groom in church and donated to the Black Madonna. A double necklace of gold coins, the groom's customary gift, broke the brightness of her white attire like a shower of sparkles on fresh snow. Michele next to her stood tall and straight as a young tree, and not even his doublet of black velvet could make him look somber, with happiness and pride shining from his soul.

Kallyna sat at the far end of the women's table. Nobody paid any attention to her. Her girlfriends had vainly tried to draw her into their circle, but then had given up and now crowded around the bride, chatting and laughing. Neia was too busy serving spongecake, Aunt Tresa refilling the pitchers with sweet malmsey wine. Gheorghe di Nico wouldn't even look at her now that Raimo was there; and Arni, very much in the same mood, looked as dazed as a little boy, awkward in his Sunday best. As if caught in a bad dream, alone in all that crowd, she stared at Sila's and Michele's fingers entwined on the tablecloth, and Michele was pressing so hard that Sila's hand looked tiny in his grip.

She was wearing the dress she had made for special occasions. It was a beautiful dress in the traditional cut for girls not yet married, pleated red satin with the bodice embroidered in gold, the two flat bows on the shoulders and the long fringed apron for which she had chosen pale pink; but she hated how it made her look lovely for Raimo's exclusive benefit. She had noticed the way he kept glancing at her from the other table. Vasili had wanted Raimo to sit at his right-hand side, and that honor seemed to have gone to Raimo's head. He busied himself with the wine jug, pouring one noisy toast after another. Vasili, even though he wasn't at all accustomed to drinking, obliged him willingly at every glassful. This was a special night, a night that would not come twice in his lifetime.

Suddenly Kallyna realized that she had made a mistake in setting herself apart. Seeing her all alone Vasili leant toward Raimo and with a smile nudged him discreetly into going over to her. Raimo was only too pleased to receive that sanction. He bowed his head low to Vasili, making a show of respectful gratitude, then stood up and quickly approached her from behind.

He wasn't tall, and the showy clothes of brown velvet made him look even stockier. He had the bad taste of wearing a dagger even in the most inappropriate occasions, like a lord; and like a lord he always knew when it was time to be humble and when to attack, and with whom, and why.

"Donna Kallyna d'Àrgira doesn't enjoy herself at a wedding feast," he said in her ear. "She likes to be by herself and to make a long face, as if she were at a funeral instead."

There was anger in every word, and his breath was foul with wine. Kallyna wanted to stand up, but he grabbed her hand. "Watch out, shrew," he whispered. "Try just for this once to behave."

"And you try to leave the scolding to my father while you're not yet my husband," she spat back.

As always, the look of hatred in her eyes seemed to amuse him enormously. He loved that game, because in the end he was going to win it. She could run from him forever and he would simply follow her, angrier and happier. He smiled, and let go of her.

"I'm going to bed," Kallyna said, starting to walk toward the house. "Find yourself another pastime. There are plenty of women… or what do *you* call them?"

He went after her without hurry. "I think you're not going anywhere," he said. "Look."

Vasili was beckoning her, his arms raised to embrace her.

"Daughter," he called her warmly, tenderly. "Please be happy, daughter. After we go down into our graves, no lost minute of our lives is ever going to be paid back to us."

Astounded, she could only stare at him. In all her life she had never seen him like that, and he had never spoken like that to anyone, certainly not to her. Now all of a sudden he was telling her how much he loved her, begging her to be happy as if he were to die in an hour.

Again a thousand words of sorrow and love came to her lips. Before she could say any of them Raimo took her by the hand and spoke for her.

"Be at peace, Mastro Vasili. You know that I'm here to make your daughter happy."

Smiling, Vasili patted their hands, as if giving them his blessing. Then, while Kallyna still tried to hold back, Raimo pulled her away and deftly began to march her toward the other side of the square, snaking through the crowd.

"Where are you going?" she whispered. "Are you mad? Where on earth are you going!"

Raimo stopped briefly to greet a guest, never loosening his grip on her wrist. Then again he began to walk ahead of her. "Keep quiet," he grumbled. "You're not going to start a scene right now, are you?" The guests, shouting congratulations at them, parted to let them through and then quickly forgot them. Kallyna tried to pull her hand away, tugging against his clutch. Soon the music and the light seemed to drown behind them. She knew what came next. At the first corner of darkness he was all over her with his hands and his mouth.

"Let me go back. Leave me alone. If you don't leave me alone I'll wake up the whole town."

Raimo locked his sweaty hands around her face, trying to bring her lips back under his own.

Two shutters slammed open at a window above them. "Why don't you children go make love somewhere else and leave us to sleep in peace?" shouted a woman's voice.

Kallyna kept still against the wall. The shutters closed. Again Raimo's hands ran down feverishly to her breasts.

"Dried-up old hag," he cursed up at the window. "You want to fight, my love?" he panted, pawing her all over. "Now and forever after? Of course you do. We're going to have so many fights you won't have breath left to talk."

She began to sob quietly. "Please let me be. Please… may God strike you dead before my eyes!"

The slap came hard against her ears, making her stagger. He pulled away from her. Though he was silent now, she could feel how angry he was, angry as her father when he got angry. For a moment she hoped he had left, because she couldn't hear him in the dark.

"You still haven't learned anything," he said then in his teeth. "But don't you worry, shrew. I'll straighten you up if it takes me a lifetime."

Another slap would come at the first word she would say. But she didn't care.

"It won't take you that long, Raimo Trani. I'll make your life so wretched that you won't get to be forty."

She swung her face toward the wall; but after a while, abruptly, she heard him burst instead into a loud laugh, as if she had said something very witty.

"Good God, my love, will you listen to yourself? You were *born* to be a wife!" Again he was all over her. "That's why I don't believe you for a minute," he said, and now his voice had all the tenderness he would ever be capable of. "They say the toughest customers are the ones who buy first... You're going to buy with pieces of gold... You will love me, you will love me..."

She was sobbing like a small girl, shaking her head, feeling dizzy and defeated. Again he started to drag her by the hand. "Please don't," she begged. "Don't do anything foolish."

He was paying no attention. "Shh. Your father's drunk, and in a month we'll be married. Just come along."

Past the dark corner they had turned shone the light of a torch set in the wall of a house that she had never set foot into but that she knew. A painted raven stood guard on its thick door, black wings outspread. Now she was truly in a panic.

"Look, be reasonable. You'd better let me go or I'll start screaming."

"God, how you chatter," he cursed. But when he had to let go of her hand to reach for his keys, she slipped away from him and started running down the alley. Raimo uttered an oath and pulled the key from the lock.

Her silk slippers didn't make any sound on the smooth cobblestones. But soon Raimo's boots were echoing behind her. And while she was running blindly in the dark, he must have taken the torch from the wall, because a smoky flicker of light was chasing her past the low arches between house and house.

She didn't know where she was, perhaps near the Portammare. She stopped, trying to remember her way back to the square. At that moment a deep pounding of wood on wood thundered in her ears. It was louder than

Raimo's footsteps, louder than her own wild heartbeat, like a giant hand knocking at the doors of the night.

Horrified, she stood listening. Once again, twice, three times. The heavy cadence sounded immensely strong. When Raimo finally found her, she no longer cared about him.

"They are battering down the Portammare," she whispered. "They are battering down the Portammare!"

Raimo lowered his torch, frightened by the look in her eyes. He too stood listening. For a while there was silence. Then there was a cry from the walls above, and the pounding resumed, at closer intervals.

"It can't be," Raimo said. "By God, it cannot be!" But the knocks behind him were the stubborn answer to his confusion.

"Let's go to the Castro," Kallyna blurted out.

"There's nobody there at this hour. The guards should all be on the walls... Then why didn't they sound the alarm?"

The pounding was already changing in pitch, as though the gate were starting to yield. There was a flurry of footsteps, the slamming of a door, the shriek of a woman. Raimo glanced back in the direction of his house and seemed rooted to the spot.

"Give me that torch," Kallyna cried out, reaching for it. "Why are we standing here? Let's go tell my father. Let's go tell somebody, for the love of God!"

Raimo pulled the torch away, leaving her with a handful of sparks. He kept staring toward his house. "Keep quiet. I know what to do. There isn't time to tell anybody, not anymore."

From the balcony above them came another woman's cry. "The Saracens! O Mother of God!"

The ugliest sound of wood beginning to splinter under the thrust of the battering ram boomed into the dark streets that were finally waking up in a surge of terror. Stumbling over Raimo's feet, Kallyna started to run. Two men crossed her way, and they too were running, with daggers in their hands.

"The Saracens! The Saracens!"

Now the streets were swarming with torches that looked like maddened fireflies, and she could see where she was going. In her frantic hurry she could think only that she must be with her family. She must tell her father that she loved him, she must thank Arni for his shell. So many things to do!

A hand grabbed hold of her hair. She screamed, thinking it was a Saracen and she was going to die there, away from them. It was Raimo instead, who had seized her by both arms and was dragging her back, where she didn't want to go. She started shouting for help, but now her voice was lost in the din of the attack. Where was he taking her? What in God's name was going on?

The painted raven flashed again before her eyes. Two women and their children dashed past her. She tried to grab one of them, but Raimo's hands were ropes pulling her inside the house. He slammed the door shut behind him. She pounded on it and scratched it with broken nails.

"Let me go back to my father! I don't want to die with you. Let me go!"

In the dark, Raimo was fumbling desperately for another key. "Stop this barking," he ordered. "Stop it, damn you, you'll draw them all here."

But as soon as he moved one step away Kallyna began pounding on the door again. "Somebody out there… Somebody please let me out!"

Somewhere at the other end of the courtyard Raimo's key cracked inside a hidden lock, and she smelled mold. Again his arm closed around her waist. He had taken the torch again, and the flame danced dangerously close to her hair.

From outside the house came a clatter of iron, a strange confusion like that of a busy armory shop. Hauled across the inner courtyard to what looked like the door of a cellar, Kallyna found herself standing at the top of a dark, narrow stairway that seemed never to end. Raimo threw her in and locked the trapdoor behind him, keeping her at bay with his whole body.

Through her mind flashed the memory of rumors she had laughed at, rumors about Raimo cutting a passage from his house into the walls when he had made the repairs after last year's earthquake. It was all true, she thought.

"Down," he ordered.

She fought him as though he were pushing her into her own grave. "I'm not going anywhere. I'm not budging from here."

"Move or I'll kill you!" he shouted, shoving her down the first two steps.

Tugging, struggling, cursing, she halted after him. "You coward, you coward. If you were really a man you'd be out there, you son of the devil himself, you—"

Suddenly she tripped over the long hem of her skirt and fell down with a cry. Raimo pulled her up; pain shot all over her.

"My ankle... Oh God, my ankle!"

"The hell with your ankle. Get up."

Every step down became torture. She kept sobbing and begging. "What's the use of saving my life? Please let me go to them. Please, if you love me."

Raimo dragged her on in a grim silence, down an endless coil of steps. The light of the torch spread like a rusty wing, forcing old cobwebbed shadows out of their corners.

"My ankle hurts so much. I'll do anything you say if you let me go. I promise, I promise."

Still on and still down, inside a pit dark and narrow as a throat. Her blood was pounding in her ears.

"At least let's bring the others here. All right, Raimo? Let's bring them here, let's save them, too."

He wheeled around, sallow-faced. "Listen to me. There's no time to go back. There's nothing we can do, and don't you *dare* call me a coward." He bent over her, threatening. "And if you so much as breathe a word to anyone about what you saw tonight, I swear by the blessed souls of my mother and father that I'll lash you to death. Now shut your mouth and wait here for me."

"No, Raimo, no. Please!"

"I said be quiet, damn you!" She slumped onto the steps, gasping for air. She thought she could see a faint light ahead, and smell a faint smell of sea and grass. Raimo stamped the torch out under his boots and disappeared for a few moments that to her were like all eternity tied up into one knot of darkness.

Curled up against the damp steps, she saw in her mind her mother and father pierced through by the long crescent swords, Sila carried away screaming, and Michele lying in his own blood, and Arni chased by the Saracens up the steps of the house. She hammered her fists on the stone, sobbing.

Raimo was back. "It's going to be day soon. Get up."

She wouldn't move, and he had to force her up and then through the exit. This was just a crack in the rock, enough for one person to pass sideways almost bent double, and covered from the outside by a tangled curtain of ivy and branches. Then he followed her; once they were out he stopped for a moment to listen.

It all seemed quiet, except for some noises high above them, atop the black granite bulk looming in the pale glimmer before dawn. Muffled, terrifying noises, and the glare of fires.

"Let's go," Raimo whispered.

Struck silent, Kallyna held onto his arm and limped after him in the wet grass, wherever he might lead her. Besides, she thought, none of this was true; none of this could be true.

Raimo groped onward blindly, whispering an oath every time a tree stood in his way. Once in a while he turned around to cast a glance over his shoulder. After some time the grass became a dirt slope, a beaten path deep in the hillside. Kallyna's ankle throbbed. The harsh breathing that dried up her throat had become the most frightening sound she had ever heard.

It felt like an endless time before they were at the end of the trail. A wall took shape out of the dimness, shadowed by a tall wooden cross. Kallyna let go of Raimo's arm and slipped down to the ground.

"Padre Elias!" Raimo called softly. "In the name of God, open up."

A face came up behind the peephole in the door. "Who are you, son?"

"Raimo Trani, the master builder. The Saracens have broken into town."

"*Kyrie*!" the monk whispered. "*Kyrie eleison*, God!"

Raimo lifted Kallyna on his arms and waited for Padre Elias to let them in. Her hair blew gently around her, like a black sail.

III

T HE TOWN WAS WAKING UP TO A NIGHTMARE. The Portammare was
reduced to nothing more than a blind hole. The walls around it were
black with the ashes of the burned gate, strewn with bodies and weapons.
Houses still smoldered here and there. The streets were a shambles of broken
furniture thrown from wide-open windows.

In Piazza Portercole the tables of the wedding feast were overturned, and
what was left of the bridal trousseau was scattered all over the bloodied
cobblestones. A white nightgown hung from the paw of the bronze lion that
decorated the fountain. No one would ever forget Sila d'Àrgira's wedding
day.

Vasili's house was very quiet. The front door was shut. One might have
thought that inside everybody was still asleep. Gheorghe and Tresa Casali
moved like two shadows between the two beds. On one lay Vasili, his arms
crossed on his chest, his chest cleaned of the blood; on the other was Arni, his
head wrapped in a bloodstained cloth, the edge of the wound reaching down
to his temple.

Tresa's eyes were dry. She sat by Arni, staring at him, breathing every breath he took, and thinking of nothing. Gheorghe picked up the things scattered on the floor and heaped them up in a corner, slowly. At least Vasili had died a happy man. His face was at peace; perhaps he hadn't even felt the cold of the blade.

✳   ✳   ✳

The monastery of San Nilo rose isolated, almost hidden in the craggy hills that surrounded the town, built in the shape of a Greek cross. It had been made by men who yearned to flee from the world; now the world had intruded upon it, the same old, unwelcome guest.

From the window under one of the five small domes the light spread slow and ashy into the cell and on the narrow bed guarded by a great black crucifix. Padre Costantino, dressed in his threadbare black habit, sat by the bed with his hands joined in the usual gesture of prayer. His seventy years of age rested oppressively heavy on him that day.

Kallyna was all wrapped in a blanket, but still shivered. Her eyes were closed. Only her ragged breathing revealed that she wasn't sleeping. Next to her, on a stool, were a bowl and a mortar and pestle. The old abbot had been mixing healing herbs for her, but hadn't been able to find any healing words.

She knew, he had told her everything: Vasili killed, Arni wounded, her mother, Sila and Michele carried off by the pirates. Kallyna hadn't cried. She had railed against God, shunning her survival as an act of supreme injustice that she would never accept. In her grief she was twisted like a sapling in a storm.

Only the poppy could soothe her. Under its effect, she seemed to be groping through an endless darkness crowded with faces, eyes, voices. But her eyelids couldn't lift, and her whole body felt like lead. While she struggled through that thick twilight she threw her arms out of the blanket, and Raimo's fingers had left marks around her wrists, like manacles.

On the third day a thundershower put the fires out, leaving blackened beams pointing upwards like fingers reproaching the heavens. Gathered in a hurry at the Castro, the council had begun to send messages to the neighboring towns, asking for help in the reconstruction of the Portammare. Cosimo Falizza, acting as temporary governor, wanted to have the few captured Saracens tortured so they would reveal where they came from and rescuers could be sent. But there weren't enough soldiers left to man such an expedition; so the pirates were taken to the *Scoglio della Galera,* the Gaol Rock where all Saracen prisoners were executed. There they died a slow death, chained to the cliff with the sea up to their shoulders.

Down at the Marina the fishing boats lay abandoned on the wet sand. Some the Saracens had stolen, others they had sunk. The southern watchtower had burned along with the sentries in it, leaving nobody to guard that stretch of coast. Tropea was left defenseless, a gull's nest plundered by hawks.

Gheorghe and Tresa Casali hadn't had any sleep in two days and nights. They had waked over Vasili and watched over Arni, who was recovering slowly between fits of fever. Because Tresa didn't want to leave Arni alone for a moment, she sent Gheorghe around to learn what had become of Kallyna. Gheorghe found about her at San Nilo from Padre Elias. The monk had told him also that it wasn't wise to move her yet. Then Padre Elias had gone back with Gheorghe to take Vasili's body.

It hadn't been easy to persuade Tresa to let go of the body. As soon as she had heard the mule's hooves in front of the door, she had jumped to her feet, as if realizing only now what had happened. She had started to call Vasili over and over, as she would have done on a morning he had overslept. Then she had burst into tears, after so many days, and she had let them take him.

As a sign of respect, Padre Elias had him buried in the upper right corner of the chapel, and he had the green and black oars from the boat planted on the grave. The oars rested against the wall next to the overturned Grecian capital that was used as a footstool. The sunlight coming through the window high behind the altar would keep shining on them, as though they were still lifted in the *ontre* at the end of a fishing day.

❄   ❄   ❄

On the fourth day, in the cell above the chapel, Kallyna woke up. She was alone, and for a moment she couldn't tell where she was, what day it was.

33

Then everything came back to her like a great bitter wave — the attack, the escape, her family destroyed.

From the hallway she heard moans of pain. It seemed that pain was all around her, and that hiding would not help. She lifted aside the blanket and put her feet on the floor. Her left ankle was bandaged tightly, and it hurt. But she set her teeth and limped to the threshold, holding onto the wall.

The hallway was crowded with people, wounded and refugees. The monks had been treating them as best they could, tearing up even the altar cloths for bandages. Children cried, women prayed. She recognized Daniele d'Andria, one of her father's friends, and by the look on his face she knew he was dying. A woman was nursing Melissa Yeraki's baby daughter, whom Kallyna herself had held at the baptismal font ten days before. Melissa had been killed while trying to hide her daughter in her cellar. Palma Scordo screamed without comfort, clutching a torn shawl. It was all that remained of her two daughters, carried off by the raiders. The servants from the household of Rannulfo Massara had nowhere to go now that their master's family had been wiped out. Two soldiers were carrying away the body of a third, dragging his sword along.

Kallyna scanned the devastation before her. What a big lie, she thought. Raimo had made it all up to scare her to death.

Then she saw Maddalena di Nico, Gheorghe's mother, crouched in a corner like a puppet with the strings cut. She limped toward the woman, and at every step an absurd hope rose inside her. Maddalena had been at the wedding, Maddalena would finally tell her the truth. Yes, yes, Kallyna thought, her mother was waiting for her back home and her father was going to give her a sound thrashing for staying out all night.

"Maddalena," she whispered. "Maddalena?"

The woman raised her face, wondering who that stranger could be.

"It's me, Kallyna d'Àrgira…your goddaughter."

Maddalena frowned. "I don't have any goddaughters. I don't know you, go away. I'm waiting for Gheorghe to bring me some pears, I like pears." She smiled wide. "Do you like pears? Then I'll save some for you, sweetheart, we'll eat them together."

Kallyna stepped back. She couldn't see Gheorghe anywhere. She felt someone behind her; it was Padre Angelo.

"What is she saying?" she asked the young monk. "For the love of God, what is she talking about?"

The boy didn't look at her. "I don't know. She's been like this for four days now... Maybe she's better off like this."

"Gheorghe," Kallyna whispered. "My Gheorghe. Is he dead too?"

Padre Angelo kept his head low and didn't answer.

Maddalena pulled herself up and shook her head. "No, dear, he's not dead. Nobody's dead. I know where they all are, I'll tell you if you keep it a secret."

The woman's vacant smile horrified her. She tore herself away and stumbled toward the end of the hallway, seeking sanctuary. She hobbled down the worn stairs, not knowing where they led. She saw the open doors of the chapel and went in.

A sea of candles burned inside, their flames fluttering like soft petals. The walls were alive with the wings of angels flying in the golden night of the frescoes; and Jesus the Pantokrator, the Ruler of All, curved high on the ceiling, his large eyes staring from his gaunt face.

She dragged herself to a bench and fell down on her knees, sobbing. In her mind she sought desperately the words of a prayer. The thought of being alone filled her with dread. There was no one left who could tell her what to do, and life wasn't a weight to be carried all on one's shoulders.

Then she saw the oars in the upper right corner, so very familiar and so horribly out of place. They seemed to beckon her from beyond the sea of candles, like crossed arms.

She forced herself up and went over to them. She could feel the smooth packed earth of the chapel's floor rise and fall very gently under her feet, where Vasili was. She stopped in front of the oars and ran her hands over the weathered wood, feeling every small crinkle in the green and black paint. Unexpectedly, she remembered.

"Please be happy, daughter."

How did he know? she wondered.

"No lost minute of our lives is ever going to be paid back to us."

So many regrets in those words, and still so much acceptance of what was true. Strangely, her pain was soothed, like a musty room sweetened by a gust of good wind.

She pressed her lips to each one of the oars. In his heart of hearts Vasili d'Àrgira had always understood. She wouldn't have to ask for his forgiveness.

❊   ❊   ❊

On the morning of the fifth day the monks met to decide what was to be done about the refugees. It was decided that the monastery would take in all males from the age of ten who had been left without support. The younger children were entrusted to the families of their closest relatives; some girls would earn their living as servants in the homes of the lords. Kallyna offered her house to Maddalena di Nico, but she kept refusing, claiming that Gheorghe was going to take care of her. In her madness Maddalena would soon become a recluse, and from then on all that Kallyna could do for her was bring her some food whenever Maddalena could be persuaded to accept it.

At midday, when the first group of people left San Nilo, Kallyna sent word to Uncle Gheorghe Casali that she was waiting to be taken home. While she waited, she found out from a man who had been at the wedding that Michele had put up such a savage resistance, refusing to be separated from Sila and Neia, that the pirates had been forced to take him along.

The news comforted Kallyna enormously. It seemed to her that as long as Michele was with them, nothing could be so bad. She set about looking for more news.

A boy who lived near the Portammare told her that the three were still together when he had seen them being marched down the stairway to the Marina with the rest of the captives. Someone else said that at a certain point, when again the Saracens had tried to pull Michele away from the two women, he had made as if to push them both to their deaths off the staircase; and the pirates, frightened at the thought of losing in that manner two, in fact three pieces of merchandise, had allowed them to stay together for the time being.

Some hours later Gheorghe arrived at the monastery. Kallyna kissed again the earth on Vasili's grave, then hobbled into her uncle's arms. Gheorghe promised to put aside some bushels of wheat from his fields as a thanksgiving to the monks for their help. Then he eased Kallyna up on the saddle of his mule and prodded the animal toward the main road.

As they neared the town, it seemed to Kallyna that she had never seen it more beautiful than now, etched against the raw edge of the sky, with the Porta Vaticana opened to her like two open hands. But inside the walls was a world she didn't recognize.

Burned houses stood around her, heaps of rubble where next spring the woolly dandelion would grow. To some she had gone to deliver the linen she had embroidered and the blankets she had woven; in others she had played when she was a little girl, with Sila and their friends. She could see her mother coming back from the fountain with the heavy clay jar balanced on her head. The market stalls were empty; emptiest of all was the one where Vasili had sold his still-wriggling catch to his haggling customers. All of what had been her life paraded before her eyes, like relics in a glass case.

Aunt Tresa was waiting on the doorsteps. She looked ten years older in her *saia*, the long shawl of black woolen cloth. The good humor and the energy Kallyna remembered about her were gone.

Tresa wanted to smile, but couldn't. "Look at your best dress, it's ruined," was all she could say.

The house seemed to have grown larger, and so silent. But in the kitchen coals were burning under a crock of food after five days, and in the garden the two turtledoves were still in their wicker cage hanging from a branch of the lemon tree.

They went up to Arni's bedside. The room was dim, and smelled of sweat and medicinal herbs.

"Sometimes he raves," Tresa whispered. "He calls Vasili, Michele... you."

"Padre Elias looked at the wound," Gheorghe said. "He says he will live."

Kallyna felt gently Arni's forehead, then wiped it with a corner of the sheet. "I will take care of him. We will get by."

They had supper as the daylight waned. They tried to put together everyday matters, but the conversation went on listlessly, fitful.

"We might use the pantry room to store all this furniture," Tresa said. "We'll sleep upstairs... there's plenty of room."

"What about the *ontre?*" Kallyna asked.

"It will have to be sold," Gheorghe said. "I spoke to Demetrio Pentelica. He says he's willing to buy it for a hundred and fifty *scudi*."

"A hundred and fifty?" she cried out. "But it's worth more than three hundred!"

Gheorghe nodded sadly. "I know. But what good will it do to have it rot on the beach?"

There was a long silence. In the garden the cooing of the turtledoves mixed with the chanting of the first crickets in a soft ripple of sounds.

"Can't we keep the ontre for Arni?" Kallyna whispered. "Vasili was master of a boat when he was twenty."

Gheorghe shrugged. "And how will he man it? Who can he pay to be his lookout, his spearer, his oarsman? He'll have to thank the Lord if someone hires *him*."

Kallyna felt sick with pain. Arni so proud forced to beg for his livelihood. She simply couldn't let that happen. She would think of something else, anything else.

Tresa hadn't said much, numb with grief. "I wonder what has become of Raimo," she ventured then.

"I don't know," Kallyna said.

Tresa's face took on a look of admiration. "It was a miracle, the way he saved you... and at risk of his own life! That man has courage."

Kallyna cleared the table and didn't speak. Then she went to close the garden door. While she did that she heard the horn call three times from the Porta Vaticana.

"Do they still sound the curfew?" she wondered contemptuously. "I thought the Normans had better things to do than take care of this town."

Tresa crossed her arms. "This time it's not their fault. It's the devil who put his tail in front of them, or else they would have been here a week ago... and nothing would have happened."

Kallyna slammed the door shut. "If it's the devil's doing, then to his finest hell he ought to take them," she said.

IV

They took turns watching Arni, and Kallyna wanted the first part of the night. She sat by his bed, holding his hand and measuring every breath he took, stifling the tears that came back to choke her.

When she woke up the morning after, she heard Aunt Tresa talking with a neighbor who had come to bring the *ricònsolo*, the offer of food made to comfort families in mourning.

Tresa thanked the woman hoarsely.

"May the black soul of Mohamet drag them all to ruin," she cursed fiercely, busy by the hearth. "Pagans that geld the men and make whores of the women…" Her voice cracked. "Poor Sila, still in her wedding gown! I see her in my sleep and I want to scream."

A little later the neighbor left. Kallyna went downstairs and put her arms around Tresa. "Let's eat something, Aunt," she said.

In the afternoon, after taking care of Arni's wound, she sat again by him making alterations in a black dress that had been her mother's. When she put it on, Tresa looked at her, heartbroken at seeing her so young wearing the color of nuns and widows. But she bowed bravely her graying head and smiled.

"You could wear rags and still look like a queen," she said.

Toward sundown, when Gheorghe was about to return from the farm, Tresa went to draw water from the fountain, leaving Kallyna to make supper. While Kallyna sat in the kitchen cutting up a piece of salt meat and thinking about Arni, the front door quietly creaked open, making her start. It was Raimo.

"What are you doing here?" she asked. "Why didn't you knock?"

"Tresa saw me, outside."

"I didn't. What a way is this of entering a house, like a thief?"

Raimo went to the cupboard and poured himself some wine from a jar. Everything about that terrible night seemed to have barely touched him, like a storm that never ruffles the lowest branches.

"Keep your voice down and don't start with your nonsense," he muttered.

"Why not?" she countered. "You don't want to be noticed? To be asked *how* you got away? Don't worry, everybody thinks you're a hero, the savior of Kallyna d'Àrgira…. But you didn't dare show your face in town for five full days."

He drank his wine. "Never mind what happened. You're just too thick to understand. Some gratitude I get!"

She nodded once with a jerk of her neck. "Never mind what happened, right. All you lost were stumbling blocks."

"I *loved* your father," he countered vehemently. "I was up at San Nilo this morning, to pay the monks for a headstone of red marble that the governor himself will never have on his grave. Or my own father."

Kallyna was astounded. "A marble headstone! And who on earth gave you permission to do a thing like that? You must have heard him say a thousand times that he wanted to be buried without vanities, like a true man of the people." Her voice was twisted with anger. "You, Raimo Trani, you… Not even dead will you leave us in peace!" She forced herself to sit down and went back to cutting the meat with short, furious strokes of her kitchen knife.

Raimo shook his head. "You don't know a thing about life," he said. "What's all this garbage about being 'a man of the people'? Your father could have lived like a lord, instead he chose to work every day of his life until the last day, like a serf. Work is nothing but God's curse upon Adam. What is it that makes you d'Àrgiras so damn proud of everything, even things no one in his right mind would be proud of?"

Kallyna didn't look at him and didn't reply. She thought of her father, and tears welled again in her eyes.

Raimo came closer to her, taut with anger. "And how long do you think you can play the fussy princess with me now, uh? You're nothing but a woman, and there are only two things a woman's good for, to be mounted and to make children!"

She jumped up, with the knife in her hand. "Maybe what you say is true," she said. "I've heard it so many times I almost believe it. But whatever it is that I'm good for, it won't be for your enjoyment, because I'll end up buried alive in a convent first."

"I'll tell you where you'll end up," he spat out. "With the whores at Santuzza's tavern, that's where. And then I'll come and see you, for five *scudi* a night."

Kallyna lunged against him, chasing him toward the door. "Get out of my house. Get out or I'll kill you!"

Raimo slammed the door shut, leaving her sobbing.

Tresa was back some time later. Seeing her crying frightened her to death. "My God, is it Arni?"

"Why did you let him in, why didn't you tell me he was here?" Kallyna moaned. "Now he comes to insult me in my own house!"

Tresa stroked her head. "All right now, all right. I'm sure he didn't mean to upset you. You're so tired, you've been crying so much…. He just cares about you being alone."

Kallyna stopped crying and left Tresa's arms. "Everybody seems to worry about me being alone," she said bitterly. "Sometimes it looks like you're all trying to get rid of me with this marriage, and the sooner the better."

Tresa frowned. "Get rid of you? You know that's not true. But you also know that's not going to be easy for you without a man. A man is everything in this world of evil."

Kallyna limped back to her chores. "No, Aunt," she said. "I want you and Uncle Gheorghe to give him back his bride price. The pledge my father made to him is broken now, and he knows it. My father never understood who Raimo Trani is. None of you understands."

Tresa folded her black *saia* and put it away. "All right, my treasure. We'll talk about it when Gheorghe comes back. Calm down now." She went to check on the pot that was bubbling on the fire. "Besides," she added, "you couldn't marry while in strict mourning even if you wanted to. Hand me a ladle, the chicory looks done."

❋ ❋ ❋

It was almost daybreak when the guards opened one of the doors cut in the Porta Vaticana and let in a lone messenger on horseback. The first glimmer of light was creeping from behind the hills like a shudder of pink. After the messenger had called at every appointed house, the Castro filled with the voices and the hasty footsteps of the members of the Council abruptly awakened from their sleep.

Guillaume Auriac and Eude of Berwick were going up the stairs to the main hall, speaking between themselves in French.

"By god, Guillaume," Berwick was saying, "why can't these stubborn Calabrese understand? They've even marched at night, with little or no sleep in between!"

Auriac shook his grey head, pulling up on the side of the sword the belt he'd had no time to buckle up properly.

"I know, I know. But if we let them in with the usual pomp and circumstance, we'll only stir up a hornets' nest. You weren't out there in the streets during the past days. They blame us Normans for the raid, which means they blame the king and his new man. Falizza is not a fool. If he says no giving of the keys, let him have his way for this once."

In the council hall sleepy servants were hastening to light torches and candles. Cosimo Falizza was sitting at the oak table, with the messenger by his side.

"Please, Your Lordships, be seated," he called out. He exchanged a few more words with the messenger under his breath, while the councilors filed each into his seat marked by the coat of arms of its owner. Then he stood up and cleared his throat nervously.

"Your Excellencies, notables of the Crown. We have just learned that a squadron of one thousand soldiers is about to enter our town. Their commander is the lord d'Hancourt, whom the king has appointed new governor of Tropea."

He paused, pressing his hands on the table. "Now let me be blunt, and may God enlighten my judgment. It is my opinion, which I have pondered quite carefully, that the usual public ceremony of the giving of the keys to the town should be — as an utterly exceptional case, of course — omitted in our present circumstances."

A murmur of surprise from the council interrupted his speech. Then Berwick stood up, his great height held straight as a ship's mast.

"That would indeed be an utterly exceptional case, my lord Falizza," he thundered in his heavy foreign accent. "No town has ever received the right hand of King Roger as a common man, and even, as I seem to understand, in silence and secrecy, as if he were a thief. The ceremony of the keys is the very symbol of our loyalty to the king, and as such it can never be omitted!"

Guillaume Auriac slapped his thigh with his glove. "You talk like a blockhead," he exclaimed in French, so that the insult would remain within the circle of his peers. "There isn't a single door in all Tropea that hasn't been battered out of its hinges, beginning with the Portammare. What the hell would d'Hancourt need keys for?"

"Don't forget," added heatedly Francesco della Scala, "that we ought to call ourselves lucky. A better organized raid would have left no stone standing."

"Precisely," said Auriac. "What we fear now is that those stones will be used to greet our new governor. And *that* would be a truly worthy welcome for the right hand of King Roger!"

"True, true," Falizza pressed. "The people are angry. They demand to know what we are going to do about their houses, their boats. And we are already in debt up to our necks, my lords, merely to rebuild the Portammare!"

In the wake of his words everyone was silent. Then Falizza waved his hands, calling again for attention. "However, your Excellencies, I do have a proposal. I beg you to hear it."

"I'm not going to hear anything," Berwick grumbled.

Auriac pulled him down by the hem of his cloak. "Sit down and don't be a mule."

"What I propose is," Falizza began with hesitation, "that the keys be given privately, here in this room, in the presence of the Council alone. This way we shall, hopefully, fulfill our duties to the Crown and also avoid confrontations with the townsfolk."

Auriac hammered his fist on the armrest of his chair, nodding at each stroke. "Amen, my dear Falizza. You are a born diplomat."

But Falizza's eyes were fixed on Berwick, who was conferring under his breath with the man sitting next to him on the opposite side. At last Berwick surrendered. "It does sound reasonable," he said.

Falizza sighed with relief. "Thank you all, my lords."

The council broke up amidst a murmur of comments. The servants opened the doors, while the torches paled already in the light of the new day.

Auriac fastened his cloak around his neck, then put his hand on Berwick's shoulder. "Don't fret, my friend," he said. "I know the young d'Hancourt. It's his first official appointment, and I bet my horse he won't even know the difference."

❋   ❋   ❋

Early in the afternoon, while Kallyna was at the fountain to draw water, a woman from the neighborhood came by in a hurry to give her the news.

"They're coming! They're on the main road!"

Kallyna looked up from her jar. The woman was already striding off toward the Porta Vaticana, and now Assunta d'Andria was coming, too, with her baby in her arms. Assunta looked distraught with rage.

"Cosimo Falizza wants to hide our wounds from the eyes of the Normans," she said. "But we are going to show them anyway. If they are here when it's time to collect taxes, they must be here also when our men are butchered!"

Without a moment's hesitation Kallyna put down her jar and followed Assunta. Not even the pain in her ankle, still bandaged, could stop her.

A quiet stream of people, mostly women and children, was trickling down from streets and alleys toward the Porta Vaticana. The guards on the turrets saw it and called out to the soldiers below, who instantly clustered into a cordon bristling with lances. Beyond the gate was a slow cloud of dust coming closer and closer with the weariness of the very last miles.

The crowd broke against the soldiers' line like a dark wave against a reef. Shouting, the soldiers tried to push it back. Kallyna was behind a red-haired man who spoke to her angrily in French. She couldn't understand his words, but his look was enough to make her step back a little.

Looking up at the Castro, she saw that Cosimo Falizza was at one of the balconies with other lords. He seemed to be hiding behind the shutters, fidgeting. The eyes of all were riveted to the main road, those of the women peering grimly from the folds of their long black shawls. Even the children dared not whimper.

"Here they are," said a young man under his breath.

The first four rows of soldiers passed through the gate. They walked on stupefied with exhaustion, treading the road as if it would never end. The banners on their lances were white with dust and hung limp as rags.

"They do look bad," said an old woman standing next to Kallyna.

Kallyna didn't hear her. While the anger of the crowd seemed to be melting away at the sight of those worn-out men, a dark anguish was rising inside her. If those men had been there only a few short days ago, her life would still be in one piece. No one, no one had the right to walk in now and proclaim himself governor of the people he had forsaken in their direst need. The red-haired soldier pushed her again with the shaft of his lance, but this time she didn't budge.

Two riders were now approaching the gate, mounted on good Arabian horses. One seemed to be in his thirties, bearded and big, the other was younger. She couldn't see their faces well, with the sun in her eyes; but the head of the younger man seemed to gleam with the same light, a head of thick blond hair, sweet as a boy's.

His eyes were of a dark, solid blue. The dust of the road was all over him, on his tunic, on his cloak, on his boots. As he swept with his gaze the crowd around him, his face had a wild, astonished look of fatigue and defeat. It was like the look of a wounded wolf that limps back to his den and finds it empty. He had gambled with time, he had lost, and no one would ever forgive him. Kallyna could not take her eyes off that apparition. The old woman next to her crossed herself with a sort of superstitious fear, as though she had just seen a wrathful Saint George made flesh.

The crowd stirred, pressing against the breakwater of soldiers and lances. Suddenly Assunta lifted her baby in the air and showed him silently to the young Norman. With her ragged dress and tangled black hair, offering him that tiny bundle, she seemed to loom as terrible as a nemesis. After her two, three more widowed mothers held up their babies, or pushed forward their children for him to see.

The Norman threw back his head, averting his eyes. At any other time Kallyna would have seen that gesture for what it was, the touchy pride of a boy trying desperately to be brave; in her grief she saw instead the arrogance of foreign lords who would not even look upon the misery of their subjects. She started to push her way along in the crowd, and the more the Norman rode impassively on, the more her outrage grew.

A little girl slipped away from the crowd and stood in the middle of the road. The Norman saw her, and without slowing his horse he motioned her to move out of his way. The girl skipped aside, laughing in her innocence; but to Kallyna that gesture of his was like a spark to kindling.

She ducked under the arms of the soldiers and flung herself at the Norman like a black butterfly, nearly pulling the reins from his hands. "Traitor! Deserter!" she damned him, her face glowing with anger. "Where were you when they died? Is this how the king watches over our lives?"

The horse reared up with a frightened neigh. The Norman had to jerk the reins back and struggle against the animal to avoid trampling her. Everything was confusion. A soldier rushed forward to restrain the horse, two more to seize her by the arms and pull her away.

When a measure of quiet was finally made, the Norman looked down at her from high on his unsteady mount. His face wore an expression of wrath such as Kallyna had never seen, not on her father's face, not on Raimo's face, not on the face of Christ the Judge painted in church.

The young man fingered the horsewhip he carried tied to his saddle. Then he tore it off and tossed it to one of the soldiers.

"Give her five good lashes," he said in his teeth, and reined away.

The older Norman put his horse closer to that of the young man and leant over to say something. Kallyna caught only some of the words. "By the True Cross, Dàlibor d'Hancourt, have you lost your mind?"

The young man was already riding away.

She was pushed to the side of the road and down on her knees. The crowd around her was swaying with a murmur of horror. Two women took the hand of the soldier who was holding the whip, begging him to let her go. The soldier himself didn't know what to do. He stood there confused, until another soldier had to take the whip from him and carry out the order.

The first lash came as Kallyna was looking across at the young Norman riding away toward the Castro, so that she thought the sight of him would forever after be linked in her mind with that onslaught of pain. She shut her eyes. The second lash came, and the third, and the fourth, and the fifth. She bit her lip until she tasted blood, while the voices behind her seemed to drown in a sea of thunder.

Tresa was fighting the guards to be let through, screaming.

❋　　　　❋　　　　❋

After the hasty giving of the keys at the Castro, no one dared to speak of the incident at the Porta Vaticana. Falizza, who had performed the ceremony, considered himself lucky that the crowd had not protested in a worse manner. Still, he was appalled by that first encounter with the man who was now, to everyone's misfortune, the new governor of Tropea. Too young, too impulsive, and lacking the most elementary skills of a ruler, which include mercy toward the ruled. His opinion was shared by all those who had witnessed the scene, together with a good deal of apprehension for the future.

However, when Falizza was told that the girl who had provoked the incident was Kallyna d'Àrgira, he locked himself in the council room with the bringer of the news and vented out his anger with him.

"Five lashes?" he seethed. "Well given. Those d'Àrgiras are going to be my death. Wretched breed of troublemakers, as if her father hadn't been enough."

While the afternoon waned, the soldiers took up quarters in the Castro, crowding for their rations of food and wine. D'Hancourt and his companion retired to their room on the second floor. They sent for someone to wash their clothes, and then for someone to bring up a tub of water.

No sooner had the servant closed the door than the older Norman confronted his younger friend with an infuriated look. "You *had* to do it, didn't you? I suppose there simply was no civilized way to show them who's master."

D'Hancourt unbuckled the belt that held his sword and tossed it away. The heavy weapon landed with a din of iron on the floor next to one of the two beds and lay there like a big toy discarded by a bored child. Then he unbuckled the belt that held his clothes and he took off his cloak, his tunic and his boots, which all ended up in a heap by the door. The coat of mail came out last in a jingling of links, as he jerked it off his neck with a grimace of disgust.

"You still have breath left to talk, haven't you? Save it for when you'll be under the noose and let me be!" and the coat of mail flew clear across the room, collapsing on the steps of the fireplace.

The other man took a sardonic bow, then went to open the window.

"Have mercy, sweet lord! I'm just a lowly bastard son who couldn't possibly comprehend the many points of honor of a purebred knight such as yourself." He threw the shutters open. "And may we thank all the blind angels for that. At least there's still one of us who can afford to be sane."

From the courtyard came a sound of marching feet and the curt orders of the master of arms.

D'Hancourt slammed his fist on the table. "Did you *hear* what that little witch called me? In front of the whole town! How else can you teach obedience to people who jump at you the moment you set foot into their stinking walls?"

The older man wheeled around with a motion of annoyance. "By the skirts of Saint Anne, Dàlibor. If you lose your patience so quickly with some hysterical girl, what are you going to do when the real trouble begins?" He shook his head. "You have much, much to learn if you intend to keep that stubborn head of yours on your shoulders."

D'Hancourt took a step forward, pointing a finger at his companion. "And I should learn from Geoffroi de Vire, right? Well, my friend, we're no longer at court, and it's no longer fencing and jousting for the ladies of Palermo. Here you will kindly keep your advice to yourself, while I make my own mistakes."

De Vire grinned, but with an air of compassion. "I feel sorry for you… You're going to like your new job a lot less in the days to come. There's a bit more than pageantry to it, you know."

There was a knock on the door; de Vire went to open. Two boys brought in a wooden tub, then one by one several buckets of water.

"That is none of your business," d'Hancourt said. "If you really want to know it, yes, I had to do it. I like people to know from the start who Dàlibor d'Hancourt is."

"And now we all know who he is," de Vire mumbled. "A snapping cub fresh out of King Roger's kennels."

D'Hancourt chose not to listen. He took off his sweat-stained undertunic and his hose and he lowered himself in the lukewarm water with a shudder of pleasure.

"Oh Lord," he muttered. "What an abominable life this is. When I was fifteen I couldn't wait to be given a title. Knight, governor, any damn thing at all, just so I could start biting into some power. Now the more I taste power the more it gives me a bellyache."

He reached for a pitcher of wine from the table. "All that horrible trek for nothing… for nothing. And they were looking at us as if we were the ones who drove the nails through Christ's own feet!"

He took a long draft from the pitcher. "At least I can still get drunk. I don't want to see anything, hear anything, think of anything anymore," and he kept drinking and mumbling.

De Vire pulled off his boots, then started to pummel his saddle-sore buttocks. "I bet you didn't even notice how lovely she is," he said.

"Who?"

"The little witch you had to thrash like that. A girl like her has every right to a far different treatment, even from an oaf like you."

D'Hancourt plunged his head into the water and snorted, half asleep. "Then you go mount her for me. I'm so damn tired I couldn't do it if she came to dance naked before my eyes."

De Vire stopped. He cocked his chin to one side, conjuring up the scene with a lecherous grin caught in his beard. Then he shook his head.

"You wretched fool," he sighed.

❀   ❀   ❀

The bed seemed to be pitching like a ship on a choppy sea. Kallyna lay face down on it, trying to fight the pain that rang through her. Tresa was sobbing, glancing at the bloody streaks and rocking her body back and forth in anguish.

"Look what they've done," Tresa sobbed. "Look what they could do to a child!"

After a while she forced herself up and went to get the ointment she had used for Arni. Arni had regained consciousness the night before. He had heard the commotion when Tresa had brought Kallyna home, and had asked to know what it was all about. Tresa had told him that Kallyna had hurt himself falling with her water jar.

Coming back to the bed she saw that Kallyna's eyes were wide-open, as though she were quietly daydreaming. Kallyna hadn't said a word yet, and her staring look worried Tresa more than anything else. She gathered Kallyna's long hair to one side and began applying the ointment on her shoulders, trying to put down her stubby fingers as gently as she could. But no response came, not even a moan.

"Kallyna?" she whispered. "Will you tell me what happened?"

"Nothing happened," Kallyna said slowly, absently. "I'm all right. It doesn't hurt."

She burrowed her face in the pillow and closed her eyes. She yearned to be alone. She had never dreamed that somebody standing in the same room with her could all of a sudden intrude so much upon the island of amazement that the world had become. One more word from Tresa and she would start to scream.

Tresa resigned herself to leaving. She went to close the window. Kallyna raised her hand to stop her. "No." Tresa reopened the shutters. The evening seemed to pour in like a dust of blue stones, with a scent of sea and lemons.

Kallyna had to dig into a thick golden fog to remember his face, the gold of the afternoon sunlight and of his head. In her mind she kept hearing the endless shuffling of the soldiers' feet as they went by her, and the frantic screams of Tresa begging the guards.

It doesn't hurt, she thought. He could do it again a thousand times and still it would not hurt. Still she would trust him. Even though she knew nothing about who he was, she already knew beyond all doubts that he was a good man who for a moment had forgotten himself. She too had forgotten herself, she thought; she had hurt him first, with the same mindless fury.

Arni called her softly from the next room. She remembered that he was in love with her and that up to this moment she had never been able to understand what went on inside him.

"Kallyna… are you asleep? Are you in pain?"

She stared at the open window, at the sky beyond it.

"You are so dear, Arni," she said. "So very dear."

V

BOTH SLEPT LATE THE MORNING AFTER, Kallyna under the effect of the herb infusion Tresa had made for her, d'Hancourt drunk with wine and exhaustion.

Cosimo Falizza was forced to act as governor for one more day. He had the market reopened, the rubble cleared; then he sent for Raimo Trani and entrusted him with the reconstruction of the Portammare. Trani had no trouble finding men willing to do the work. All those whom the raid had left penniless crowded at his door to be hired.

Even so, it would take weeks to complete the rebuilding, and the gate was vital to the town. So Falizza went to ask d'Hancourt for some of his soldiers to be employed as woodcutters and cart drivers. As soon as d'Hancourt was able to stand on his feet again, he selected a dozen of his men and sent them over to him.

Whether the people of Tropea liked it nor not, the Normans' arrival reminded them that life must resume its usual course. Soon the familiar sounds of hammers, cartwheels, bells and hooves merged once again in their comforting hum after days left entirely to the lonely heartbeat of the sea.

Kallyna didn't set foot out of her house for the time it took her shoulders to heal. It was during that time that Tresa brought her a commission. The old baroness Irene della Scala was having the monks of San Nilo say a mass a day for her grandson kidnapped by the Saracens, and she wanted to pay them with a fine altar cloth. Eager for the distraction that work afforded her, Kallyna began to weave the moment the skeins of white and gold thread were delivered to her.

Arni was up and about the last day of July, still quite weak but finally out of danger. He knew nothing about the lashing. Tresa and Kallyna had done the impossible to hide it from him. But one day Maddalena d'Andria came by to return a water jar she had borrowed, and asked Kallyna how she was doing.

Tresa motioned Maddalena to lower her voice: Arni was upstairs and might hear her.

Maddalena embraced Kallyna. "I'm so proud of you, daughter," she said under her breath. "None of us had the courage to speak out before the Normans. Like a flock of dumb sheep! But you are just like your father, made of fine silver. You spoke out for all of us… and you paid, too, for all of us."

"No matter," Tresa couldn't help putting in with pride. "Vasili too went to his grave with scars on his back, and they only made his skin tougher."

Maddalena left. As soon as the door was closed behind her, Arni came running down the stairs. His face showed so much horror and rage that Tresa stepped back, frightened.

He strode up to Kallyna, made her turn around, pulled down the neckline and looked at her shoulders. "What are these?" he gasped. "These belong on *my* back, not yours! O Lord, O merciful Lord. The bloody bastards, even the women now."

Tresa tried to take him by the arm, but Arni wouldn't calm down. He demanded to be told everything that had happened, and he kept cursing as he had never cursed in his life. He wanted Kallyna to be as angry as he was. But she just sat with her face in her hands, infuriating him more. Finally he stormed out of the house.

Kallyna picked up again her basket of thread. "He's right," she said, almost speaking to herself. "I should have stayed home. I should not have insulted that man. It's not his fault... It was never his fault."

All afternoon she sat at the loom, pressing the treadle, tossing the shuttle. For small fragments of time the repeated motions took her mind off that dark hidden thing inside her, that love she carried the way a mother carries her unborn, always inexorably together day and night. Raimo was back, but even her fear of Raimo should have been there and suddenly was not, and that too for a reason she could not think of. All she could think of was the new one who was there, like a gold coin found under a heap of laundry.

She rocked back and forth at the loom. The creaking of the wooden beams was like an old voice to her. *White thread, gold thread; white thread, gold thread.* She could almost hear what Vasili's words would have sounded like.

Out of all the men you could have chosen! Vasili would have said. *Now you've really done it, daughter. Now you really have no way out.* And in her mind she could hear her own answer, too. *Yes, Father, I know. Lock me in the cellar if you want. This time I won't say a word. This time you're right.*

❋   ❋   ❋

The following day Uncle Gheorghe came back from the farm earlier than usual. He had spoken to Arni about selling the *ontre*, but Arni would have none of it. When he had invited him to go meet Demetrio Pentelica, the prospective buyer of the boat, Arni had curtly refused. But Kallyna begged Gheorghe to go with him, and Gheorghe didn't have the heart to refuse her.

It seemed to her that years had passed since the last time she had felt the smooth cobblestones of Piazza Portercole under her feet. It was a cloudy afternoon. Sultry gusts of *scirocco* blew from the sea, raising angry grey waves. When she heard the hammering of mallets coming from the Portammare she couldn't help wincing. They still sounded like the pounding of the battering ram of that terrible night.

The gate was a hub of activity and noise. Carts full of logs and planks rumbled by, bricks by the dozen were laid out to dry, ropes and pulleys hoisted big blocks of granite up the scaffolds.

A small army of masons shouted to one another above the din in a mixture of tongues — Calabrese, Italian, French, Greek. The Norman soldiers lent by d'Hancourt worked in a group apart. Light-skinned and unused to the heat, they toiled sullenly in the stifling wind, stripped to the waist. A woman dressed in black went around pouring wine from a clay jar, while a troop of children sat solemnly watching.

As she made her way through the gateway, Kallyna clung instinctively to Uncle Gheorghe, all too aware of how the men were looking at her. Atop one of the scaffolds a soldier nudged another, smiling.

The *ontre* lay canted on the sand, still covered by the burlap sheet that Vasili had left on the last time. Demetrio Pentelica was scrutinizing it in all its seams with careful eyes and hands. Grief stabbed Kallyna at that sight, as though in place of the boat her father's own flesh were up for sale.

"Have a good evening, Mastro Demetrio," Gheorghe said.

"And you too," the man replied. "I see you brought along your niece," he added, and his voice trailed as if asking why.

"The boat belonged to her father," Gheorghe said evenly. "And it still does."

Demetrio raised his hand in a conciliatory gesture. "It's all right. If it pleases you."

Gheorghe lifted the burlap sheet. "Everything's here," he said. "Rudder, planks and two spears. Only the oars are missing."

Demetrio nodded. "Yes, yes. I did offer you one hundred and fifteen *scudi*."

"One hundred and fifty," Kallyna corrected him briskly, laying her hand on the gunwale.

A patronizing smile thickened the wrinkles on the fisherman's face. "That was before it sat in the rain and in the night dew for almost two weeks," he said, "when the cracks in the hull weren't as big as my thumb."

"And how much will it cost you to pay for a good caulker?" Kallyna asked.

Demetrio started to wave his hands. "But, well…"

"Kallyna," said Gheorghe sternly.

"Wait, Uncle. Mastro Demetrio is a good man, he can tell us."

Her clear gaze forced the man to lower his own. "Certainly, certainly," Demetrio said quickly, and crossed himself to show that he was speaking the truth.

"Ten, there. Ten *scudi*."

"Then you can have the boat for one hundred and forty *scudi*, if you still want it," Kallyna concluded.

Demetrio thought for a minute, looking at the boat. Then he nodded reluctantly, and put out his right hand. "It's agreed then, Mastro Gheorghe. One hundred and forty *scudi*, may Saint Peter guard us all."

Gheorghe laid his right hand on the one offered to him. They shook them together three times, and the sale was made.

"The money's at my house," Demetrio said. "Come take it tonight before the curfew."

"I will," replied simply Gheorghe.

"A good night to you," Demetrio said, and walked away.

Kallyna stood by the boat, feeling the rough wood under her hands for the last time, and looking at the waves breaking against the cliff. Perhaps, she thought, if she waited long enough and patiently enough, some day they would all come back to her.

Gheorghe came closer. "I remember the day we bought it," he said under his breath, staring at the horizon.

Kallyna couldn't speak. Then she wheeled around and walked away from the beach.

They had reached the last step of the stairway when she saw Raimo. He was with Adelmo Stratta, a friend of his from a neighboring town, and he was showing him how the work at the Portammare was going on. Kallyna had to fight the impulse to run away and hide. Raimo was the very last person she wanted to see that day or any day. Then she set her teeth and marched up stiffly.

As soon as Raimo saw her, he left Adelmo and went straight to Gheorghe, but didn't bother to greet him. "I've been looking for you, Mastro Casali. Where's that crazy niece of yours?" He looked up. "There she is."

Gheorghe wanted to know why he was so upset. "You know very well why," Raimo replied. Then he took hold of Kallyna's arm and walked her to a less crowded corner, away from the gate.

"I ought to keep you locked up with a double lock," he began. "Whatever in hell possessed you to go yelling insults at the governor, huh? By God Almighty, have you gone completely out of your mind?"

Kallyna tried to pull her hand away. "You're hurting me. Let go of me!"

Raimo's anger, suppressed for so long, would not be silenced. "You're lucky we're outside, or else by now I would have made you black and blue all over… And that Norman bastard," he spat out, "that filthy son of a whore, making a spectacle of you!"

Alarmed, Gheorghe joined them. Raimo let go of Kallyna's arm and turned on him. "You please keep a good eye on this girl, Mastro Casali," he said furiously. "If she were my wife, she wouldn't go running around like a loose dog, you know."

Gheorghe looked Raimo squarely in the eyes and spoke quietly. "Are you going to tell me what to do with my own kin, Mastro Trani? I'm a few years older than you, I should well know."

Raimo walked away without replying and rejoined Adelmo by the gate.

"Let's go home, Uncle," Kallyna said, fighting tears of rage. "Let's go take that cursed bride price of his and throw it back in his face."

As she started to move, she felt the blood rush to her head: d'Hancourt was approaching the gate, walking straight toward them. He must have come to call his men back. While he went by the men dropped their hammers and saws and picked up their shirts, scrambling down the scaffolds.

Raimo greeted him with nervous deference. D'Hancourt pointed at the gate, at the surrounding wall, commenting on the work done; and Raimo explained, smiled, moved his hands up and down. So calmly now, Kallyna thought, so politely. He would have killed a lesser man in a moment for what d'Hancourt had done to her, but he fawned abjectly before the Norman my lord who gave him work and money. Her face was a grimace of disgust.

D'Hancourt listened absently, nodding once in a while. He seemed to be in a hurry, and when Raimo was done he quickly turned around to leave.

Raimo stopped him. He went to take Kallyna by the hand, made her walk up to him and stand in front of him. Stiff with shame, she couldn't look higher than d'Hancourt's spurs.

Raimo's voice sounded strained. "This, my lord, is Kallyna d'Àrgira, who will soon be my wife."

A frown of deep vexation appeared on d'Hancourt's face. During the past days he had had plenty of time to regret the lashing; then after he had found out who the victim was, he knew that sooner or later he would have to confront the anger of a man as important as the master builder of the county. But his vexation was short-lived. He bowed his head as impeccably as he would have done among his peers at the royal court.

"Congratulations," he intoned, blankly. "She's truly lovely. It would be hard not to notice her, even in a crowd."

Raimo tried his very best to smile.

.A clash of angry words made them all turn their heads. One of the Norman soldiers had started an argument with the woman in black who sold wine to the workers. The man had grabbed the empty jar from her and had smashed it to pieces against the wall. Both were shouting at the top of their voices.

"I tried to tell him I had no more wine," the woman cried out. "What can I do if I don't speak Frankish!"

D'Hancourt excused himself, strode over to the soldier and with a punch in the jaw sent him to join the broken shards on the ground. No one understood a word of the abuse he lavished onto the soldier in French; but the soldier must understand very well, because he kept his arms raised to protect his head.

One last insult had the man shuffling out of everybody's sight. Then d'Hancourt took two ducats from the leather purse he wore hanging from his belt and called the woman. "Here. Buy yourself another jar." The woman kissed his hand twice.

Kallyna, who hadn't moved a muscle, finally blinked. She would have been appalled, if she weren't instead gratified to see that those incredible outbursts of temper were entirely impartial. She allowed herself to think that perhaps that was just what he had meant to show her with this particular outburst, because when he turned he was now looking only at her.

"I must go now," he said. "It's been a pleasure meeting you all." When they raised their heads from their bow, he was gone.

The woman in black was fingering her two ducats with a look of disbelief. "Look, it's real gold…. Enough to buy *twenty* jars!" Raimo brushed her away curtly.

"Jesus," Adelmo Stratta marveled. "That man is God's own scourge!"

"Uncle, please let's go home," Kallyna urged.

"Eh, what a hurry!" Adelmo said. "You don't put her to bed at the same time as your chickens, do you Mastro Gheorghe?"

"No," Gheorghe replied, "and I don't stay up drunk all night braying at the moon like you do. I'll see you both tomorrow at mass."

Adelmo grinned. "Sure, Mastro Gheorghe, sure. Look for us under the cassock of the priest."

As she left both behind, relieved to be going home, Kallyna couldn't see the way Raimo was stalking her with his eyes. Then he looked at Adelmo, and Adelmo nodded with an air of agreement, as though the two of them had made a deal of some sort.

Then Raimo turned his back to his friend and his expression became one of bewildered desperation. "Why does she have to make me do this?" he wondered. "Why can't she be like every other woman?"

Adelmo loitered around him, shrugging.

"I can tell you all the numbers you need to build a church, a bridge, a tower seven stories high," Raimo said, shaking his head. "But I can't tell you that I ever learned one thought that's in her head."

He spat on the ground with an air of disgust at his own impotent confusion. "God damn the day I fell in love with her!"

❁   ❁   ❁

Tresa and Gheorghe, as they did every evening, sat on the steps of the front door chatting with some neighbors. Kallyna instead joined Arni in the garden. She sat on an old tree stump, watching him water the young turnip plants that spread in their furrows like thin green fingers.

"We sold the *ontre*," she said after a while. "One hundred and forty *scudi*."

Arni didn't look up, careful not to crush the plants with his feet.

"That's not the real price," he said grimly. "The real price are twenty years of sweat and blood gone forever with it."

Kallyna hung her head. "What are you going to do now?" she asked.

Arni put the wooden bucket down. "To begin with, I'm not going to beg Demetrio Pentelica to take me on *his* boat. I don't know what I'm going to do. Don't ask me."

She leaned over toward him. "Listen, tonight when we went to get the money for the boat I heard that Demetrio's youngest son is going to Vibona to become an apprentice in the house of a goldsmith. He said the entire stay will cost him only sixty *scudi*. So I thought you too could—"

Arni cut her off. "I won't even touch that money. You're going to be married soon. It would be like taking money from your husband, and I don't want to be in debt with Raimo Trani… or with anybody else."

She got up from the tree stump. "This must be your blockhead's way of thanking me," she said in anger. "I'm only trying to help you. The money is mine, do you understand, and I'll do whatever I please with it." Her lips began to tremble.

Arni nodded. "All right. Sit down and don't start crying. You know I cannot stand to see you cry."

She sat back down, trying to collect herself.

"Then will you take the money?" she asked again after some time. "Will you go to Vibona? You can learn a good trade, one that pays well. You wouldn't have to work for someone else, I could not bear that."

"And what are *you* going to do?" Arni replied. "Don't *you* need the money to get married? Or do you want Trani to buy you everything down to the last apron, as if you were the daughter of a poor man? That is something *I* could not bear now."

She looked at him with a bleak smile. "I will never get married. Don't you understand?"

Arni frowned. "No, I don't understand. You keep making fun of me, as though you didn't know how I feel toward you..."

She looked him squarely in the eyes. "I know how you feel toward me," she said. "Go to Vibona. Make yourself more respected than Raimo. Then come back and ask for me."

Arni said nothing. He searched her face, taken aback by the tone of challenge in her voice.

Again she leant over toward him, almost begging him. "I want you to become the best goldsmith in the county, just as you were the best lookout. I know you can do it." She took his hands and opened them up. "Look, if you wait too long, your hands will get too rough."

The touch of her fingers on his own moved Arni in his deepest heart. At last he smiled.

"All right. I'll think about it. It really is not at quite as easy as you put it, you know."

"It's my gift, Arni. A gift to both of us."

He nodded. "Just the same. I'll find a way to repay you. Vasili too started out barefoot, like me." There was a long silence. The night was seeping like ink over the walls of the garden. They listened to the sound of the horn announcing the curfew. The town was raising the gangplank, like a ship ready to set sail in the dark with her heavy cargo of hope.

"And please don't be so hard on me, all right?" Kallyna begged softly, holding onto Arni's sleeve.

"Me?" he wondered. "I would cut off both my arms for you... and you would still go your own way, like a blind lamb."

"It's not my fault," she said dully. "Do you think I *choose* to get into so much trouble all the time?"

Arni smiled. "Of course you do. That's why I care so much about you."

❀   ❀   ❀

August brought day after day of *solleone,* the hammering 'lion sun' that parched the whole world into submission. On the hills the chanting of the women who picked broomflower sounded like a prayer for mercy. The boats seemed suspended above the flat sea, striped butterflies hovering motionless in the glint of the heat.

Arni had taken to going to the farm with Gheorghe every day, needing to feel useful. Tresa kept house and watched over Kallyna like a hawk. Sometimes she would join her niece by the loom with wool and spindle, and entertain her with the latest gossip. Then she would realize that Kallyna wasn't paying attention, and Tresa would lapse into silence.

But not even Tresa's keen eyes could detect the little boy who followed them everywhere and then quickly scuttled out of sight. The little boy would rush to d'Hancourt and report everything he had seen, and d'Hancourt would put a few coins in the boy's hand. In just a couple of days he had learned all there was to know about her.

For her part, Kallyna saw d'Hancourt always from a distance and always with his bearded companion by his side. She always made sure neither one noticed her, going out of her way if she had to. Every Sunday at Mass, sitting with the common folk in the last pew, she saw him sitting in the front pew with the nobles. At the moment of the Offertory he climbed the marble steps to leave on the altar the customary offer of a loaf of bread and a small jar of wine, his symbolic duty as keeper and protector of the town. Sometimes she heard from the town crier's voice the orders he issued — a house rebuilt, a new toll levied, a thief jailed.

She couldn't know that every time he passed by her house he memorized a different detail of it — where her window was, how the garden was laid out; and that seeing a trash heap he had thrown on it his whip. She wove her cloth, eyes low on the shuttle, hands low on the thread; and he seemed to go with her wherever she went, making her scream in every fiber of her being. She wove and she cursed herself before God who wouldn't deliver her from that obsession.

Day followed day in the heavy summertime peace. The boats left every morning before sunup and came back every evening before sundown.

Somebody was born, somebody died, somebody got married and somebody ran away. She worked almost in a frenzy, even by candlelight, as if trying to race ahead of her own thoughts. The cloth was finished in three weeks.

It was a magnificent piece, shimmering all over with large and small stars grouped together into golden constellations. She had made beautiful things before, but this one took after her love. Tresa sighed in admiration, begging her to keep it at home for a few more days so she could enjoy it a little longer. But the morning after it was finished, one of Donna Irene's servants came to remind Kallyna that the cloth had to be delivered to San Nilo as soon as ready.

"You're not going alone, are you?" Tresa fretted.

Kallyna folded the cloth into a length of white linen and put it in her basket. "It's broad daylight, Aunt. You're always afraid of something."

Tresa waved her hands in the air, as if shooing away the ghosts of her own worries. "I don't know, daughter... Too many soldiers all over the place."

"Lidia has to go to the river for her laundry," Kallyna reassured her. "She said she'll come with me."

Tresa saw her to the door. "Good. But mind yourself, and don't be late."

The ripe summer morning was like a great sail unfurled all around her. It seemed as if every bird were singing perched on her shoulders.

Lidia met her in front of her house, carrying her laundry basket on her head. She insisted to see the altar cloth, then praised it endlessly all the way. Kallyna barely heard her. She had been forced to the girl's company because she lived in a world where she could not walk alone, and that galled her. There were invisible fetters forever rubbing at a woman's soul, she thought bitterly.

They were passing under the tall grey walls of the Castro when Lidia dug her elbow into Kallyna's side.

"Look, it's the governor," she said. "At the window, up on the second floor.... I think he's looking right at us."

Kallyna lowered her head and quickened her pace. "Let him look all he wants."

"Can I see your scars?" Lidia whispered. "Are they still there?"

"No," Kallyna lied, motioning her to hurry along. "There's nothing to see anymore."

Once they had walked through the Porta Vaticana, the walls hid from them the Castro. They couldn't see that d'Hancourt's black and blond figure had disappeared from the window. Soon they were out of the main road and on the pathway to San Nilo.

Such a small load of laundry was in Lidia's basket, Kallyna wondered. Even more suspicious was that tone of anticipation in her voice, underneath all her prattling. When the girl told her she had to go pick soapwort plants for her laundry, Kallyna was only too happy to part company. She would rather walk the rest of the way alone than listen to any more of Lidia's chatter.

They said goodbye. A few moments later Kallyna heard a muffled giggle somewhere behind her, and then a furious rustling of bushes. She told herself she'd better go on and mind herself. Then curiosity got the better of her. She retraced her steps and stood peeking through the bushes. Instantly she shrank back. Lidia was lying on the grass, her skirts pulled up to her waist and her hands groping in the curly hair of a young man who had been courting her all summer. Kallyna ran away.

The path became steeper, shaded by a thick vault of chestnut trees. It was cool and pleasant there, she thought, before remembering with a shudder that the last time she had gone up that path had been the night of the Saracen raid.

There were some big ripe blackberries on a bush, peeking like shiny eyes. She scrambled up the bank and reached for the closest one, but couldn't grab it. She stood on tiptoe to try again, and gasped. A hand had come out of nowhere and had plucked the berry for her.

"Here, take it. Aren't you afraid of going around all alone?" Adelmo Stratta was looking at her with an insolent smile on his face.

She threw her head back and clicked her tongue in the gesture that meant no, and quickly stepped away from him. "I don't want it anymore. Get out of my way."

Adelmo was faster; he spread out his arms to trap her against the thorny blackberry bush. He skipped left and right every time she tried to escape him.

"Always in a hurry, Kallyna d'Àrgira! What am I, the devil? Do you see any horns on me, huh?" He ruffled the hair on his forehead like a buffoon.

Whatever his game was, Kallyna had no intention of playing it. She put both hands on his chest and pushed him away with all her strength. "I told you to get out of my—"

Adelmo's hand fell on her mouth. She dropped her basket with the altar cloth inside and fought him until she was almost choking in his stranglehold. He dragged her to the side of the path and gave a low whistle. A horse appeared out of the trees. He hoisted her onto the saddle, then mounted behind her. She tried to gather enough breath to scream, but his hand was clamped hard around her mouth.

The horse started off at a canter. She couldn't see in what direction, as her face was covered by Adelmo's hand; soon he was slowing down as if for a pleasure ride, pushing deeper and deeper into the chestnut woods. She tried to throw herself off the saddle, but Adelmo was holding her tightly. She began to feel dizzy. She stopped struggling, hoping he would at least loosen his grip a little.

At last the horse stopped. Adelmo dismounted, pulling her down along with him and then into an old ruined building that had once been a barn or a stable. The ceiling had collapsed into a heap of beams and bricks, but the four walls were still so solid that Adelmo had to lock the door behind him. Kallyna knew well to whom that stable belonged. She stumbled down onto the straw that covered the floor, in a sweat.

"You're going to pay dearly for this," she panted. She lunged for Adelmo's face with her nails. "Both hanged I'll have to see you, both dancing from a rope!"

Adelmo didn't even hear her. Every move of his was quick and precise. He looked like a craftsman quietly plying his trade.

From inside his shirt he pulled out a piece of rope and a rolled-up handkerchief. Kallyna twisted furiously in his arms, but he had calculated everything, down to the amount of strength he would need to counteract hers. All her tossing and fighting didn't bother him much, and he had her tied and silenced in a matter of moments, without ever uttering a word. When he was done, he stood up and left, locking the door from the outside. An instant later the sound of the horse's hooves died out.

The first thing she did was throw herself against the door. It rattled in its hinges but held fast. She saw that the bolt was brand new. They must have changed it for that purpose. She butted her shoulders against the thick wooden planks, to no avail. Her mind was racing in all directions like a startled flock.

Perhaps Lidia had noticed something, perhaps she would go tell Tresa or someone else…. The little strumpet in the bushes, she damned her, God knows if she even remembered by now. Up at San Nilo no one would wonder about her being late, since no one knew when she was coming. She thought of the altar cloth dropped and lost back on the pathway, trying to remember whether Adelmo had picked it up, tossed it away or what else: all that work gone.

Then her thoughts switched to how she could defeat him. Her own frenzy made her think that it would be enough to split his heart open; but it was only rage, not strength. She studied the stable around her. In one corner the ruined bricks formed a heap so high it almost reached the rim of the walls.

She put her feet on the bricks and started to climb, wobbling on the broken edges. But with her arms tied behind her she couldn't keep her balance. Soon she lost what little ground she had gained and slipped down on her knees, her arms scraped and bruised, her eyes blinded by the gritty dust. Gasping and crying she lay where she had fallen.

Some time went by, she couldn't tell how much. No matter what would happen, she knew she had already lost. Raimo didn't even have to force himself on her now. All he had to do was keep her there for a few days, enough to make everyone believe that they had eloped and spent those days together as husband and wife. To the world she would become second-hand merchandise, belonging to the man who had first taken her or to no man at all. It was a "marriage of honor," the true and tried custom of centuries. She knew many women who had been so ultimately coerced to marry a man they loathed, and coerced by their own parents before anyone else.

The door had opened, and she hadn't even heard it. She huddled against the whitewashed tree trunk that had once supported the roof, her wrists working frantically against the rope. Raimo was in no hurry, and paced around at ease.

"Finally you keep your mouth shut," he said. "I was beginning to think I'd never live to see the day." He came up to her and pulled her to her feet. "You really gave me no choice, you know. I had to put the fear of God into you one way or another." He sounded truly earnest, almost apologetic.

She was so tight with rage that he fingered the rope around her wrists to see if it was steadfast enough. It must be, because it had left its mark already.

He put his hand on her throat. "Now, my love, what do you suggest we do for the next few days?" He pinned her against the tree trunk and started to undo the strings on the front of her dress.

The feel of his hands on her body made her retch. There wasn't even any lust in them anymore. There was only a cold, methodical desire to punish her. She ground her teeth together, as if wanting to sink them into his flesh.

Her dress fell around her waist. He kneaded her viciously, to hurt her. He pushed her to the ground, then took off his belt with the dagger. He looked at her shoulders, where five scars crisscrossed her skin, and cursed fiercely at d'Hancourt.

"Bastard from a race of bastards, ruining other people's property... May the grass grow on the steps of his house!" He started to pull down his breeches, still swearing under his breath.

Almost as if a messenger had summoned him, d'Hancourt was heard shouting outside the door and pounding to be let in. An instant later the door crashed open in a cloud of dust, with a noise that to her was like the bells on Easter morning. D'Hancourt's tall shadow stood blotting the sunlight on the threshold, his horse behind him.

Raimo scrambled to his feet, fumbling at his breeches, and grabbed his dagger.

"What the hell is this?" he yelled hoarsely. "Who are you?"

After he did realize who it was, instead of turning humble he confronted d'Hancourt with the righteous anger of someone who had been wronged.

"This is *my* stable, and *my* door you broke down! Not even the governor can do that, my lord!"

D'Hancourt didn't move, knowing Raimo was right. He kept peering at the girl crouching on the floor and turning her back to him. All he could see of her was a mantle of black hair spread out on a naked back. He held up the basket he was carrying. It was the one with the altar cloth in it.

"I found this on the pathway. It belongs to your betrothed." He sounded in a hurry to leave alone the two lovers he had intruded upon.

Raimo's hands were shaking. He went to take the basket and tossed it onto the heap of bricks. "Well, then…" he muttered in his teeth. "I will take care of it. And… thank you."

D'Hancourt glanced at the girl one last time, then turned around to leave.

Suddenly Kallyna raised her face to make him see that she was gagged, and stretched out her wrists to make him see that they were bound. She moaned frantically to call him.

D'Hancourt knit his eyebrows, realizing this was no lovers' assignation. He looked first at her and then at Raimo, with an air of astonishment and disgust. "By god," he muttered, "what way of making love to women is this?" He crossed the room in three steps and knelt down to untie her wrists without a moment's hesitation.

Raimo was standing behind him, with his dagger in his hand. "Let her be, my lord," he said venomously. "You weren't sweet yourself when you had her flogged before the whole town." He came closer. "I said let her be!"

D'Hancourt glanced at him with contempt. "How come you're so brave all of a sudden, Trani? No more bowing and scraping? It certainly took you a while to show your true colors." He threw away the rope and pulled down the gag. "She instead had the courage to speak her mind to me right when she felt like it."

Kallyna hurriedly wrapped her dress around her. She looked up at d'Hancourt; Raimo's dagger flashed behind his back with a sound of torn silk cloth. D'Hancourt jerked around to clutch his arm and retrieved a handful of blood.

Raimo sprang away from his reach and called him from the middle of the stable.

"Come on, come on, come on," he whispered. "I've been wanting to cut your throat from the very first day. You came to trespass right onto my property... Now I can kill you with all of God's commandments on my side!" He looked like a madman; and mad he must be, Kallyna thought, to be doing such a thing.

D'Hancourt got up slowly, waiting to see if Raimo would come to his senses, for surely he couldn't mean to kill him. But Raimo was challenging him in earnest. Crouched over, dagger in hand, he beckoned d'Hancourt to come closer. In a flash d'Hancourt drew his sword and held it high above his head.

Kallyna couldn't move for terror. She grasped the tree trunk and whispered God's name over and over. She looked at Raimo and hoped he would run; she looked at d'Hancourt and hoped he would scare Raimo to make him run.

Raimo would not run. He jumped clear of the first blow, while the sword hissed past him like a sickle mowing wheat. The second blow struck closer, tearing his shirt. Still Raimo kept taunting and lunging. The third blow drove into him like a wedge, between shoulder and neck. Blood spurted from the severed vein. Raimo dropped down to his knees with his eyes wide open. Then he fell forward and was still.

Out of breath, d'Hancourt stood where he was. He planted his sword into the ground and gasped out a string of curses. "Damned fool... Bloody, damned, goddamned fool," and it wasn't clear whether he meant Raimo or himself.

Kallyna watched him from her corner and didn't dare breath too loud. She put her hand on her mouth. "O Jesus," she whispered. "O sweet God."

At the sound of her small, terrified voice, d'Hancourt turned around and looked at her. He wiped his forehead, leaving a wake of blood across his hair. He put his sword back in its sheath and waved his hands at her. "What the hell are you looking at? Put that dress back on."

Her fingers too numb to work properly, Kallyna groped for the strings and tried desperately to make a knot.

D'Hancourt picked up the piece of rope he had taken from her before, looped it around his arm and twisted hard to stop the bleeding.

"Why do I have to keep running into you," he muttered angrily. "Nothing but trouble every time, from the very first instant!" He looked at her, glowering. "You didn't curse me with this thing you people call the evil eye, did you?"

"Your Excellency… my lord," she blurted out, shaking her head.

He came behind her as she was about to tie the last few strings of her dress. "Wait." He parted the two corners of black cloth on her back, then started to graze the lash marks one by one from end to end.

She shuddered. The same hands that had just split Raimo's throat in half, made rough by the reins and the hilt of the sword and the strap of the shield, were now probing her skin as delicately as those of a goldsmith putting together the tiny links of a necklace.

"Not much damage done," he concluded. Quickly he stepped away from her.

He went to Raimo's body. She could only guess that he was dragging it, because she couldn't bear to look. Instead she tried to tidy up her dress with a strained fussiness, just so she could keep from screaming.

"Can you find your way back to the path?" d'Hancourt asked, busy at covering the bloody tracks on the floor with handfuls of dirt and straw.

She nodded. "I… think so, yes."

"Good girl. Then get out of here as fast as your legs can carry you."

More strange noises came from his corner, hideous scrapings and bumpings. "What about him?" she cried out. "What's going to happen now, what am I going to do?"

He left his grisly tasks and went to stand in front of her with a look of threat. "No crying! I will take care of this mess."

She kept shaking all over, until he had to grab her by the shoulders. "Calm down and listen to me," he ordered.

The simple thought of provoking his anger was enough to make her come to her senses.

"All right," she gasped.

"Now. Where were you going with that altar cloth?" he asked.

"To San Nilo…. The monastery, up the hill."

He nodded. "Then you're going to go to San whatever, you're going to deliver your cloth, you're going straight home and you're going to stay home until tomorrow night. It they ask you anything, make up a story." He lowered his face close toward hers. "Did you hear me well? I don't want any trouble from you."

She motioned yes. "But what about Adelmo Stratta?" she asked then. "The one who brought me here? Won't Adelmo think maybe that I killed him?"

D'Hancourt went to get her basket and slapped it into her arms. "With a left-handed blow that took me four months to learn?" he sneered, shoving her toward the door.

Kallyna held out against him, raising her voice. "But he was my betrothed!"

"Well, did you love him?" he countered. "Forgive me if I have a few doubts. If you did love him, I don't think you would have forced the poor bastard to go to such extremes."

She wheeled around, astounded. "How come you know so much about me, who I love and who I don't?" She thrust out her chin. "And another thing, why were you following me, and how did you find me here?"

D'Hancourt jabbed his finger furiously at the basket. "I found you with this, and you should thank all the saints in Paradise that I followed you and that I found you!"

"Oh, but…."

D'Hancourt clenched his fists. "If you don't get out of my way, so help me God I'm going to deflower you myself, so this will be the last time I go around killing people to safeguard your damned virtue!" he snarled.

Kallyna wouldn't budge. She kept staring at him in astonishment, with her mouth open. He raised his good arm and pointed at the door. "Move."

She threw back her head, swallowed the tears left in her throat, then shuffled out of his sight. When she glanced over her shoulder, he was untying the blanket he kept under the saddle of his horse and carrying it into the stable, and he gave no sign of noticing her presence.

❋   ❋   ❋

Tresa had been waiting in the marketplace; one could see how worried she was by the half-hearted way she haggled. When she saw Kallyna coming down the square, she gave up and handed the fisherman the money he wanted. The fisherman lifted out of a wooden bucket a big wriggling octopus, dispatched it with a bite between the eyes and dropped it into Tresa's basket.

"I did ask you not to be late," Tresa began, in tones of complaint.

"I know, Aunt. I'm sorry."

Tresa eyed her torn apron. "It got caught in a branch," Kallyna said quickly. "I'll sew it."

"Did they like the cloth?"

"Yes, very much. Only, Padre Costantino's eyes are still bad, and he couldn't see it."

They crossed the square and got home. Tresa closed the door, then went to the flat stone she used as a chopping board and began to clean and cut the octopus. Kallyna carried a pot of water to the hearth and stirred the coals, sliding firewood under the trivet. She had to tug at her sleeves to hide the red streaks left by the rope around her wrists.

"Oh, I almost forgot," Tresa said. "Raimo came by soon after you left, to say goodbye. I told him where you'd gone, in case he wanted to catch up with you. Did you see him?"

"No," Kallyna said.

"He's going to Nicastro, to buy a new lot of chains for the Portammare." Tresa shook her head, worried. "He shouldn't travel alone when he has all that money on him... But God be with him."

Kallyna kept waving the wicker fan to revive the embers. Her hands shook so hard she could barely hold it. "How ugly is that headstone he put on the grave," she said after a while. "Red, like blood…. Every time I see it it looks more awful."

Tresa clucked her tongue at the grey cat and tossed a handful of fish scraps. "I think it's very fine instead. Don't be so hard on him. After all, he never wronged you in any way."

Kallyna put down the fan and headed upstairs. "I'm going to sew my apron."

"Won't you wait for your meal?" Tresa called out.

"I'm not hungry. I'll eat tonight, with Uncle Gheorghe and Arni."

Tresa sighed loudly to herself.

It was only late at night, while she tossed and turned in her bed desperate for sleep, that she finally realized how terrified she was. Raimo was really gone, gone like her father, never to come back. It occurred to her that now she had become the sole owner of her life; there was no longer anybody to tell her what to do. She had dreamed of that so many times; now the thought filled her with dread, like a bird that has only known its cage and then finds itself free.

Every last tie that bound her to her past was severed. Her life had become like the weather, impossible to forecast.

VI

NOT A LIVING SOUL knew where the governor of Tropea had been all morning.

Around midday he was seen riding in from the Porta Vaticana, carrying across his saddle what was unmistakably a corpse wrapped in a blanket. Ahead of him went the town crier announcing that Mastro Raimo Trani, most esteemed foreman of the masons of the county, had been most treacherously and most unfortunately killed by robbers on the road to Nicastro. The culprits, he cried on, would soon be found and brought to sure justice.

The body had been stripped of the dagger, of the money purse, even of shirt and boots. Women crossed themselves as it rode down Piazza Portercole, whispering in horror. From the church of the Black Madonna a priest came out to give it absolution. Others carried it into the church and sent for the coffin-maker.

In a flash the news bounced from house to house. Tresa almost fainted when she heard it. Kallyna began to shake all over, as though she were hearing it for the first time. Then Tresa went to the church to see the body, begging Kallyna to stay behind with the neighbors. Tresa was heartbroken, and terrified by that destiny of grief and mourning that seemed to persecute the d'Àrgiras.

Women came to the house to wake with her, wailing prayers and laments, noisy. Kallyna could only think of d'Hancourt and of the secret she now shared with him.

Of all possible bonds, what a wretched one. She had seen him kill a man in a fit of his terrible anger, although in self-defense, and he didn't want any trouble. No one who valued his own life would ever dare to question the governor's word. Adelmo Stratta would never speak out, since he was no less involved in the affair. D'Hancourt might even falsely charge that Adelmo was the one who had killed Raimo. The entire incident was very neatly closed.

Kallyna was racked with guilt and confusion. She thought that perhaps she could make a clean breast of the story to a priest in confession. But d'Hancourt had ordered her to say not a word to anybody, and she was too frightened of him to risk even the sanctity of the confessional. Like God, he might find out somehow, and punish her again.

Raimo was buried the following day. To Kallyna the funeral mass seemed to last an eternity. Arni held her hand, and Tresa wept all the time, but Kallyna felt utterly alone in the midst of all those people. She kept telling herself that Raimo had caused his own death, and not for love of her but for hatred of the Norman lord who had "ruined his property." Still, as she watched the shrouded body disappear into the ground, she joined her hands and put together a desultory prayer of mercy for him. Outside the church a thunderstorm was brewing, rolling down from the hills like a rumbling of cattle hooves.

They were standing on the church steps saying goodbye to the last of the mourners when the sound of the town crier's horn echoed across the square. The crowd, already scattering in anticipation of the rain, gathered again. The sellers who were beginning to herd away their flocks and to cover up their baskets, stopped to listen. Amidst a clucking of chickens d'Hancourt and de

Vire were approaching the carved dais used for public announcements. D'Hancourt climbed it and waited to hear silence.

"Orders from our king and lord Roger," he began, "concerning the recruiting of arms for the war against Naples." His ominous words merged with a distant flash of lightning. Tresa cast a worried look at Arni, the only able-bodied man left in her household.

"All the men of Tropea from age twenty to age forty must report to the Castro within four weeks, to be selected for enlistment." D'Hancourt paused, studying the crowd. It was clear that he didn't like to say what he had to. He closed the announcement in a hasty, almost cursory manner. "Do not try to evade the call. I can well assure you that the king is as fair in his exemptions as he is harsh in his punishment."

Tresa crossed herself with a sigh of relief. "Twenty to forty. Thank God Arni is still with us."

The town crier sounded his horn again. D'Hancourt stepped down the dais and jostled his way back to the Castro, deaf to the angry murmurs caused by the news. From a distance he raised his arm to point Kallyna out to de Vire, then went his way.

"Are they looking for me?" Kallyna whispered, startled.

"You, girl," de Vire called her, towering above the small group like a mountain pine.

"My lord?...." she answered under her breath.

"I've been told you're good at making clothes."

"Your Excellency," Tresa chimed in with pride, "she's the best in all Tropea!"

De Vire shrugged his enormous shoulders, unimpressed. "I need a tunic, a good one. "I'll pay you well if I like it. The cloth is going to be delivered to me tomorrow around midday. Come to the Castro around that time."

Kallyna stiffened. "I'm sorry, lord, but I don't take commissions at the houses of men, honored as I am to accept this one from you."

De Vire made a tremendous effort to stifle a laugh, with the result of an amused growl.

"And where would you want me to stand in my underwear while you take my measurements? In *your* bedroom?"

"My lord!" Tresa said.

The Norman walked away, still laughing. "My name is de Vire. Be sure you mention it to the guards tomorrow, or they won't let you in."

Arni grunted an oath after him. Then he turned to Kallyna. "You are not going anywhere tomorrow. He can have his tunic woven by the tarantulas."

Kallyna was much more upset by Arni's imperious attitude than by de Vire's insolence. She faced him closely, her hands on her hips. "I'll be the one to decide. It's my craft, and my commission, and we don't reap money in the fields these days, in case you hadn't noticed."

Arni's eyes flashed with rage. "And what is that supposed to mean? That for a bit of money you're now at the beck and call of the lords and make the rounds of their houses like a whore?"

Tresa interposed herself between them, flushing with indignation. "Enough, for the love of God. Arni, don't you swear in the streets like a drunkard!"

Arni ducked away, striding toward home. Kallyna jumped after him.

"It means no one orders me around, neither the lords nor you, Arni d'Orta. You think I have no pride? I have as much pride as you, but I also know how to keep my head on my shoulders."

"You won't keep much else this way, believe me," Arni muttered.

"Children, children," Tresa cried, rushing to get the key she kept in a crack under the doorsteps. "Save it all for when we'll be inside, where no one can hear you!"

"Listen to me," Kallyna addressed Arni. "Things are no longer what they used to be when my father was alive. I can no longer afford to turn down a commission because it comes from the lords or from the Normans. Who else pays in cash for their things? Do you want us to starve?"

"I don't want you to go to the Castro, that's all," Arni replied. "You tell her, Aunt Tresa. Tell her what happens to women of the people who go too close to the lords, like so many dumb moths to the fire."

Tresa opened the door, eyeing the neighbors' windows, then pushed both of them inside.

"She knows, she knows, she's not stupid. Now leave her alone. I'm sure she'll change her mind even without all this squabbling."

Kallyna didn't seem at all willing to change her mind; she was already heading up to her room.

"You can go get the cloth tomorrow," Tresa said in Arni's ear. "This way we'll save both the parson and the church."

"I heard you, Aunt," Kallyna shouted from the top of the stairs. "And if he has to go for the cloth, he might as well sew it and embroider it, too."

Arni beat his fist on the cupboard, making it wobble with a clatter of dishes. "Lord in heaven, that is precisely what I'll do!" he swore.

From the top of the stairs came Kallyna's laughter. "Remember to pull the thread back when you do the chain stitch," she sneered, and slammed the door.

✻   ✻   ✻

It rained all night. In the morning the garden had a lovely scent of wet earth and wet leaves. Arni waited all morning for Kallyna to come out of her room, patient in his anger. Kallyna came out only when it was time to go to the Castro. By that time Arni had left the house without telling Tresa where he was going.

"I won't be late," Kallyna mumbled, picking up her small bundle.

Tresa was so upset that she didn't even turn around from the hearth.

Kallyna made her way to the Castro at a smart pace, looking about for Arni. Younger than her, she fumed in her mind, and already he wanted to lord it over her just because he was a man. But this would show him, she thought, him and all other men like him.

Before leaving the house, however, at the last minute she had wrapped herself in one of her mother's big black shawls. That belated concession to modesty turned out to have been wise once she arrived at the gate of the Castro and faced the two guards.

"Name and business," one of the men ordered in a heavy Greek accent, eyeing her askance.

She kept the folds of her shawl crossed over her breasts. "Kallyna d'Àrgira, the daughter of Vasili," she answered. "I have been asked to sew a garment for the lord de Vire."

"What's in that bundle?" the soldier inquired.

She opened it up and put the contents under his nose. "Cloth and rope. But I won't strangle anybody with it, I promise."

The two men burst into laughter. Then the Greek let her in, looking her up and down with a leering grin. "Good enough to eat, isn't she?" he winked to his companion.

She left them behind, twisting her mouth. Then she remembered that she didn't know where she was going, and panicked. The long, dim hallway ahead of her was empty. She could hear men's voices and a rattling of bowls and spoons somewhere. She wandered for a while, determined to find her way on her own. Eventually she was forced to go back to the gate and ask the guards for directions.

"I'll tell you if—" the Greek replied, and whispered an obscenity in her ear.

Kallyna spat on his shoes and ran back up the stairs. Past the corner she almost butted into someone coming down; it was de Vire himself.

"My lord… the tunic?" she gasped.

De Vire eyed her from the top of his six-feet-three, puzzled. "My, what a hurry. Right this way."

She followed him down the hallway. Under the high vaults drifted smells that to her were uncomfortably new. Leather, wine, horses, the very air of the Castro spoke of men and their rituals. She looked at the battle axes hung in rows on the walls, not knowing how they could lift them, at the shields made of iron and wood behind one of which she could easily hide. How many times, she wondered, had she woven together cloth that a man's sword had then split apart along with the flesh underneath?

De Vire pushed open the door of his room and showed her in. The room was a shambles of weapons, clothes, dirty dishes, playing cards. The one thing she would have never expected in all that confusion was a beautiful Norman harp with a gilded handle lying on the floor next to a small puddle of wine.

"Good God, what a pigsty this is," de Vire cursed, kicking away a heap of shirts. "Come in, come in. I don't bite."

Kallyna did go in, but didn't close the door behind her. De Vire began to undress with all the ease in the world, while she kept measuring the distance between herself and the door with quick, sharp glances. When he stood in nothing but his knee-long undergarment, he dragged a stool in front of him and motioned her to climb on it.

"Are you going to take these bloody measurements or aren't you?" he grumbled, planting his feet apart.

At last Kallyna opened her bundle and took out a piece of rope knotted at each nine-inch span; then she stepped onto the stool. Even on the stool she only came up to de Vire's beard, and it was a most awkward stance. She carefully avoided pressing her fingers and meeting his dark, deep-set eyes.

Yet the way he was looking at her was placid, almost innocent. He seemed to be simply enjoying her presence. For the time being, at least, because when she spread out her arms to hold the measuring rope at both ends of his shoulders, she could have sworn he was about to throw his hands around her and squeeze the breath from her with one mighty hug. When he didn't, in her mind she thanked him.

"Four spans at the shoulders," she announced, blankly. "If you would kindly keep the measurements in mind, we can check them when we mark them down later."

"Damn it," de Vire blurted out. "I loathe enough already this business of having to stand here stiff as a rooster…. All right, three spans."

"Four, lord."

"Four, four."

Then she stretched the rope from the top of his shoulders down to his knee. "Seven spans in length if you want the tunic to the knee."

"Yes, yes, to the knee. And long sleeves, uh, nice and wide for the chain mail to fit under."

"Yes, lord. Then four spans for the sleeves."

"Four spans, Mother of Jesus. Is it done?"

"It's done."

"Hallelujah."

She stepped down from the stool, while de Vire went to get his clothes. From her bundle she took out a piece of parchment. "Can you write, lord?" she asked.

He turned around and glowered at her. "Me, write? Are you making fun of me? Writing is for priests and monks. Do I look like a monk to you?"

"I'm sorry, lord," she said. With the tip of a knife she found on the table she scratched on the parchment four crosses, seven circles and four arrows; then she put the note in her bundle together with the measuring rope. "As for the design," she said, spreading out on the cluttered table half a dozen small squares of cloth. "These are some of the ones I did for other commissions. The cross and sword, the two-headed eagle, the—"

"Never mind," de Vire interrupted. He had found a wine jug, and was drinking what was left of it. "I have no family crests to show off, I'm a bastard son. All I care is that you make it sturdy and wide. Especially wide, I like to eat. The cloth seems enough for two garments… God knows I paid that thief of a merchant for two."

"But lord, don't you like any of these?" she insisted, sliding her embroidered patches toward him.

De Vire glanced at them with an air of disapproval. "Lions, griffins, dragons, the whole menagerie. I'd end up wearing someone else's beast." He wiped drops of wine off his beard. "Do something new," he said. "Something out of your own head. It's a pretty head, something good will have to come out of it."

Kallyna wrapped up her samples, nodding uncertainly. "I'll try… hoping to meet your pleasure."

"Oh, it would take more than embroidery to… meet my pleasure," he laughed. "However," he sighed, taking his eyes off her. He went to the door and poked his head out. "Saìd!" he shouted. "Where's that package I told you to bring me?"

A hasty shuffling of feet came from the hallway. A young Arab appeared; he bowed to de Vire and handed him a bulky package. "My lord master, here it shall be" Saìd said in his faltering Italian. "The merchant brings it now." He glanced at Kallyna from under his spotless white turban.

Kallyna lowered her eyes. She had never seen an Arab up close. The only thing this one reminded her of were the pirates of that night. As soon as Saìd had left the room, she looked at de Vire with an air of reproach.

"You keep an infidel as your servant, lord?"

De Vire weighed the package, holding it by the rope. "Why on earth shouldn't I?" he said. "Saìd is so clever he says his prayers when he thinks I don't notice him." He saw that she was making a face. "I see… You country girls think they're all robbers and rapists. Truth is, there are more breeds of Arabs than one."

"I'm not a country girl," Kallyna snapped. "And it just so happens that I lost my entire family to Arabs, whatever was the breed they belonged to."

De Vire adjusted his belt and headed for the door, with a smile on his lips. "I know. They cost you five lashes, too."

"Where are you going?" she asked after him.

"Just wait there one minute," was the reply from the hallway.

She kicked the package with the wool, irked.

Not one minute but several went by. Kallyna began to pace the room, looking at its messy contents. From under one of the two curtained beds she could see something peeking out, a garment that seemed familiar; it was the black silk cloak d'Hancourt wore. Suddenly the room took on a whole new meaning. It was his room, too. Here he slept, drank, played cards and made love. She grazed the soft folds of the cloak, as if wanting to pick it up.

Where on earth had de Vire gone? she wondered then in annoyance. She remembered Arni's rage, Tresa's silence, and the whole world outside that would never forgive her for setting foot into the Castro. She made up her mind that she was going to leave right away. She picked up her cloth and turned toward the door. There at the door d'Hancourt's arms, opened wide to stop her, made her understand that she wasn't going anywhere.

"Where's the lord de Vire? He gave me the cloth, it's all done," she said in one breath.

"All right, all right," d'Hancourt replied. He quickly stepped into the room and nudged the door shut.

For a dizzy moment Kallyna stood counting one by one the iron loops of his suit of mail, frightened to feel the golden mass of his hair so close to her head.

"Please, lord," she begged then. "Please?"

He tightened his grip around her arms and pushed her, as if to remind her that he had all the power and she had none, and not because he was the governor but simply because he was a man. Then he let go of her.

"If I weren't such a fool," he said in a dull voice, "I would have taken you from Trani long before I killed him. But this black dress of yours…"

Kallyna twisted the corners of her shawl with a motion of anguish. "With five dead… what else should I wear?" she whispered.

His eyes clouded with anger. "Stop reminding me of your sores, damn it! When will you understand that I have nothing to do with your dead?"

"I know, lord, I know," she hastened to say. "And I'm sorry for what I said that day at the gate. I'm sorry, lord."

"So you are," he grunted. "You know something else? You are the first person who ever called me a traitor and lived to tell about it."

Kallyna hung her head.

After a while he calmed down and went to sit on the bed. "Can you play the harp?" he asked at random, not knowing what to say.

Kallyna shook her head.

"Geoffroi wants to teach *me*, imagine that… Did anybody ask you about your betrothed?"

Kallyna shook her head again.

D'Hancourt put his hand under his pillow and took out a full purse. He offered it to her.

"This is the money he had on him. It's yours now."

Kallyna stepped back. "Oh no, no. I don't even want to touch it."

He nodded. "As you wish. Then I shall make a very generous donation to the church of the Black Madonna. That ought to stop somebody in this town from complaining behind my back at everything I do."

He let out a deep sigh, tousling his hair with quick, repeated strokes of his hand.

"The damn hot nights you have here in Italy," he complained. "How can a poor wretch ever sleep?"

Kallyna summoned up her courage. "Where were you born?"

"Saint Jacques d'Hancourt, Normandy."

"Where is Normandy, lord?"

"Very far from here, on the French side of the Straits of Calais. When I was a boy of thirteen my father dragged my mother and me all the way down to Monreale. I didn't know a thing about this country… I had to learn fast."

"Where is your father now?"

"Dead. Left his bones in Salerno during the rebellion of the barons of Puglia." He paused, staring off at nothing. "My father lived and died the way he wanted… making war."

It took her a moment to notice how much he had answered her, beyond what little she had asked him. She was almost as startled as she was pleased.

Then he looked up at her with a tender look. He patted the bed. "Come. Sit down."

She shook her head for the third time. "They're waiting for me at home. I don't understand why you're keeping me here." She put her hand on the doorknob.

D'Hancourt sprang to his feet. "I keep you here because I want to keep you here. And I can always call my men out there to tie you up spread-eagled to my bedposts if I so like!"

She stood facing the door for an instant. Then she spun around with a great fanning of black hair. "If that's the only way you think you can have me, why not. Just like Raimo Trani, only *you* can do it without losing your neck because you're the governor."

Her words seemed to strike him like a slap in the face. From his flabbergasted look it was clear that he had never dealt with so much brazenness in his life.

He eyed her askance. "Are you sure your mother didn't make you with some duke or something?" he marveled. "You have a way of talking back just like a damned lady… and by Saint George, what a tongue!"

Kallyna bowed curtly and opened the door. "Have a *very* good day, lord."

Before she could step outside, d'Hancourt's hand clasped her shoulder with a gentle, warm grip. All his anger had vanished.

"Don't go to sleep tonight. Go down to the garden… You'll see what other ways there are."

She stared at him. Then she nearly ran out of the room, without glancing back.

When she was down at the gate she saw that the two guards were pushing away Arni and Arni was pushing back, amidst shouting and cursing from all three. Passersby had stopped to watch.

"Here she comes!" yelled the Greek guard, letting her through with a laugh. "All in one piece except the cork!"

Arni closed his fist and rammed it into the man's stomach. Rushing between them Kallyna managed to get Arni away before the man could return the punch. The guard chased them briefly, knowing he couldn't leave his post. Then he had to return to the gate, where he stood calling insults for as long as they could hear him.

"You fool, what do you think you're doing?" Kallyna scolded Arni. "Instead of making so much noise, take this thing off my hands and let's go home."

"Pigs," Arni said, panting. He took from her the package with the cloth. "They wouldn't let me in… What did I tell you yesterday? You'll end up the laughing stock of the town."

Kallyna set her teeth and faced him squarely. "Listen to me. I've had enough of being told where I'll end up and what I'll end up. First my father, then Raimo Trani, now you. All right, so I'll end up a whore. Is there a law against it?"

Arni stopped abruptly and looked at her. Nobody would ever have the last word with this woman, he thought, because words were the only thing Kallyna had to defend herself from the nastiness of the world.

He dropped the package with the cloth before her feet and turned his back. "Go to hell."

Kallyna watched him walk away from her. Then she burst into tears.

A small boy stopped to look at her as she sobbed in the middle of the square. "Go home," she shouted. "Go away, scram!"

The boy stood there, curious.

✻   ✻   ✻

By the time she reached home she had stopped crying. She took the cloth package inside, making as much noise with it as she could, as though she were trying to cover the clash of her own thoughts. D'Hancourt's last words to her seemed to echo in her mind like a possession, a haunting.

Tresa was in the kitchen with Rachele Tedesco, who lived next door. They were sitting at the kitchen table with a plate of food in front of them, talking somberly.

"I tell you, Tresa," Rachele was saying, "the Normans will never have enough. When they came here they owned nothing but the shoes they walked in. Then they took half of our land, but still they weren't happy. Then one day King Roger wakes up and says, *'I'm in the mood for some of those fine mussels that grow in the Lake of Lucrino.'* And they tell him he cannot have them, because the Lake of Lucrino belongs to Naples. *'And who commands Naples?'* the king asks. *'The Duke Sergius,'* they answer. *'Then,'* says the king, *'let's make war on this Duke Sergius!'*"

Kallyna said hello to both women and went up to her room. She closed the door and picked up the dress she was embroidering. The window was open. She put down her needle and stood up. She looked at the garden beneath her. The tiles of the roofs around it were still shiny with yesterday's rain. The grey sky looked like tangled wool. She pressed her hands on her hips, and her whole body felt like a tree heavy with fruit.

Arni came back at suppertime. He was no longer angry, but nobody spoke much around the table.

After supper Kallyna took de Vire's cloth upstairs. She stared at the soft wool, thinking about what to do with it. Arni put his head in the doorway. When she didn't snap at him, he came in and stood behind her for a while without talking.

"Look, I'm sorry," he finally said. "At least I hope you know why I did it."

"I know why you did it. Where have you been all day?"

Arni waved his hands around. "Walking... thinking. Tomorrow I'll go to Vibona, to see if that goldsmith you told me about wants to take me as apprentice."

She nodded, happy. "That is good. Everything will work out." She smiled. "Blockhead."

Arni smiled back to her before leaving.

Night was falling, and now she had made up her mind. Even if he never came to the garden and he never spoke to her again, for the first time in her life she was the one who had decided, who had weighed the consequences and dismissed them.

It started raining after sundown, a fine drizzle that washed down the tiles with a soft rustle. Inside the house there was only the heavy silence of sleep. She had slept fitfully for a while, tossing and turning in the stifling warmth of the room. From the window left ajar seemed to come an urgent call, like the one she had heard in the voices of fruit sellers warning that their grapes wouldn't last forever. Neither that night would last forever. At last she left the bed. She walked over to the window and pressed her face to the shutters. She couldn't see anything.

First she searched for a nightgown, which she recognized by touching the embroidery around the neckline. Then she took off her robe and patted herself dry of the sweat all over. She felt for her tortoiseshell comb and combed her hair with long, careful strokes like a bride. After that she slipped on the nightgown, and it fell around her like a shiver. Finally she left the room. She made her way down the stairs. The kitchen door opened noiselessly under her hands. She closed it behind her, forever, and stepped into the garden.

It seemed like a whole new place, almost the earth in the very first rain that ever fell. As she walked towards the farthest corner, drops of rain touched her shoulders like the tips of quick cool fingers. The lemon tree sheltered her under its black limbs. She grasped the rough wood above her head and closed her eyes.

The soft sound of feet jumping down the wall reached her together with the murmur of the rain and was lost in it. Before she could see him she felt his arms folding around her, casting out the emptiness that had surrounded her for so long.

"Little witch!" he said out of breath, grateful. "You didn't keep me waiting."

"You did, lord. All of my years."

His mouth tasted like rain, and had no patience. She moaned when he stepped away from her to unbuckle his cloak and spread it on the grass by the trunk of the tree. Then quickly he undid every knot she had left loose for him, and the white nightgown fell softly onto the black silk of the cloak.

She became precious glass in the hands of a maker of rose windows; deft, gentle hands that seemed capable of holding all of her at once. When he made her lie down she complied trustfully with the ritual. His tall body covered and hid her. He held her wrists tight above her head. Then suddenly he thrust his face in her hair, like a child startled by a crash of thunder, and breathed in deeply her fragrance of warm bread.

"Don't scream now," he whispered; and as her lips were about to part, he muffled them with his own. Her eyes opened wide for an instant, and her forehead creased with a small grimace of pain. But instead of shrinking from him, she moved with him who moved like the sea surging and falling in long slow tides.

The rain was warm, scented with grass and leaves. All memories and all time seemed to be washed away from her, along with the pain that had always been with her. She felt as if she were being born, and this time she was the one who had wanted to.

❉   ❉   ❉

"Kallyna. Kallyna?"

"Yes."

The way she said that one word made him think that she would say it to anything he might ask. After he had moved away from her, he had dressed himself; now he was leaning on his elbow, watching her with a pensive look. When she opened her eyes she was proud to see him so perfectly at peace.

It had stopped raining, and it was almost light. She sat up, groped under him for her robe and slipped it on in a hurry. He seemed amused by that sudden modesty. He reached out to help her tie the strings, but she politely refused his help. When she was finished she began to braid her hair with the same haste.

"Perhaps you should go now, lord," she said. "My uncle leaves for the farm in a while."

"Your uncle works on Sundays?" he wondered with a gently mocking grin.

She stopped. "Oh… It's Sunday, isn't it?"

He played with her long braid, wrapping it and unwrapping it around his fist.

"If I had known…" he said almost to himself.

"Known what, lord?"

"That you are like this… so beautiful. I would not have wasted so much time."

She lay down beside to him. After a moment's silence she said, "How could you be sure that I would be in the garden?"

He laughed softly. "Can't a man take a guess?"

That pleasant answer made her bolder. "So what would you have done if I hadn't come to the garden?"

He shook his head. "Don't ask me questions I don't like. I have my pride to look after… whether I want to or not."

Kallyna turned her head and said nothing. On the wall behind them a snail was climbing toward a crack. Some drops of rain from the lemon tree fell on his hair. He measured his large hand against hers, and seemed surprised at the difference.

"Will you want me some other time?" she asked, pushing her fingers into his.

Suddenly he saddened. His eyes became restless, and his voice hard. "I'm off this morning. Recruiting men all over the county. I don't know when I'll be back… and when I'll be back you will surely be married to someone." He ran his hand on her head. Then he got to his feet and picked up his cloak.

She too stood up. Tears were welling up in her eyes; but she would not cry in front of him, so she hoped that he would go quickly. He bent down to kiss her again briefly, eyeing the wall he had to climb and the sky that was growing brighter.

"If I won't be married," she said as he put his foot on the lowest branch of the lemon tree, "I will wait for you."

He looked down at her and nodded, smiling. "All right. I'll bring you a silver buckle. A very pretty one, like the ones they make in France. Goodbye, Kallyna."

She smiled back. "Good keep you, lord."

She closed her eyes. She heard the rustling of the leaves, the muffled thump of his boots on the grass from the other side of the wall, then the cries of the first swallows circling above the garden.

When she went back to her bed she retraced lightly the wake of his hands on her body, as if trying to make the memory of them stay. Tresa woke and went to take a peek in her room. Kallyna was sleeping soundly, curled up in a corner of the bed. Not even the sunlight streaming on her face from the window could rouse her from her peace.

❃　　　　❃　　　　❃

It was almost midday when the soldiers riding in her dreams pulled the horses to the side of the road and dismounted near the fountain, a moss-covered gargoyle spitting water into a stone cockleshell.

The yellow hills quivered in the grip of the sun, which the rain of the day before had only made harsher. Along the rocky coves the sea glittered like armor. The soldiers drank greedily from the fountain, then gathered armfuls of cool fern fronds and lay down on them, ridding themselves of the weight of swords and lances. Out of their saddlebags came pieces of salt meat and loaves of bread. They ate slowly, munching food and thoughts tiredly.

Geoffroi handed Dalibor a canteen filled with water, then wiped his neck drenched with sweat.

"What did I tell you, sweet lord? The sun of this country is going to shrivel the man out of us. A few more years of this life and we'll be ready to lower our flags forever."

Dalibor drank and grunted absently. He was looking at the ravine that opened up at the side of the road and rolled down toward the beach in a tangle of weeds. The wedge of sea peeking beyond it seemed to entice him like the corner of a woman's dress glimpsed through a half-opened door.

Geoffroi took back the canteen and splashed what was left of the water all over his face, snorting with delight. "Are you going to keep your backside nailed to that saddle or are you coming down to eat?" he asked.

Dalibor waved his hands at him, still staring at the sea and fidgeting with his reins. Then he drove his spurs into the horse's flanks and hurtled down the ravine in a cloud of dust.

Dumbfounded, Geoffroi watched him disappear.

"That son of a don't-know-what wants to crack his bloody head," he said in his teeth. He turned to the men in the grove. "Bohemond, keep an eye on the road and take it easy with that wine!" he yelled. He mounted the horse nearest to him and followed Dalibor down the ravine.

He found him when Dalibor was beyond the narrow pebbly shore, his horse wading lazily in the low surf.

Geoffroi jerked his reins up. "Have you gone insane there or what?" he called out.

Dalibor ignored him, looking down at his own hands. Geoffroi got worried at the silence. He bent over in the saddle to search Dalibor's face. "By the skirts of Saint Anne, will you look at this now," he muttered. "Hey, did you hear me? Are you sick?"

Dalibor raised his head. "Look, leave me alone. I had no sleep at all last night."

Geoffroi burst into a loud laugh. "Oh yes, but it wasn't my snoring that kept you awake, was it?"

Dalibor didn't answer. He turned his horse around and spurred it up the steep slope. Geoffroi tried to keep up, sweating and swearing.

"I thought I'd get her out of my mind once I'd have her," Dalibor said angrily. "At least that was *your* advice."

"Well, and it didn't work?"

"No, damn it, no!" Dalibor said, and there was almost fear in his voice. "I should have left her alone. I've had enough trouble already on account of her." He waved his hands. "I tell you, Geoffroi, that woman is bad luck. I haven't had a moment of peace since I set foot in that blasted town."

Geoffroi shook his head. "You're making a lot of noise for nothing. We've both been idle too long... A nice meaty war by now would have cleared all the cobwebs from that hard head of yours."

Side by side the two horses climbed the edge of the ravine and ambled back to the grove. The soldiers were dozing in the shade.

"Are you in love?" Geoffroi asked.

Dalibor flashed him an infuriated glance. "For the love of God, don't talk like a madman!"

Geoffroi smiled broadly. "You sound scared to death..." He nodded. "Good. That's the way it should be. It would be better for you if you lost your eyesight than if you fell in love with a woman. Maybe you'd gain as a man, but as a soldier you'd become perfectly useless. And can you tell me what good are we men in this day and age if we're not soldiers?"

Dalibor twisted his mouth. "Amen, Padre. You never get tired of preaching the same old sermon. It must have been going around ever since soldiers were invented."

From the grove one of the men came to hand them bread and meat and two full wineskins. They sat together under a tree, away from the others.

Dalibor ate listlessly, looking at his food as if wondering why it seemed to have no taste.

"But do tell me, my son," Geoffroi whispered with a rakish grin. "Did you *enjoy* the girl as a good Christian should? Did you have a good time?"

Dalibor smiled to himself. "Good isn't the word for it."

Geoffroi's eyes grew wide with curiosity. "Ah! Then there must be hope for you. You're not just a whip-cracking maniac after all." He broke his loaf of bread in two and emptied half of his wineskin. "I still can't understand how in hell she ever came to like you, after what you did to her... but I imagine it's none of my business."

He threw the wineskin down on the grass. "Me, I have no idea what it's like with a nice girl," he rambled on. "I make it a rule never to fool around with virgins, especially in this country where they have fathers and mothers who call the constable if you tell their daughters hello."

"She has no father and mother," Dalibor said slowly.

"How lucky can you get," Geoffroi mumbled. He got up and turned to the soldiers. "On your feet, move!" he roared. The men stood up grudgingly, dragging their feet.

"Here comes the finest part of the trip," Geoffroi complained as he mounted his horse. "The whole afternoon ahead and not a leaf overhead."

The soldiers closed ranks, waiting for the command. Dalibor raised his arm, and the horses resumed their sleepy gait down the dusty, sun-baked road.

VII

A UTUMN, AS ALWAYS ALONG THE COAST OF CALABRIA, came without a color of its own, still caught in the wake of the long hot summer. It was more like a shiver, a foreboding, to be felt more than seen. The tang of new wine was everywhere. There must be men and women working in the vineyards; but the land is so rugged that they could not be seen, and nothing but their song rose from the bottom of the steep valleys.

Kallyna's house was empty. At the beginning of September they had moved to the farm for the grape harvest. She had taken with her the tunic for Geoffroi de Vire, already sewn together. At the end of the day she would sit on the steps of the farmhouse and embroider it until late. She had found the design for the garment, or perhaps it was the design that had found her.

The monks of San Nilo had begun to dig an irrigation channel from a spring uphill to their well-tended vegetable garden. On the feast day of Saint Michael, when Kallyna and her kin had come to hear mass, one of the monks had chanced to strike with his hoe a large slab of carved stone. Padre Costantino, the most learned among them, had been summoned. His hands had recognized the hands of men long dead and gone. The Grecian sarcophagus had been eased out of the ground and taken inside the monastery.

It was still sealed, untouched, a boat of white marble downstream the river of time. It would be used again as a bench in the chapel, or perhaps some learned lord would want it for his own coffin. The bones of the ancient, nameless dead were scattered outside the consecrated boundaries of the monastery, since they belonged to a heathen.

When Kallyna had gone to see the sarcophagus, she had been struck by the beauty of the carvings that ran all around it as if to tell a story. It was the story of a sailor king who roamed the seas after a great war. Here he was shipwrecked on an enchanted island; here he met a lovely young princess; here he escaped a monstrous giant with a single eye in the middle of his forehead.

She had never seen anything like it. The story caught her imagination as forcefully as the biblical scenes carved along the walls of the chapel. But compared to those crude, dwarfish figures, the creatures that graced the Greek tomb seemed to her as perfect as she thought heaven should really be. However, when she had asked Padre Costantino if she could copy some of them for her design, the abbot had frowned; those were the pagan myths of a people who had never worshipped the true and only God.

"But they're so beautiful!" Kallyna had begged him. "How can something so beautiful be evil?" Then, a little at a time, while sitting in the chapel pretending to pray, she had fixed the images in her mind. At home she had copied them from memory, arranging them on large strips that she would sew all around the hem and the wide sleeves of de Vire's tunic.

While she plied her needle, Aunt Tresa and Uncle Gheorghe would sometimes come to look at the work, and Kallyna would start making up her own stories about the sailor king. Gheorghe shrugged, puzzled. Tresa liked the bright colors of the ship's sail and the quaint helmets of the ancient warriors; but she crossed herself in horror when she saw the one-eyed giant.

October had the new wine bubbling in the great oak casks, and the wide hopeful gesture of the sowers. Along the coast the sea was loud, like a somber reminder. Soon it would be time to pick the chestnuts. The green spiny burrs were dropping softly from the trees. The woods were one huge carpet of wild cyclamens, and the fat mushrooms were cries of delight hidden under the dead leaves.

Arni had begun his apprenticeship in Vibona. He now came and went from the neighboring town, but he would move in with the master goldsmith as soon as the work at the farm would be over. In Tropea, now that d'Hancourt was away, the recruiting of men for the war against Naples had been left to Robert Saintecroix.

Not every young man was training under him at the Castro. Many were at the grape harvest, and Tresa never missed any occasion to coax Kallyna into joining them. Kallyna did join them; but she had her ways of keeping them all at a distance.

A change had come over her. She moved and she spoke more slowly, strangely calm. It was as if Sila had come back in her sister's skin. Far from being pleased by that change, Tresa almost wished for the other Kallyna, the one who scratched and bristled like a cat.

The only spark of rebellion came when Tresa reminded her one more time, but not as tactfully as before, that she must find herself a husband.

"I don't need any husbands," Kallyna had replied curtly, and that had been the end of that. The nails were still there, Tresa thought. Only the purring that hid them was new.

Kallyna would often wander away from the others, with her basket only half full of grapes. Once, Gheorghe had to go looking for her. He found her by the spring, crouching so silently in the grass that a big spotted hawk had come out of its nest and was circling above her. Gheorghe had chided her; she had smiled to herself as if hiding a secret.

Then the first cold evenings came, and the rain. Tresa stirred the chestnut jam that bubbled in the hearth, and Gheorghe sharpened his tools. Kallyna took the great copper brazier out to the steps and heaped up coals, straining her eyes in the darkness that spread over yellow slashes of sky.

But the night was too vast a space to let her soul wander in it. She knew that worrying about him would only make time seem as dreary as forever.

Better to close the door to the wind and to curl up by the fire, following the colored thread in and out of the warm grey cloth. Better to simply wait, like she had waited for him the night he had come to the garden.

✻   ✻   ✻

The second Sunday of October they locked the farmhouse and went to town for market day.

The sounds of a great excitement reached them even before they had approached the Porta Vaticana. The whole town was buzzing. The bells rang from every church, the horn was blaring from the turrets, people milled around in the streets. Out of the doors of the Castro marched soldiers in full dress. Other soldiers were unfurling the great town banner at the main bacony. From every other balcony hung damask blankets, lace shawls, anything resembling festive decoration.

Trapped in the excited crowd, the three newcomers from the farm looked around nervously.

"What's going on?" Tresa wanted to know. "What's all the commotion?"

"The king!" answered a man next to her. "Can you ever believe it? The king is coming to Tropea!"

With a great squeaking of rusty hinges the soldiers pushed open the entire Porta Vaticana. A couple of sergeants shouted to clear the streets of people, herding them to both sides. One man went around looking for the prettiest girls. He motioned Kallyna to come forward with the others he had picked. He thrust a basket of flowers into her hands and hurried off. The girls elbowed Kallyna to her place, whispering and giggling. She craned her neck looking for Tresa and Gheorghe; they were nowhere to be seen in all that crowd.

The bells wouldn't stop ringing, making the air shake with waves of sound. She saw Cosimo Falizza striding to the square, accompanied by his wife and every other blueblood in town. They were followed by a little boy who carried two enormous gilded keys on a red velvet cushion. They got there just in time, as a squadron of Sicilian cavalrymen passed through the gate and made way for the royal party. Flustered with excitement, Kallyna

100

raised her eyes to look at Roger d'Hauteville, king of everything south of Rome.

Sturdy and tall in the ample folds of the cloak that covered the back of his horse, he looked like a golden ghost out of the page of an illuminated book. Age had taken suppleness from him, but not strength. Not even war, the universal necessity of his times, seemed to have dimmed the vigor of his body and of his mind. In the shadow of the crowned helmet his grey eyes were sharp as a boy's, and in the cowl of mail his face resembled almost that of a monk, lean and attentive.

Behind him rode Prince Guglielmo, whose appearance revealed none of his father's wisdom. His extravagant display of garments and armor eclipsed even Roger's. Roger's good looks were lost to a brooding, mistrustful glare of his dark eyes, and the thin mouth seemed like an unlikely place for a smile. Though still a boy, he appeared already as the future ruler whom his subjects would brand as Guglielmo il Malo.

The man who accompanied Prince Guglielmo must have a very special place in the Hauteville household to be allowed to ride side by side with a royal prince. What made him repulsive to the sight was a deep, badly frayed scar that ran the entire length of his cheek. If on Guglielmo's face a smile would have seemed like a mistake, on the face of his companion it would have resembled a sneer.

Coaxed by one of the girls beside her, Kallyna took a handful of yellow asters and tossed it in front of the hooves of Roger's horse. As he entered the town, the crowd broke into a spontaneous cheer simply because he was the king, since little or nothing was still known about the man; in fact until now even the way he looked had been a mystery to the people of Tropea. Mothers lifted their children for him to touch, Cosimo Falizza pulled down nervously the hem of his brocade coat, and Donna Vittoria, Falizza's wife, spread her beautiful ivory fan in front of her flushed face.

Kallyna was searching among the many heads for one that would not make her long for the sunshine in that cloudy autumn morning. First, in between rows of Sicilian foot soldiers, an extraordinary array of men passed before her. There was George of Antioch, admiral of the royal fleet, a native of Greece; Abu Abdallah Al Idris, court geographer, an Arab; and the young son of Robert of Selby, an Englishman.

Each man wore the garb of his country of origin: George of Antioch the ivory-white Byzantine *dalmatica* hemmed with pearls, Idris the brown *burnous* and a magnificently draped turban, Selby the kite-shaped English shield with the golden lions. Never before had anyone seen such a variety of faces; it seemed as though the whole known world were enlisted in Roger's army. Last came the familiar pair of d'Hancourt and de Vire, one light as the other was shadow. Dalibor's hair had grown longer, and it escaped from the hood of chain mail like gold spilling from the smelter's ladle.

Kallyna dipped her hand into her basket, grabbed a bigger handful of flowers and tossed it high just as he rode by. He reached out and caught a blossom in mid-air. He pretended not to be looking at her, but a smile rippled irresistibly his mouth, because she had come so close that his big grey horse nuzzled her hair.

As soon as he rode on, she handed her basket to another girl and started to follow the crowd down toward Piazza Portercole. After the very last row of soldiers three carts came trundling through the gate. They carried half a dozen huge coffers bolted with chains, and a cage full of hunting hawks feeding on chunks of raw meat.

At last the bells died out in a clanging echo; the bell-ringers, too, rushed down to see the king. Waving their arms like windmills, the guards managed to restore some silence. Then Cosimo Falizza took the velvet cushion from the hands of the boy who followed him and, keeping his head bowed as far down as he could, offered the keys to Roger.

"To our most gracious sovereign and lord," he intoned solemnly in Latin. "May he live and reign forever."

Roger grinned very lightly at that last word, as a man who knew well the brittle value of time and power. Patiently he took up the keys, kissed them and put them back in their velvet nest, as he had done in every other town he had passed along the way.

"And so may also our noble and loyal town of Tropea enjoy perpetual prosperity," he answered, as he had done in every other town he had passed along the way, changing only the name of the town. The worn-out ceremonial words sounded a bit world-weary on his lips.

On hearing the king's voice, again the crowd broke into an outburst of salute. Kallyna was standing on tiptoe. Dalibor had come down to hold the king's stirrup, as was his duty as governor. Once Roger dismounted, the king was surrounded by a throng of lords all wanting to kiss his hand, greet him, present wives and children.

Falizza formally invited Roger to be his guest. Roger accepted by offering his arm to Donna Vittoria, who stood back as if terrified to touch him. A procession took shape, with men and women arranging themselves in couples after the first one. Dalibor picked at random one of the daughters of Corrado Altamura; Geoffroi took under his wings not one lady but two.

Behind the procession the crowd lumped together into smaller undisciplined groups. No one wanted to go home. News and rumors were passed on, corrected, denied. From what Kallyna could hear all around her, Roger was on his way to Naples, to launch a final offensive against its ruler, the Duke Sergius. The army he gathered as he went was pitching camp on the hills around Tropea.

"He has made a solemn vow that he will hear Christmas mass in Naples, in the church of Sant'Elmo," someone said.

"May God grant him his wish," someone else replied, "but I'm afraid the mass will be Easter's, not Christmas'."

The women crossed themselves. "And may my husband … my brother… my son come back with him soon and in good health."

Kallyna decided it was time to find Aunt Tresa and Uncle Gheorghe. She followed the procession all the way to the Castro. It was there that she saw the young women clustering around the king, dressed in their fine gowns and fancy jewels. Dalibor moved around at ease in their midst. She had never been so far from him, a black speck lost in a crowd of black specks.

Envy and despair took her. She ducked into a doorway, leaning out to see. The daughter of Corrado Altamura, the little baroness, was running her beautiful white hands on the hilt of Dalibor's sword, admiring the silver inlays. As Dalibor walked on, holding her on his arm and chatting with her, Roger put his hand on his shoulder and smiled affectionately to him.

Kallyna turned around and made her way back to the square. Escorted by a small army of Arab attendants, the carts with the king's trunks rolled by past her. Suddenly the grey hawks in their cage shrieked, their red throats gaping like those of laughing witches.

Keep your place, country girl, they seemed to screech at her. Keep your place!

❊   ❊   ❊

The nobles had withdrawn as if on a ship's high forecastle, busy at their exclusive task of entertaining the cream of the kingdom.

Strains of music came from the tall barred windows of their mansions deep in quieter streets. Armed men stood by the doors, to keep away the intruders who still tried to catch a glimpse of the king.

In Piazza Portercole the townsfolk gathered in their usual parlor, the marketplace. Falizza's servants were ransacking the stalls for the best each had to offer, and for once they even paid the full price of the merchandise. Even Gheorghe had left mass earlier, and was now making the best deals of his life selling his plump black grapes by the bushel. Kallyna had found him and Aunt Tresa, but now all she wanted to do was go home and be by herself. All that bawling, excited crowd was making her dizzy.

"He is positively the handsomest man I've ever seen," Tresa declared once more with a look of rapture, while all the women around her nodded their agreement.

"They've told me he can speak all the four languages of the kingdom as if his own mother had taught him," one of them said.

"That is nothing," a second woman chimed in. "I heard he consorts with magicians and witches. The Pope says he's a heathen and should be excommunicated."

"Is it so, really?" the first woman marveled, passing on the tidbit to her neighbors.

"And all those tall fair knights," Tresa sighed on, picking up her scales again.

A girl leaned in with an air of mystery. "That man with the scar?" she whispered. "I've heard he's a good friend of the prince's. A really *good* friend, if you know my meaning."

"Yes, yes," a man added. "His name is Falco da Torre."

Tresa nudged the girl, giggling. "But he does look more like an owl than a falcon, doesn't he?"

Kallyna had had enough of all that gossip. She told Tresa she would wait for her at home, then left in a hurry. The empty kitchen was a haven; she welcomed its dim silence fragrant with herbs. For a long time she just sat at the table with her head on her arms.

Why hadn't somebody told her that d'Hancourt wouldn't always be prowling at night like a lover? Arni was right: there was nothing to be gained by going too close to the lords. Perhaps when the king left and all that excitement passed d'Hancourt would send her a message... She beat her fist on the table, burning with shame at her own foolishness. There she was, she damned herself, reduced to waiting for the wink of a Norman, whenever that might come!

There was a knock at the door. Sullenly she went to open it. She was startled to see that it was Saìd, de Vire's young Arab servant, greeting her incomprehensibly in his own tongue. She motioned him to speak.

"The lord de Vire sends me about the tunic you are fabricating for him," he said. "He shall have it delivered to him tonight."

"But it's not finished!" Kallyna said, alarmed. "He gave me three months, and it's only two!"

Saìd nodded politely. "That shall not matter. It is... presentable?"

"Some parts aren't filled in yet. If he wants to show off with the king, he won't do it with *that* tunic."

"Mistress, it shall be quite all right," Saìd insisted patiently. "The tunic is needed tonight around the setting sun. You press it, please, and you bring it to the house of the lord Falizza, please. I shall be present to escort you."

"Wait," she called him. "I'll press it, yes, but why must I deliver it, too? Can't you do it yourself? I don't care about the money, he can pay me later."

This time Saìd almost threw to the winds all his diplomatic skills. "Mistress, please. The lord de Vire gives me such orders. I not know why he wishes that you bring the tunic. But I think that it shall not be too..." he frowned, searching for the correct word "too unseemly if you do once what a slave such as I shall do always: obey, no questions."

Dumbfounded, Kallyna watched him disappear down the square with his slightly bowlegged walk and the dignity of a prince — which, for all she knew, he might very well have been in his own country. Then she slammed the door shut. She paced back and forth for a while, thinking quite a few unkind thoughts about Geoffroi de Vire.

At last she stopped. "All right," she grumbled. "I'll *go* to the Falizzas'. And I'll raise the roof if he pays me less because it isn't finished."

Sundown came with a sharp wind that rustled through the narrow streets carrying a smell of seaweed from the damp beach. Saìd waited for her in the square, holding a torch. Kallyna wrapped herself in her shawl and followed him quickly across the Piazza.

The mansion of the Falizzas rose on a smaller square circled with old palm trees. A tall arched door took up almost entirely the façade. At the top of the arch was the family crest carved in stone. The door rose to hold up a single stone balcony, upon which the roof leant like a frowning eyebrow.

A valet opened the door and showed them to a small waiting room. From the underground kitchen came the sound of a tremendous fluster. A meal truly worthy of a king, and lavish enough to feed his army, was being prepared. Above the excited voices of the cooks and the steady clatter of pots and pans rose the stern commands issued by Donna Vittoria Falizza.

A few moments later de Vire came in and dismissed Saìd. "Hello there," was his greeting for Kallyna.

"Have a good evening, lord," she replied glumly.

"You don't seem too happy to see me," De Vire teased her.

She followed him out of the waiting room, with the tunic draped on her arm. "That is not true. I'm worried about the tunic, it's—"

"It's not finished, I know. It's all right. I won't have you whipped."

She blushed. Her mood was getting worse by the minute.

The house was like a cave. What little light there was seemed to be absorbed by the massive furniture — huge cabinets, thick draperies, tall overstuffed chairs. The few scattered candles cast long, bizarre shadows on every curve and shape of the heavily carved furniture. On the tapestries that covered the walls all sorts of wild animals roamed, side by side with snarling imaginary creatures. Kallyna felt ill at ease, a small ghost prowling behind a big one.

The valet lit all the candles on a wrought-iron chandelier as large as a cartwheel, bowed to de Vire and left.

"If you don't mind, lord," Kallyna said evenly, "I would like to know why you asked me to deliver the tunic in person."

Geoffroi squinted at her, amused. "I was right, you definitely aren't happy to see me. I hope the lord d'Hancourt at least will receive a more pleasant welcome."

Kallyna shut her mouth.

Geoffroi took the tunic and brought it under the chandelier. He stared at it very carefully. The sailor king had reached home at last, and sat in a beautiful palace on an island girdled by the sea.

"Lord in heaven," he finally muttered. "I've never seen anything like this."

"You did tell me to do something out of my own head," she reminded him. "Do you like it?'

He threw up his hands. "I guess I do," he said. "Who on *earth* are these people?"

"Ancient Greeks. I found them on a stone tomb. It's the story of a famous warrior, you should know about such things better than I."

Geoffroi was still studying the garment from every side. "The designs are fine," he said. "The colors, too…. I like the colors."

"Why don't you put it on," Kallyna prodded.

So he did. The tunic fell around his big body without a crease. He flexed his arms, shrugged his shoulders, tossed and turned, looking for a flaw and finding none. "By god," he surrendered, "first time in my life I spent my money wisely."

Kallyna's eyes lit up with relief and pride. "I'm glad to hear you say that, lord."

"But this one-eyed monstrosity," he groaned. "You made him look like me!"

The hallway filled up with lights and hasty footsteps. "Maria, the tablecloth of white damask and the silver vessel for the spices. Both must be without a single spot, mind you, or else…. My lord de Vire!"

Donna Vittoria Falizza stepped into the room, followed by a retinue of maidservants carrying candlesticks and silverware. The look of flattery in her eyes became one of cold detachment as it moved from Geoffroi to Kallyna.

"I say," she worried, "you look like a king yourself… You could make yourself more conspicuous than Roger…" It was clear from her voice that she didn't approve at all of that involuntary breach of etiquette. She turned sharply to the servants, waving her well-groomed hands. "The rooms, the rooms. What are you all standing here for?" The women left in a hurry. Donna Vittoria came forward, looking de Vire up and down.

Geoffroi was fumbling impatiently with the ribbons of red silk wrapped around the scabbard of his sword. "What do you think, eh?" he gloated. "Isn't this a beauty?"

The lady bent her head, reluctantly. "Our little d'Àrgira has always been good with her hands. A bit odd, if you will, but… good."

Kallyna knelt down to help de Vire with the ribbons and tied a plump knot around the hilt. Her eyes avoided carefully those of the marquise, and the latter knew well that it wasn't because of deference.

Geoffroi took from his belt a chamois pouch trimmed with mother-of-pearl and opened it. He took out a handful of ducats, started to count them, then dropped the money back into the purse and pulled the strings shut. He handed it to Kallyna. "Here, take the whole thing. Must be sixty silver pieces, give or take a piece."

Donna Vittoria frowned, startled. Kallyna's eyes opened wide in amazement. She held the heavy purse in her hand, gingerly. "Sixty silver pieces is a handsome sum, lord," she said.

Geoffroi gave a pleased grumble. "I know. But I figure it's worth it. A garment to me is like a woman, if I'm comfortable insid— " He froze, aware of two pairs of women's eyes pinned on him. "Dear God, I talk as if I were drunk already," he said by way of an apology.

Kallyna tied her purse around her waist and picked up her shawl. "Thank you, then. I'll have to be going now… if that is all?" She waited for de Vire to say something about meeting d'Hancourt. But de Vire, so taken with his new tunic, had forgotten all about it.

"Tell Saud to walk you home," he told her. Kallyna wanted desperately to say something, anything that would make him stop and remember. But he just stuck out his chest. "Let's see if I can find a mirror somewhere," and started toward the door.

At the door he stopped, plunging into a back-cracking bow. Donna Vittoria curtseyed low, while nudging Kallyna to do likewise. As all three of them stood so bowed, King Roger walked into the room, followed by Prince Guglielmo, Falco da Torre and Dalibor d'Hancourt.

"My friends, look," the king said. "Tonight the lord de Vire wants to dazzle our eyes with the stories of Odysseus worn around his body in fine thread!" He took Geoffroi's hand to raise him, then came closer to look at the tunic.

Glancing up, Kallyna saw that from behind the prince's shoulders Dalibor was looking at her with a puzzled air, moving his lips as if to ask her what was going on.

"What an excellent garment," Roger said. "I do believe Idris would love to see it."

Promptly Donna Vittoria stepped forward. "I'll send for him, sire," and left.

De Vire hastened to show the king to the tallest chair available. Kallyna had shrunk against the wall as if trying to make herself invisible, but Roger was looking at her inquiringly.

"Is she the one who made the tunic?" he asked.

"Yes, *Mon Seigneur.*"

"Well, let me see her."

De Vire reached out to take her hand. With her heart in her mouth, Kallyna kneeled down in front of Roger and didn't rise until she felt Geoffroi tugging at her hand. Roger kept studying her with a look that was at once mild and implacable. "You have a taste for beauty, my dear Geoffroi," he said. "In more ways than one."

Geoffroi smiled an embarrassed smile. "Thank you, *Mon Seigneur.*"

Now standing in the middle of the room, Kallyna could barely keep from shaking. Every man was looking at her, each in his own different way. Prince Guglielmo had stopped pouting with boredom as soon as he had seen her, and now studied her with a thin smile. Falco da Torre ran his fingers on his cheek, where the scar was. Dalibor was just pleased that she was there, proud himself inside of the praise being paid to her.

"Now, though," Roger addressed Kallyna, "was it your *own* idea to show scenes from the *Odyssey* of the good poet Homer? Yours and no one else's?"

She drew her breath in. "Yes, sire. I saw them on a stone tomb… I liked them because they seemed so different, more beautiful than the usual…"

"Precisely," Roger agreed. "It's their originality I like. So much around us nowadays is unimaginative… How can we create something fresh when the Church of Rome dictates what is proper or not for an artist to do?"

No little confused, Kallyna kept silent and still.

Escorted by Donna Vittoria, Al Idris came in. He was a spark of a man, small and bony, with a goatee framing the old creased leather of his face. He carried an armful of parchment scrolls, and the feather in his turban was a quill stained purple with ink.

"*Jalaltu Al Malik* Great Sovereign," he saluted Roger. "So many interesting things are to be found in every corner of your dominion!"

Roger greeted him and his familiar enthusiasm with a benevolent smile. "I see you've been collecting material for your book again," he commented.

Idris cut a big swath of air with his hands. "Indeed I have. Our host the lord Falizza has supplied me with much information. For instance they say there is a treasure of the ancient emperor Trajan buried right nearby in the country..." he consulted his maps, "here, in the country of Vibona... And of course you know that Calabria is the land that gave Italy its name, the Greeks who ruled it many centuries before us called it Vitalia..."

Roger interrupted him quietly. "All this is fine, my good Idris. But have you thought of a title yet?"

Idris stood thinking for a moment. "Ah, yes. This is what I have in mind: The Avocation of a Man Desirous of a Full Knowledge of the Various Countries of the World."

Roger shook his head. "Too long. People will end up calling it *Kitab Rujar*, Roger's Book."

Idris took a bow. "Quite possibly, sire, but no matter. As long as it shall perpetuate your name, promote your glory, and further our enlightenment!" he concluded, nearly out of breath.

Roger showed him de Vire's tunic. "This is why I called you, Idris. One more thing worth your attention."

Idris squinted, nodding his recognition. His hands ran on the thick woolen stitches.

"*The man who saw mighty Troy fall to ashes, crafty Odysseus who much pain did suffer from the gods,*" he recited emphatically. Circling slowly around de Vire, he followed the design all around the hem, bent low.

"What a remarkable piece," he said then. "Reminds me of the tapestry I saw in Bayeux, the one depicting the glorious conquest of the Saxons by your Norman forebears. Nothing like this was ever made in our royal workshop of the *Tiraz*."

He pointed at Kallyna. "Is this her work?" De Vire nodded.

Idris' face took on an expression of regret. "It is most unfortunate that we don't have more talented young people like her in Palermo."

Dalibor seemed struck by an idea. He turned to Roger. "*Mon Seigneur,*" he said, "perhaps I could, with your permission, find a place for her among the craftsmen of the court. If she can please you so with a garment made for one of your subjects, she will surely do even better in the service of her king."

Roger nodded. "Brilliant suggestion. I'll be glad to write you a note of recommendation." He looked at Kallyna. "But say, we still don't know her name... Are we raising a statue to the Unknown God, like the people of Athens once did?"

Donna Vittoria prodded Kallyna with her hand. This time Kallyna was quicker.

"My name is Kallyna d'Àrgira, sire," she said with her head bent. "You are far too generous in your praise of my work, you are far too kind."

Roger stood up and put his hand under her chin, raising her face to the light. Then he turned to Donna Vittoria. "My lady Falizza, you have taken so much care in preparing our meal. Please add a crowning touch with the company of this young woman. Not only is she beautiful, but she has a fine mind, and to me a fine mind is as precious as gold."

❋   ❋   ❋

Her heart felt like a wheel rolling loose down a hillside. She had expected to find a crowd at the king's table; it was instead a mere group of eleven. The frightening thing was that at that table only she and Donna Vittoria were women; and the stunning thing was that nine of those eleven were the foremost men in all the kingdom, including the highest man of all. Luckily, her place was between Dalibor and Robert Saintecroix, an arrangement that gave her some courage. If only Prince Guglielmo would stop staring at her with that little smile of his, though.

Cosimo Falizza, her involuntary host, still hadn't been able to swallow his surprise. When he had heard about Kallyna d'Àrgira's unexpected dinner invitation, his jaw had dropped in disbelief: the daughter of his enemy of ten years, the little shrew flogged at the Porta Vaticana!

Three months ago he had suggested to d'Hancourt that she be thrown in jail; now the king wanted her at his table and d'Hancourt himself, turned silly as a jackass by a few smiles of hers, seated her in her chair and treated her like a princess! In the end, after no little arguing with his wife, he had been forced to put a good face to the entire affair, and to pray God that the girl wouldn't stir up some other disgraceful incident in his very house.

The valets made the round of the table with bowls of rose water for everyone to wash his hands. At the far end of the large hall four musicians began to play. Crouched by the marquis's chair his two big hunting dogs waited for their meat scraps, tails wagging.

Two servants brought in a pair of huge trays heaped with plump ducks stuffed with wild mushrooms and surrounded by a smaller flock of roast quail. Under Roger's amused gaze, Robert Saintecroix and Dalibor pulled Kallyna's plate from each other's hands, both wanting to carve the meat for her. The dish ended up in Dalibor's hands. He gave her a grin of triumph, wielding the silver knife.

Prince Guglielmo nudged Falco da Torre sitting next to him. "Idris was right twice when he spoke about interesting things to be found in the kingdom. Wasn't he, Falco?"

The scarred man nodded. "Absolutely, my lord. Do notice her skin. Young noblewomen have that white, powdery look that makes them seem so artificial. She instead has a healthy sort of complexion... A bit suntanned, of course, but it suits her."

Kallyna didn't like a single word of that double-edged compliment. She lowered her eyes to hide her embarrassment.

"Falco, you're making her blush," Dalibor said evenly.

"Oh" Falco said. "And you would like me to... apologize to her?"

Dalibor returned his look briefly, sharply; then he addressed Richard of Selby.

"So, Richard, you haven't told me what's new down in Palermo."

Selby looked up from his plate. "Not much there, really. I'm afraid the news will all be in Naples, at the war."

From the head of the table King Roger shook his head. "Please, my lords. Let's leave war out of the conversation. There is no worse condiment for a meal, and this meal is far too delicious to be ruined." He turned to Idris. "Why doesn't Idris entertain us instead with tales from the *Odyssey*, in honor of our lovely guest?" He looked at Kallyna and winked. "But skip the heroic details and stay more on the love stories."

Idris didn't need coaxing to talk. But soon he was getting off his Homeric subjects and beginning to intersperse them with a great deal of other things taken from the geography book he was writing. He said that some Norwegians were born without necks; that Britain had the shape of an ostrich's head; and even that the earth was round, like the apple he held in his hand.

That last piece of information caused a stir among the guests. Falizza in particular thought it bold to profess an unorthodox opinion contrary to the teachings of the Church. At once every man wanted to make known his opinion, with the exception of Geoffroi de Vire who simply shrugged, digging into his second duck. Dalibor and George of Antioch took Idris' side, while Robert Saintecroix and Richard of Selby took that of the marquis. Finally the king was called on to pronounce final judgment on the matter.

Roger put down his wine cup. "I will have to confess that I share whole-heartedly Idris' belief. I am a descendant of the Vikings, who sailed into the unknown ocean and reached the shores of Vinland. This is one unorthodox opinion of which I'm not only very fond but, believe me, quite proud."

In his mind, Falizza wondered how Roger could be so deluded as to give credit to fairytales that had been real only in the mind of some Scandinavian bard of old; but he held his peace, and clapped his hands at the royal verdict along with everyone else.

More courses kept being brought by the servants. Falizza's Arab cook had outdone himself that night. The guests had nothing but praise for his creations. The time had grown late. The candles dripped; the dogs under the table were dozing off.

At the end of the meal, over cups of warm wine fragrant with cinnamon and cloves, Roger accepted a challenge at backgammon from George of Antioch. He was in such high spirits that he encouraged everybody to bet on their favorite player.

They left the dinner table and moved to a smaller game table, talking and laughing while the board was set up. Only Prince Guglielmo didn't seem interested in the game. He paced the room looking idly at a collection of ancient Grecian weapons hung on the walls.

Kallyna stood by one of the windows, waiting for Donna Vittoria to dismiss her. Donna Vittoria wanted first to make sure the rooms for her guests were ready, and left to see to that. The moment the lady was out, Prince Guglielmo walked over to her. Kallyna understood that he had been waiting for that moment all night. She looked anxiously at Dalibor, who was beside the king, and started to walk toward him. But Guglielmo was already in her way.

"It's a pity that you must leave so soon," Guglielmo said. "I have another invitation for you, and it's certainly not to my table." He sounded as arrogant as he was awkward, like the boy he still was.

Her hands clasped behind her back, Kallyna tried to smile and to look as unaffected as she could. "I'm very sorry, my lord, but I have to go now. I did enjoy your company more than words can say," she managed to answer.

She thought he would say something else. Guglielmo didn't reply and didn't smile back. Falco, who followed him everywhere like a shadow, plucked the strings of a mandolin left behind by one of the musicians. A moment later, to Kallyna's great relief, Donna Vittoria was back, motioning her to come.

Kallyna bowed in a hurry to the prince, then went over to Roger and knelt down before him.

"Sire, I am bound to remember your graciousness for the rest of my life. Please accept my thanks for this night, from my heart."

Roger put down his ivory dice and smiled. "Do think about coming to work in Palermo," he said. "The lord d'Hancourt will see to it, if you so decide."

"I will most certainly think about it, sire," she answered. "May God keep you all."

Donna Vittoria walked her to the stairs. Roger followed Kallyna with his gaze as she left; then he threw the dice, and it was a good throw.

Guglielmo was still with Falco near the window. He looked grim. Falco paced short paces behind him, studying the carved floor.

"Damn it," Guglielmo muttered furiously. "It can't be that she misunderstood me."

Falco smiled contemptuously. "She's woman, my lord. She understands, but she likes to pretend that she doesn't. It's all in the little games they play. They just cannot talk straight and honest like men do."

Guglielmo was silent for a moment, sulking. Then he turned sharply on his heels.

"I'm going to bed," he said. Falco went after him without a word.

No sooner had the two men left that Dalibor took Geoffroi by the arm and marched him toward the staircase.

"Go tell Saìd to stay where he is, if he's not sleeping already," Dalibor whispered.

Geoffroi squinted slyly at him, leaning heavily onto his arm. "Praised by a king, complimented by a prince, and now courted by a governor... By god not even my mother ever drew so much attention, and all modesty aside she was the best courtesan in Palermo."

Dalibor kept shoving him downstairs. "Keep your mouth shut. You smell like an old cask."

But Geoffroi was drunk and felt very much like talking.

"You know?" he slurred. "I was remembering that time we borrowed from Roger's harem that pretty Armenian girl... Seat of Mercy, just fresh from the market she was, new as a new door lock..." He chortled under his breath. "Never for the life of him could he figure out how she came to be pregnant only a couple of weeks after he bedded her."

"I was with my back to the side of the guards," Dalibor reminisced in his turn. "Didn't you remember that too?"

"Hey!" Geoffroi snapped. "To get her through that window you pawed her all over worse than a horse in the market."

Dalibor pushed him on with one hand, fastened his cloak with the other. "A horse I never even got to ride. Move now, go call Saìd."

Geoffroi stumbled down the stairs, still laughing. Then he turned around and pointed his finger. "Nor have I ever laid hands on your little witch, just like you asked me. Damn it, though! I don't even know why I'm keeping that stupid promise you forced out of me." He sounded plaintive, almost resentful. "We've always been good friends, sweet lord, shared all we had… Why not this time?"

Dalibor stormed down on him and grabbed him by the arm. "Listen up. If you call me 'sweet lord' one more time, either in private or in public, I swear I'll wring your neck, either in private or in public. You want people to think we're lovers? You haven't had enough of Guglielmo and Falco?"

Geoffroi made a face with an air of repulsion. "Those two are bad, and that's an entirely different story. There is nothing wrong with the thing itself, and I say again that we ought to try it, me and you… There he goes, looking at me with those big blue eyes of an angel."

Dalibor waved his hand at him crossly. "You know I'm not inclined. But should I ever become inclined, I give you my solemn promise that I will keep my virginity for you."

Kallyna had been waiting for Saìd in the small anteroom by the front door. When she saw Dalibor coming instead, holding a torch, she sprang to her feet.

"Put your shawl on," he told her tenderly. "This is definitely your night."

She looked behind him. The hallway was empty, except for two marble griffins looking as if they were snatching at each other from the opposite walls.

"Do you really want me to go to Palermo like you said?" she asked under her breath.

He put his finger to his lip. "Shhh. Not here."

They walked out side by side. In the light of the torch tormented by the wind, the palm trees in the small square stood like feathered lances. Kallyna pulled the corners of her shawl more tightly around her shoulders.

"Are you cold?" he asked.

She held her hands together. "No, lord."

"Bull-headed and a liar, too," he snorted, laughing. Then he plunged the tip of the torch into the bowl of holy water by a niche of the Black Madonna cut in the wall of a house and pulled her into his arms.

His kiss was still as impatient as that of a soldier between battles. Eagerly, happy, she clung to him, lifting her face to his mouth like a thirsty woman.

"Yes, I do want you to go to Palermo," he said with his lips in the cold skin of her throat. "But first I want you to come to the Castro... Make a tunic for me too."

She laughed, pressing him closer to her as he filled his hands with her small round breasts.

"A tunic, a robe, a blanket, just say what you want!" Then she stood back, frightened. "They were talking about the war... You're not going to Naples with them, are you lord?"

Something inside him that he preferred to call compassion made him lie. "No, not me. I'm going to stay here with you. You looked so beautiful tonight! Did you see how everybody was looking at you? I hope you don't like any of them better than you like me."

She thrust out her chin. "Why? There was someone else?"

He took her under his arm, wrapping his wide warm cloak around her. Together they walked toward the Castro, followed by the distant sound of the sea as if by the breath of a sleeping giant.

At the gate of the Castro someone was waiting for them. It was one of Falizza's young errand boys, still hot from the run. Kallyna ducked into the shadow of an empty sentry box, while Dalibor went to meet him.

The boy made an awkward bow. "I have a message for you, from the lord de Vire. It's urgent."

"What the hell is this all about?" Dalibor snapped.

In the dark, Kallyna could only grasp a few words that made no sense to her. She was worried more about being recognized by the boy. She kept still until Dalibor dismissed him with a curt gesture and the boy disappeared down the square.

His face had become hard, ashen. He took her by the arm, turned around and started to walk in the direction of her house.

"What is it, lord? What does he want?"

His fingers hurt her, clamped around her arm. "Nothing," he said. "Bloody stupid nonsense."

They crossed Piazza Portercole. He made her stop in the corner of darkness of a shop's lean-to. "Tomorrow we'll go hunting with the hawks. Where will you be?" he demanded to know.

"At the farm... Why?"

He brushed off her question with a move of his head. "Can you stay home instead? With your uncle or Arni....with *men?*"

From behind the door of her house she thought she heard someone's voice.

"I don't know. My uncle will not miss a day's work, and Arni lives in Vibona now. If I stay home I'll be alone."

"Then go to the farm," he said. "But listen to me. Don't stay by yourself, don't wander away from the others. Don't make anybody notice you, if you can." His voice became flat, and his arms went rigid. "That is all I can do," he whispered, more to himself than to her. "May God have mercy on my idiocy."

"Wait!" she called out, baffled and vaguely terrified. "Won't you tell me what this is all about?" He had left already.

A candle flickered on the threshold and Gheorghe opened the door. "Kallyna, is that you?" She hung her head. "Yes, Uncle," and went in.

❋   ❋   ❋

Geoffroi was waiting in the entrance hall of Falizza's house. He seemed to have sobered up instantly. As soon as he heard the knock on the door he ran to open it, motioning Dalibor to keep his voice down.

"What's all this garbage you send after me now?" Dalibor asked.

Geoffroi shook his head and looked at the wall. "If we thought our friend Falco had changed since our good old days in Palermo, were we ever wrong, sweet lord." He eyed Dalibor. "As you may well have guessed by now, he's asked to borrow Kallyna for a night. Says he wants to make a present to Guglielmo."

For a while Dalibor couldn't speak. "And what did you tell him?" he asked then.

Geoffroi shrugged with an air of impotence. "I told him I never had anything to do with her except for woolen cloth and needlework."

"I don't suppose he believed that?"

"No," Geoffroi said. "And he's going to ask *you* the same thing the moment you go up those stairs."

Dalibor sat down on a bench, drawing his breath in.

"If I hadn't told her to do something out of her own head, none of this would have happened," Geoffroi said shaking his head. Dalibor made a gesture to mean there was nothing for him to feel guilty about.

"Maybe she won't mind," Geoffroi said, scratching his beard. "He's still the prince… She might even brag about it with her girlfriends."

Dalibor looked at him in a way that made him shut his mouth.

"God *damn* the man," he said then. "If she was the daughter of a lord, Falco wouldn't even dare to look at her. But as long as she's one of the common folk, she's everybody's game."

He stood up. "Everybody's game."

VIII

I T HAD BEEN THE FINEST DAY FOR HUNTING EVER MADE. The sky held nothing but a few clouds, brush strokes left at random on a blue canvas. The sun was pale, almost warm, and the air had the translucence of glazed china.

The hawks had soared gracefully, plunging onto their prey and then returning with slow sure flight. The hunters looked like splendidly colored shadows on the rusty grey of the trails. As the day progressed, the royal party had split into smaller groups, each following its quarry in the thick of the woods or out in the open. Clusters of people had gathered everywhere to watch and to cheer.

At the farm nobody had worked much. There was too much excitement about the king, everybody wanted to share in the great event. Tresa couldn't wait to add her own great news about Kallyna dining with him at the Falizzas'. Last night she had kept Kallyna awake till late, wanting to know every smallest detail, what everyone was wearing, what they had eaten and what they had talked about. But Kallyna, for reasons that Tresa could not figure out, didn't want anybody to know. She had begged both her and Gheorghe to keep the secret for the time being. Eventually, puzzled as they were, they had both promised her.

All day Kallyna kept trying to guess why d'Hancourt had left her so abruptly the night before. Angry and bewildered, she could only do as he had told her, skulk around in the crowd and attract no attention.

She went home with the others at sundown, as always. By then the royal hunters had returned to town and were now banqueting in some other nobleman's home. Even the curfew sounded later that night. Finally, after much talk, everybody settled down to supper.

Tresa had prepared a special meal in honor of the occasion, and Gheorghe had opened a bottle of old wine. Assunta d'Andria had come to borrow a sieve and to chat. Her two oldest children kept looking at the full pot with a look of appetite; Tresa invited all three to have supper with them.

They were just gathering around the table when they heard a knock on the door. Gheorghe went to open. Two soldiers broke in, boots stomping loudly on the floor. Frightened, Tresa drew Kallyna into her arms. One of the men pushed Tresa aside and tore Kallyna away.

"In the name of the Almighty!" Tresa cried out. "What is this? What has she done?"

The soldier said something in French, unintelligibly. Assunta too began to ask questions, with the two children crying in fright around her skirts. The second soldier drew his sword and held it up like a peasant waving a rag to scare away birds.

"The next one of you who lets out a word is going to get a good taste of this," he threatened.

Blanched with terror, Tresa pressed her hand on her mouth to keep herself from making a sound. Silence fell into the kitchen. The first soldier again laid hands on Kallyna and started to lead her to the door.

Gheorghe stepped forward. "Please don't take her away," he begged. "Please don't. She's only—"

The soldier turned around with a curse and brought the hilt of his sword down hard on Gheorghe's head. Gheorghe fell to the floor, as Tresa ran to him in tears. The man prodded Kallyna out the door, then slammed it shut behind him.

The time it took them to reach the Castro seemed like an eternity to her. She tried to think, to steal a few moments of lucidity; but fear was stronger, numbed her. The streets were empty and dark. At the Castro only two or three windows were lit in the high front wall, making it look like a giant jack-o'-lantern.

The soldiers escorted her in, as though she were a thief they had just caught, and dropped the iron grid behind the heavy oak door. At the foot of the stairs one of the men went his way, the other marched her up to the second floor.

Light poured out of the only open door. She knew which room it was; she had been there before. The man led her into the room but he didn't lock it behind him; for those who went into the Castro for the wrong reasons, the whole of the Castro was the safest of jails. Her heart was pounding so hard she barely heard Falco's steps as he came in.

He walked toward her, looking at her with a cold, indifferent stare. In the reddish light of the candle the scar on his cheek looked as raw as if the sword had just split it open.

"Please don't come any closer," she whispered.

Falco twisted his nose, as if he had smelled something unpleasant. "Oh, *I* won't come any closer. Now, if you would please put up the appearance of a fight... scratch and bite and all those other things women do, that would be good. He likes it that way."

She shook her head. "No. No!"

The shout annoyed him. He shook his hands up and down. "Please be quiet." He turned around and left.

After a few moments footsteps echoed in the hallway. Not of one man; of two, perhaps three, she couldn't tell. Then their voices, loud and carefree. Falco ushered them in grandly, like a majordomo showing his guests to a banquet.

"Here she is, our little embroideress," Dalibor said, stumbling on the edge of the carpet with the unmistakable walk of a drunk man. "All nice and ready like an apple."

Prince Guglielmo threw away his cloak. "By God, finally a little fun! My learned father is the king of all bores, and this town isn't fit for my horse to shit in..." He patted Dalibor on the shoulder. "Thank God our good d'Hancourt has been considerate enough to find us something that might just about make up for everything."

Then he looked at Kallyna. "Last night she must have mistaken me for another one of her stable boys, or else how could she say no to *me*." Dalibor burst into a hard laugh.

Only Geoffroi seemed a little out of place in that company, a little more sober than the others. He glanced at her, shrunk in a corner with those astonished eyes of hers, and for a moment he looked like a tame dog thrown by mistake into a cage full of wolves.

Dalibor took Kallyna's arm and dragged her out. A stench of wine was all over him, and the front of his shirt was stained red. He made her stand up straight in the middle of the room, then he called Guglielmo with a flourish of a bow.

"*Mon Seigneur!* Your faithful subjects wish to present you with this prime piece of merchandise as a tax of obedience from your land of Tropea. Be so gracious as to accept it with good and fair will."

Kallyna shut her eyes. The hand that touched her cheeks, her throat, her breasts was the prince's. She could feel the heavy signet ring around his forefinger. Tears welled up from her eyes and rolled down her face.

"My lord d'Hancourt, we most certainly accept it," Guglielmo replied, with another bow. "Now, what was it that you had in mind for our amusement?"

"Only a humble proposal," Dalibor said with a wink.

Guglielmo took him under his arm. "Yes, yes, say it."

"Well," Dalibor began, "we all love to hunt, right? And what do we hunt... deer, fox, wild boar. But a quarry like this one, my lords... Isn't she worthy of our best efforts more than any dumb creature?"

Falco's eyes suddenly lit up. "By god, he's right! We let her loose, and the first one who catches her takes her first, like a good hunter. My dear d'Hancourt, you are a *master* !"

Guglielmo was frowning. "But she has no spirit," he complained. "She just stands there like Saint Sebastian tied to the stake!"

Geoffroi finally seemed to overcome his listlessness. He went to the fireplace, picked up the poker and with a show of ferocity thrust it under Kallyna's chin.

"This will make her run, my lord."

Kallyna stepped back with a frightened cry from the white-hot tip. Guglielmo rejoiced. "Much better. Let's start then, let's let her loose!"

"Wait, wait," Dalibor called out. "We must be blindfolded, or it will be much too easy." From the sleeve of her dress he ripped off a strip of cloth and waved it up in the air.

"Here we go, my brave hunters. Now we can begin!"

Each man took his strip of cloth from her sleeves. Falco led Kallyna to the door and there released her. The men stood around her at even distances, tying their blindfolds on. Dalibor shoved Geoffroi back. "Hey there, no cheating!"

Falco swung the hot poker like a battle ax. "Fly now, my dove, fly," he shouted. The four of them started after her, groping along with arms outstretched.

This wasn't a bad dream, she told herself at last. She looked at the far end of the hallway, which led to the stairs and to the main door. Falco's hand grazed her skirt. Horrified, she tore herself from his grasp and started to run toward the staircase, beyond the corner where only darkness was.

When she was at the top of the stairs she saw the two soldiers who had taken her there, standing at the sides of the locked door. She knew they would bar her way as if they themselves were made of stone. There was no way out. They had wanted it so. She leant back to catch her breath, and the shield hung on the wall clanged like a bell behind her.

She ran back to where the hallway turned. She had seen doors opening onto the hallway. Perhaps she could slip into one of those rooms and hide.

She peeked out. They were still far enough. Geoffroi stumbled and fell down on all fours, uttering a horrible oath. The other three pulled him up to his feet and goaded him on with a volley of obscenities and laughter.

She started cautiously along the wall, toward the first door she could see. She reached it, put her hand on the doorknob: it was unlocked. She turned it very gently, then pushed the door open. The door gave a long, slow screech that seemed to echo down the hallway like a sneer.

"I know where she is!" Falco shouted. "I know which door I left unlocked!"

Unable to move, she watched him skip closer and closer to her, his hands stretched out toward her.

"My dove... Here, my dove..."

And now there was something wrong, she thought. One of the four men had started to run straight toward her as if no longer blindfolded. She threw the door open and was about to lunge into the dark room when two arms fastened around her, two bars of living iron from which nothing could deliver her. She screamed and kicked and scratched. He dragged her out of the room and into the arms of Geoffroi, who was still blindfolded and thought he had found her first.

"She's mine," Geoffroi cried out. "I've got her!"

"You bloody liar," Dalibor shouted back. "I found her first, I had her long before you came and grabbed her!" The two of them kept yelling and shoving and pulling her from each other's arms.

Guglielmo ripped off his blindfold and threw it away. "All right," he fumed with disappointment. "No need to argue among friends. You will just have to share her, and so will we after you."

Geoffroi gave up the tussle too soon. He started to walk toward Dalibor's room with his bear-like gait, muttering unintelligibly under his breath. Dalibor lifted Kallyna up, tossing his head this way and that to get her nails off his face, and burst into a happy laugh of triumph.

"But please be good to her," Guglielmo pouted, stroking Kallyna's legs under her crumpled skirt. "Try for our sake not to damage her more than strictly necessary."

Dalibor tried to nod, while still fighting with her who wouldn't be still. "Yes, my lord," he replied with another laugh. Then he carried her into his room and kicked the door shut behind him. The laughter instantly died in his throat.

Geoffroi wasn't there. The window was open, and strange noises came from the street below. Dalibor dropped Kallyna on his bed. She was out of breath, shaking with sobs. He went to the door, listened with his ear to it; then he went to sit next to her and took her in his arms. "Enough now," he whispered quietly. "Please."

Kallyna kept gasping out broken words, clutching at his shirt as though she were drowning.

"Why this... not even a stray dog..." she stammered. "Why all this, lord?"

"Shhh... They might hear you. Please stop crying now." He started to stroke her hair, her face. After a while his gentle, reassuring touch quieted her into a stupefied and exhausted silence.

"Geoffroi will take you home," he said. "I *had* to do it. Guglielmo asked me yesterday to let him have you. I lied to him, I told him I didn't even know you. The truth is, they can take anything they want... no, we can take anything we want, so we take it!"

"But the hunt.... you said it yourself..."

"I know, I know. I had to do it, or else by now you'd be with them and not with me." He took her face in his hands and kissed her eyes. "Please, please understand. I'm so damn sorry." He looked disgusted from the depths of his soul.

"All right," Kallyna gasped. "I understand. But what will they do to you now? Won't they punish you now?"

"No," he answered. "There's no need to. They've punished me already when they ordered me to follow them to Naples... with a rank of captain."

"No!" she shouted. "Not to Naples, not to die!" He pressed his hand on her mouth, but still her eyes cried out in a wordless horror.

From the street Geoffroi's voice rose up to them, muffled and impatient. "Skirts of Saint Anne, what are you two doing up there?"

"Don't send me away," Kallyna begged. "Don't leave me, lord."

Dalibor stood up and raised her to her feet in front of him. "Listen to me. It might be years before I see you again. One thing I want to tell you. If I'm alive next Easter, if I come back, I'll take you with me. Remember that. Remember me."

He lifted her on top of the windowsill and kissed her with a new fury, the hurry of a condemned man. Her skirt hung for a moment from the window, as he whistled to Geoffroi below; then she plunged into Geoffroi's arms and into the darkness of the street.

Geoffroi wrapped his cloak around her. "Come on, little witch, come on," he said under his breath. "The Black Mass is over."

She strained her face upward to catch a last glimpse of Dalibor, but she couldn't see him.

Geoffroi's arms hauled her, more than held her. She could barely keep up with his giant's stride. The streets were cold and empty, and the sea pounded the cliff. She had to stop for a moment to catch her breath. Above her was the light of an oil lamp burning in front of an icon nailed to the wall of a house.

Geoffroi looked at her, shaking his head. "Jesus, you look terrible." He reached out to touch her face, then instead beat his fist on the wall. "Damn," he cursed in his teeth. "Damn!"

Kallyna took off his cloak and gave it back to him. "Thank you, lord. I'll pray for you."

"God is deaf," Geoffroi said. "Go now. It's cold out here. Go home, sleep."

She drew herself up, glancing toward her house. Suddenly, without a word, Geoffroi ran back to her and pressed briefly his lips on her forehead, so hard that she was startled. An instant later he had disappeared.

Dizzy, she walked to her door and sat on the steps. She braided her hair on her shoulder, wiped her eyes and tidied up her dress. Then she knocked on the door. Tresa came to open, with Assunta cowering behind her. Weeping, they took her in their arms.

"My child," Tresa sobbed. "My child, my baby."

❋　　　　❋　　　　❋

Cursing to himself all the way, Geoffroi went back to the Castro and up to his room, cautiously crossing the hallway that was now quiet and empty. As he walked in he saw that Dalibor was turning the room upside down, strewing sheets on the floor, smashing jars and uttering a shower of oaths that could have awakened the sun before its time.

"That little bitch. That little bloody bitch. If only I get to have her back in my hands I swear to God I'll rip her open!"

Geoffroi flung his arm around Dalibor's throat. "Stop this raving," he said in a hoarse whisper. "You won't fool anybody with it. Jesus, sweet lord, you do play the nastiest games."

"Is she safe?" Dalibor whispered.

"She is. The ones in trouble now are you and me."

Dalibor sat on his ravaged bed with his head in his hands. "It's over," he said. "Tomorrow we leave. It's all over." Then he jumped up in a rage. "By the Holy Cross, Geoffroi, why couldn't that royal bastard pick some other woman!"

Geoffroi had been looking in vain for some wine. "That is most definitely not the point," he said. "Some other woman you would have handed over, but not this one. You certainly went to very imaginative lengths to keep this one to yourself." The gruffness in his voice could barely disguise a touchy sympathy. "Why," he said, "you wouldn't let *me* have a bite of your apple... It figured you wouldn't make an exception for those two vultures out there."

Dalibor stopped by the window and wiped his cheek, where Kallyna's nails had left thin red streaks.

"We must go tell them," he said. "Oh God, how scared she was. What must have gone through her mind all that time..."

"Tell them *what*?" Geoffroi wanted to know. "That two bulls couldn't keep one heifer? How in hell do you expect to explain something like this?"

"She jumped out the window," Dalibor hissed. "She kicked us in the groin, she wore an iron belt without a lock, God damn you leave me alone!" He shoved Geoffroi out of the way and strode out.

"May I be gelded with a dull knife if I know what's come over that man," Geoffroi wondered.

When he reached the door of the prince's room, up on the third floor, Dalibor stopped. There was much too quiet inside. Guglielmo and Falco, busy at games of their own, must have forgotten about her.

He stood at the door for a moment. Then he turned around and walked away.

※　　　　※　　　　※

The following day was the last of the grape harvest and someone had to go to the farm. Tresa left at the usual hour; Gheorghe, with his head badly hurt by the soldier's blow, could not move from his bed.

Later in the morning the town crier made the round of the streets announcing that the king was about to be escorted most solemnly out of town, and inviting all to be at the Porta Vaticana to bid him a worthy farewell. Kallyna begged Gheorghe to let her go to the gate, and Gheorghe consented.

The gate was crammed with people. So were the windows of every house nearby and even the roofs. The royal procession filed out of the door of the Castro between two lines of guards holding the crowd at bay.

There were priests dressed in wide stiff robes that shimmered like scarabs' wings, deacons swinging censers that puffed out clouds of fragrant smoke, boys and girls spreading a carpet of flower petals before the mounted party. Shields and swords gleamed in the crisp autumn air. The horses' manes were braided with ribbons like women's hair. Blue, red, brown veils fluttered above the velvets, the silks, the furs. There was a forest of flags and banners, a sea of heads, helmets and caps. All that Kallyna saw was a strip of cloth tied around the right arm of Dalibor d'Hancourt, captain of King Roger d'Hauteville, leading a squadron of two thousand men to the war against Naples; the little strip of cloth he had taken from her sleeve the night before.

His face, enclosed in chain mail, wore a look of distant, determined calm. It could be simply resignation, she thought, for he knew he had been born to war. He kept his eyes fixed ahead, with that poise of the head she could have recognized among thousand. The sound of the bells, the cheers of the crowd, everything seemed to bounce off him like arrows off a wall. God alone knew what was in his mind as he moved out of Tropea, out of her life.

She made herself small in the throng that surrounded her. The king went by, and then Prince Guglielmo and Falco da Torre and Geoffroi de Vire. But they seemed to have become an army of dead splendidly dressed and marching toward heaven.

She kept following with her gaze the strip of cloth around Dalibor's arm, like the wake of blood left by a wounded man, while the air between them stretched wider and emptier.

If only she could become that piece of cloth, she thought.

PART TWO

IX

D ECEMBER WAS SO MILD that the lemons on the lemon tree ripened
much ahead of time, small yellow suns hanging from fans of glossy
leaves. Down at the Marina the boats had been pulled into niches that the
wind had scooped into the soft pale sandstone. In good days the fishermen
spread out their nets like brown cobwebs and mended them, crouching in the
sand with the hoods of their cloaks drawn over their heads. Most of the time
the beach was the noisy domain of tall billows that came crashing against the
foot of the cliff. Sometimes the crows left their hidden holes in the walls and
swarmed over the roofs, cawing hoarsely.

Arni came from Vibona for Christmas. His apprenticeship had begun
well. The master craftsman spoke in praise of the young newcomer. Kallyna
went with him, and with Tresa and Gheorghe, to Christmas Mass at midnight.

That night all the candles were lit in all the houses; happy groups of
people gathered in Piazza Portercole. Two snow-white oxen, their horns
festooned with mistletoe, were led to the center of the square. They pulled a
plow to which were tied four huge olive trees that lightning had struck down.

The trees were heaped together with kindling, while everybody stood around them in a great circle. A priest blessed the pile. Cosimo Falizza lit the kindling with a torch; soon the flames were roaring high, painting giant frescoes of shadows on the walls. Kin and neighbors exchanged the kiss of friendship, wishing each other peace and prosperity. Then there was light and dancing and music from the bagpipes.

The following morning nothing was left in the square but ashes and pieces of charred wood crumbling in the cold wind. A young man with curly hair, alone, went to pick up one of those pieces of wood and laid it on the doorsteps of Lidia's house. It was the ancient way of asking for a girl's hand in marriage. At midday he returned to her door. The piece of wood had been taken inside; he had been welcomed into the family.

A few days later Lidia stopped by Kallyna's house to invite her to her wedding. Lidia looked so happy that Kallyna wanted to curse at the top of her voice. Arni found her looking out her window intently, as though she were seeing something down in the garden that no one else could see.

Arni's feelings toward her had begun to change. He had discovered that he harbored a consuming grudge against her, that at times he almost hated her. If she didn't want to marry him because he was too young and too poor, why did she keep rejecting everybody else as well? Now it wasn't because of Raimo anymore, it wasn't because of Vasili. Perhaps Raimo had made her hate all men? During his long hours at the workbench he racked his brain trying to find an explanation to the mystery she had become.

Uncle Gheorghe told him that sometimes she disappeared briefly with an excuse or other. Arni followed her on one of those occasions, unseen. He found her talking to Rachele Tedesco, who had two sons at the war against Naples. When he had asked Rachele what the conversation had been about, the woman replied that Kallyna must be secretly in love with a soldier, because every Sunday now she had been coming to ask her news of the war. Arni found it hard to believe that explanation. Surely Kallyna would have said something about this man after Raimo's death; unless this man was married or for any other reason couldn't be hers.

Toward the middle of January she became ill. She ate little or nothing, and grew small in her black dresses. She turned down all of her commissions and left unfinished on the loom the ones she had already started. Tresa sat on the stairs by the door of her room, out of her sight, trying to catch a sob or a half-spoken word. But there was so much silence that the room could have been empty. Kallyna didn't cry and didn't talk. She just lay on her bed with her eyes open. After weeks spent like that, one day Tresa was frightened enough to send word to Arni in Vibona. Arni rushed home and sat in the kitchen all night, crying.

The morning after, while the bells rang for Lidia's wedding, a soldier from the Castro came looking for him. To Tresa's horror, since she thought they wanted to enlist him, Arni was ordered to go meet Robert Saintecroix, who had become the new governor of Tropea after d'Hancourt's departure. Arni came back holding in his hands a small square of red velvet cloth.

It was a silver buckle, heavy and finely chased, the most expensive thing the house of the d'Àrgiras had ever had within its walls. "It's for Kallyna," Arni said. "That's all they told me, nothing else."

"Who sends it, what for?" Tresa kept asking while she followed him upstairs.

"I told you, Aunt, I don't know. The lord Saintecroix gave it to me. He said it was for Kallyna d'Àrgira and sent me on my way."

He entered Kallyna's room and stopped by her bed. "Kallyna?" he called her softly, touching her hand. "The governor gave me this today. He says he forgot to give it to you before."

Kallyna turned her head and looked at the silver buckle in Arni's hands. It was a thick, sparkling little tree made of delicate filigree branches. It seemed to have been made for her and no one else, for her eyes that were accustomed to following coils of silken thread like magical mazes leading to a secret center.

She took the buckle in her hands and pressed it into her palms until it hurt. Then she gave it back to Arni. "Thank you. Could you please put it in the chest with the rest of my things?"

"Seems like a very expensive present," Arni said as he opened the lid of the walnut chest. "Who sends it?"

Kallyna sat up, searching with her eyes beyond the closed shutters. "Is it a sunny day?" she asked. "Has the wedding started yet?"

Tresa smiled. "We just saw the bride leave her house… and it's a day to make one's heart sing."

Slowly Kallyna put her feet on the floor and reached for her shawl. "Let's go then, Aunt," she said. "The buckle is from the lord de Vire… for that tunic I made him. He did tell me he wanted to spend a bit more after getting so much praise for it. I could not have imagined that he meant this."

She started going downstairs. Tresa and Arni, far too relieved at her unexpected recovery to dwell on doubts, followed her.

"Such a generous man, the lord de Vire," Tresa said pleasantly. "And such fine tastes, for a grouch of a Norman."

❊   ❊   ❊

She went to Lidia's wedding, she ate and danced and laughed for a few hours. Everybody wanted to know about that night at the Falizzas' with the king, and she quietly obliged them. Not that Tresa had ever let out a word about it. It had been Falizza's servants who had trickled the story out of their master's walls.

January was long and bitter. The trees were covered by crackling gauntlets of frost, and the sea pummeled the cliff with thundering knocks, wrecking galleons of foam onto the sharp rock. Padre Costantino was gravely ill, and waited to be released from life with a comforting patience. Kallyna wove a shroud of plain white linen for him. When the abbot died, it was wrapped around his naked body and followed it into the arms of the earth.

The endless winter nights were heavy on her soul. There was no escape from the deadening uniformity of her work at the loom. Still, with its repeated rhythm it seemed to lull her into a sort of unwanted resignation. She still went secretly to ask for news of the war from Rachele. The woman's brother was an armorer at the Castro, who passed on to her whatever scrap of information he heard from the governor or from others.

There wasn't much new. The Norman army was camped all around Naples, holding the neighboring towns in its stranglehold, and the siege went on between outbreaks of cholera. Pisa, Naples' ally, helped by sending soldiers, crossbows, and the highly flammable liquid used to make the horrible thing called Greek fire. The formidable Pisan warships stormed repeatedly the galleys that George of Antioch had linked together with chains to block the mouth of the harbor.

Who lived, who died, God only knew. Messengers on horseback were hampered by the impassable winter roads and often stopped altogether by the bands of robbers that infested the mountains between Calabria and Campania. As for the burials, if it wasn't the sea or the crows, more often than not it was a mass grave marked by an old notched sword. It was a world clamoring from afar like the frescoes showing the End of the World on churches' walls.

February came with raw winds and tales of the snow that capped the peaks of the Sila mountains. Kallyna had never seen snow, just as the people of the Sila mountains had never seen the sea. The man who took Arni to and from Vibona on his cart said that in the inland the wolves roamed up to the very doorsteps, and that the charcoal-makers had to chase them away from their huts with fire and poison.

At baptisms and weddings Kallyna could forget the winter for a day or a night. It was pleasantly warm in the church lit by a carpet of candles. Behind the wrought-iron grill the face of the Black Madonna was an oval moon with soft pensive eyes, her shoulders covered by a mantle worked in gold. All around the icon hung necklaces, bracelets, rings, and the veils of brides folded into white triangles like resting butterflies.

One day Kallyna went into the sacristy and pressed into the hand of a priest a tiny bundle wrapped in a scrap of cloth. The priest accepted the beautiful gold cross that Vasili had given her on the day of her Confirmation, and assured her that he would hang it in an inconspicuous corner of the icon.

"Is it for someone you love?" he asked her. "Someone in danger of his life?"

"Yes," Kallyna answered simply. "Please pray for him, Padre."

March was a wild month of thunderstorms. Every bush along the river sported a flapping cape of freshly-washed laundry. The sun bathed the hills in sudden green light, then hid again behind the passing grudge of a cloud. In the windy days there was a harshness that drove fledgling hawks to try their wings against the changing currents.

After the dead truce of the past months, Kallyna was restless again. Now she almost stunned herself with work, as she always did when she felt threatened. Even Donna Vittoria Falizza, the wife of the man who had fought the d'Àrgiras for years, was persuaded to commission her a new gown.

Sometimes, pausing from her long hours at the loom, Kallyna opened the trunk next to her bed and looked at her belongings. There were the gold chains she was to have worn with her wedding gown; the tortoiseshell comb her father had bought her on the day of her betrothal; clothes she could not wear, money she could not spend; and a silver buckle.

"If I'm alive next Easter, if I come back, I'll take you with me," he had told her.

Easter was close, and he may never come back. So immensely brief had been the time with him that sometimes she thought she had only dreamed of it, maybe during one of her bouts of fever. She couldn't remember his face, or the way words had sounded in his mouth. It was as if he had already become a stone warrior lying on the lid of a tomb, his hands joined peacefully on the hilt of the sword.

She knew that peace was not for her. She wanted to shake her fists at God, to run from that prison of useless days that were smothering her. Something must happen, she kept telling herself; a sign, a word, a way that would wake her up from her own sleepwalking death.

X

ONE AFTERNOON DURING THE LAST WEEK OF MARCH, someone knocked on the door with a light and patient hand. Kallyna put the wicker screen in front of the hearth and went to open.

"Padre Elias! Come in, come in."

"*Pax vobiscum*, daughter."

Tresa pulled a chair for him by the kitchen table. After the death of Padre Costantino, Padre Elias had become the new abbot of San Nilo. This didn't exempt him from going for alms door to door on foot. But this time it didn't look like he had come for the usual offering. He didn't have his bag with him, and he seemed to have come in a hurry on some unforeseen business.

"I've come to ask you for an act of charity, my dear Tresa," the monk began.

Tresa opened her hands. "If we can be of help. Just tell us."

"A small group of pilgrims came to the monastery today, four souls headed for the tomb of Pope Gregory in Salerno. One of them is a woman, late in her forties or perhaps younger, the widow of a merchant from Monreale."

His eyes wandered for a moment. "I might be mistaken, but she looks weak in the body for such a long journey. I saw about her an air of suffering, of waste..."

From the hearth, Kallyna stirred the lentil soup and listened.

"Now," Padre Elias went on, "these pilgrims had hoped we could put them up for the night, but as you know, since last summer the monastery is so full of orphans that we can't spare a single cell for travelers as we used to do. Then I remembered that your house was large enough to give shelter to these four good people," he concluded. "Only for tonight, mind you, no more."

Tresa nodded. "You thought well, Padre. We'll be happy to host them, and I'm sure I speak for my husband too. Don't you think so, Kallyna?"

"Of course, Aunt. Arni's room is free for the lady, and we can put a cot and a couple of pallets down here in the pantry room."

"They are willing to pay," Padre Elias added quickly. "The same price they would have paid for a good inn." Tresa almost didn't let him finish. "That we won't agree to. We won't take money for an act of charity. Of what we have, we'll give."

Padre Elias smiled, very pleased. "I knew the house of the d'Àrgiras, bless it, could not say no."

He stood up and was about to leave when he turned around, as if remembering only now something he had left out.

"Oh, my good Tresa, please don't be surprised if one of the pilgrims will look like... like an infidel. The woman has assured me that he's a convert, born and raised in Christian Sicily."

At those words, the good Tresa nearly winced. She looked the monk in the eyes. "If he is a convert as you say," she said sharply. "If he is *truly* a convert..."

Padre Elias took her hand. "I have no doubts he is. Besides, he's a very quiet fellow, minds his own business, as a good servant."

Tresa nodded again, uneasily this time. "Fine, Padre, fine. When will they be here?"

"Soon before the curfew. Right now they're hearing mass up at the monastery."

"All four of them?" Tresa inquired suspiciously.

"All four of them," the monk replied convincingly. "Peace be with you. And thank you, in the name of Jesus who was denied a house to be born in."

Gheorghe was busy moving tools and baskets to make room on the floor of the pantry room, and Tresa and Kallyna bringing downstairs pallets and blankets, when the curfew sounded along with a clap of thunder.

"If they don't hurry up they'll get soaked to the bone," Tresa grumbled. "What was I supposed to do, after he came to my own door asking for an act of charity?"

"Calm down now," Gheorghe replied patiently. "It's only for a night, infidel or no infidel."

"They're here," Kallyna announced from the front door.

It was already dark. Rain clouds hung heavily over the square, and the wind brought a screeching of hinges from the gates being closed in the face of the night. Four horses came to a halt in front of the house; lifting her candle, Kallyna searched with her eyes the four newcomers.

"There's a gate to the garden, on this side," she directed a husky, slow-moving young man with red hair braided at the sides of a face full of freckles.

The young man mumbled a thank you with a heavy foreign accent. "Lupo, give me a hand," he called then.

The second young man coming to help him was a good head shorter, but lean and almost cat-like in his movements. The light of the candle revealed curly black hair, a thin beard and sharp, restless eyes that lingered on Kallyna longer than necessary. Like his companion, he wore a dagger at his belt.

"There's also a water trough in the garden, for your horses," Kallyna told him. "We don't have any hay, though."

"We have our own, mistress. Please don't bother," he replied. His accent instantly revealed him for a Sicilian.

Then Kallyna helped the woman dismount. "Come in, come in. It's still a bit chilly, maybe this year we'll have Easter by the fire, as the proverb goes."

143

The woman stopped on the threshold and took Kallyna's hands in her own — long, soft, magnificent hands.

She was tall and slim in her cloak of coarse blue wool. The thin half-moons of her coif peeked from beneath the hood, adding paleness to a face that was already pale and smooth as a death mask. Her eyes were blue, large and steady. They seemed incapable of tears, yet retained their invisible, indelible mark.

"My daughter, you are most kind," she thanked Kallyna. "There seemed to be no place for us tonight, and the storm is close. Bless you all, good hosts."

Tresa and Gheorghe came to the door to welcome her. Their smiles froze when they saw the pillar of a man who entered the house after her.

Easily the tallest head in the room, the Arab was an impressive sight. His garb alone was enough to draw attention, a wide brown burnous and a thick striped sash with a curved, ivory handled dagger tucked in it. He stood on the floor as if on the deck of a ship, like someone who has lived at sea for many years, his feet poised at the point of perfect balance where no wave could sway him. His face had the warm color of the finest cordovan leather, and it seemed that nowhere one could escape his eyes.

The widow noticed the awe-struck expression of her hosts. "This is Mansour Ibn Hamid, my... well, bodyguard, scout, treasurer and physician, a little of each."

The Arab bowed lightly his head. "A very good night to our generous friends," he greeted them in flawless Italian.

"And thanks, from our hearts," the woman added. "My name is Leonora da Monreale. Padre Elias must have told you about my pilgrimage. It's an old vow I made when my husband was still alive and then never fulfilled. I hope to do it now, with the help of the blessed soul of Pope Gregory."

Kallyna was first to recover from her surprise and lead the guests to their chairs.

"Sit down," she invited them. "You will share our supper with us, won't you?"

Leonora's beautiful but colorless lips stretched into a rueful smile.

"I wonder how much we can possibly intrude on your peace, my friends. We thought we would find an inn somewhere in town and have our meal there, but—"

"No more talk," Tresa said, almost rude in her zeal. "Four or ten, we'll be honored to have you at our table."

Somebody knocked at the door. Mansour went to open to the two servants, both loaded with bundles, saddles and canteens.

"The horses are provided for," said the Sicilian, dumping his cargo on the floor of the pantry room where the beds were. "I wish I could say the same for myself. I'm so hungry I could have stolen the hay from their mouths."

"Lupo, Erik," said the woman sternly.

The two young men eyed their hosts with some embarrassment, then took off their felt caps. "A good night, a good night," they mumbled together.

Tresa waved them over to the table. "Come, come. Our lentil soup is better than any inn's. Eat all you want."

She started ladling out the hot rich porridge, while Gheorghe passed around slices of bread. They all huddled around the table, close to the warmth of the brazier placed underneath.

It was only after a while, as the young servants ate their meal with noisy gusto, that anybody seemed interested in resuming the conversation. They talked of the weather, of the bad conditions of some roads, of the impossible number of tolls.

Kallyna barely listened. She only picked at her food, feeling suddenly and inexplicably anxious. She kept glancing at the widow who sat across from her and who sipped from her wooden spoon with the unmistakable manners of a noblewoman.

She found it hard to believe that this was the wife of a merchant. There was a self-assurance in the woman's gestures, an easy, almost commanding way of talking and of moving that reminded her of someone else. Who, she couldn't tell. Perhaps her eyes, she thought, that compact blue that was not azure or turquoise or greenish but real blue without thinness, like steel.

"So you're going to Salerno," Kallyna finally blurted out. "Aren't you afraid of the war?"

Leonora looked at her with a long steady look. "My daughter," she replied, "war has already deprived me of my husband, and now it has taken my only son away from me. If fear is a Christian virtue, I'm afraid I lost it long ago, may God forgive me."

Kallyna took those words like a punch. Wasn't... wasn't Dalibor's father buried in Salerno?

With a bowl of almonds and raisins the meal was over. Lupo belched, satisfied and ready for sleep.

"Your room is upstairs," Tresa said to the widow while clearing the table. "Kallyna will show you to it. If there's anything you need, just say it."

"Perhaps a cup of milk, if you can spare it?" Leonora asked. "I do intend to pay for everything. Thank God I can afford not to be selfish."

"Then we will afford to be as ungrateful as lords," Tresa cheerfully replied, "and we won't take a single *scudo* from you."

The widow smiled. Gheorghe turned to her. "But please do remember us in your prayers to Saint Gregory. May he give you a good journey and a safe return."

❀   ❀   ❀

Mansour, Lupo and Erik had already closed the door of the pantry room. Kallyna eased the hot brick out of the brazier's ashes, wrapped it into several layers of woolen scraps and took it upstairs to the widow's room.

"Donna Leonora?" she called.

"Come in, daughter."

She stepped into the room wondering again, straining her memory. Then she slipped the brick into the woman's bed. "This will keep you warm. I'll go get your milk now. Shall I put some honey in it?"

Leonora took off her cloak and undid her coif made of starched lace. "No, thank you. You're very sweet."

With the coif removed, a head of hair of the most splendid shade of blond gleamed around Leonora's shoulders in the light of the candle. Kallyna almost staggered, unable to take her eyes off that golden haystack. Now there was a shadow behind the woman, a ghost sharing her every feature. She looked like Dalibor d'Hancourt.

Leonora noticed the way she was being stared at. She folded neatly her cloak and put it under her pillow. She smiled with some amusement.

"Why do you call me *Donna* Leonora? I'm no countess, you know. Oh, my hair…" she added, touching it. "No, no, I'm no blueblood. Maybe some great-grandmother of mine was from Germany or some other land to the north."

"It's not your hair alone," Kallyna murmured. "It's just that you look… you look very much like someone I used to know."

Leonora's mouth seemed to harden a little. "Oh?"

"Yes," Kallyna said without hesitation. "Somebody named d'Hancourt."

She waited almost nakedly for a reaction.

The woman shrugged. "That's a Norman name, isn't it?"

"I'll go get your milk," Kallyna said.

She spilled half of it on the table. Her mind was going like a startled horse. His sister, she thought; a cousin of his, his mother, his aunt. She thought at random, struggling to drive away her own bewildered hope.

A roll of thunder gave the start to a furious rain that pelted the tiles of the roof with a fast tapping of a hundred fingers. The small pitcher of goat milk warmed pleasantly her chilled, unsteady hands. She took it up to the bedroom and put it on a stool near the bed. She saw that Leonora was bent over a piece of parchment, writing on it with a small charcoal pencil.

"How wonderful, you can write!" Kallyna said. "I so wish I could too…"

Leonora made the parchment rustle between her hands, nervously. "I used to keep my husband's book, back in our store in Monreale. Now I just try to keep track of the days of my pilgrimage, of the stopping places and so on. But I leave most of it to Mansour, he's got a much better memory than I."

Kallyna puttered around the room, buying time. "I sleep in the next room, call me if you need anything," she said. Then she smiled, a smile that was almost a grimace of pain. "You know, you do remind me quite a lot of the lord d'Hancourt. He used to be our governor, and, well… it's funny how people look alike sometimes."

Leonora turned around with a look that made Kallyna feel like a scolded child. "He seems to have left behind rather persistent memories of himself," she said evenly, wanting to silence her.

Kallyna blushed, lowering her eyes. "I'm not trying to be a gossip, Donna Leonora, believe me. It's such a long story anyway… a very old story." She headed for the door.

"Wait," Leonora called, pinning her on the threshold with that single word as if with a knife. "Close the door, the others must be asleep already," she added gently. "Now, sit down and tell me this very old story."

"Aren't you tired?" Kallyna whispered. "Shouldn't you sleep now?"

Leonora made a face, as if despising her own body for failing her. "I have a pain that seems to come expressly at night, to torment me in my hours of rest. Mansour gives me a most bitter medicine that he makes from some herbs he knows, but it starts to work only after some time."

"But I have nothing to say," Kallyna claimed. Then her voice broke. "Does Mansour have a medicine that makes one sleep forever?"

Leonora stood up. "Yes," she answered sofly, "but he doesn't sell it at any price." She put her charcoal pencil and her parchment away. "This… d'Hancourt? Did he make you pregnant?"

Kallyna shook her head.

Leonora breathed in. "Were you in love with this man? Was he with you?"

"It doesn't matter anymore," Kallyna said. "He's gone to the war… He might be dead already." She grasped Leonora's hand. "Please don't tell my aunt and uncle. I told you because… I don't know, because it's been a long time and I can't tell anybody, but—" She didn't finish.

Leonora was silent for a while. Then she sat down in front of her.

"I wish there was something I could do for you," she said halfheartedly. "But misery loves company, so all I can tell you is that I am without news of my son since more than eight months. He's at the war, too. He too might be dead already."

"You're going to look for him, aren't you?" Kallyna said. "Isn't that what your journey is all about?"

Leonora's face clouded. It seemed clear that she didn't want to answer that question.

"You're a smart girl," she sighed. "Yes, that is why I'm going to Salerno." She smiled a worried smile. "You're smart and you talk too much. Go to bed now. By the way, I saw some beautiful work as I went by your room before. You are very good."

Kallyna smiled. "The lord d'Hancourt wanted me to go to Palermo, to work in the *Tiraz*... Could I show you something he gave me?"

Leonora nodded tiredly. "All right," she said, clasping her hands together in her lap.

Kallyna was back right away with the silver buckle. "Isn't it truly beautiful?" she asked, handing her the big sparkling thing.

Leonora touched the jewel briefly, as if it were too much for her to handle. "Indeed," she said dryly. She lifted her face and studied Kallyna with new interest. "It might well be that he really loved you, you know," she wondered. She laughed a little harsh laugh. "Why, even my husband never made me a present like this, certainly not before our engagement."

Kallyna bent toward her. "Listen, when you are in Salerno... could you please ask after him? He's very well known, the king himself loves him like a son. You could write me a letter, I'll find someone who can read it for me."

Her voice became hard. "No, wait. Better not to know anything. Better to keep waiting." She wrapped up her buckle and pointed at the bed. "I'm sorry. Your bed must be cold again, and your milk too. Please forget all about my nonsense."

Leonora eyed her with a taut, frightened compassion. "You shouldn't wear yourself out like this. You're so pretty, don't you have a beau?"

Kallyna shrugged. "He was killed not long ago... by the lord d'Hancourt."

Leonora whispered something to herself that sounded like a moan of pain. Then she stood up and gently led Kallyna to the door.

"It's quite late, dear. We must leave early in the morning. If you see Mansour before I wake up, please tell him to... Well, never mind. I don't want that big dark fellow to scare you."

"I'm not scared of him," Kallyna said. "The lord de Vire had an Arab servant, too."

"The lord de Vire..." Leonora repeated.

"I made him a tunic. The king told me it was excellent."

Leonora's eyes opened wider. "*Roger* told you that?"

Kallyna nodded. "The lord Idris, too. To tell you the truth, I have no idea why those embroideries made such an impression. But if you stay in town another day you'll probably hear half of Tropea mention this famous tunic that the king praised. They don't have much to talk about, you know."

"My dear child," Leonora blurted out, "it would seem that you've come to know quite a big piece of the world!"

She put her hand on Kallyna's shoulder. "I do like you," she added earnestly. "I kept wishing so long for a daughter. At least now I wouldn't be left empty-handed. There isn't much reward in raising a son... Not when you know that sooner or later the time will come when you have to hand him over to war." She patted her shoulder. "Sleep well, now."

"You too," Kallyna said.

❃   ❃   ❃

It rained all night. There must be an owl hidden in the fig tree. From her bed Kallyna could hear a low cry wafting through the dark like an endlessly unanswered question.

She had asked for a sign, she thought; now fate's own horse had come to her door with an empty saddle. She would come back, of course. Yet she knew already that from a flight like that there was no coming back. Tossing and turning she fought her own thoughts. The worst thought of all was that even if she did go looking for him, even if she did find him, then what?

But her heart was good at reasoning, and it made her remember something her father used to say when she was a little girl. The sea, Vasili used to say, has many names. It's called Aegean around the islands of Greece, and Tyrrhenian around the southern coasts of Italy. To him it was everywhere the same old childhood friend, and Vasili's childhood was many thousands years old. One blue day he had packed all his hopes into one bundle and he had sailed away, leaving a home to find another. The gods all live by the sea, Vasili used to say; only the dead don't need boats.

She glanced at the candle. There was enough light left for what she had to do. She opened the walnut chest and looked at its contents, sorting them out with her eyes. Her gold and her silver disappeared into a handkerchief knotted up tight; into another handkerchief went the chamois pouch with the money de Vire had given her.

Then she took the dress she had worn for the first time the day she had been betrothed to Raimo. It was the color of the lilac flower, with strips of blue and of paler pink embroidered in designs as delicate as those of the Moorish tiles that shimmered on the domes of Palermo. She laid the dress on top of the blanket. Then she took two more dresses, one made of wool and one made of linen, two cloaks, two pairs of slippers, a pair of soft ankle boots that had belonged to Arni, three shirts and a white handkerchief with a big swirl of a *K* done in silvery stitches.

She drew the corners of the blanket together, tied them, and weighed the bundle in her hands. It was as light as her heart.

XI

I T WAS A FINE DAWN. The rain had stopped, yielding to a wide orange sky dappled with grey wisps of clouds. Kallyna left her bed, walked quietly out of her room and went to knock on the door of the room next to hers.

She noticed that Leonora too seemed to have been awake for some time. Leonora lay stiffly on the bed, which she had already made, and she was all dressed and ready.

"Good morning," Kallyna greeted her. "I hope you slept well."

Leonora sat up, put her coif in her lap, then began to roll up her hair. Her smile was as crumpled as her pillow. "Very well, thank you. Is Mansour up?"

"No," Kallyna lied. "I came to tell you that perhaps you might want to wait an hour or two for the road to dry up a little."

Leonora kept her head bent to pin her hair. "Oh, that won't be necessary. We rode on many a muddy road before." She made a face when one of her brass pins pricked her skin.

"I also came to tell you that I want to go to Salerno with you," Kallyna blurted out headlong.

Leonora let go of her hair and looked up at her. "My dearest—"

Kallyna cut her off. "I can pay with money of my own. Are one hundred ducats enough to buy me a horse?"

Leonora raised her hand in alarm. "Money is *not* the point, my treasure. If I wanted a lady-in-waiting, don't you think I would have chosen one back in Monreale?"

Kallyna clenched her fists. "I don't want to be a lady-in- waiting. I want to be a pilgrim, like you. If there's anything I cannot pay for, I'll work. I'll cook, I'll sew, I'll wash clothes. I can ride, I can swim, I'm in good health and I sleep anywhere."

"No, no, wait," Leonora called. "You still haven't told me *why* you want to go to Salerno."

"I don't know why," Kallyna replied. "I'll think of a reason on my way there."

Leonora's eyes showed a thin edge of controlled rage. "It's because of that man you told me about?" Kallyna hung her head. "You came all the way from Sicily to look for your son..."

Leonora threw her head back with impatience. "There is a difference, you know. Your brave Norman knight may have forgotten you were ever alive."

Kallyna stiffened. Then she realized that Leonora hadn't spoken out of spite. She drew her breath in. "All right. I'll take that risk, too."

Leonora was shaking her head no.

"Look," Kallyna pleaded, "I'm alone in the world. I have no family, no obligations. All I'm asking for is an act of charity, like you asked when you came to my house. If I stay here I'll go mad."

"Nobody goes mad because of that," Leonora snapped. "Don't try to soften me with your tears. You're too young, too... everything! I already have my hands full with Lupo and Erik, and everywhere I go people stare at Mansour as if he were the walking ghost of the Prophet Mohammed. I simply cannot afford to draw any more attention," she concluded earnestly, "and instead look at you, with that hair, that face and all the rest."

Kallyna took hold of the braid that reached down to her waist. "I'll cut it like a man's. I'll wear man's clothes."

Leonora sighed. "You'd end up at the stake, my dear. You know very well that the Church thinks women who dress as men are witches."

There was a long silence, as both of them seemed to be running out of arguments. Leonora paced to the window, glanced down at the garden. "I guess it's useless to ask you what your aunt and uncle think about all this. You clearly aren't accustomed to asking advice from people."

"What will it be, then?" Kallyna said dully.

Leonora turned to face her. "What if anything at all happens? What if I decide to stay in Salerno and never go back home? Would I leave you to fend for yourself in the middle of a war?"

She grinned in disbelief. "This is all so very strange... If we had stayed at the monastery I would have never met you. I wonder whether there's some plan of fate to all this... whether I was *meant* to run into you." She eyed Kallyna with a small frown. "You're such a peculiar child. First you tell me that I look like a Norman governor, then you share with me all your love labors, and now you ask me to take you to nowhere... I'm sorry, dear, I can't. I can't take you with me."

Kallyna set her lips. "Then I will do something stupid, and may God forgive me. I will tell everybody that you *are* a Norman lady, a very rich one, the mother of a governor. And then you'll be bound to attract all the attention in the world." Her voice broke into muffled sobs.

Astonished, Leonora stared at her.

"You cry too much, too," she said after a while. "But at least one thing I can say in praise of you... You're just too stubborn to die, like my son."

Kallyna tried to wipe her face. "Please tell me that his name isn't Dalibor. Please tell me I'm wrong."

Leonora shook her head again, firmly. "Of course you're wrong. I can't even pronounce it, that name. If I were the mother of a governor, one the king loves as dearly as you say he does, don't you think I could have kept him by me instead of sending him to his death like every other man?" She raised her head and looked Kallyna in the eyes. "My son's name is Carlo, like his father's."

Kallyna drew her breath in. "What will it be, then? Are one hundred ducats enough to buy me a horse?"

There was a brief silence. Then Leonora bowed her head. "Better a mule. You'll need to save all you can."

At once Kallyna swallowed all her tears. She took Leonora's hand and kissed it, but Leonora tugged away. "Come on, I'm not the Pope. Let's put our minds to this fiendish plot, rather." Her voice was almost that of a little girl contemplating a prank.

"I've packed my things already," Kallyna said. "I'll take the bundle to Mansour as soon as I can. Now, I need you to please write a note to my aunt and uncle. I love them both very much, but I will not rot here."

"No, I guess you won't," Leonora chuckled. She took one of her small pieces of parchment and looked for her charcoal pencil; but before setting her hand to it she looked intently at Kallyna for a moment.

"Oh God, I do hope I'm doing the right thing," she said. "'Dearest Aunt, dearest Uncle'" she recited as she wrote, "I do love you both very much and I am very grateful to you for all you've done for me. I shall be back soon, and I shall pray for you in Salerno. The lady from Monreale will take good care of me. Your niece, Kallyna.'"

Kallyna followed the mysterious signs appearing on the page, nodding along. "It sounds fine. The priest can read it to them. I so wish I could read and write too…"

"Listen," Leonora said, "I'll teach you during our journey. Better still, I'll have Mansour teach you. He never loses his patience. He tried to teach Carlo, back in Monreale, but my son would rather handle sword than quill."

"Would you, really?" Kallyna exclaimed. "I can't believe my good fortune!"

Leonora's eyes dimmed. "Don't speak so soon about good fortune. You may have just made the worst choice of your life."

"Worse than this?" Kallyna replied with quiet passion. "Worse than waiting and waiting for something that may never come at all? Please don't fret, Donna Leonora. You won't regret it."

Voices and footsteps rose from downstairs; everybody must be up.

"My aunt and uncle will leave for the farm in a while," Kallyna whispered. "I will tell them that I'm not well today, that today I'll stay home. If you wait for me just outside the Porta Vaticana... no, by the custom house, I will join you there as soon as I can."

"Sounds devilish enough," conceded Leonora. "Of one thing, though, I want you properly forewarned. Mansour is not a eunuch, to say nothing about Lupo and Erik. Don't go bathing naked in the brooks like Susannah of the Bible, and if you ride like a man, wear a man's hose under your skirts, like I do."

It was clear that Kallyna had understood everything except what Mansour was not.

"What I mean is," Leonora explained, "there are three men out there, and all we women were taught about men is to be on the lookout. So be on the lookout. I won't be responsible in this sort of matters."

Kallyna nodded wisely, then stood up and headed for the door.

"One last thing," Leonora called, coming behind her with a grim face. "We are specks of dust in the lap of the Almighty," she said. "We might reach Salerno only to find that those we look for are dead. Even faith, hope and charity might not be enough."

Kallyna didn't speak. She lost herself for a moment in the woman's eyes, trusting her from the depths of her soul.

Leonora took her in her arms. "Perhaps the Lord is putting you by my side for reasons we cannot know yet. But neither you nor I were promised sure rewards. And unlike me, you can still receive from him the most bitter rejection you can dream of. Do you know all this?"

Kallyna wasn't afraid. She held Leonora back like a young tree planted next to an older one to help it weather the wind.

"I know," she answered. "But you and I must try just the same."

❋   ❋   ❋

Mansour took the new bundle from Kallyna's hands without saying a word. Tresa and Gheorghe, suspecting nothing, left for the farm as they did every morning and now must be already off the main road.

Kallyna put on her cloak. Her hair, tightly braided on the back of her head, was unnoticeable under the hood. Arni's hose was a bit tight around her hips, but comfortable and warm. She gathered the house into her eyes, saying goodbye to it in her mind, then slid the key into its crack by the doorsteps. Piazza Portercole was still empty. The sentries at the sides of the Porta Vaticana were still sleepy.

"Come on," Leonora called her softly with a smile, helping her to mount behind her.

"*Bismillah'i rahmani rahim*," Mansour prayed. "In the name of God the Merciful, the Compassionate ." The horses started out.

The road stretched along the high edge of the coast, between olive groves and vineyards. The sea was quiet, and the gulls seemed to sew the fine fabric of the sky with grey stitches. The morning was so lovely it seemed almost to breathe, with the wind blowing softly in and out of the world as it did in and out of one's breast.

Kallyna closed her eyes and sighed with delight. She felt more wonderfully free than she had ever been even in her dreams. Then she felt Mansour's black, probing eyes on her, and blushed. Lupo yawned noisily behind her, while Erik kept chewing on a sage twig with a most pensive air.

The three men had learned about their new travel companion while they waited for her by the custom house. Mansour had engaged in an animated exchange of alarmed comments with Leonora; however, knowing when to be more of a servant and less of an advisor, he had ended the discussion without forcing his mistress to remind him that she was such. Erik had shrugged his thick shoulders, only grumbling when it came to fastening the extra bundle to his saddle; and Lupo had unwisely let out a descriptive Sicilian adjective in appreciation of Kallyna's good looks, only to be silenced by one of Leonora's withering glances.

The morning was ripening into midday when they left the coast and began the ascent to Vibona. The town rose on an even taller crag than

Tropea. A cascade of grey houses dripped down the steep slope, dominated by a forbidding castle whose main wall was one with the chasm below. From its windows — so ran the rumor—unwelcome guests were thrown into the windy lap of the valley.

Shouting to be let through, Lupo spurred his horse past carts and flocks, headed for the main gate. Erik took custody of the remaining three horses, while Leonora, Mansour, and Kallyna made their way on foot to the market-place of San Leoluca.

It was of course Mansour who took charge of the choosing of the mule, of the inspecting and of the haggling. At less than fifty ducats and complete with saddle, the animal turned out to be a true bargain. Its seller, no little intimidated by his imposing customer, didn't dare refuse the price he offered.

Leonora bought some delicious honey loaves of *mastazzola*, after a lengthy selection among the great variety of shapes and sizes. There were prancing horses, birds, fish, couples of man and woman; all had tiny ribbons baked in to underline hearts, fins or hooves. Leonora was delighted by all that colorful parade.

They were leading the mule back to the meeting place with the two servants when Kallyna noticed, in the midst of the many unknown faces, a very familiar one. It was Arni, sitting on the steps of a large basin where women and girls were washing their laundry, slapping it on the wide sloping rim.

She ducked behind Mansour, trying to hide; but Arni's eyes, accustomed to scanning the underwater swim of the swordfish, nailed her with a single glance. His surprise turned into a frown when he saw that she wasn't with anyone he knew. Instantly he got up and pushed his way through the crowd to her, calling her name.

Kallyna rolled her eyes in annoyance; Leonora and Mansour looked at one another, puzzled.

"Have a good day, my lady," Arni began with nervous politeness. "My name is Arni d'Orta. I see you have with you somebody I know."

Leonora raised her eyebrows. "It would seem that we have. We are pilgrims going to Salerno."

"Quite a long journey, may God keep you. Is she showing you the market? Then I will take her home as soon as you're through."

Kallyna looked him in the eyes. "No. I'm not showing them the market. I'm going with them."

Predictably, Arni was quite baffled. "Just a moment. Before you do anything like that, I'd like to talk to you, if you don't mind."

"My young friend," Leonora said, "our time is precious. But if you two have things to settle, we'll leave you alone for a while."

Arni bowed his head. "Thank you."

Leonora rode away with Mansour, looking at them over her shoulder. Arni led Kallyna to a quiet spot by a mulberry tree, where some sections of ancient Grecian columns lay scattered in the grass like snowy millstones.

"Now, may we please know what this is all about?" Arni demanded.

Kallyna fidgeted. "There's not much to tell. In fact, there's nothing I'm *supposed* to tell you."

"Supposed?" Arni said. "No, supposed you are not. But maybe if I got down on my knees and begged you, who knows."

She turned her head. "Sometimes you sound just like Raimo Trani," she whispered. She twisted her hands together. "This woman is from Monreale. She's asked me to go with her as a... sort of lady in waiting. She pays me well."

Arni shook his head. "I don't believe you. And if you don't come with me I'll have the guards stop you at the gate."

"I will not come with you," she replied quietly. "You know I won't. Don't make me feel as if I didn't have you on my side anymore."

He looked away. "You had me on your side long enough to make up your mind... and you still do, or I wouldn't be standing here making a fool of myself in front of all Vibona." He stooped toward her, hands forward. "But patience has its limits, you know. Even my patience."

Kallyna was trying very hard not to cry, and she didn't know for whose sake, his or her own.

"If I tell you the truth," she whispered, "will you let me go in peace?"

Arni jerked his head. "The truth! From your mouth I don't even know what that sounds like anymore."

She raised her face to him wildly. "Then here is what it sounds like, Arni d'Orta. I'm going away because I love a man, a soldier, and because I intend to find him before death does!"

The words had shaken all of her as she blurted them out. After a moment Arni opened his eyes with a gentle amazement that was also relief.

"So it did come out at last, praise the good Lord," he murmured.

He was silent for a long time. Then he nodded to himself. "All right. I feel I ought to thank you. This thing had begun to fester inside me. You're a good surgeon."

He looked at her with a painfully steady look she dared not meet. She took a small step toward him, as if asking him to take her in his arms. But Arni didn't move.

"It's all right," he said again. "I told you I don't mind. Come, the lady is waiting for you."

"Let her wait," Kallyna snapped. "How will I leave you?"

Arni smiled, opening his arms. "How will you leave me. As good friends, as always."

His arms were not open to her, but she wedged herself into them just the same, and he folded them into a wary embrace, as if she were made of glass.

"Tell Aunt Tresa and Uncle Gheorghe," Kallyna said. "It's been some time now, but I can't tell you his name yet."

Arni let go of her. They stood face to face. "I'll set my soul at rest, then," he said. "After all these years.... He's the one who gave you the silver buckle, isn't he? Is he a good man?"

"He is, or I would not have chosen him."

"Can he take good care of you?"

"Yes," she lied. "And he loves me as dearly as you do," she lied again. "Wouldn't you do the same if you were in love with someone who's away?"

"You've been away from me all this time," Arni said, "and I've always come looking for you." He started walking back to the marketplace. "I'll let you go now."

161

"How's your apprenticeship going?" Kallyna asked as she followed him.

"I'll be a master craftsman in three months."

She smiled. "Really, so soon? I knew you could do it. And then? No, wait. I'll be back long before then."

"God willing," Arni said. "I'll make you a wedding ring. Go now," he urged her. "And remember, my debt is still unpaid."

She touched his hands. "So is mine, for everything you always did for me." She turned with one last look, and left him behind in the crowd.

The four travelers had been waiting for her at the side of the main road.

"All settled?" Leonora asked gently.

"All settled," Kallyna answered while mounting her mule. "Arni is my brother, and he worries, of course." The horses started out again.

"They've told me the inland road's given way in several places," Lupo said as they rode out of town, "and the next inn is in Nicastro. I wonder what the hell's in between, damn it."

"The Plain of Santa Eufemia," Mansour replied, "where the rivers can be forded even at this time of the year if one knows the right place. There is no need for us to take the inland road."

"What about tonight?" Leonora asked. "Do you think we should ride on and sleep wherever we can?"

Lupo twisted his mouth at the prospect of having to spend yet another evening looking for lodging. But Mansour shook his head. "No. We should sleep here. If we ride all day tomorrow we should cross the Plain and reach Nicastro in time, God willing."

"God be praised," Lupo mocked with a snort of relief.

The thick archway of Vibona's main gate stood above them. To pull her mind off Arni, Kallyna observed the small prayer rug tied behind Mansour's saddle. She had seen him roll it up in the pantry room where he had slept. For a convert, she thought, he seemed to have kept many of his old ways.

The inn was a two-story house sitting on a sun-streaked alley full of children and chickens. The bed in the women's room was big enough to accommodate a convent of nuns, and hard enough to be used by nuns who slept on wooden boards as penance.

Kallyna helped carry the bundles upstairs, and Leonora closed the door. "Let's take a look at what you packed," Leonora said "and if there's something you need for the journey we can buy it right away."

Kallyna handed her her bundle. "Of course. Here."

While they sorted out its contents, Leonora discreetly asked about Arni. "You didn't tell me you had a brother living in another town."

"You didn't tell me Mansour is not a convert," Kallyna replied in a very even voice.

Leonora glanced up at her and grinned. "It's hard to hide things from you... I'd say it's time we told one another what we left out before."

"I think so too," Kallyna agreed. "Arni is not my brother. We grew up together in my parents' house, but I have no obligations toward him. I told him where I'm going, and he has nothing against it."

Leonora spread out the lilac dress and admired it. "This one is lovely. I wonder whether you plan to wear it for your brave Norman knight."

Kallyna blushed. "Do you think he would like it?"

Leonora bent her head sideways. "I know my son would... No, Mansour is not a convert. I hate to lie about him, but that depends on where I go asking for lodging. I didn't think it would be a good idea to knock at the door of a monastery with a Muslim along."

She saw the tight, heavy bundle tucked inside the clothes.

"That's my money," Kallyna explained, "and some jewelry I took if I need to sell it."

"I have the feeling you'll keep this one for the very last, though," Leonora commented, holding up the silver buckle.

"Oh, not that one. I'll never sell that one if I starve."

Leonora sighed. "Blessed youth... I think it would be much safer if you gave this rather expensive collection to Mansour to carry. It's what I did myself at the very start of our journey. Lupo and Erik know nothing about it, of course."

"I certainly will," Kallyna said. "But where does he keep everything? I didn't see any purses on him."

Leonora winked. "Did you happen to notice how thick his sash is? It's all in there. I sewed it in myself." She laughed. "This extra roll is going to make him look as fat as a pasha."

Kallyna finished making the bed. "You have great trust in him, don't you?" she asked.

Leonora nodded. "You could say that I have most willingly inherited the trust my husband had placed in him. My husband bought him when Carlo was fourteen and needed a tutor. And Mansour certainly did teach Carlo many things, including an ungodly way of cutting off a man's head with a single stroke of the sword and only one hand."

She stood up, shivering with cold. "I'd better go call him now. After our meal he'll be off to say his prayers."

"What about your servant Erik?" Kallyna asked as they went downstairs. "Is he a Norman?"

Leonora chuckled. "A Norseman more than a Norman. Up to a few months ago he spoke in syllables and ate his meat raw, like his Viking grandfathers. I tried to have him baptized, but he almost bit the priest's hand in half."

The innkeeper busied himself around the five travelers with unusual zeal. He must have sensed that they had money to spare, and plied them with a meat roast, which he himself probably ate only at Christmas and Easter.

"Might we at least know your name," Lupo asked Kallyna while they were eating. "From your own pretty lips," he added quickly, ignoring Leonora's stern look.

She kept her eyes on her bowl. "Kallyna."

"Ah. Nice. My name is Lupo, because I'm strong as a wolf."

"Then how come you always make me carry the stuff you should be carrying?" Erik griped with his mouth full. "He's lazy as a lizard, too, mistress. All Monreale knows that."

Lupo slammed his fist on the table and stretched out with a threatening air.

"Do you want to fight, or will you swallow what you just said down that freckled throat of yours?"

Erik only swallowed his mouthful of food, then sent into hellish exile all of Lupo's Mediterranean ancestors with a single Scandinavian curse.

"Can we please eat in peace with neither wolves nor lizards prowling around our table?" Leonora scolded them both.

"He must apologize to me first," Lupo insisted, his hand on the kitchen knife.

Erik grumbled another string of unintelligible Nordic oaths. "And for the fourth time today I apologize, may Thor smash you to bits with his hammer."

Kallyna couldn't hide an amused smile. Lupo's eyes flashed at her in rage, and she lowered hers again.

After the meal Mansour took into his sash the new little bundle with Kallyna's money and jewelry, then borrowed the privacy of the room for his afternoon prayers. Leonora and Kallyna went to sit on the doorsteps of the inn, talking and laughing with some neighborhood women. Lupo snored, sprawled on the straw. Erik scrubbed the horses with dogged, sluggish strokes.

After sundown the innkeeper lit a brazier at the foot of the bed. Leonora swallowed a spoonful of the medicine Mansour made for her, and with that she was soon asleep. In the light of the candle Kallyna looked at her while she slept. She told herself again that no, Leonora da Monreale didn't look like the older sister of Dalibor d'Hancourt; that she had nothing of him at all. Then she took off her boots and slipped under the blanket. The candle dwindled out, and so did the voices of the children in the alley.

XII

THEY WERE UP AT SUNRISE, and ready to go after they bought food from the innkeeper and refilled their water skins.

Mansour put the saddles on the horses, tied his rolled-up prayer rug behind his own, and pronounced the words he would utter at the beginning of each day of their journey. "*Bismillah'i rahmani rahim,* in the name of God the Merciful, the Compassionate." The horses' hooves sounded softly on the cobblestones, breaking the grey silence of the morning.

A little later they were again on the Via Popilia, the Roman road whose large white flagstones worn smooth by centuries of use emerged here and there from under clumps of wild oleander.

Kallyna had steeled herself in anticipation of the long day of riding she wasn't accustomed to, but the morning seemed endless just the same. Bare trees in row upon row, Byzantine churches with domes as white as skulls, farmhouses enclosed in stone walls, wheat and barley, oat and rye, sheep and goats passed before her eyes under the low leaden sky. By the time they stopped to eat within sight of a watchtower, every bone in her body ached.

On top of everything she was forced to fend off Lupo's awkward gallantry, since he wouldn't stop buzzing around her. When the time came to set out again, he grabbed her around the waist to boost her up in the saddle. She had to dig into her repertoire for one of her sharpest retorts.

In mid-afternoon they enjoyed another brief rest. Then they forded their second *fiumara* of the day and headed toward Nicastro.

Seeing how tired everybody was, Mansour suddenly became talkative. "I want to tell you what happened to a friend of mine who was traveling through England, a guest of Norman lords there," he said.

Leonora perked up her ears with a flashing smile. "If it can take our minds off the saddle, my good Mansour, you're welcome to tell us the entire *Arabian Nights* all over again."

Mansour grinned. "This friend of mine was called Ali Ibn Issa Al Hasan," he began, and the name alone sounded like a tale. "While on his way to meeting his hosts, he stopped to eat at a country inn. To make sure that he wouldn't be served the meat of pigs, righteously forbidden by the Prophet, he asked the innkeeper for a meal of chicken. But since Al Hasan didn't speak the language of England, the innkeeper could not grasp what he was saying. So Al Hasan tried to make the man understand by means of gestures."

Leonora listened, rubbing her hands together in the cold wind. Kallyna strained her eyes between flatland and sky searching desperately for anything resembling the town of Nicastro.

"Unfortunately," Mansour went on, "all the gestures that Al Hasan could think of failed to make the innkeeper understand. So finally Al Hasan took a piece of charcoal and he drew the picture of a chicken. And to make the picture clearer, he also drew an egg next to the chicken's feet." He paused, doubtlessly for the sake of effect. "Not long afterwards the innkeeper was back bringing a dish of ham and eggs."

Laughter burst from everybody's lips. For a brief moment Kallyna forgot her aching body and the long day of riding. And while they were still laughing Lupo raised his arm and pointed ahead.

"Nicastro," he said happily. "Finally we're there."

The town rose on a hillside, deep within a mantle of woods. Old, dilapidated Byzantine ramparts still propped up the houses here and there. Kallyna saw little or nothing of it. She was tired, hungry and in a miserable mood. As they neared the cathedral, however, the five were stopped by a crowd of people blocking their way.

"Do you know what this is?" Leonora asked Mansour. Mansour shook his head.

On the last steps of the cathedral's stairs sat a bishop in full vestments, flanked by rows of deacons and priests. Arrayed at their feet were large baskets decked with flowers and ribbons.

"It's the *incanto*," Kallyna said, "the auction. It's a long ritual too."

"We might watch a little of it while Lupo looks for the inn," Leonora said. "We can't go through this crowd anyway."

They brought the horses to the side of the road. Mansour took out of his burnous a purse full of money and handed it to Lupo. "Here. Twenty silver *dinar* should be enough."

"And don't you borrow any of it to buy wine like you did in Scilla," Leonora warned. "Or else this time I'll sell you off, I swear it by the blessed soul of my husband."

Suddenly meek, Lupo took a deep bow. "My lady, I won't. I give you my word of honor."

"Hah!" Leonora said, and then watched him snake through the crowd, smiling at every girl. She shook her head. "No need to worry about losing our purses tonight. A couple of these good townsfolk will."

The head of the congregation started the auction with a spin of his wooden rattle. Then one of the deacons lifted out of a basket a loaf of bread shaped like a newborn baby and held it up for the bidders. Shouts of, "Five *scudi!*" "Ten!" "Fifteen!" rose from the men in the crowd. At the highest bid the auctioneer spun again his rattle and handed out the life-size loaf. Then from the baskets came heads, arms, legs, hearts, all made of bread and all as big as the real thing. Leonora wanted to know from Kallyna the meaning of the ceremony.

"The loaves are offerings from those who've been healed from sickness, or want to be," Kallyna explained. "They bake them and donate them to the church to be sold in this way."

"Look!" Leonora pointed. "Another little baby!"

With her eyes riveted to the noisy, bizarre pageant unfolding before her, she kept her arms drawn against her body, as if to stop the pain inside her. "Perhaps I ought to bake a loaf too," she whispered.

Lupo was back, much too soon and in a rage. He tossed the money purse back into Mansour's hands. "That damned bitch at the inn won't take *dinar!*" he shouted. "She says she's never seen that kind of money before."

This time even Mansour seemed on the verge of losing his patience. "This is most annoying," he muttered. "I imagine it would be useless to look for a house of change."

"No, but perhaps a lord of this town," Kallyna intervened. "The bishop!" she said, pointing at the man sitting on the cathedral steps. "He will have to know what *dinar* are."

Mansour looked at her. "A good idea," he said, "with one drawback. We will have to wait for the end of the auction."

Kallyna's shoulders fell. Lupo spat out an oath.

"All right," Leonora quieted them all. "I'll go ask myself as soon as this is over. And let us take this penance in good spirits. I have the feeling it's going to be much worse in Purgatory."

As God in his mercy meted out, the auction came to an end. Leonora, accompanied by Lupo, went to ask the bishop of Nicastro to take a purse of Arabian *dinar* in exchange for the local counterpart, and the bishop agreed. It was night when they could finally sit to a table and eat whatever the inn had to offer. By the time she stretched into bed, Kallyna had forgotten Dalibor, Arni, the war and everything else. Wishing that she could sleep till midday, she sank into a dreamless sleep of exhaustion.

They had been asleep for perhaps five hours when a horrible rumble shook the inn from foundations to roof like the belch of an underground giant. Jars and dishes crashed down from the shelves, the shelves beat against the wall, the wall creaked and strained as if about to burst open. With a terrified scream, Kallyna sprang out of bed and dashed out the door of the room she shared with Leonora.

"Wait!" Leonora called her in the dark. "Not the stairs!"

But Kallyna was already in headlong flight, together with every other guest of the inn. Lupo ran by her while trying frantically to tie up his breeches, followed by a disheveled girl clutching in fear at his sleeve. Outside the inn she found herself engulfed by a crowd of people all rushing toward the same spot, the cathedral square. Screams and calls and prayers ripped the night in half. Another rumble, stronger than the first, ran the length of the street, as though the earth were trying to shake free of mankind's small weight.

Alone, not knowing where she was going, Kallyna was swept away by the crowd as if into a river of terror. The only open space in town, the cathedral square, filled up with people whom nothing would persuade to return to their houses: as closely built as an anthill, these would surely collapse at the next jolt. Women wept and children clung to them with wide-open eyes. The men pushed open the doors of the cathedral and lit torches to show the way in. In an instant the cathedral was full and echoing with prayers.

Shivering, Kallyna sat on the steps and thought she could no longer move. After some time she heard Mansour's voice calling her name. She stood up, trying to see him in the dark, calling him back. He pushed his way through to her, found her and started to lead her back to the inn.

"It's over," he said, panting. "It's all right."

"How do you know that? I'm not going back to the inn. The street's too narrow, the houses will bury us alive!"

Mansour kept pulling her along with an unquestionable grip. "If it is written on the forehead of God that we die tonight, not a thing in the universe will change that."

"I don't want to die," Kallyna cried out. "I want to go back to the cathedral like everybody else!"

"The bell tower has come down in pieces at the first shock," Mansour said. "If there is one unsafe place, it's the cathedral... yet half of Nicastro is in there."

People still dashed past them, some carrying bundles they had hastily put together. Then Erik came running from the inn, rambling in his unknown tongue.

"Where is your mistress?" Mansour asked him.

"She is all right," Erik sputtered. "Still at the inn. O mighty gods."

They were reunited in front of the inn's door. Pale but calm, Leonora took Kallyna into her arms. "Please, Donna Leonora," Kallyna begged her. "Let's get out of here."

Leonora was looking at Mansour, waiting for his decision.

"Come on, what do we do, huh?" Lupo demanded angrily, shaking with fear.

"We stay outside, like the others," Mansour finally said.

"But it's freezing!" Lupo whined. "Lord, what a bloody damned night this had to be."

"Go get our things," Leonora ordered him. "I guess we'll have to leave the horses where they are. Quick."

The old woman who kept the inn was sitting on the doorsteps, rolling her rosary beads between her hands, motionless as stone. Her eyes were raised quietly to the dark heavens.

Lupo was back in a flash. They wrapped themselves in their cloaks, glancing at the houses around them in apprehension. Then they went back to the cathedral square. Mansour had to fight to find a place in the huddled crowd.

Leonora and Kallyna curled up in each other's arms, with the three men around them for protection. The cold of the night was cut by a wall of bodies whose hearts all beat with the same helpless dread. There was no hope or desire for sleep left. A very long night had just begun, and only to be followed by an even bleaker dawn.

At the first ray of sunlight Erik went to get the horses. There was nothing else to do but leave. In a gloomy silence, while the crowd began to break up, they took the road to the coast once again.

For several hours the only noises Kallyna heard were the dull creaking of the saddles and the snorts of the horses as they picked their way along a steep, uneven trail engulfed in fog. They rode through marshes and past the ruins of fields washed away by the swollen rivers of early spring. Then at last the fog lifted. The road now stretched between sea and hills, among pale expanses of heather and thistle heaped at random like yarns in a prickly carpet. Kallyna's body had reached the point where no single pain could be recognized in the general misery. She swayed in the saddle, struggling to stay awake.

"Where are we headed?" Leonora asked Mansour after some time.

Mansour looked at her with an air of concern. Her face had lost all color, and her shoulders were stiff. "To the town of Longobardi, my lady," he answered, "where our night stop is scheduled."

Leonora shook her head. "No. We'll stop and get some sleep now. If we can't reach Longobardi on time, we'll stay at the first village."

"As you wish," Mansour said.

At an isolated farmhouse they bought food and water. Lupo cajoled a reluctant peasant into selling him two rabbits, which he killed and skinned expertly; then he cooked them on a hearth he improvised with stones and branches.

After their meal Leonora and Kallyna made themselves beds of grass and slept for a few hours, while the men took turns standing guard. When Mansour gauged from the curve of the sun that it was time to go, he woke up his four companions.

Now the rest of the day's journey didn't seem like such a dreadful prospect anymore. It was a beautiful afternoon. The road ran side by side with endless white beaches, at times merging with them. The sea was like the polished floor of a magnificent hall, where they could almost ride forever toward the blue backdrop of the horizon.

"Were you very scared last night?" Leonora asked Kallyna.

Kallyna tried to smile. "Of course I was. I'm not like you... I wish I were."

Leonora shrugged lightly. "It must have become a matter of habit," she said. "And yet I've seen men who in their lives had killed scores of people being seized by the terror of death... Old soldiers, scarred like olive trees notched by the ax... When their time comes, they too call on the Virgin Mary as if She were their own birth mother." She was silent for a moment, looking at nothing.

"By the way," she said then, "with all this fuss I almost forgot that we haven't started you on the alphabet. My dear Mansour, did I tell you that our lovely friend wants to learn how to read and write? Won't you please think of a way to teach her while we travel?"

Mansour eyed Kallyna impassively. "It might take more than the length of our journey" he answered blankly.

"Or it might take less," Kallyna replied with a hint of indignation.

Mansour accepted her challenge with a nod of his head.

"Very well. I shall write down the alphabet tonight, for you to learn before we reach the border."

"That will be fine," Kallyna concluded.

Atop a rounded hill was a town all gathered around a castle high on the sea and the beach below. "Amantea," Mansour announced. "We should be in Longobardi in about four hours, *inshallah*."

Kallyna looked at the rocky crag, then crossed herself. "I do hope we won't have to stop up there tonight," she muttered.

"I don't think so, but may I ask you why?" Leonora said.

"You mean you don't know about the Duke of Amantea? My mother used his name to frighten us when I was small."

Leonora looked at Mansour as if asking for an explanation, but Mansour shook his head.

"That man loves to torture innocent people for no reason at all," Kallyna said, fidgeting on her saddle. "Men, women, children... and he has such a horrible love for his dogs that God should cast him down to hell for it."

Leonora was still baffled. "I can't see what's so horrible about loving dogs. My husband had half a dozen of them... True, in winter he let them sleep on our bed, but other than that..."

"That's not it," Kallyna insisted. "The Duke of Amantea forces new mothers to nurse them!"

In the silence that followed, the dark castle passed high above them, surrounded by a flight of crows. "Dear God," Leonora murmured.

They were in Longobardi only minutes before the curfew, as the guards were about to shut the single huge gate. There was no inn to be found anywhere. The one Mansour had scheduled months before had been razed by a fire. In the pressing dusk the five travelers looked for a convent first, a monastery then. Soon after nightfall the group split, the men bound for the monastery, the women for the convent.

The convent was ancient and lovely, its sculptured pillars covered with geraniums and ivy. Kallyna pointed out to Leonora some lay sisters showing them to their cell: red or blond hair, blue eyes, milky complexion spotted with freckles. Like many of Longobardi's inhabitants, they were of Nordic stock, descendants of those Lombards who had settled in the region a hundred years before.

While Kallyna was undressing, she pressed her hands on the small of her back and tried to suppress a moan of pain. "My bottom's killing me," she chuckled. "I'd never put a horse to a gallop before... I thought I was going to smash my head!"

Leonora looked at her in alarm. "But you rode as if you were born to it... Why didn't you tell me?"

"And slow us all down when we were already so late?"

Leonora smiled. "Sometimes when I see you it seems that I see my son... On the day he started to train as a soldier he came home covered with bruises from head to toe... The horse, the shield, the lance, all at once... But he would have sooner gone to hell than utter a word of complaint, just like you, and I was too afraid of his father to go comfort him. Poor boy, what a sad night he must have spent. And the day after that it was the sword, an iron thing that weighed almost as much as he did..."

The sound of a bell came from the hallway. It was the guardian nun making sure the cells were closed and the lights out. Kallyna blew the candle out and slipped into bed next to Leonora. They were silent for a long time, each lost in her thoughts. Beyond the narrow window there was a full moon, and the night was lovely. The cell smelled of lavender and soap.

"Have you thought of what you're going to do once we reach Salerno?" Leonora asked.

"No," Kallyna whispered. "I'm too scared to think about it. Something will happen. Something always happens."

A night bird cried out from a tree outside. The scalloped window looked like a lacy frame set around a shimmering icon of moonlight.

"I want to tell you everything, Donna Leonora," Kallyna murmured then. "Everything that happened between the lord d'Hancourt and me."

"Yes," Leonora said.

Quietly everything poured out of her, as a final bond of trust. Leonora listened in silence, fighting the tears that came to her eyes in the dark. Afterwards, Kallyna felt as if a great weight had been lifted from her heart.

"Good Lord, I talk so much," she apologized at last with a little laugh.

"There's nothing to apologize for," Leonora said.

"Now that you know everything," Kallyna ventured, "what do you think? Am I a fool to go looking for this man?"

Leonora's voice had a determination, almost a harshness that comforted Kallyna in her deepest being. "No. There are certain "foolish" things that we are bound to do only once in a lifetime, things that belong in God's order like spring and summer. What we do when we fall in love for the first time is the seed of destiny… and I hope it's going to be like that forever." Another drop of silence fell softly between them.

"You'll find him," Leonora said. "You need no other reason but this."

XIII

MORNING WAS A GENTLE BELL, then the rolling of a cart in the street and the first birds chipping the silence with their song.

As soon as they were again on the road, Mansour solemnly handed Kallyna a sheet of rolled parchment. "This is the alphabet," he said. "I shall tell you the name of each letter, and you shall learn them all by heart."

Kallyna opened the sheet and looked very carefully at the twenty-one mysterious signs neatly spaced on it.

Lupo, who was making a bow with a willow branch and a length of ox sinew, twisted his mouth in disapproval. "It's all a waste of time," he declared. "Women were born to different things than learning the ways of the quill."

"Nobody ever asked your opinion," Kallyna replied, holding her precious piece of parchment to her breast.

"I never would let my sister or my wife do it," Lupo went on, unruffled.

"Then thank *God* I'm neither your sister nor your wife!" she silenced him. Then she returned the parchment to Mansour. "Now, tell me what this is," she commanded.

"This is the *Aliph*," Mansour began.

A magnificent spring morning spread all around them. White hawthorn bushes dotted the side of the road, and the bare branches of the trees looked like grey veins in the flesh of the sky. Great sandstone bastions rose against the clouds, and dark green pines climbed them in long processions.

"So this is the *Aliph*," Kallyna said, letting the mule rock her gently on the gravelly path. "How do you write my name?"

Mansour smiled. "That will come later."

When it was almost time for their midday stop, their lesson was suddenly interrupted by the sound of a peculiar argument that seemed to have broken out between Erik and Lupo. Lagging behind as usual, the two were waving their arms at each other while shouting names of holy shrines, venerated relics and saints, mostly female saints.

Leonora frowned. "Mansour, please go see what those two ruffians are doing." Then she winced when she heard the name of God followed by an enormously gross oath. Mansour had a hard time raising his voice above the uproar. The two young men kept yelling at one another a flood of elaborate and ghastly curses. Eventually Mansour reduced them to silence by lashing them with his reins. Erik rubbed his neck with the humbled fury of a dog kicked out of a church, but Lupo kept laughing and taunting him.

"Six *dinar* you owe me," he rejoiced. "By Saint Mary Magdalen all naked in the desert, six whole *dinar*!"

Muttering to himself in anger, Mansour rejoined the two women.

"What was *that* all about?" Leonora asked him.

"A bet," Mansour answered in his teeth. "They had wagered a week's pay on the most awful curse they could come up with. Wretched heathens!" he let out in his anger.

Leonora immediately confiscated the six *dinar* of the wager. Outraged, Lupo declared open war on her, beginning with an entire day of silence. Kallyna heard Leonora tell Mansour to start keeping a closer eye on both servants.

At midday they camped on the beach, in the comforting sunshine of late March. Fishing boats rocked on the water at some distance, and the wind was as gentle as the voice of a lover. The horses grazed on grassy dunes spilling from a thicket of pine trees.

Kallyna couldn't resist taking off her cloak and her boots. "Can I walk around a bit?" she asked Leonora, who was dozing off leaning against the trunk of a tree.

"Certainly," Leonora said. "But keep in sight."

Kallyna rolled up her cloak and put it under Leonora's head as a pillow. "Are you very tired?"

Leonora smiled. "A little. Go stretch your legs now, while you can." She followed her with a look of affection as Kallyna became smaller in the expanse of sand.

It was all so quiet as she walked toward the edge of the water. She rolled up her sleeves and sighed with delight at the warmth of the sand between her toes. She stopped in front of the sea with her hands clasped behind her back, as if to ask the sea a question. The soft ripple of the waves became the clash of iron blades, the mad gallop of horses, the shrieks of dying men. She forced herself to put all that out of her mind and to follow instead the wake of the boats rowing toward a faraway cove.

"Can I keep you company?" Lupo asked, coming behind her out of nowhere so silently that she flinched.

Irritated in her deepest being, she strode on along the surf. "I am my own company, thank you."

"You're too pretty to be by yourself," Lupo tried again.

"That I've heard before. Never from somebody I liked, though."

"Jesus, how nasty can you be!" he said resentfully. "After all we're travel companions. If we don't stick together, who will?"

"Horseflies, for one."

She eyed the pine grove where the others were, and then made up her mind to go back to them. Lupo wheeled around at one pace with her.

"I've been in Salerno many times," he chattered on. "I know the place as I know my own pockets. I have many good friends there. You might need help, and I'd sure be glad to help you."

She was about to start yelling in exasperation. But Mansour saw her, and started walking toward her. As if by magic, Lupo peeled away from her the moment he saw him loom out of the pines' shade. She sat down next to Leonora without saying a word.

"Perhaps you should keep your cloak on," Leonora suggested, shaking her head at Lupo with a look of blistering reproach.

❋　　　　❋　　　　❋

By sundown Kallyna had fathomed the mysteries of the alphabet up to the letter *L*. Judging that it was enough for one day, she handed the dog-eared parchment back to Mansour. Then she flashed a scowling glance at Lupo and Erik riding behind her. Lupo had been serenading her with saucy stanzas improvised under his breath, while Erik giggled his red head off.

"I hoped *him* at least would keep his mouth shut," she said pointing at Erik, "and save what few teeth he's got left."

"Pay no attention, dear," Leonora said. "Their bark is much worse than their bite, like all mongrels." She turned to Mansour. "How does she learn?"

Mansour's face, as usual, revealed no emotion. "Faster than I had imagined."

Kallyna gave him a smug look that made Leonora burst out laughing.

During the night a wild wind kept rattling the shutters of the house where they had found lodging. At dawn, low thunderclouds still hung low in the sky. The road turned into a causeway stretching between sand and marshy ground. The five travelers soon regretted setting out under the impending threat of rain. But they pushed on along with the swelling clouds, heads bent against the dust. Leonora shivered in the damp wind, her forehead beaded with sweat. Kallyna had pulled the hood of her cloak down on her face and kept her eyes on the side of the road, where the embankment crumbled away here and there at the passing of the mounts.

The storm brewed for several hours. There was not a town, a village, a house in sight, only rugged hills sloping toward the sea in a fretwork of caves. The five ghosts edged their way against the wind in dread of the first raindrop.

180

Soon the blanket Kallyna had wrapped around Leonora's shoulders was soaked through. The rain began to pour with a rumble of fast thunderclaps; the lightning's skeleton fingers dipped into the fringe of brush hemming the hills above them.

"Do you know where we are?" Leonora called out to Mansour, her cloak pasted to her face.

"A little past the county of Diamante," Mansour answered. "The next town is five hours away."

"We can't go on in this rain," Leonora shouted again. "Let's find some sort of shelter, and then we'll see."

Mansour turned his horse from the road and disappeared in the direction of the hills, leaving the others to fend for themselves along the treacherous way. Blinded by the rain, Kallyna struggled to lead the mule through marsh water and reeds to higher ground. The legs of the mule wobbled and splashed; a stumble, and she knew she would find herself knee-deep in mud.

Finally the marsh gave way to a strip of sand on which they pushed the mounts with frenzied impatience. Mansour reappeared from a curtain of willows shaking their flaxen strands in the storm.

"There is a cave nearby," he said. He took Leonora's horse by the bit and led the slow party to a dark mouth gaping in the sandstone wall.

Leonora almost collapsed into Kallyna's arms, short of breath and racked by shivers. While Kallyna tried to wring their cloaks dry, she called Mansour and together they talked for some time in a low voice, away from the others.

Leonora seemed to speak in a pleading tone of resignation, as if she were hearing death close behind her. Mansour kept shaking his head gently, comforting her; then he gave her an extra dose of his medicine. Finally Leonora fell into a restless sleep, still racked with chills. Mansour called Erik to go out with him, ordering Lupo to stay with the two women.

Outside the rain kept pounding hard. The angry roar of the sea was one with that of the thunder. In the dimness of the cave lit now and then by flashes of lightning, Leonora's breathing sounded ominously harsh. Lupo, crouched by the entrance, studied Kallyna with his sharp eyes and rolled the handle of his knife between his hands.

Some time later Mansour came back, having found almost by miracle a bundle of dry branches. He kindled it with the spark from two stones and it soon began to warm them with its uncertain flames. Nobody spoke much, with hunger and cold prowling among them like bad companions.

Before the fire started to dwindle, Leonora sent the three men to the mouth of the cave, ordering them to keep their backs turned. She quickly changed her wet clothes while Kallyna kept a blanket around her. Then it was Kallyna's turn to change. For the space of a few moments the blanket Leonora held around her bore the graceful contour of her body etched against the fire. Braving Leonora's anger, Lupo turned his head and looked over his shoulders. No one saw him, and he didn't avert his eyes until the very last minute.

Slowly the storm abated. A strip of blue peeked from under the clouds, and the thunder rolled away beyond the hills. It was time to set out again, while the damp afternoon cleared on a sea ravaged by long white breakers whose roar could be heard for miles. To ease her mind, Kallyna kept repeating to herself the letters of the alphabet. Leonora looked better now, but for a moment she had feared for her. She didn't know what she would do if something happened to Leonora.

Five hours later they reached Scalea. True to its name, it was a stairway of stone houses fanning out from a hilltop like a Grecian theatre and facing the immense stage of the sea. There was almost no level space within its massive walls. Long flights of steps substituted streets and alleys, many running under thick arches that stretched like bridges from house to house. The marketplace was decorated with faded figureheads and crowded with Saracen slaves from faraway ports of call. It was a town of sailors, narrow as the hull of a warship and as secure.

The young innkeeper, his wife and their six children were kind and helpful people. After that rough day, their every favor was twice as welcome to the five exhausted travelers. While they sat to a hearty supper, a pitcher of wine and a plate of dried figs stuffed with walnuts, the couple took care of their wet clothes, hanging them to dry around the large copper brazier. The youngsters, all shaven-headed to ward off lice, stood guard to make sure that none of the clothes would end up in the luggage of some other guest.

When it was time for bed they offered Leonora and Kallyna a tiny but prodigiously clean room graced with white embroidered linens. The bed even had wool mattresses. So many unexpected luxuries in Scalea, Kallyna thought, and stopped cursing the day she had embarked upon that uncomfortable adventure.

XIV

T HE FOLLOWING MORNING UPON WAKING UP Kallyna discovered that
Leonora had sent Lupo ahead a few hours earlier, to the castle of the lord
of Aieta, to inform him of their arrival. The lord of Aieta, Leonora explained,
was a friend of her late husband's, and had offered months before to house
her and her fellow travelers on their way to Salerno.

They set out in a warm sunshine that seemed to make everything sing.
The coast now reached out into sharp headlands and long sickles of sand.
The sides of the mountains rose from the sea like the knuckles of a huge
hand. Islands were scattered along the coast; Dino, the tallest one, was high
and flat as the deck of a ship. Beyond that last sentinel of Calabria, Lucania
stretched out in a breadth of blue and green.

The castle of Aieta rose halfway up the ridge as if on a rocky balcony,
with rigidly rectangular walls and two round towers ranged closely together.
Banners waved on the covered catwalk atop the roof, from where hundreds of
miles could be commanded in absolute sovereignty. Standing on the walls of
the castle of Aieta one could imagine he had taken the wings from an eagle.

The four visitors were escorted to the main gate shadowed by the twisting branches of a huge oak tree. Mansour read with impeccable pronunciation the inscription in Latin carved on a slab of white marble above the gate. "The Lords Rocca of Aieta, Sires of the Counties of Aieta, Maratea, Summuranum and Praia. Built in the year of Our Lord One Thousand and Sixty. To Persevere."

As they entered the grassy yard that separated the double curtain wall, Leonora asked one of the servants about Lupo. The man said he didn't know anybody by that name. No matter, Leonora replied, he would be looked for later. The servant had them wait in the courtyard while he rushed to call an old woman who would show them to their room. The courtyard was a vast square surrounded by workshops and stables. On the farthest corner was a lovely chapel draped in wisteria, with a bell tower full of pigeons and sparrows.

The old woman summoned by the servant greeted Leonora with a warm embrace, as though she had been her own nurse. She was a small, bony woman with withered braids and a smile like winter sunshine.

"Well arrived, all of you! Everything is ready. We didn't know you had female company, but we'll find a nice room for her too, won't we?" She led them up the staircase, happily talking on.

"Do you know that we hadn't seen women in this castle ever since the marquise died, God rest her soul? My name is Gemma. Are you hungry? Would you like a warm bath?"

Beyond the staircase was a great hall furnished with a marble table, Roman chairs and sheepskin rugs. A small arsenal of weapons hung on the walls, interspersed with long banners clustered under the vaults.

Ever since she had set foot into the castle, Kallyna hadn't spoken a word. Suddenly she felt uncomfortable, dwarfed — like in the house of the Falizzas, like in the Castro. She still hadn't learned to trust any place in which lords lived.

Leonora seemed well aware of her discomfort. "I know you were expecting us yesterday," she told Gemma, trying to break the silence. "I hope we haven't inconvenienced you too much?"

"Inconvenienced us?" Gemma said briskly. "*We* are the ones who should apologize. The marquis went hunting this morning, when he should have waited to hear news of your arrival."

Leonora bit her lip. She knew Kallyna must be asking herself why the lord of Aieta should have to wait for the wife of a merchant. She smiled wanly to herself and kept her peace.

Their rooms were on the third floor. Leonora's was furnished with a canopy bed of crimson velvet and chairs covered with the same royal fabric. In niches carved in the walls were lined up bottles of costly perfumes and ivory chests finely carved in the Moorish fashion. The window opened onto a magnificent view of the coast.

"I hope the room is to your liking," Gemma said. "If you come with me across the hallway, I'll show you the one for your young friend."

The room across the hallway could very well have been the bedroom of the marquis's own daughter. The bedspread was a spring field of pale green brocade, matched to the draperies hung on gleaming brass rods. There were silver candlesticks and books bound in leather and gold leaf. On the marble floor lay a brown bearskin rug and fur cushions.

Kallyna kept her mouth shut and her eyes open. This was no time for questions, she thought, although she did have quite a few of them in mind.

Gemma put her arm on her shoulder. "I'd really like to know if the room suits her," she wondered, "but... has she by any chance taken a vow of silence?'

Leonora burst into a laugh. Kallyna shook her head, blushing. "I'm sorry," she stammered. "I was just... thinking."

"You don't like the room?" Gemma fretted.

"Oh, I do, I do," Kallyna blurted out. "It's perfect, believe me."

"Good," Gemma said, pleased. "Then I'll go downstairs to see to your meal. Call me if you need anything at all."

Leonora thanked her, then turned to Kallyna. "Let's see how you look in that lovely lilac dress of yours."

A little later, while Kallyna was putting the dress on and combing her hair, she heard Leonora sing softly to herself in her room.

"Do you need a mirror?" Leonora called her. "I have one here, if you're ready."

Kallyna brought her braid over one shoulder and tied it with a ribbon. "Yes, I'm coming."

When she walked into the room, Leonora looked her from head to toe with a look of frank admiration. "Well, I must say you cut quite an impression when you're not trying to pass for a man. Here's the mirror."

A round sheet of polished brass showed Kallyna what she had never seen before in a mirror: herself, looking like the spring day outside. She pursed her lips. "Uhm. At least I'm *clean*."

Leonora asked her to comb her hair and pin the soft muslin veil around her face. Kallyna put some hairpins between her lips and picked up an ivory comb. Leonora's hair felt like silk in her hand.

"You're as nervous as a bride," Leonora said. "Don't let all this impress you too much... Enjoy it. For one day we're both ladies of high rank!"

Gemma came back, clapping her hands. "You look just like two stars in the sky," she praised. "Ah," she sighed then, "it was so nice when the marquise was still alive... I keep telling the lord Filippo that he should remarry, but he loved her too much."

From the open window came the sound of a horn followed by hoof beats. Gemma threw her hands in the air. "It's him, it's the master! Come, come."

They went downstairs, while the hunting party dismounted in the courtyard. Grouse and pheasant stained with their blood the backs of the hunters' shirts. The dogs made a happy noise barking around them. Mansour crossed the courtyard to go meet the lord Rocca. The two men greeted each other with the warmth of old friends. Then Mansour pointed at the top of the staircase, where Leonora and Kallyna had appeared.

Filippo Rocca, a handsome man with graying hair and the bearing of a Roman leader of legions, came up with his arms extended toward his guest. When he stood in front of Leonora, he bent his knee and took her hands into his own with the utmost devotion.

"Welcome with all my heart," he said, "my lady d'Hancourt."

Kallyna took a step backward, as if something had hit her in the face. She clasped her hand to her mouth to keep from crying out.

Between Leonora and Mansour ran a glance that was like an arrow.

"Lupo," Leonora said in her teeth. She turned to Rocca. "My dear Filippo, please ask your men to find my servant Lupo. And when they find him, have them give him a dozen strokes of the lash."

Rocca nodded. "As you wish, but may I ask… "

"Dearest Filippo, I will explain," Leonora said with a bleak smile. "My young companion here was not—"

Kallyna was running up the stairs to her room.

❋   ❋   ❋

A warm midday sun shone on the coast and the sea. From her window Kallyna could see the beach, the island and the watchtower. The door of her room was bolted. No one had come looking for her, and for this she was thankful. She knew she wouldn't be able to face anybody until she had sent her every thought back to its proper place. A little later Lupo's screams had reached her from somewhere in the courtyard, and she had pressed her hands on her ears to shut out that horrible sound.

"Kallyna," said at last a voice from behind the door, softly.

Her hands shaking, she went to open. It was Leonora, confronting her with her calm and inescapable presence. She let her in.

"I would have told you," the woman began. "In fact, I simply *should* have told you. You're far too smart." She searched Kallyna's face. "Are you afraid of me?"

"Afraid? No," Kallyna said. "But I don't know how to treat you anymore. Everything is different now."

"Is it?" Leonora wondered quietly. She paused. "I sent Lupo ahead this morning to let the lord Rocca know that I was traveling, out of necessity, under a false name… He was drunk even before setting foot into the castle. They found him snoring in a cellar."

"You shouldn't have punished him," Kallyna said with passion. "It seems to me that you d'Hancourts make great use of your whips."

Leonora was stung. "When we deem it necessary, yes. It is our prerogative."

"I know all about your prerogatives," Kallyna rebutted. "I still wear them on my back."

Her voice was full of bitter resentment. "What I find hard to believe is that you are the same person who only a few hours ago chatted with innkeepers and haggled over the price of a loaf of bread. I knew who you were from the very first instant, and I was honest enough to tell you. You could have trusted me. I had no reason to do you harm."

"My girl," the woman snapped curtly, "I once told Roger d'Hauteville that I didn't trust him. Distrust is the one luxury we lords cannot afford to do without in any circumstance."

Kallyna recoiled. The woman was hiding behind the shield of her aristocratic pride; she couldn't let that happen.

"All right," she said. "To begin with, who are you?"

Almost unconsciously, the woman straightened herself up. "Malva, duchess of Hancourt and Monreale, widow of a councilor of the Crown, mother of a captain of King Roger, and carrier of an illness that will rob me of my days before one hair on my head turns grey."

She made the last statement with the same high bearing with which she had given all her titles. Kallyna was struck silent.

"I may not have trusted you enough," Malva said. "I may have put you to the test. But I never made a mystery of the fact that I like you very much." She smiled. "As for chatting with innkeepers and haggling over the price of bread, it comes naturally when one gets to see things from my point of view. An emperor and a leper don't look much different to the eyes of death. Thank God this at least I've had the time to learn."

Kallyna got down on her knees. "Forgive me," she begged. "I understand."

Malva pulled her up and close to her. "Come on. I hate it when you try to be humble. It doesn't suit you at all."

She held Kallyna in her arms. "The ways of God, truly!" she wondered. "I had stopped in Tropea to see Robert Saintecroix and ask him news of Dalibor. Shouldn't we both be grateful that we met? I certainly am. I wish I could will your loyalty and your love to my son when I die... If I must trade it all now for mere obedience simply because I'm a Norman, *then* I would regret that you found me out."

Kallyna shook her head. "No. You know I love you even more now."

Malva smiled, almost mischievously. "We'd better be friends, you know. I know too much about you and you know too much about me." She hugged her again, then started for the door. "We must go now." She looked at the silver buckle threaded through Kallyna's belt and smiled from the depths of her heart.

Kallyna ran her fingers on the beautiful jewel. "Your son has very fine tastes," she whispered.

Malva nodded. "In everything."

As they went downstairs, Kallyna remembered Lupo. "Please see that Lupo is taken care of," she asked. "In a way, it's my fault."

"All right. He will be taken care of, because you asked. And of course it's not your fault."

Gemma had set the table in a small room that looked like the inside of a jewel chest, lined from floor to ceiling with red damask cloth. Mansour and Filippo Rocca were seated side by side.

"My dear Mansour," Rocca was saying, "You shouldn't be so quick to blame us if we don't seem capable of governing ourselves. After all, we were never masters of our own country. Even the ancient Romans, whom everybody praises, were nothing but a foreign breed of conquerors to us... And ever since them we've only known one foreign conqueror after another — Greeks, Germans, Arabs, Franks, God only knows how many more will come in the future." His fine mouth curled into a melancholy smile. "We have learned how to be good subjects, and that we have learned all too well, but learning to be our own rulers will take quite a long time."

"Please allow me to contradict you, my friend," said Malva d'Hancourt, as she came in holding Kallyna by the hand. "The Italians have one great talent, which in the end will ensure your survival."

A servant hastened to show both women to their seats. Rocca opened his hands. "I would very much like to hear it," he said.

"If you don't rid yourselves of your conquerors by the sword," Malva said, "it's because you do it not by shedding blood, but by mixing it. Look at how many of us Normans have become Italians, and how very few Italians have gone the other way around. One more generation, and we'll be nothing but a memory to you."

Rocca smiled. "Perhaps. But in the meantime, may we both live together in peace."

"Indeed," Malva said with a wink, "history is made in the bedroom even more than on the battlefield."

The servants handed out scented linens for the guests to wipe their hands with. Malva bent toward Mansour and spoke under her breath. "Please see that Lupo's sores be treated." Then she turned to Rocca and offered Kallyna to his pleased but still very much puzzled gaze.

"This, my dear Filippo, is Kallyna d'Àrgira from Tropea, whom I love as a daughter of my own."

Her words made Kallyna blush with joy. Rocca studied her with a look of admiration.

"She has every hallmark of our people," he praised her. "Perfect companion to one of the most beautiful women who ever graced King Roger's court."

Malva picked up a pheasant drumstick with two fingers and placidly shrugged her shoulders. "Fifteen years ago, perhaps."

In came Gemma, holding a huge silver platter heaped with roast wild boar and slices of bread soaked in its juices, the whole surrounded by rosemary sprigs. She seemed to burst with pride as she lowered the platter onto the table.

Rocca stood up to tackle the carving of the roast.

"You know, I am tempted to join you in your journey to Salerno," he confessed. "I'm not too old to offer my services to the Hautevilles one last time. But my lands need a good caretaker, as I modestly consider myself nowadays."

"Far too modestly," Malva countered, addressing Kallyna. "You should have seen him when he returned from the Holy Land, where he fought side by side with Tancredi."

"What a perfect warrior Tancredi was," Rocca said, "at nineteen the flower of the Hautevilles… and the only one compassionate enough to stop the massacre in Jerusalem!"

Mansour nodded. "Different times," he mused. "Now we no longer need to hack another to pieces."

"Truly," Rocca said, "this young kingdom of ours is the work of a man of genius. Look at what happens in the North of Italy, where Florentines kill Florentines and Milanese butcher Milanese. Down here for once in our history we have tolerance and peace. You see the mosque rising side by side with the cathedral, the synagogue next to the Greek chapel… And Roger *will* bring Naples into the same fold."

He lifted his cup of sparkling Falernum wine. "Long live the Hautevilles," he toasted. "Long live Roger."

All raised their cups with him, and the servants applauded. Gemma, from the threshold, was beaming with satisfaction.

✻   ✻   ✻

Beyond her fondest dreams Kallyna found herself plunged once again into Dalibor's world, a world that called out his name as loudly as a battle cry. Since he was the reason for the journey, during the meal they spoke mostly of him, of his courage, of his temper, and of his harrowingly fast rise.

She saw him wobbling on his father's stallion in Normandy while Godfrey d'Hancourt swung the big horse around in fast circles; training with Mansour in the courtyard of their house in Monreale, sparks flying from their crossed lances; waiting with other young squires on Queen Elvira and her ladies; listening to lessons in warfare from Greek and Arab teachers; dubbed a knight by King Roger himself, on an Easter Sunday glittering with Sicilian colors; sitting in the shadow of miles of mosaics while his father conferred with the king; and lying at death's door with a gash opened in his side by a Saracen spear. Malva talked for her, as an intimate favor, knowing that of all that tale she and Kallyna were the only ones who shared the latest pages.

In the afternoon Filippo Rocca led his guests on a leisurely ride around his estates. He owned lumber mills, fishponds, kilns; he lived alone, keeping his holdings for his sons, should they come back some day to that land he loved so much.

Back at the castle, Erik was having a high time in the company of a girl and of a jar of wine. Lupo wasn't so lucky; his flayed back was first washed with sea water, then smeared with a foul-smelling salve made of deer's grease. His curses could be heard all over Aieta.

Upon their return, the three guests and Rocca headed for the chapel, where they would hear a mass of thanksgiving for their safe arrival. Malva took the seat of honor that had belonged to the dead marquise, Kallyna the velvet bench used for weddings. The castle's folks pressed behind them to see them. Kallyna looked aglow with happiness, and lovely in her lilac finery.

Sitting beside her, Malva d'Hancourt cast a tender glance at her, smiled quietly between herself and God, and collapsed onto the chapel's floor.

The small crowd stirred in alarm, the priest on the altar turned around. Mansour rushed to Malva's side, then lifted her up and carried her out. Four shadows hurried from the chapel to the room on the second floor, while the last of the sunset lingered on the empty courtyard.

"She's only unconscious," Mansour said after he felt Malva's pulse.

Kallyna loosened the veil around Malva's face and brought another pillow. Rocca stood with Mansour by one of the windows.

"How long ago did it start?" Rocca asked under his breath.

"One year, perhaps two that I know of. She is so very brave," Mansour whispered.

"Isn't there anything you can do?"

"I have done all I could."

Kallyna winced. "Oh God. She's come so far…"

"Such a valiant woman," Rocca said. "What will you need to treat her? Ask for anything."

Mansour shook his head. "We will only have to wait."

Rocca kept his peace; after some time he left. Gold poured from the open windows. The sun sank into the sea like a burning ship.

"I'll stay with her," Kallyna said.

Mansour stood watching the two women for a moment. A little later Kallyna heard him recite his sunset prayers, and there was like a quiet wrath in his voice.

XV

ALL NIGHT MALVA LAY IN THE GRIP OF A PAIN that must be unimaginable, unable to see or hear. Twice Kallyna snapped at Mansour when he tried to send her to her room. She dozed fitfully in a chair next to Malva's bed, while he chose herbs and mixed them in a mortar.

Dawn brought a respite. As soon as Malva could speak she ordered Mansour to put her in the saddle. Rocca offered her his carriage, but Mansour cautioned them both that it was best to wait for a recovery.

Out of sheer willpower, Malva got up at midday to eat with the others. Afterwards she went back to bed, after ordering Kallyna to get some sleep. Kallyna obeyed reluctantly, and Gemma remained posted by the door. Once she was alone, Malva rolled up a piece of cloth and clamped it between her teeth to keep from crying out, like she had done when she had given birth.

That afternoon Kallyna went to Mansour, demanding again that he find a way to cure her. Mansour was in the main hall with Erik and Lupo, whom he was about to take along in search of medicinal herbs. Lupo was naked to the waist, his back a grating of bloody scabs. When he saw Kallyna he glared at her as though she had whipped him with her own hands.

At her request for a cure Mansour replied curtly that he was doing everything in his power.

"Is she dying?" Kallyna wanted to know.

"Yes," Mansour said.

"Then what herbs are you looking for?"

Mansour put his saddlebag over his shoulder. "Hemlock. The pain is great, and she knows there is no hope. She might want help, and that is the only help I can give her."

Kallyna sat at the marble table and cried. When she looked up, the three men had left.

She resumed her watch by Malva's bedside. Malva was resting, her beautiful hair loose on the pillow. Even that morning she had asked Kallyna to brush it for her. Her eyes shone with tears, and she was rigid with pain. She took Kallyna's hand, whispering to herself. "We break our bodies in childbirth, risking our lives every time... We nurse our sons and we raise them and we watch them day and night... and then as soon as they've barely reached manhood their fathers take them from us and throw them into the battlefield to become meat for the sword... No choice is given... Do the fathers want their sons to love them or just to fear them?"

A cloudy sunset was gathering outside. The sea looked like the skin of a snake, all rough with overlapping waves.

"Please don't die now," Kallyna begged. "It's only seven days left to Salerno..."

Malva twisted in pain as she tried to smile. "It doesn't matter anymore. *You* will get there."

"I'm not going alone! I'm not going without you."

Malva moaned. "You must," she rasped. "That is the reason why we met, don't you see? You cannot turn me down."

"But there is no need... We'll be in Salerno together."

"Now it's you trying to fool me," Malva whispered dryly. "Listen," she said, laboring to speak. "As his mother, it falls to me to find him a wife. I came upon you while I wasn't even looking for one."

Kallyna shrank back. "You cannot mean that. I'm nothing but the daughter of a fisherman!"

Malva squeezed forcefully her hand. "The daughter of nothing but a tanner gave birth to William, the Conqueror of England," she said. "And please, should he be stupid enough to balk, do remind him for me this particular page from our illustrious Norman history."

Kallyna didn't know what to reply.

Malva summoned her closer. "You told me about Prince Guglielmo, that night… He risked more than you will ever know when he let you run. No one defies the Crown Prince with impunity. And he would have never dreamed of doing such a thing unless for love, plain and simple as that. You are the first… Do you understand?"

Kallyna hung her head. "But he never told me that," she whispered. "Not even when I needed so much to hear it. Is it because of pride?"

"Pride!" Malva said. "No, it isn't pride. It's fear. I've known so many like him… To a man who must wear a sword even when he sleeps, love comes as the ultimate enemy… An enemy he can neither see nor fight, one that grows inside him like an illness, a curse… You say he never told you he loves you? I wouldn't be surprised if he were terrified to tell that to himself."

Torn by her own thoughts, Kallyna kept silent.

After a few moments, when Malva sank back into exhaustion, she pulled gently her hand from her grasp and slipped out of the room. Before sundown Mansour was back with the hemlock. He pounded it into a lethal drink and hid it in his room. Stunned by a powerful mixture of wine and poppy, Malva spent a quiet night.

The morning of the third day Filippo Rocca called an old woman he knew to the castle. Under Mansour's skeptical eye, she cut off a lock of Malva's hair, then with it she prepared a poultice in whose powers Rocca seemed to have great faith. She applied it to Malva's chest, while mumbling incantations over icons of saints. At midday Mansour sent her quietly away.

The ripe spring afternoon outside the castle went on with the full flow of life, the flow that had clotted around Malva's bed. She knew she had many things to cram into few hours. She called for Mansour and had him rewrite her will, adding a clause he alone was to know. Then she instructed him about the burial. Church bells were to ring not a knell but a full peal, and food was to be handed out to the poor. As soon as it could be done, her remains were to be moved to their final resting place next to those of her husband, in the cathedral of Salerno. There the great marble vault built at his death bore the name and the coat of arms of the d'Hancourts, but contained only two niches, because Dalibor's death must not even be thought of. When she was done, Mansour rolled up the parchment sheet and left.

After him she called for Kallyna. Malva's eyes seemed to be searching for her through a thick fog. "Take all I have," she said. "Take my very place. Now you are both of us looking for him. Don't let his stubbornness defeat you. You know what's underneath it."

From the windows came shafts of sunlight that looked like gleaming lances wielded by an army of ghosts. The sky was an immense pink cockleshell.

"Now, promise me that you'll find him," she commanded. "That is all I can ask of you. The rest is in God's hands. I cannot arrange your lives any more than I can save my own."

Kallyna couldn't bear to look at her.

"I promise," she whispered. "If you ask for my life, I promise you that too."

A long silence followed. Malva's nails scratched the bedspread, her jaws grinding together in agony. "This could last for months," she worried. "The pain is nothing... but it breeds loneliness, defeat."

Kallyna remembered the hemlock, wondering whether Malva was trying to ask for it. She bent over her and gently moved a strand of hair away from her cheek.

"Not loneliness, no. You are loved by so many... He's alive. The war will end. All wars end."

Malva closed her eyes. "May God hear you.... May he hear you, my daughter."

At day's end Rocca dismissed his overseers and came to stay with his guest for a while. He had ordered the castle's noisy shops closed and every man, woman and child gathered in the chapel with the priest to wrest her from death with prayers. An air of mourning had come over Aieta, an ominous quiet rippling with words spoken low.

Night fell. The black shape of the castle soared against a sheet of blue that seemed to resound like a great bell. Stars appeared, transfixed on candelabra of pine branches. Kallyna got up without making any noise. She looked at Malva: she was asleep, the light of a lone candle flickering on her closed eyelids. Gemma sat on the stairs whispering her rosary; she greeted her on her way downstairs with her tears.

It had grown dim; the castle was full of shadows. She was looking for Mansour. There seemed to be no one else who could give her advice except that impenetrable man who had become her guardian by virtue of some unspoken agreement. She was going to hear a word of comfort from him if she had to yell it out of him.

His room was empty. She went down to the kitchen and asked some servants she found dozing by the hearth. They shook their heads; one of them went to light a few candles for her. She looked for him in the courtyard, in the chapel, in the stable; Mansour was nowhere to be found. More and more overwrought, she could have cursed him for deserting her in her hour of need.

At last she went back to the main hall. First she stopped by the armed man who guarded its entrance. "If you see the Arab, please tell him to come to my room as soon as he can," she told him.

Room after room the castle echoed with her uncertain steps. She went to check on Malva, who was still sleeping. Then she crossed the hallway to her bedroom. She closed the door and lifted her candle to light another in a candlestick. The tip of a knife came out of nowhere and stopped hard against her ribs. A hand clamped around her mouth, smothering her scream.

"Give me that candle," Lupo whispered in her ear. "And don't even *think* of opening your mouth."

She didn't move. The knife poked a little closer at her side. Lupo took the candle from her and snuffed it out. The window was open, and a dim light lingered from the evening sky.

"Please don't do anything stupid," she whispered.

He jerked her back. "Kindly shut up. Now and forever after, or I'll turn that pretty face of yours into a mess of scars."

Slowly she started to slide away from him, but while she still faced him, to keep track of the knife.

"Tell me what you want. Money?" she asked quickly, before he could silence her again. "I'll speak very softly... They'll think I'm praying."

Lupo's teeth flashed white.

"So very wise of you. Praying never hurt anybody."

He sounded out of breath. He moved closer to her, the knife now held flat against her cheek. "Now you're going to do each and every little thing I tell you, nice and obedient as you can be when you want to. One little thing for every lash I got on account of you."

"It wasn't my fault!" she whispered hoarsely. "I had nothing to do with it, and you know it."

Suddenly the edge of the bed cut her legs behind her, making her stumble and fall back on it. When she tried to jump up, the knife forced her to stay.

"Isn't that fine," Lupo praised her. "You sure know your trade well. I didn't even have to tell you to lie down... I bet my life you're just waiting for it, aren't you?"

Her voice choked her.

"Lupo, don't. For the sake of that woman who's dying out there!"

Lupo got rid of Malva with a ferocious oath. He put the knife down on the bed next to Kallyna's head, leaving his hands free. Clawing at her in a frenzy, he recited at leisure the list of obscenities he demanded from her. He tore at her neckline, pressing on her the full weight of his body rank with sweat.

"Blood of the Virgin, you're even better than I ever thought you'd be!"

Kallyna's nails sank into the welts on his back, but not even that pain would stop him. Each time she tossed her head the tip of the knife pricked her ear. She didn't know where all that strength of hers suddenly came from, but she fought him coldly, silently, made more skillful by her own outrage. She didn't hear the knock on the door. Lupo did. He stopped abruptly and raised his head to listen. The knock came again, louder. He smothered her mouth with his hand.

"Kallyna... are you there?" Mansour asked from behind the closed door.

She could have almost touched Lupo's fear. He ran his hand on his hair, knowing he was lost.

In the instant he let go of her, she remembered the knife. She grabbed it from the bed and stabbed blindly at the air. The last stroke brought to her nerves the ghastly feeling of flesh being torn into. Lupo sprang away from her, screaming. The door burst open under Mansour's push. The light of his torch revealed Lupo crouching on the floor, blood trickling from his chest. It was only a scratch, but terror had struck through him worse than any knife could. He stared at his own blood with the look of a crazed man, waiting to die.

"She's killed me," he wailed. "Oh God, she's killed me!"

Mansour planted the torch in a sconce and went to the bed. Kallyna hadn't moved from where she was. She summoned enough strength to cover her legs with her skirt. His face was a study in wrath. She was more afraid of him than of Lupo before. He pried open her hand and tossed away the knife. She sat up stiffly, her eyes shut against the alien presence of both men.

Lupo was still whining and groaning on the floor. Without a word Mansour walked over to him, raised him to his feet and made him stand. The back of his hand fell across Lupo's face with a sound like the flat of a sword, sending him staggering against the door.

"With you I will deal later," Mansour said in his teeth. "Out of my sight."

Lupo limped out of the room.

Kallyna remained alone before Mansour. From his expression she thought that he would offer no sympathy. He looked at her again, scanning the hair heaped around her, the neckline of the dress that she was trying to fold together. She knew that at the first word he would say she would start screaming.

Instead he put his hand very gently on her shoulder, making her flinch at that sudden touch. Sobs came to her throat, against her will, and now she let them all out wildly. Mansour stood waiting patiently while she cried, close to her. Finally she regained her composure and stepped away from him.

"Are you all right?" he asked in a very even voice.

"Yes."

"I will send up Gemma."

A moment later the old woman came to her room. She combed Kallyna's hair, washed her face and put her to bed as if she were a little girl. She also gave her a cup of something warm and sweet to drink. While she drifted into sleep, Kallyna realized that Mansour had put a soothing drug in the drink.

❀   ❀   ❀

A little before dawn she was jolted awake by Malva's delirious screams. She threw on her robe and rushed to her room. Mansour and Rocca were standing by Malva's bed. Destroyed by the pain, left defenseless before death, Malva raved and wept without anybody's comfort. Kallyna couldn't believe her eyes. How could Mansour in all his wisdom let that happen?

She stormed toward the bed.

"My lady Malva," she called her. "Please look at me. Do you know who I am?"

Malva clung to her, almost unrecognizable with fever and tears.

"Godfrey, why can't we stay here in Normandy? Why can't we all die in the same place we were born?"

Appalled, Kallyna looked at Mansour as if asking for his help. Mansour stood and said nothing.

"Please, my lady," she begged Malva. "Please."

Malva twisted her head wildly.

"I beg of you, and you know how hard it is for me to beg... Your son is not a token of obedience... You can't just give him to Roger as you would a new horse. And for what, to feed your ambition?"

Mansour wanted to lead Kallyna away from the bed, but she fought him to stay.

"Listen to me!" she shouted at Malva. "How can you fear so for him, as if he were a child? Have you forgotten who he is? Have you forgotten that Roger loves him as dearly as a son of his own? Stop this. In the name of God, stop it!"

The pride, the almost blasphemous love spilled into the room was what Malva had hoped to hear. She fell back onto her pillow; stunned, pacified, grateful for that humiliation inflicted upon her, and restored to herself.

Mansour observed in silent amazement the change that had come over her. He saw that the two women were of the same soul, and that they must be left alone together. He quietly led everybody out of the room and left.

"My daughter," Malva whispered. "Truly my daughter. Now I can go."

Another day dawned over Aieta. April in the splendor of its new green seemed to cover the earth and the sea in a blissful embrace. Malva had made her peace with death. Exhausted, but thankful that the end wasn't going to drag on for a torturing length of time, she slowly drifted out of life's known sea toward the other, unknown one.

At nightfall, while the lord Rocca waited outside the room patient as a beggar, she had both Kallyna and Mansour by her bedside. There wasn't much to be said. Neither Malva nor they knew what lay ahead, except that both journeys must be made.

"You know you were never a servant in our home," she told Mansour. "We have all loved you from our hearts, beyond race and creed. If you wish, I will set you free."

Mansour shook his head. "No. The last d'Hancourt alive may have to do that."

Malva nodded. "Then please be as faithful to Kallyna as you've been to us. She and Dalibor are the ones who need you now."

Mansour looked up. With the easiest of gestures he took Kallyna's right hand and placed it on his head, thus becoming her servant. Kallyna's fingers shook on his hair. She wondered how she could ever command a man so much older and so much wiser than she. But Mansour was pledging his priceless friendship with his usual, steadfast generosity.

"I have a last gift for you," Malva then told Kallyna.

She pulled from around her neck a gold chain and asked her to take it off. It was a beautiful signet ring bearing the coat of arms of the d'Hancourts.

"Keep it always on you," Malva said. "And when you meet Dalibor, show it to him. He will know."

Kallyna kissed the ring and fastened it around her own neck.

Malva sighed. "It's all done."

Kallyna started to cry. Again Mansour tried to ease her away from the bed, and again she refused. Mansour brought her a chair, then let in the lord Rocca.

Rocca kissed Malva's hands.

"I mourn you as I did my own beloved wife," he said in a cracked voice. "As dearly and as deeply."

Malva took his hands. "Thank you, my friend. I'm glad I could see you. In your house even dying becomes a gesture of exquisite hospitality."

All night Kallyna stood watch by her. Dawn wafted down from the mountains like a violet wing, the hour of deepest silence.

Malva put her hand on Kallyna's head and caressed it. "It takes much patience to be the wife of a soldier," she said, her voice already growing free of the pain. "Much patience to sit through a war. Can you do that, my daughter? Can you wait?"

"My father was a fisherman," Kallyna whispered. "I grew up waiting."

A smile appeared on Malva's face.

"How much you please me. I wish I could have seen you two together… Your hair like a winter night, long, dark… his like a June afternoon… What a beautiful sight."

Her breath rose and fell for a few more instants, then stopped. Mansour felt her temple: the vein was mute. He closed her eyes.

Kallyna looked at her. The world seemed suddenly too wide, like a room without furnishings, with nowhere to lie down and rest.

Gemma hastened after her as she went out the room.

"Please help me dress her," Kallyna told her.

✻ ✻ ✻

At sunset the body was carried to the chapel on a velvet bier, with Mansour and Rocca among its bearers. Rocca had it buried in the place of highest honor, in front of the altar. Kallyna graced the bare grey stone with yellow broomflower. None of them knew when the body would join that of her husband in Salerno, not until Dalibor was found.

Because she looked so lonely sitting on her bench, Mansour came to stand by her side. Throughout the Requiem Mass she clutched in her hands Malva's prayer book. She wondered whether Vasili would meet her, wherever they might be now, or whether even beyond death lords and commoners walked separate paths.

After the funeral she listened to Mansour and Rocca as they spoke about the rest of the journey that lay ahead. She heard them talk of mountains to be crossed, of malaria-infested marshes to be avoided, of caves inhabited by robbers and of unsafe roads. It seemed like such a long way, she thought, frightened.

Before going to bed she packed Malva's bundle into her own, as Malva had told her to do. It was impossible to distinguish Malva's clothes from her own. Every sign of rank and wealth had been removed. She knew now that Malva d'Hancourt was the richest woman in Monreale, who could have traveled with the ease of a princess yet had chosen to be truly a pilgrim, stripped of everything but her hope.

Loneliness that night was crushing. Without Malva, she didn't know where she would find the courage to go on. Now there was nothing but men around her, and men were and would remain a world apart. But Malva had entrusted her with a mission, and she would not deny her. So be it, she thought. Let another day come.

✻ ✻ ✻

The following morning she was torn from sleep by the sound of an uproar coming from the outer courtyard of the castle. Leaning out the window, she saw Lupo and Erik being hauled by Rocca's soldiers toward the main entrance, surrounded by an angry crowd. One soldier was looping a rope around a limb of the great oak tree. Erik shrieked and twisted; Lupo, whom one would have expected to make even more noise, walked instead with an impassive, almost scornful bearing, only jerking his head away from the mob.

Kallyna dashed out of her room in her nightgown. On her way downstairs she met Gemma.

"What a terrible way to bid you farewell," Gemma whispered. "What a bad omen this is..."

Kallyna didn't try to ask her what that was all about. She ran across the courtyard, where she saw Mansour. "Mansour," she called him, and it was the first time she was calling him by his name. "What is going on? What have Lupo and Erik done?"

Mansour didn't stop for her but kept walking, stiff with anger. "They were found stealing last night, while we were at the Requiem Mass."

"Stealing?" Kallyna repeated, panting after him. "Stealing what? Food, silverware? Is theft such a crime that we should hang them?"

They stopped by the main entrance, while the crowd settled in a circle around the towering oak. Erik's face was a mask of terror. The rope slid around the branch. The guards tugged at the noose, making it dangle like a snake.

Mansour wasn't looking at her. "They broke into the lord Rocca's own coffers," he thundered. "A wretched offense, for which I am partly responsible. I should have locked them both in jail long ago. If the lord Rocca hadn't already ordered their execution, I would have done so myself."

Erik was dragged to a stool set under the noose. He kept praying and shouting; he called out to Kallyna, begging her for mercy, claiming that he was innocent and that it had been Lupo's evil persuasion to bring about his ruin. Lupo didn't care to deny the accusations, so it was clear that Erik was telling the truth.

Kallyna's voice probed an uneasy tightrope between authority and arrogance as she pleaded with Mansour. "But they are *my* servants now, aren't they? Shouldn't *I* be consulted when it comes to my own property?"

"The law here is what the lord of the place makes it," Mansour replied. "And need I remind you that theft is not Lupo's only crime? You cannot save their lives. Indeed I wonder why you want to save their lives. Perhaps because you have never seen a man being hanged?"

Kallyna's cheeks turned crimson. Mansour was right; for a moment she hated him from the bottom of her heart.

Filippo Rocca was coming, looking incensed.

"Taking advantage of death and mourning to do such a thing," he said. "Hang them now, or else the noble guest who just died in my home won't be able to rest in her grave."

Kallyna turned to him, straining to find the right words to say. Rocca gave the signal before she could speak. She heard the crowd let out a long murmur, and turned around to see Erik swinging from the oak tree, his eyes and his mouth wide open. Nausea came to her throat; her words died on her lips. Dwarfed by Mansour on one side and Rocca on the other, her eyes ran desperately over the scene until it became a featureless blur.

Lupo was prodded toward the stool. He looked resigned to his fate, as if he had always known that that was going to be the end of his road. He climbed on the stool with a last flash of bravado, spitting in the face of the soldiers.

Mansour seemed to possess the diabolical power of looking at two opposite places at once. Kallyna saw him watch the soldiers, yet she knew also that he was checking her without mercy. She was forced to stop her gaze on the noose.

For as long as she lived she could not erase from her mind the memory of Lupo's eyes in those last moments. She suddenly noticed how young he was, and how little he cared about everything, including his own life that the rope was about to cut. The soldiers kicked the stool down.

Death kept mowing people around her like ripe wheat, she thought.

※   ※   ※

Gemma was right, it was a bad omen. The two travelers were ready. Not a word had been spoken between them while they prepared to leave. Kallyna mounted the good mare that had belonged to Erik. Her mule followed Mansour's horse, loaded with all their bundles. Rocca accompanied them on horseback to the gate. Gemma tagged along carrying a bowl full of water.

The bodies of Lupo and Erik still hung from the oak tree. Aieta's folk went about their usual business around them. Kallyna's heart was heavy as a boulder inside her. She had never felt such despair.

At the main gate they stopped. Gemma poured the water in front of the hooves of their horses. "May you travel as lightly as this water," she said, trying to hide her tears.

Mansour and Rocca held one another's arm in farewell. Rocca saw Kallyna's dismal look, and smiled sorrowfully to her. "I wish you luck in your search. I wish us all the luck... the wisdom, rather... to never have to live through a war."

Mansour nodded his assent.

"My lord, thank you," Kallyna said dully. "Thank you for all you did."

"May God give you of His bounty without counting the measures," Mansour said as his farewell.

The horses started out. Kallyna looked one last time at the tall castle behind her, the place where Malva lay. Her hand went to her ankle, where her newest travel companion was hidden. Mansour had bartered Lupo's knife for a short dagger sharp as a hairpin, made for a woman's hand, and had forced it into her boot. Her lips stretched into a bitter smile as she felt the little hard hilt secretly stroking her. Knives were the friends of unloved souls, the badges of fear and distrust. She had never owned one before. Iron had prevailed over flesh.

XVI

A LITTLE PAST MIDDAY, Aieta now far behind, Mansour and Kallyna were again on the coast road, headed north past the long curving headland of Capo Palinuro. All around them rose tall mountain ranges, indigo triangles wrapped in a soft haze. The sea, blue and green along the barren cliffs, was becoming more and more distant behind them.

Mansour rode ahead, studying in his mind the itinerary he had set down with Rocca before leaving. This was going to be the hardest part of their journey. Mansour had planned an entire day of riding for a distance that on flatland would have taken a few hours.

Kallyna eyed the peaks looming ahead. The feeling of dread creeping inside her at the thought of being now literally at Mansour's mercy was made deeper by the fact that he still hadn't uttered a word.

"There are nothing but mountains around," she finally said. "Which way are we going?"

Mansour turned around and observed her for a moment. She frowned at those eyes that seemed to hold a universe of secrets.

"We are headed for the valley of Diano," he replied. "It is not a short way. We will have to stay in Lauria tonight, and cross the mountains tomorrow. If God wills it, the valley will take us to Salerno in five days."

Kallyna played nervously with her reins.

"And then?"

"Then we will find lodging for you in Salerno and I will go on to Naples."

"Why would you leave me behind?" she said, alarmed.

"Because beyond Salerno it is all a battlefield. You will be so patient as to wait there until I find my master."

This was the first time Dalibor was mentioned between them. Kallyna felt a chill down her spine. How terribly precise could Mansour be in his choice of words. He had said 'my' master: to whom on earth did she belong?

"You can always leave me right here and go on alone," she said harshly. "I don't intend to be in your way. Or in the way of your master."

Mansour grinned that devastating grin of his, elusive as a will-o'-the-wisp. Then he raised his arm and pointed at a crossroads marked by a tall rusty crucifix. "We should be in Lauria before nightfall."

Kallyna's irritation became anger. She kept repeating to herself that crying in front of Mansour was like walking around naked, yet tears were coming to her eyes. "If you think that I have no business with the lord d'Hancourt, why don't you say so?" she asked.

They had reached the crossroads. Unruffled, Mansour spurred his horse up the mountain road. Only when they were halfway up the slope did he answer.

"I have lived with the d'Hancourts long enough to know that they have never misused my services," he said in a calm, musing tone. "If the lady Malva has ordered me to deliver you into the hands of her son alive and unhurt, it is certainly not without a sound reason."

Kallyna took those words as she would have a bunch of roses. For once, being delivered into the hands of someone seemed to her like the most wonderful thing any man could do for her.

She smiled. "Thank you."

Not a yard of that blessed road to Lauria was straight. It looped and it twisted around every boulder, and the boulders on the ledge above teetered like eggs in a broken nest. Lush, thickly wooded ranges came into view. The air became cooler, and the underbrush lit up with endless expanses of wild violets. One towering peak was covered with snow, the first snow Kallyna had ever seen.

Then the road became a narrow, unpredictable path on which nothing stood between the horses and the green chasm gaping below. Kallyna had to force herself to keep her eyes open; but at a certain point, overcome by dizziness, she let out a moan of panic and reined in. Mansour suggested that they dismount and continue on foot.

From some woodcutters they met further up he asked for directions. The men offered to lead them to Lauria, where they too were headed. Mansour accepted, but not before taking Kallyna close to him and introducing her as his daughter. Only when they were in sight of the town did he leave her to return to his horse. After the woodcutters went on their way, Mansour took advantage of the occasion to tell her that from now on she was to pass for his daughter whenever the circumstances required it.

False identities were not needed at the house of the lords Terranova, to whom Filippo Rocca had directed them with a letter. Donna Chiara Terranova treated Kallyna like one of her own daughters, that is with the same smothering indulgence. Kallyna was exhausted by the long day of riding, and the lady's insistence only made her stay more uncomfortable. Then at last Lauria, too, became another crown of walls growing smaller behind them.

Mansour uttered his *Bismillah* with unusual strength. Soon the going got quite rough. They had to make their way through deep, dim forests that had given Lucania its very name. They wound laboriously up and down steep gravelly trails without ever sighting a farmhouse, a hut, a human being, only startled foxes and deer. The day was damp and windy, and at times their feet sank into marshy undergrowth.

While crossing a wooden bridge over a deep glen, the mule dug its hooves in and refused to budge. Kallyna cried out in terror as the animal began to kick madly behind her, shaking the weathered wooden slats that seemed ready to break open underneath them and send them all hurtling to their deaths. Mansour had to shuttle back and forth between the bridge and the opposite side, first leading Kallyna to safety, then the two horses, finally the mule, which he managed to soothe into inching its way along the swaying bridge and on the trail again.

After midday the river Tanagro appeared, marking the border with Campania and the beginning of the Valley of Diano. When she saw the thin silver line down below, Kallyna thought she would fall to her knees and kiss the ground. They were now finally and truly on their way to Salerno. Her heart shrank as she thought of Malva who wasn't there.

They stopped for their meal at an isolated abbey, then took the easy route along the river. The afternoon was waning fast. They had already lost precious time at the crossing of the wooden bridge. It was even later when a smaller stream meeting the Tanagro stopped them. Mansour wanted to look for someone who could direct them to a barge. But the countryside was deserted for miles around. There was nothing left to do except try to ford the river; it seemed shallow enough.

Kallyna could only agree. Mansour tied together the reins of their three mounts, took off his burnous and stepped into the water. Kallyna watched him anxiously from the bank. The water rose to his chest but not higher. He walked carefully, testing the bottom for holes. Eventually he emerged out of the water and landed on the opposite bank.

"Wait," he called her as he tethered the horses to a tree. "I am coming back."

She already had the water up to her hips and was picking her way toward him, arms outstretched for balance.

"Easy," Mansour directed her. "Walk in a straight line from that point on…"

The river was wrapped around her like a great chilly hand. She wobbled in the pull of the current. He waded closer to her from the opposite bank. She looked up at him, reaching out to grasp his arm. The sudden move threw her off her balance. She felt the current cutting the ground from under her. Her scream was smothered by a mouthful of water, and she plunged like a stone into the pothole below.

Mansour stopped abruptly to avoid the same fate. He tried to circle his way around to her. She came back up splashing in panic, her long hair blinding her. With her mouth barely above water she cried out desperately for him, trying to swim.

Mansour dived and began to swim after her. She grappled against the current, crying out frantically. He grabbed hold of her as she was about to give up. She fastened her arms around him as he pulled her along. Finally she felt the soft muddy bank rise beneath her. Mansour dropped her on a flat boulder, where she lay out of breath, still too terrified to speak.

"Next time—" he began.

"Next time I'll stay home, I swear it to God and to the Virgin Mary," she wailed.

"Enough," Mansour said. "We must reach Diano, or else we will be stranded here all night." He helped her to her feet. He scanned the overcast sky and the light that was waning behind the mountains.

Kallyna let him hold her up like a baby. "I have to change my clothes," she begged him, "or I'm going to die of cold."

"There is no time. If they told me right back at the abbey, Diano is still two hours away. *Yallah.*"

She clambered back onto the saddle and took the reins. Her hair and her clothes, clammy around her, made her shiver all over. The wind began to glue them to her flesh. Mansour had already spurred on his horse. She stood looking at him in desperation; clearly being soaked to the bone was not a bother to him. Then she dug her heels into the mare's side.

The valley stretched on for two hours of agony. She could hear her teeth chatter. She lagged more and more behind but Mansour never stopped, while she cursed herself and him with equal fury. At long last, out of nowhere came a road leading to the town of Diano.

Mansour handed her over to the nuns at the convent of Sant'Anna and left. Kallyna changed her clothes, burrowed into two blankets and was asleep a moment later.

✳   ✳   ✳

A caravan of merchants left Diano the following morning, twenty men traveling with laden mules and armed to the teeth.

Mansour asked to join them up to the town of Atena, and the merchants accepted. But they began to grumble when Mansour left them waiting at the gate, having to rush to the convent and urge the nuns to wake Kallyna up. She was still half-asleep in the saddle when the caravan took the route along the Tanagro River. Mansour asked about the conditions of the roads beyond Salerno.

"I wouldn't set foot out of Salerno if my mother lived there," replied a fat, bald merchant. "Besides, with your daughter along…"

"What is the news from Naples?" Mansour asked.

The merchant shrugged.

"The Germans have come back to give Roger more trouble. As for the Duke Sergius, one day he swears he's ready to hand over Naples to the Normans, the next day he kills the messengers sent to discuss the terms of the surrender. It will never end, never."

The merchant's son put his horse closer.

"I was in Amalfi about a week ago. Prince Guglielmo's there. He's safe, but there was a big commotion . Some of his own men made an attempt on his life. They say Sergius paid them."

Kallyna shivered from head to toe. "Anybody dead?"

The young man looked at her shyly. "Two knights of his escort, from what I heard."

"You wouldn't by any chance know who they—" Kallyna began.

Mansour pointed at her saddle. "Watch that waterskin, daughter. It is not tied up properly."

She glanced at him, then pretended to adjust the waterskin.

At Atena they parted from the caravan.

"Your daughter seems ill," the merchant remarked before leaving.

Kallyna looked flushed, her eyes gleaming with fever. But she shook her head.

"I'm fine."

The merchants wished them good luck and rode away.

About an hour later, as Mansour was counting the money for the toll at the bridge of Campestrino, he again turned to look at her.

"If you want to rest, there is an inn by the guardhouse."

Kallyna shook her head again. "I want to go on. I want to be in Salerno," she grumbled.

Three hours later the fever rose. She shuddered all over, her body knotted in pain. Mansour stopped his horse and faced her with a stern look.

"You are stubborn. We could have stopped at the bridge. We will ask for shelter at that farmhouse."

She bobbed her head.

The horses ambled off the main road. At the farmhouse, a man, two young boys and a dog came to greet them. Their look of suspicion must be as old as the land itself.

"Good friends," Mansour began, "may God keep you. We are pilgrims headed for Salerno. My daughter is ill, and—"

The peasant turned around even before Mansour had asked for anything.

"Please, we can pay," Mansour called.

The dog started to bark. The man kept shaking his head, his hand on the handle of his pitchfork. "I don't want money," he said. "I don't want strangers."

Kallyna pulled back her hood. "For the love of God, we're not criminals," she said.

The man ran his hand on his stubbly beard, looking at her with only a little less mistrust.

"No, mistress," he said, and walked away. The two boys stood staring with their grimy faces, sniffing.

Twilight was coming with the ominous slowness of a dangling ax. They went back to the main road for want of a better thing to do. Then Mansour reined in. "There should be some caves nearby," he said, leaning on his elbow. Kallyna didn't answer. She was slumped forward in the saddle, her cheeks the color of brick.

When she came to, she looked for the sky above her. There was instead a stone ceiling all hung with stalactites like the vault of a Moorish palace. They were on the banks of a small pond. Mansour had lit a fire, and was now feeling her pulse.

"Where are we?" she asked. Her voice echoed softly all around, bouncing on every icicle of limestone above her. The fire cast shadows that looked like demons alive. In her fever she could see them cavorting in every uncounted nook of the underground chamber.

"We are in the caves I told you about," Mansour replied. "The lord Rocca had mentioned them. We are not too far in. They must go on for miles."

The horses gave out warmth. Their breath seemed to smoke from their nostrils. The fire was steady.

"Please give me something for this fever," Kallyna said.

Mansour took his waterskin off his saddle. "It will not last long. Drink."

She drank, then she curled up inside her cloak. Mansour seemed to know what he was talking about, she thought.

"Eat," he said then. He handed her a slice of bread, a piece of salt meat and a handful of hazelnuts.

She shook her head. "I'm not hungry."

Mansour put the food back in the saddlebag. Then he started to eat his own, hunkered down by the fire.

"I want to reach Salerno as soon as we can," Kallyna whispered. "Are we behind schedule?"

"No."

"Do you think that one of those knights in Amalfi, the one the merchant's son spoke of…?" Suddenly she started to shout. "God, why don't we go back? Why don't we forget all about this?"

Mansour stopped cutting his bread. He came closer to her and saw that she didn't even know he was there.

"I can't go on, I can't," she whispered to herself, in tears. "Father… mother," she cried again, tossing about. "Take me back. Please take me back with you."

Mansour took her wrists. "Kallyna. Please open your eyes. Please look at me." But she moaned and spoke broken words.

He went to rummage hastily in his bundle. Her voice was beginning to touch him in a way he didn't like. He found one of the small horns in which he kept his medicinal powders. He opened it and put some of the content in a cup with some water.

"My love, my love," Kallyna said.

He brought the cup to her mouth and held her head up.

"I don't want any water. Michele, why don't you speak to him? He always listens when you speak to him."

Mansour poured some of the water into her mouth. She choked and spat. His hands tightened around the back of her head.

"Drink it all," he ordered.

She made a face and swallowed the bitter, gritty brew. Then he lowered her gently onto her pillow of rolled-up clothes. She sighed, looking at nothing.

He took out his prayer beads and started to roll them between his hands. Some time later the fever went down a bit and she sank into sleep. Mansour pulled the hood of his cloak over his face and pushed his hands into his sleeves. The fire crackled; the stalactites looked like blades hanging overhead.

When she woke up, she saw she was alone. She called Mansour in a wild panic. Her clothes were soaked with sweat; the air was dank.

"Mansour! For the love of God, where are you?"

Footsteps sounded from beyond the small pond. Mansour loomed out of the shadows like a *jinni*. In surprise, Kallyna watched him bring more firewood to the dwindling fire.

"We don't need that," she said. "We're leaving."

He spread the dry branches evenly within the circle of stones. "Not today. You cannot ride in those conditions."

"What conditions?" she argued. "Can't you see I'm fine?"

Mansour watched the fire as it rose to engulf the branches, then sighed. "That the Calabrese are stubborn people is well known," he said, but not without sympathy. Then he stood up, his hands on his hips. "If there is no fever all day today, tomorrow we will set out again."

She stretched toward the fire. "Good."

"I will go to get food," he said then.

Kallyna jerked her head up. "I'd rather starve. Don't leave me alone here!"

He smiled very lightly, raising his eyebrows. Then he bent down and pulled her dagger out of her boot. "From now on *this* will have to be your company." He waved the dagger in front of her. "Let me see how you handle it."

Wrinkling her nose with distaste, Kallyna grabbed hold of the dagger with a sudden move, of which he seemed to approve.

"Between the ribs, in the throat, and right below the left nipple," he went on, directing the tip of the knife to each place on his own body as he spoke.

She eyed him askance. "I won't need it. I've never needed it so far." Then she remembered Lupo, and blushed.

Mansour buckled up his cloak and chose not to remind her of the incident.

"Do not move from here and do not make any noise. I will be back in a short while."

"What am I going to do in the meantime?" she cried out after him.

"Finish learning your alphabet. If you do not know all the letters by the time I come back, you will not eat." He grinned on his way out, but she couldn't see him.

She plunged her head into her arms, terrified by all that hollow loneliness of stone around her. Mansour's steps died away. She reached into her neckline for her alphabet sheet. As she did that, her hand met the chain on which she kept Malva's ring. She pulled it out and held it close to her cheek like a good-luck charm.

With the food, Mansour had bought some milk. He made her drink it so hot it scalded her throat. He cut her food and made her eat it. Then he built a roaring fire and went to look for a more comfortable place in the cave. The cave opened into many chambers, each leading God knew where. It was best to come back, he decided, and to stay close to the entrance.

For most of the day, with a high fever, Kallyna slept or lay in a daze. At times, when she tossed about moaning, Mansour thought she looked as if she were being made love to. He noticed that she never let Dalibor's name escape her lips, and this pleased him; but every now and then she would whisper, "My love, my love." He wished he had bought some beeswax to plug his ears with.

During the night it rained. The sound of the rain came into the cave like a soft shuffling of angels' feet. Mansour gave Kallyna another dose of his medicine that he had pounded from the bark of a willow tree. While she quieted down under its effect, for a moment he hovered over her as a father might do, waiting until she drifted back to sleep. A little later, when he went to check on her, he saw her stir in her cloak.

"You did want me some other time after all," she said in her sleep, smiling.

At sunset she woke up with a deep sigh. The fever had halved already. They ate together.

"Is it true that he can cut off a man's head with a single stroke of the sword and only one hand?" she asked.

"Yes. And with either hand."

"I wonder what you used for practice."

"You would not like to know."

"You're right."

She wrapped herself into her cloak again. "God, let us out of here soon," she prayed. "Please, please, soon."

Suddenly Mansour took her hand, startling her. He looked her somberly in the eyes.

"All of this is my fault. I was foolish not to give you such a little time to change your clothes. I shall not forgive myself."

Kallyna smiled. She held his hand with the same good grip.

"And I shall not forgive you," she said. "Ever."

The next day dawned clear. Sunlight reached down into the mouth of the cave. It broke along the pillars of rosy stone, the ribbed garlands, the jellyfish and toadstools supporting the roof, all the slow secret masonry of the centuries.

Kallyna stood up and held her hands out for Mansour to feel. "I'm fine. I slept without fever all night."

His dark eyes softened with a quiet joy. "Yes, I can see. *Al hamdu lillah.* God be praised."

They gathered up their things. "I wish I could wash myself and change my clothes," she said to herself.

He heard her. "Tonight, in Eboli," he said. "Or tomorrow night, in Salerno."

Her face lit up. "So close! My God, we've really made it, then."

A noise like a clap of thunder echoed from the mouth of the cave. Men were talking loudly and laughing, with a clanging of swords. Mansour motioned Kallyna to stand still and silent. Her hands froze on the saddle.

The voices boomed again from the end of the tunnel.

"I tell you, next time the bishop of Sala will think twice before traveling with all his silverware along."

"We should have cut his throat, like we did to his men…"

Mansour pushed Kallyna behind a curtain of stone and waited.

When the newcomers saw the three horses by the pond, they stopped abruptly. Mansour counted them: four, at least the ones he could see. The stolen silver made a great ringing in the burlap sacks. Clearly the visitors weren't aware that the cave magnified their voices for the ones inside, or they wouldn't have spoken so freely.

"Tonio, go see who's in there. Be careful."

Slowly a man came forward, bent in half with caution. Mansour drew his crescent dagger. The man's wary steps sounded closer. At the right moment, Mansour sprang out. The man swung his sword high enough for Mansour to parry the blow and sink the dagger in his chest. From her hiding place Kallyna heard a long rattling groan.

"Tonio?" someone called from the mouth of the cave. "Blood of the saints… Tonio!"

Mansour retreated toward where Kallyna was. Cautiously she took her little sharp knife out of her boot and finally, her heart pounding inside her, she took a step forward to see what was happening: the other three men were rushing onto Mansour all at once.

For a moment she stood watching. Mansour defended himself well, with savage skill. She saw blood oozing from his thigh. One man was thrown against a hard pillow of stone. Skull bones cracked.

That ghastly sound startled her out of her daze. Her fingers were numb around the hilt of her knife. She wondered how she could ever strike. Outnumbered, Mansour still held out. The horses pawed the ground with frightened neighs. Then Mansour dropped his dagger. One of the men jumped at him from behind to choke him, while the second scrambled to pick up the crescent dagger. The inlaid handle was already in his fist.

If Mansour died, Kallyna thought.

She thrust her arm out. The man's back snapped like a rusty lock under her blow. Unable to move, she almost let him fall on her. The second man, surprised to see her come out of nowhere, was caught unaware for an instant too many. Mansour kicked the dagger from his hand and twisted his neck into the crook of his elbow until the head lolled to one side.

Kallyna had to steady herself against the wall to keep from slumping to the ground with the four dead. Mansour came to lead her to the horses. She felt blood on her wrists as he helped her with the reins.

"I do believe you owed that to me," he said with his mouth dry. He pulled Kallyna's knife out of the dead man and gave it to her.

Kallyna tried not to step on the bodies lying around the pond while she followed him out.

"We don't even know who they were..." she whispered. "My God, who did we kill?"

Limping on his left leg, Mansour took the horses out of the underground chamber. In the dim tunnel lay the burlap sacks with the stolen silver.

"Robbers," Mansour said. "The lord Rocca had warned me. They travel in bands in these mountains... There will be others coming, we must move quickly. What they stole will remain here, it is not our property."

As if in a trance, Kallyna watched the blood drip from the tip of her knife. Then she wiped it on the hem of her skirt like a greasy kitchen cleaver and returned it to its sheath inside her boot.

The sunshine outside hurt her eyes. All around the mountainside from which they had emerged etched orchards of apple and cherry trees, a storm of pink and white petals. Swallows and larks flew high above green fields and melon patches dotted with gold. She had never seen an April day as sweet as this one.

She pushed her signet ring back into her neckline.

"My love, my love," whispered a voice she had heard in a dream. Who knows, she thought, perhaps if someone came to those caves a hundred years from now, the echo of those words would still be there.

❋   ❋   ❋

As they neared Salerno, the countryside began to show the signs of the war that had ravaged it for so long. Villages lay deserted; the ruins of burned castles grew tangled with vines, becoming nests for the vipers. Long files of refugees walked along the road; starving women gathered dandelions and wild herbs, boys looked for snails. The bodies of hanged soldiers dangled from trees or from gallows atop town walls. Once it had been *Campania Felix*, the Happy Campania of the Romans, the land where bells were invented. All her gaiety seemed to have been swept away by a tide of grief.

"My love, my love," Kallyna kept hearing in her mind. Dalibor's heartbeat seemed to sound closer and closer as she pushed toward him amid the desolation. At times she daydreamed that he was riding behind her on her saddle.

At sundown the broken stumps of an ancient aqueduct pointed the way to Eboli.

"I want to buy an Easter candle for the tomb of the lords d'Hancourt when we reach Salerno," Kallyna said. The she twisted her hands together, glancing at Mansour. "Please tell me what you're thinking," she whispered.

Mansour's eyes wandered. "I think we are alive. I think God knows what He is doing. Do not be sad."

She smiled to him, grateful for his sudden tenderness.

He didn't smile back. "I think I shall find you a female servant to take care of the talking."

"How far is Amalfi from Salerno?"

"One day's ride, the road is difficult." He paused. "Amalfi," he said then with a startling tone of affection. "Such a lovely city. They say the day its inhabitants will go to paradise will be a day like any other."

Kallyna's eyes widened with wonder. "Really… You will go looking for him there, won't you? He could be with the prince."

Mansour nodded. He took out of his sash the safe-conduct bearing not only the seal of the d'Hancourts but that of King Roger himself. They waited to be let into Eboli along with soldiers on foot and peasants with their donkeys.

"I don't know what the lady Malva told you about me," Kallyna said then, hesitatingly. "There are certain facts, about the lord d'Hancourt and others I have met…."

"I know what is enough for me to know," Mansour calmly interrupted her. "Please do not worry. We have always managed to keep our distance between us and Falco da Torre."

Kallyna breathed in. "How long have you known him?"

"About five years. It is most regrettable that young Prince Guglielmo should be so fond of him. The power games they both indulge in can be quite unpleasant." He counted out the money for the toll. "My master has always been wise enough to avoid such games, but in war it will not be easy."

The guards took the money. They had their sergeant read the safe-conduct, then waved them in. Other guards were arguing with other travelers who had no permission.

"Please stay with me for a while," Kallyna said after they had paid the innkeeper. "It isn't curfew yet, I'd like to go to church."

Mansour stepped down the inn's door.

Eboli was bleak. Many of the houses were scooped out of live rock, caves more than dwellings, where entire families lived. The steps of the church teemed with beggar children. Kallyna gave a coin to the one nearest to her, only to be sworn at by all the others.

The church was almost empty. She looked for a chair.

"Do they have a mosque in Salerno?" she asked in a whisper.

"Yes," Mansour whispered back. "There is one in Amalfi as well. I was a sailor, once. I know the coasts of Italy and of many other countries."

"Are you sad you're no longer a sailor?"

Mansour didn't look at her. She thought he would not answer such a probing question.

"Yes, I am sad," he replied then simply.

Kallyna drew her shawl over her face. "If you don't want to stand in a Christian church, you may go," she said softly.

Mansour clasped his hands behind his back. "If you don't mind me standing in a Christian church, I will stay."

Her eyes ran on the gleaming icons behind the altar.

"So far I've been quite a poor mistress to you," she said. "I pray that some day I will be able to repay you the way you deserve."

"I am most certain you will," Mansour said.

❋   ❋   ❋

The night Kallyna and Mansour slept in Eboli, the plain north of Naples lay under a downpour that had put out the campfires of the Norman army's tents.

The plain was bare and sandy, the far end of distant beaches. Tents made of burlap stiffened with pitch rose in low rows, guarded by tall siege machines. There was a broken thrashing about of feet and hooves, the sounds of moaning and praying. The camp was a place despised by sleep.

Under one of the siege machines was a fire of torches sheltered by overlapping shields. It cast a dim light on a larger, taller tent toward which a small group of men was walking, trudging hastily in the mud.

Stripped to the waist rather than wearing wet clothes, Geoffroi de Vire lifted the tent flap and waved in a short, heavy-set man; behind the man was a boy who carried a copper basin, a knife and a small saw. The three came to stop next one of the two low cots and one stool that were the tent's only furniture.

"Next time you decide to get yourself thrown off the saddle, try landing on your soft side, will you?" Geoffroi muttered.

226

Dalibor lay on the cot with his eyes closed and didn't speak.

The man lifted a torch and ordered the boy to put his instruments down. Geoffroi eyed the long notched edge of the saw. Then the man started palpating very carefully the left hip and thigh of his patient. Dalibor's jaws gleamed with sweat in the shadow of the beard long left unshaven. His body arched in pain when the man's fingers reached the socket of the thighbone. The flesh around it was swollen and black; the skin had been burned by the chain mail in the fall.

The man's balding head dripped rain on the worn-out leather of the cot.

"Looks like you sent for the wrong man, my lords," he said. "What *I* do is saw up bones, not set them. All you need here are two good arms to pull the thighbone back into the socket…" he eyed Dalibor's naked body "and four more arms to hold this young strapper down."

Dalibor shook his head. "Do it yourself. Now. I've been lying on my back long enough."

The man looked at Geoffroi as if asking his consent. Geoffroi nodded; he sat down on the cot's wooden frame and pinned Dalibor's arms under his own.

"I'll be enough to hold him down," he said.

"So, shall we do it?" the man asked.

"I said so, didn't I?" Dalibor growled.

"All right," the man said. He planted his feet well apart on the ground. He felt around for the best hold, then grasped the thighbone firmly between both hands.

"Scream out, if it helps."

Geoffroi made a face. "Wasted breath. He would never do anything that inelegant."

"I'm ready," the man said. "Here I go."

He gave the leg one strong, precise pull. With a small sound the bone snapped back into place. Dalibor screamed at the top of his lungs, startling the horses outside the tent. Geoffroi burst into a laugh of relief.

The man straightened himself up, stroking the rain off his neck. "How does that feel, my lord?" he asked, helping himself to a pitcher of wine on the stool set by the cot.

As his only answer, Dalibor extricated his right arm from under Geoffroi's clutches and thrust it under the man's nose. There was a deep red gash in the flesh of his forearm.

"Do something about this too," he muttered.

The man peered at the wound.

"Ah, good old lady's lips. Those will only need cauterizing. There's a bit of matter in it already, you should have had it done sooner."

"So many things I should have done sooner," Dalibor rasped. "Like being born… a thousand years ago, when there were no Neapolitans on earth."

The man took his knife from the copper basin and passed the blade over the fire of the torch held by the boy until the blade was properly hot. He wagged his finger to Dalibor as if to a naughty boy.

"Ah, lord, then you don't know much about Neapolitans… We were around long before that time. We are as old as God."

Geoffroi stood up from the cot so that the man could sit next to his patient.

"Tell him again to scream," he said. "So this time he won't do it, for the mere sake of contradiction."

The man laid the iron blade flat into the gash, and kept it there for the right amount of time. Dalibor let out only a low rattling groan, then slowly unclenched his fist.

"There you go," the man announced. "All patched up, at least until tomorrow morning."

He took his glove off.

"You know, my lords, you're lucky. Tonight alone they pay me to saw off four legs and twice as many arms ." He shook his head. "Lousy bitch of a war."

He got up and made a bow before walking out. "Sleep well, my lords." They heard him hum a song outside.

For a long time the rain fell on the roof of the tent without interruption. Dalibor tried to doze off. Geoffroi sat on the other cot scratching himself. Then Dalibor reached out for his cloak. Geoffroi picked it up and spread it on him.

"I think you need some wine," Geoffroi said.

Dalibor drank a few sips, then handed him back the pitcher. The stench of burned flesh lingered in the damp air of the tent. Someone outside let out a scream that was like a spear twanging hard against a shield. Dalibor shivered from head to toe.

"God, my belly's killing me," Geoffroi complained, raking his hair with his hand. "I swear tomorrow I'll have them hanged if they don't find some decent food. Better yet, I'll make them eat the food we have, worms and all."

"The road to Aversa," Dalibor said.

"What?"

"The road to Aversa. We must leave a couple of hundred men there, along the mountain pass, or they will pin us in between. What do you think?"

Geoffroi took time to answer.

"I think that Guglielmo d'Hauteville, as the little degenerate he is, ought to wear his breeches with the strings tied in back!" he spat out. "It's his war too, but all *he* does is sit pretty in Amalfi with that damned lover of his and—" There he attached a gross obscenity.

Dalibor waved his good arm at him. "Be quiet. By God, be quiet!"

A labored silence filled the tent. Dalibor's breathing sounded like a sob.

"The hell with loyalty," he rasped. "The hell with everything. All I want to do is leave all of this to the devil…. It's his department." Geoffroi smiled a bleak, malicious smile.

"Now you get it, sweet lord. Now we're at our very last lesson in warfare, the one our wise scholars in Palermo never bothered to teach us."

Dalibor tried to shift on his cot; rain was dripping from the sodden roof. "Leave me alone, you convent philosopher."

But Geoffroi had his eyes open in the dark, like a blind man. "What did we all think war was? The grand adventure patched together in epics, the dream of lordlings who sit out their lives, of women itching with boredom like old cats......"

His voice and the rain met at a vicious pitch. "Here's what it is.... Fear that pounds at your belly, and the wormy food, and the dysentery that sucks the life from your bowels... Not much poetry, is there?"

Dalibor winced. His hand ran up and down his hip, where the pain throbbed as hard and as strong as he was.

"Please, please be quiet," he begged. "I want to sleep."

"Think of something nice," Geoffroi said. "It couldn't hurt."

"Kallyna" Dalibor said.

The rain poured harder now. Geoffroi stretched his arms under his head.

"I wonder what she's doing," Dalibor said.

"Nursing her seventh child and washing her husband's underwear. Fat."

A sound of hatred came from Dalibor's throat. "I'll kill you, by God almighty. One of these days I'll kill you."

Geoffroi was already starting to snore.

"She could have been a princess, so fine she was," Dalibor whispered to himself. "I almost.... So many stupid promises."

"Go to sleep," Geoffroi said.

"Only a fool like me could have ever been in love and not even notice."

"Sleep," said again Geoffroi.

PART THREE

XVII

O N THE ROAD TO SALERNO Kallyna began to sing softly to herself. She had persuaded Mansour to eat their meal while riding, to gain time. They passed vast checkerboards of green and brown fields and plains where peasants pushed their slow oxen that had horns like silver crescents. The horizon filled up with small white clouds, and the sea beckoned again. Then Salerno came into sight like a white ship, white as the beach that ran in front of it. Everything else around was blue, sea, mountains and sky.

At the bridge on the river Irno they stopped to look at their long-awaited destination. Along the mouth of the river long strips of freshly-dyed cloth were spread out to dry, colored yellow and magenta. The pebbly shore was a playground for dozens of half-naked boys splashing and laughing in the water.

"Seven hundred miles," Mansour said, almost to himself.

"She knows we're here," Kallyna whispered, thinking of Malva.

Again the safe-conduct let them in. The city was swollen with refugees. The narrow alleys swarmed with people in rags. They slept under the arches of the aqueduct, on the steps of churches; they lit cooking fires among the ruins of the old Lombard gate. The air stank of fried pork fat and of mold growing in the halls of abandoned palaces overrun with rats.

Kallyna and Mansour headed down the *Via dei Mercanti*, the long, winding street where merchants kept their stores. An array of small shops, some underground, lined the cobbled way. People of all races walked the streets. In the shade of a portico, Arabs sat cross-legged on carpets, sipping mint tea; slaves of every color were led by Venetian traders; a group of Armenian pilgrims returned from the Holy Land showed off the Red Sea cockleshells pinned to their mantles. The noise was steady. In Piazza Portanova sailors crowded around a cockfight, and the curses flew like the feathers of the two combatants.

In front of the cathedral Mansour and Kallyna reined in. Mansour tied the horses to the neck of one of the stone lions crouching at the foot of the staircase. He slung the bundles on his shoulders and led Kallyna into the vast, exquisite courtyard with its scalloped arches painted in white and sienna stripes like those of a mosque. The fountain at the center was shaped like a date palm, water spilling from the top of the carved trunk.

They lingered a while, under a sky that seemed to wait for sunset as if for the last verse in a love poem. Talking gravely among themselves, three elderly men in long white robes passed by, one of them wearing a skullcap and prayer shawl. Mansour bowed to them with deep respect. They were teachers of the School of Medicine, the gift of past centuries that the Normans had restored to fame.

"Let's go in," Kallyna said then, knowing there was someone waiting for them inside the cathedral.

The huge bronze doors cast in Constantinople marked the boundary between the soft twilight outside and an immense chest full of golden shadows. So high the mosaics stretched, and the candlestick for the Easter candle was as thick as the trunk of a white marble tree.

"The tomb of the lords d'Hancourt is in the Chapel of the Crusaders," Mansour said.

The Christ Crucified guarding the door of the chapel was tall as a man and draped in black for Lent. The look on the face of Jesus was so pained that it was like seeing living flesh nailed to a cross. The sculptor must have carved his wood before the body of a prisoner executed on the public square.

In the dim candlelight the Chapel looked more like an armory. Tunics and cloaks worn by Crusaders, some still stained dark with blood, hung on the walls together with swords, shields and lances. In that chapel the weapons were blessed before each new Crusade; the silence seemed to echo with a clamor of men going to war.

Mansour pointed to Kallyna the tomb of the d'Hancourts, under a high stained-glass window. Suddenly she shivered.

Godfrey and Malva d'Hancourt lay side by side on top of the marble lid of the sarcophagus, their eyes closed and their feet resting next to two little dogs, symbols of fidelity. Malva looked like Kallyna had seen her in Aieta the last time; in Godfrey's features she searched for Dalibor's. The woman was soft in her veil, the man rigid in his armor.

She touched the foreheads of both statues and brought her fingers to her lips.

"We'll bring the Easter candle tomorrow," she said as they left the chapel; and in all of that strange city she felt that she had two good friends watching over her.

❀   ❀   ❀

The Bear's Inn was tucked in an alley past a corner with the Merchants' Street. It was a long whitewashed house, with a stable and a vegetable garden in the back. The windows were barred like those of a jail. It was the only inn that had the almost unthinkable luxury the two travelers looked for, a single room. In fact, as they found out, it was nearly empty because of its steep prices.

The real reason why it was almost empty, Kallyna thought, must be its owners. Landolfo dell'Orso was a short squat man with a big belly and a pasty face. His wife Marotta had the eyes of a hungry fox. The man's favorite occupation seemed to be counting money; the woman's, yelling with equal ferocity at the stray cats and at the children that wandered around the inn looking for food scraps. Both were so engaged when Mansour and Kallyna dismounted under a crudely drawn signboard displaying a black bear, the couple's namesake.

Landolfo quickly put away his abacus, and Marotta came forward still wielding her broom.

"Well arrived," she said, but from a distance, so she could sort out from the guests' appearance their means and rank. She wasn't satisfied, because she didn't come any closer nor did she deem it necessary to help them with their bundles. She just waved them in.

The lower floor of the inn looked like that of a farmhouse. Blankets hung on rods separated half of it from the kitchen. In the middle was a flight of wooden stairs leading to the upper floor. Two red-haired men peeked in from the partition.

"Copper merchants from Flanders," Landolfo whispered proudly. "Now, my lord, how can we serve you?"

Mansour put his bundle on the table. "A single room for myself and my daughter."

Marotta eyed him and Kallyna again, more carefully.

"A single room, eh? It's two ducats a day, a single room."

She waited; when Mansour put his hand to his money purse, she squirmed in anticipation. Clearly she had misjudged her customers, for they were willing to pay without raising objections . Her voice became all sweet.

"But it's a good room, you know. A very good room for you and your little lady."

Kallyna avoided Marotta's gaze. The chains of fake gold the woman wore under her red shawl clinked on her sagging breasts.

Marotta turned to her husband, pointing at the stairs.

"Landolfo, help His Excellency with his luggage."

The bed in the room was double. The rest of the furniture consisted of a small rickety table and two chairs. As they went in, the curfew echoed from beyond the tiny window and the blind alley it looked on.

"Here it is, Landolfo said proudly. "You'll find no bedbugs at the Bear's Inn, my lord. You and your daughter will sleep in peace."

Kallyna looked at Mansour, who didn't look back. He nodded. "I shall take your word for it," he said flatly, handing Landolfo his two ducats.

"You must be hungry," Marotta said. "Supper will be ready in no time. We have a barley soup that the Pope himself has never tasted." She left after her husband.

Mansour bolted the door. He took off his sash and forced open the stitches in the lining.

"I will leave you the money" he said. "Keep it on you, of course. I will take only some dinar. And this," he added, touching his dagger.

"How long will you be away?" Kallyna asked.

"Five days at most. Find something to do... The less you are out of this room the better."

She nodded, with a reluctant sigh. "All right. What if he's not in Amalfi?"

Mansour put the money and jewelry into a handkerchief. "I will come back, and we will decide together."

He handed her the rolled-up handkerchief. "If I am not back in one week, the best thing for you to do is go home. There is a salt caravan that leaves the day after Palm Sunday."

She lowered her eyes onto the bed's old, soiled blanket. "I hope I won't have to."

"So do I," Mansour said. "I will come back regardless, to see if you are still here." He went to the door. "I will wait for you downstairs."

Kallyna slid the bundles under the bed. She tied the handkerchief around her thigh, hiding it under her skirts like a garter belt. Before leaving she went to open the shutters. From behind the wrought-iron bars she saw that the alley was home to a small family of refugees.

A girl sat on the steps of a back door holding a baby to her breast, more to keep him quiet than to feed him, for she was too gaunt to have much milk. An old man wandered around the battered brazier that warmed them at night and the one sooty pot that fed them. A boy of about twelve clung to him with eyes full of hunger. Kallyna's heart shrank. She went downstairs with a lump in her throat.

237

Landolfo was ladling out the barley soup. The two Flemish customers sat by the hearth, eating noisily. She joined Mansour at the table. She noticed that he too had been looking at the alley.

"Have you paid already for our supper?" she asked him. Mansour nodded.

Suddenly the boy mustered his courage and came up the stairs holding out his hand.

Landolfo called his wife.

"Marotta, get that dirty mongrel out of here."

Marotta picked up her paring knife and stormed toward the door. Kallyna stepped in front of her.

"Let him be. He's just asking for charity, and there's enough food here for a dozen people."

Marotta twisted her mouth. "Dear lady, if we fed all the beggars that come to our door we'd be left without breeches!"

Kallyna pointed at the two bowls of soup, the two slices of bread and the two pieces of cheese on the table.

"Give him what we paid for," she ordered.

Marotta's face turned gray with rage. She went back to the table and slammed her knife down on it.

"It's your money, isn't it?"

The boy dashed in, grabbed the cheese and the bread and dashed out. Then he came back for the bowls of soup, careful not to spill any of it.

"Bring me back the bowls!" Marotta yelled after him, locking the door.

Kallyna and Mansour paid for another meal and ate it. Then Mansour went to buy the Easter candle. Kallyna waited for him sitting by the window, spying on the refugees with a shy curiosity born of compassion. Mansour returned with a beautiful candle all worked in scrolls and carefully wrapped in straw. It was time for her to tell him about that business of the bed.

But before she said anything, Mansour unrolled his prayer rug and spread it on the floor, in the corner farthest from the bed. He smiled to her before lying down with his face turned to the wall.

"Sleep well, daughter,"

She smiled back.

"You too, father."

She blew out the candle. The baby in the alley cried for a long time in the night.

❋   ❋   ❋

While they walked to the cathedral, Kallyna saw the old man and the boy in the street. The old man walked with his eyes closed, feeling the ground with a cane, while the boy led him by the hand and asked for alms. The boy averted his eyes when he saw her, because she knew the old man wasn't blind. But Kallyna looked at them both without condemnation. In her eyes, they were the ones who had been cheated, not the passersby who handed them their few coins.

A deacon placed the candle by the tomb of the d'Hancourts, then directed them to the shrine of Pope Gregory. Worshippers thronged the dark underground crypt all hung with offerings of gold and silver. Women wept and prayed, calling the saint with affectionate nicknames and talking to his icon as if to living flesh. The musty air filled with the smoke of incense was all astir with hands and mouths.

Kallyna jostled her way through to the iron grill and reached out to touch the rough stone of the tomb. There she named in her mind all the people dear to her. Mansour waited for her a few steps behind; then he walked with her back to the courtyard.

More pilgrims arriving for the Holy Week crowded under the arcades, the sick lying on stretchers or propped up against the wall. Mansour and Kallyna stopped by the fountain.

"I must be going," Mansour said softly, tall and near beside her.

She was terrified, but didn't want him to see it. "All right," she said, playing with the water. "I'll pray for you. I'll wait for you to come back."

Mansour took her hands. "If I cannot come back, forgive me now. You know that I will leave no stone unturned."

She smiled, nodding. "I know. You are brave. I need you."

He brought her hands to his lips. He was saying goodbye to her with tenderness and devotion, as he would have to Malva d'Hancourt. The days when he had served her simply out of obedience to his mistress were gone.

She followed him out in the street.

"Go back to the inn," he advised her, "and if you want to go out, see if someone can come with you. The innkeeper's wife—"

"That awful woman," Kallyna cut in.

"Better than being alone," Mansour said, mounting his horse. "I must be back by Palm Sunday. Do not wait an hour longer than that. One way or another, God will lead me to you again."

He rode away toward the gate. She watched him for as long as she could. Then she put her cloak back on and took the Merchants' Street.

She tried to remember any other time in her life when she had felt so alone. Desperation took her at the thought of that small dingy room at the inn where she would be a prisoner for the days to come. Everybody who glanced at her looked like a thief. She had become one more refugee.

Some sailors loitering by the door of a brothel raised their voices as she passed by; she nearly ran away. In front of the inn she saw the boy, who had come to return the bowls. He ran up to her and pulled at her sleeve. "Mistress, are you going to give us some more food today?"

Kallyna opened her hands with a sad smile.

"I'm not the queen... Don't you have anything at all? I saw you take alms."

The boy looked down at his dirty bare feet.

"With three of us, mistress, with the baby..."

She took the bowls, licked clean.

"What's your name?"

"Maso," the boy said. "Your father's gone, mistress?"

"Yes... Yes, he is." They sat down on the steps.

"Listen," Kallyna said, "if you accompany me when I have to go out of the inn, I'll give you a coin every time you come."

Maso wiped his nose with the back of his hand, his dark eyes peering at her with mistrust.

"Just to come with you?"

"Just for that."

He nodded, but still not quite sure.

"Well, all right, mistress." From the alley the old man called him. Maso jumped to his feet and ran to him. Kallyna went into the inn.

"Daughter my foot!" Marotta had been saying, while she made soap out of lye. "Can't you recognize a whore when you see one? Well treated, eh, salaamed and all."

"Mother of Christ, will you shut up?" Landolfo replied, crossed. "Stop nosing around or she'll get us into trouble."

"All right, all right."

Those last words were all Kallyna heard as she stepped in, leaving the two bowls on the table. She went up to her room, locked the door and lay on the bed until she had thought all she had to think, worried about all she had to worry about, and hoped for all she had to hope for. She must find something to do.

When she went down for her midday meal she asked Marotta if she knew anybody who needed weaving or sewing. Marotta said she didn't. The afternoon was endless and boring. Not knowing what else she could do, she started to copy on a scrap of parchment the faded alphabet letters Mansour had written for her. From the door left ajar, Marotta peeked in suspiciously; she came down wiping her chapped hands on her apron.

"And a lettered whore, too!" she muttered.

From the alley the old man's voice rose in anger. The baby began to cry again. The sound of their misery had become Kallyna's constant companion. Maso called up to her.

"Mistress, aren't you coming to see the *Vattienti* ?"

"Who?"

Maso had disappeared already. She hastened downstairs, looking for him.

Marotta, Landolfo and the two Flemish merchants were out on the landing. In the street was slowly advancing a grim procession made up of men of every age, barefoot and naked except for coarse burlap loincloths. In their hands they held brushes armed with nails instead of bristles, and at every step they took forward in unison they flogged themselves with them. Flowers of blood oozed on the penitents' skin under each new stroke. The men seemed to compete with one another for the hardest blows. The women following them down the street urged them on with a hair-raising wail, some rushing forward to kiss their wounds.

Kallyna's blood ran cold. She saw that one of the Flemish merchants had turned around, retching. The other merchant muttered something in his teeth with a tone of contempt.

Quick as a squirrel, Maso ran up to her from the street and grabbed the hem of her skirt.

Marotta scorched him with a look full of hatred.

"Always around, aren't you? If only I catch you stealing!" Fortunately, Landolfo called his wife in.

"Mistress, the baby's dying," Maso said. "My sister says he needs milk."

"I'll drop you a coin from the window," Kallyna said. She smiled wearily. "Remember, though, that means you owe me. Tomorrow I want to go to church."

Maso was already hopping away on his callused feet.

When she leaned out the window to drop the coin, the girl only glanced at her. "For your baby," Kallyna told her.

The girl stooped to pick up the coin. A small quiet bundle lay on the ground by the doorsteps.

"He's dead," she said.

❋   ❋   ❋

The girl spent the coin on a wooden box, in which she laid the baby to rest wrapped in her shawl. In the morning the gravediggers came to take it away without a word.

All day long Kallyna sat copying alphabet letters, until she could write them by herself. Mansour had written her name once in a corner of the old sheet. She scribbled it over and over; then she tore up the old sheet so she wouldn't peek at it anymore.

Maso was good company, and she could trust him. Once, however, she caught him stealing a handful of early cherries from a seller's basket.

"Mistress, I'm sorry," he apologized. "I was curious to see what these little red things taste like."

As Palm Sunday drew nearer, her worries grew deeper. One day she went to a woman who sold candles at the door of the cathedral and asked her where she could get news from Amalfi or from Naples. The old woman told her about a Norman barracks in Piazza Portanova. Kallyna couldn't muster the courage to go there.

At night she was kept awake by her own thoughts and by Marotta and Landolfo arguing in the bedroom next to hers. Often the man got drunk, called his wife the foulest names and beat her. Marotta smashed things and shrieked.

The two Flemish merchants, their business concluded, left town. More travelers came and went. Kallyna used up another sheet of parchment with her clumsy attempts at writing Dalibor's name; then she burned the sheet.

She began to copy from Malva's prayer book those words she had seen most often on the walls of churches, words whose sound and meaning she knew. She learned to write the name of God, of the Virgin, of Jesus and of the four Evangelists. Sitting in her pew in the cathedral she studied the long ribbons of legends around the mosaics; back at the inn, she tried to write them down as best she could.

Marotta went snooping in her room when she was away, but found only clothes. She was convinced that Kallyna was up to no good with all that writing. She told her husband more than once that they ought to call the guards and have her kicked out. Besides, she argued, where the hell had that Levantine gone? To find customers for his whore, no doubt; but if Marotta dell'Orso wanted her establishment to become a whorehouse, she could have turned it into one herself a long time ago, and it would have been a much more profitable business.

As new waves of refugees poured into Salerno, so did fresh news. It was said that the Germans were marching down to Naples, and that the Normans were ready to meet them at the border. Meanwhile in Rome the two Popes were at each other's throat, each backed by opposing factions on the pulpit and on the battlefield. Italy rang everywhere with war, like she had done and still would do for most of her history.

Landolfo was the one who brought the news, on his way back from the marketplace. The day before Palm Sunday he brought in two new customers, husband and wife who had just fled leaving behind a house full of valuables and an armory shop.

The woman was hysterical. "Everything they took, to the very last spoon!" she wailed, slumped on a chair.

The man was almost in tears himself. "First they came to "requisition" my horses and a suit of mail I was making for a customer. Then they came back and threw me out of home and out of business!"

Kallyna was at the stone sink doing her laundry. She anxiously perked up her ears.

Marotta came in from the kitchen garden. "The Normans, eh? Always the Normans," she said, with fierce hatred. Landolfo waved his hands to silence her, but she would not be stopped. She went to the armorer's wife. "Here, mistress, have some of our wine. We ought to keep our mouths shut, because that's what they want, but the truth is that a poor honest soul has no peace with these bloody foreigners around. Look at the taxes we have to pay for this place!"

The armorer nodded in grief. "That's right, that's right. They make their wars, we pay their bill."

Kallyna scrubbed her clothes and listened.

"But they got what they deserved, they certainly did," said the man's wife, wiping her eyes on her veil. "I pray to God they were the very same ones who came to rob us," she sobbed.

Landolfo turned from the cupboard, where he was hanging a string of pear-shaped cheeses.

"Why?" he asked. "What happened?"

"They were cut to pieces on the road to Aversa a week ago," the armorer said. "More than three hundred, all left to rot along the mountain pass."

"And one of them, a captain," his wife chimed in, "was taken alive for ransom."

Kallyna dropped her cake of soap into the sink. She had to hold onto the stone rim with both hands. Then she remembered that Dalibor d'Hancourt wasn't the only captain in the Norman army.

"Are you done with your laundry, lady?" Marotta asked her.

She fumbled in the sudsy water, looking for the cake of soap.

"No... Not yet."

"Well, soap costs money, you know," Marotta reminded her.

Kallyna's eyes flashed with fury. "I'll pay you," she snapped. "All of your bloody money."

Marotta stepped away, her fists clenched under her filthy apron.

Kallyna picked up the laundry basket and went to the garden to hang her clothes to dry. She sat on a stool there, mending her cloak. Her hands wouldn't stop shaking. She pricked herself twice, then burst into muffled sobs.

Palm Sunday was tomorrow. She had run out of money, Mansour hadn't come back and might be dead. All had been for nothing, and now it was time to look for the salt caravan that would take her back home.

XVIII

P ALM SUNDAY DAWNED WARM AS A SUMMER DAY. Children went down to the harbor to swim and to play between the hulls of the galleys, diving from the long stone pier.

Kallyna woke up in a sweat, her mind a whirlwind of conjectures. She had been wrestling all night with the thought of disregarding what Mansour had told her and waiting instead a few more days. Even so, before leaving the inn she packed her bundle. Landolfo gave her directions to the house where the salt merchants were lodged. He was going to go to market in the afternoon, he added, and could take her to meet them.

The city that morning was even livelier than usual. The cathedral was packed with a crowd waving tall branches of palm trees decorated with ribbons. A bishop in white and gold robes blessed them, his arms stretched out from the main altar. The bells rang, and an emotion resembling joy seemed to cover briefly the miseries of a city too close to war.

Kallyna had to force back the tears that were choking her. She tried desperately not to think of what she was going to do back in Tropea. The thought numbed her with grief.

Marotta saw her coming back to the inn looking haggard, and for once treated her more gently, offering her a bun that she didn't add to the bill. After her meal she went to her room to store her prayer book in her bundle. She knew that Landolfo was waiting to go with her to the house of the salt merchants. She tied her chamois pouch around her waist, dropping in it the money she would need to pay them. Then she closed the door and headed downstairs.

Landolfo must have led in a couple of customers. She could hear boots on the kitchen floor, and the innkeeper's voice as he seated the newcomers. She gathered her skirts and put her foot on the first step.

"Bring us some wine," one of the men said.

The voice seemed so familiar that for a moment she thought it was Mansour; but Mansour never drank wine. She went on down, her mind on something else. When she was halfway down the stairs she saw the two men in the kitchen. They were sitting at the table. One had his elbows on it and his face in his hands. The other was so tall the chair sagged under his weight. One was Dalibor, the other Geoffroi de Vire.

She froze where she was, and could not move a step further. To ask by what sort of coincidence the two of them were there meant to push God's mercy too far. She accepted the fact without the slightest doubt.

Neither man had seen her. Dalibor kept his eyes on the table, deep in worried thoughts. Landolfo wiped the table with a rag and set two cups and a pitcher of wine before them. Dalibor took one of the cups and turned it over and over in his hands.

Without making a noise, begging them in her mind not to go away, Kallyna rushed back to her room and ripped open the bundle looking for her lilac dress. The dress fought her as she forced it on, and the silk slippers wouldn't stay put. She kept Geoffroi's money pouch, perhaps they would not recognize her. She made a knot in the long chain where she kept Malva's ring and twisted the chain backwards so it would stay hidden under her hair. Then she dashed out again.

Dalibor and de Vire had left. In a mad panic she looked all around her: where would she look for them now? As she was about to turn around and go back in, Dalibor appeared from the side of the street where the stable was, accompanied by one of his men.

She noticed that he was thinner, that his boots were spattered with blood, that he was carrying a new sword and that he had a new scar on his forearm. She couldn't stop shaking.

Landolfo saw her. "Mistress, if you want to talk to those salt merchants, you'd better hurry."

"I... changed my mind," she managed to say. "Please forgive me."

At the sound of her voice Dalibor raised his head slowly, his mouth open.

"Not only that... " he whispered to himself. "Now I *see* things, too."

He climbed the steps, limping on his left leg. He stopped in front of her and reached out warily to touch her hair. There was such a look on his face that she almost couldn't bear to look back. Then he ripped her from where she was standing and into his arms.

"Just let me see... Heart of God, are you really there?"

The world might as well have been razed down to the piece of floor on which they stood. All her fears, all the long days and weeks and months behind her melted at once.

"You are alive, lord," she whispered. "It's Easter and you're alive."

They stood there holding each other for a long time; not talking, not moving, only breathing in their own amazed gratitude.

"What in the name of heaven are you doing here?" Dalibor then asked quietly.

She looked at him with a self-assurance that had never been in her before. "I came with Mansour."

His surprise grew wider. "Mansour Ibn Hamid? That old seawolf himself? God, wait until Geoffroi hears this!" He was looking at her as if he wanted to kiss the hem of her dress for saving his life.

She took his hands, thinking about Malva. "I will tell you everything," she said. "But it's bad news."

He shook his head. "No. You are the only good news I've ever had in my life. I want the bad ones out while I still can."

She looked at him again. His face was wasted. That smile he wore like a broken lance seemed the only thing he had left. She didn't have the heart to take it from him. He was right, she thought. Bad news could wait.

He led her to the door, his arm pressing hard around her shoulders as if he were afraid of losing her again.

"Where are we going?" she asked.

He rocked his head. "I don't know." Then he stopped to gather the whole of her into his eyes. "Look at you," he murmured. "You're so beautiful. By God you are."

He lifted her onto his horse, then mounted behind her. They rode away from the inn, past the noisy streets of Salerno where she hadn't dared to venture, past the miserable alleys full of beggars and pain. Outside the walls he found fields and orchards in full spring bloom. He didn't stop until they were deep into the countryside, where the river flowed and only the birds knew they were there.

"We came looking for you," Kallyna said slowly, as if in her sleep. "Mansour has gone to Amalfi to look for you. God has been good to me."

"My love," Dalibor said all of a sudden, listening to the words he had held inside for so long. "My love," he repeated, glorying in their sound. He caressed her face slowly, like a blind man learning to recognize beloved features by the touch of his fingers. The hooves of the big gray horse met the river's edge past a flat sandy bank, and stopped.

"I saw the lord de Vire with you before," Kallyna said as they dismounted.

Dalibor tethered the horse to a tree. He walked with her down to a bend hidden in a thicket of myrtles. The sun was warm and gleamed on the slow stream.

"I've heard also what happened on the road to Aversa," she said.

"That's where we come from," Dalibor said. "We've been hunting down the bastards who got us into that ambush. Two of them are hiding in Salerno."

They sat down by the river.

"I should thank them, then," Kallyna said with a thin smile. "I was going to leave tomorrow."

He barely heard her now. He lay down with her on the sand of the riverbank. His hands on her felt feverish in a way she almost didn't like. He must have been carrying a burden even heavier than her own. He was hurrying to claim her back with greed, desperately wanting freedom from the horror that surrounded him. She understood, and she surrendered.

"How long has it been?" he wondered. "Six months, six years? I can't even remember... But I want you like then, like always."

His hands frightened her with their mad, relentless caressing. Her clothes and his own came off with a sound of strained stitches. In one place or another they would need mending afterwards. Her silk belt swished like a snake between his fingers that war had made like leather. He pressed her brutally under him, groping clumsily as a newborn on his mother's breast. His breath grew into a harsh, husky sound that filled her ears. He hurt her more than the first time, he made her moan with pain.

Words without meaning came out of him, like broken ax heads out of the ground of a battlefield. She saw him frown, as though his pleasure were bringing him not the oblivion he wanted but only a savage disappointment. He looked haunted by some nemesis. So she clung to him, pulling him closer and letting go of every resistance, until it no longer seemed as if they were struggling against each other. She made herself into nothing more than the softness he sought with his flesh and with his soul.

Still the release came like the end of a battle. He started as if pierced by one arrow after another, then he rolled off her and lay face down as if hiding. She too lay stiffly, not daring to move or talk. Her mouth and her breasts were sore. She raised a hand to touch him; in that small moment of silence his panting breath suddenly turned into the sound of a sob.

Her hand fell back onto her mouth. The sun came out from behind the treetops, warming their bodies, and the birds were still singing. But all she could hear was the nameless grief that racked him. Never before had she heard a man cry. She drew him into her arms and held him with all the strength she had.

"So sweet an armful you are," he sobbed. "You don't know, you've never seen... You've never seen what a broadsword can do to the flesh of a baby... or mothers of small children slaughtered for nothing... for some bread they might hide, for nothing!" He clawed at the ground with his nails, tossing furiously against her. "You are clean... You are clean, my love."

She took his head in her hands. "Please... please, lord."

His voice turned into a roar of anger at that word that reminded him of his rank and of all that came with his rank.

"Lord of what?" he cried out. "The crows, lord of the crows... Sometimes even my wine tastes like blood and my food like rotting flesh!" He tore himself from her. He turned his back to her and for a long time was silent.

Kallyna stared at the trees nodding above them. She wanted to reach for her dress, but it lay under the grimy heap of his clothes. On top of their clothes lay his suit of chain mail, rusting already here and there with old blood, both of its owner and of its owner's enemies. While she looked at it, the sword lying on the sand next to her shone, glowered almost. It was nearly as tall as she was. She averted her eyes with hatred.

Dalibor turned toward her. He felt wonderfully empty now as he stretched beside her, his tears drying on his face.

"I'm sorry for the way I took you," he said. "I seem to get worse as I get older, I don't know. Jesus, like a pig." He gave her a rueful smile and took her gently in his arms. Almost unconsciously, she moved her fingers away from his forearm. The new scar felt awful, deeper than the one in his side. The body she loved, she thought, marred like that.

He noticed her gesture. "You'll have to get used to these beauty marks," he joked bitterly. "It's going to be a long time before I retire. Mother of Judas," he sighed. "Other people cut down wheat for their craft... they cut leather, wood. *My* craft had to be cutting down people!"

Kallyna was looking at the river. She rose and motioned him to come with her into the water. He did stand up but only to embrace her, and followed her only because he wanted to be forgiven.

The river's water was pleasantly cold as it rose up to their shoulders. He knelt down on the bottom in front of her. Kallyna scooped up a handful of fine sand and gently began washing him with it. Her hands were unsteady. She was in awe of his strength especially when it was resting, coiled. His face smoothed into a look of childlike, innocent bliss.

Under her hands everything was washed away from him — the grime, the crusted blood, the pain and the loathing, and the river took everything with it as it flowed on. For a few perfect moments he had no memory of the past and no dread of the future.

He plunged his head into the water and came back up splashing.

"There will come a day when I can have you in a bed like every God-fearing man," he complained.

"If we both live long enough," Kallyna said, making him laugh.

His hands were cold as he held her and stroked her. Then his fingers caught the signet ring on the chain twisted at the back of her neck and hidden in the tousled spread of her hair. He turned it around and looked at it; she instead closed her eyes, as if trying to forget that little lump of gold.

The water rippled between their bodies. He held the ring in his hand. "This belongs to my mother," he said.

"It's time for the bad news." He seemed to know already. His eyes had a look of sadness and resignation. He must listen just as she must speak, and both against their will.

Kallyna suddenly shuddered.

"I'm cold. Let's go in the sun."

As they sat down on the narrow strip of sand, a sound like muffled footsteps came from the bushes behind them. Dalibor lowered his hand on the hilt of the sword.

"It's the wind," Kallyna said. She wrung her hair to dry it, trying to buy time. She didn't know where to start, and in her mind she loathed her task.

"Why do I have to be the one to tell you," she whispered.

Her voice seemed to creep inside him like an awakening pain.

"I know she's ill," he said. "I've known it for a long time. I tried to get used to her dying when it first started, but it makes no difference."

She couldn't look him in the face.

"I still don't understand how it happened, the way we met... She was coming to look for you, from Monreale. The night she stopped in Tropea she came to my house looking for shelter. I didn't know who she was... but I knew I wanted to follow her from the very first moment."

Dalibor ran his hand on his hair, on his mouth, with a motion of anguish.

"I could have seen her at least... O God, what is it that You want from me?" He lay down and closed his eyes. "I'll bring her here as soon as this damned war is over. Where did she die?"

"In Aieta, in the house of Filippo Rocca," she said. "She died in peace, lord. Truly in peace, and surrounded by friends, honored and mourned like the great lady she was. Mansour and I went on to look for you, according to her last wishes."

"And the ring?" he asked. "Didn't she tell you to give it to me?"

Kallyna shook her head. "No, lord. She only told me to show it to you. She said you would understand."

He frowned. After a moment he waved his hand. "All right, keep it then."

"Mansour has the will," she said. "I wonder when he's coming back."

Dalibor seemed distant now, as if trying to hide his thoughts from her. "She must have loved you very much," he said.

"I hope so," Kallyna whispered. "I've loved her more than I did my own mother."

They got up. Dalibor covered himself in a hurry, with shame; Kallyna too was glad to be hidden again from his eyes. Together they walked back to where the horse was waiting.

"I *have* to see Mansour," he said grimly. "If I don't hear from him the same things you told me, I will think that I only dreamt all this."

He stopped and turned to face her. "Listen. Geoffroi and I must go to Amalfi, where Guglielmo is. We have the great honor of being his personal escort... I want you to stay at the inn until Mansour comes back, whenever that will be, and then to come to Amalfi with him."

Kallyna nodded. "All right."

"Do you have money?" he asked.

"All I have left is what I was saving for the trip home."

He opened the small leather pouch threaded into his clothes belt and handed it to her. "Take this. God," he fretted, "my squire got killed at Aversa… I don't have anybody I can entrust you to."

She touched his hand. "I'll be fine, lord. I've been through worse." She smiled. "I think you're going to tell me to lock myself in my room and don't attract any attention, like Mansour told me."

Behind the bushes the horse was snorting and pawing the ground.

"Even that might not be enough," Dalibor said. "Falco da Torre is with us, and as always he has eyes and ears everywhere. That's why I'm not taking you with me now… though God knows I cannot bear the very thought of leaving you here alone."

"My lord, it's been a long time," Kallyna said. "I'm sure Falco doesn't even remember me anymore."

"Perhaps," he countered. "But now it's not my life alone that I'm responsible for… and believe me, I'd kill Roger d'Hauteville if he got in my way because of you." He looked at her with the look she had sometimes dared to imagine.

All of a sudden he stopped, and she with him. Geoffroi de Vire was standing by the horse, trying to quiet the animal so he wouldn't snort and paw anymore.

Dalibor jumped on him.

"What the hell do you think you're doing, I'd like to know!" he shouted, snatching the horse's reins from his hands.

Geoffroi took a bow.

"Keeping watch over my lord's noble neck," he replied with the greatest ease, spitting out an unripe blackberry. "Somebody must, seeing that you so enjoy walking around naked as an earthworm. But next time do remember to keep at least your dagger someplace where you can reach it… should the need arise, of course."

Dalibor didn't speak. He waved Kallyna on and took her under his arm.

Geoffroi made her another bow.

"Skirts of Saint Anne and her underwear, too!" he said, happy. "The world is small, isn't it?"

She smiled with quiet pride.

"Small enough for us to walk it, lord."

Geoffroi's face opened into a grin of delight. He turned to Dalibor.

"May I rot in hell for double my appointed time if I know what you ever did to deserve her," he grumbled. Then he noticed that she was looking at his tunic: it was the one she had made for him, now frayed and soiled. He shook his head sadly, asking her forgiveness. "Beautiful things don't last in a war."

"Some nerve you have," Dalibor said, "lurking around like an old goat."

"Then leave me a note next time!" Geoffroi exclaimed. "I almost lamed my horse chasing down Your Excellency... Oh, it certainly is a nice place to die... a nice way too."

Dalibor saw that Kallyna was turning crimson.

"Enough," he snapped. He put her in the saddle and mounted behind her.

"When the man at the Bear's Inn told me you'd left with a girl," Geoffroi chattered on, "I told myself, I'll find him and I'll choke him with my own two hands. But by god, *that* girl! Who would have ever imagined ...Some men have all the luck."

Dalibor grinned. "Some men do."

The two horses ambled down the riverbank. Kallyna glanced over her shoulder, leaving the bend as she would have a sanctuary of peace from which the world is barred.

"You may be interested in learning that we did find those two renegades while you were... away," Geoffroi said.

"Where's Falco?" Dalibor asked.

Geoffroi slapped his thigh. "You wouldn't believe that jackass. He's still looking for his spy, the one he blames for the ambush on the road to Aversa. I figure by now he'll be busting his backside galloping around Vietri or something." He shook his head. "No wonder we can't win this war, with an imbecile like him giving us orders."

"He's lost what little brains he had," Dalibor muttered. "There is no spy, and he knows it. He's just looking for a sheep to slaughter, so he can look good to Guglielmo. He thought he'd found me, that time they tried to assassinate him in Amalfi …"

Startled, Kallyna looked at him. "Yes, I've heard about that… Did he accuse *you* of the treason?"

Geoffroi started to wave his hands. "Never mind his nonsense, little witch. He's been having delusions ever since he got tired of his job. No one accused him of anything." He wanted to sound carefree, but Kallyna wasn't at all convinced.

"Let's talk about you instead, huh?" de Vire went on to change the subject. "You know, when I saw you there at the river, for a moment I thought my lord's ghosts were beginning to haunt me too."

She lowered her eyes, blushing fiercely again at the thought of Geoffroi watching and listening before, and the conversation fell into an awkward silence. They were nearing the city; they could see the walls already.

"What are you going to do with those two we caught?" Geoffroi asked then.

"I'll hand them over to Guglielmo and let him decide," Dalibor answered crossly.

"But Falco wants them dead," Geoffroi insisted. "As for Guglielmo, he'll have them executed anyway."

"The hell with Falco *and* Guglielmo!" Dalibor cried out. Kallyna felt his hands tightening around her.

Geoffroi scratched his neck. "Don't you think we'd better hang them here and now? You know, to cut rumors?"

Dalibor threw his head back. "Fine piece of advice."

Geoffroi leant closer to him. "It *is* good advice. Don't step on the broken rung while Falco's watching you."

Frightened, Kallyna looked again at Dalibor, wanting to say something but not knowing what.

Dalibor rubbed his nose against her hair.

"You smell good," he said.

Around the Bear's Inn a crowd of people had gathered, so thick that Landolfo had been forced to lock doors and windows. On the landing were four Norman soldiers guarding the two Neapolitan prisoners. The two men hunkered down with their hands tied behind their backs and a look of terror in their eyes. One was bleeding from a wound in his neck.

The women in the crowd wept, the men cursed under their breath. They all pressed threateningly as the two horses made their way through. Suddenly Kallyna felt cold with fear. Every woman who looked at her had Marotta's viciousness in her eyes; the eyes of the men seemed to strip her of her showy dress.

Dalibor helped her down the saddle and left her by the horse. She shrank anxiously against the big mount. He went up the stairs to the front door of the inn, where the soldiers stood at attention. A soldier put into his hands the rope that bound the two prisoners.

"They're yours, my lord."

Dalibor stood for a moment holding the rope. He looked at Geoffroi, not knowing what to do. Geoffroi made a small nod of his head that meant there was no choice. Defeated by that implacable logic of war, Dalibor could only nod back. He tugged at the rope to make the prisoners stand up. The crowd was murmuring and swaying.

"Sons of whores, all of them," someone said, loud enough for all to hear.

Dalibor spoke into Geoffroi's ear. "Take her inside." Then he pushed aside the soldiers and went down the stairs with the two prisoners on the rope.

Trapped in the crowd, Kallyna tried to see where he was going. The crowd pushed her back, walling her in. Finally Geoffroi came plowing through to her and carried her away almost bodily, shoving and cursing at the throng.

"Get in and lock the door," he whispered to her.

Kallyna was still trying to catch a glimpse of Dalibor. Separated from her by a wall of bodies, she saw that he was looking at her with great worry. Then he mounted his horse and rode away. The crowd followed him like a slow flow of black lava.

"Will I see him later?" she asked Geoffroi while they walked up the stairs and then knocked on the door.

"I'm sure he'll come back as soon as he can," Geoffroi reassured her. He knocked again.

Marotta put her nose against the window bars.

"Open this damned door!" de Vire yelled.

Marotta threw her hands in the air. "Eh, coming, Jesus, coming!"

From the other end of the street came the sound of horses at a full gallop. About a dozen men were headed toward the inn, scattering the last stragglers. Geoffroi pounded his fist on the door for the third time, making it rattle. "I said open up!"

The horses came to a halt at the foot of the stairs. "Where the hell do you keep these prisoners, my lord de Vire?" Falco shouted. "Or did I run all the way back here for nothing?"

Immediately Geoffroi put his body between Kallyna and Falco's eyes. Not enough to hide the long hem of her dress, Kallyna thought. Marotta was doing it on purpose. They could hear her wooden clogs shuffling behind the closed door.

Falco dismounted. In Geoffroi's eyes there was something resembling fear. Kallyna tried the doorknob again.

"They're down in the square," Geoffroi shouted back at Falco.

Falco craned his neck to see who cowered behind him. "Why, you're not coming, my lord?" He grinned. "Oh, I see. You're up to a bit of whoring, uh?"

Geoffroi waved him away. "God willing, as soon as that slut of an innkeeper opens the door."

Falco put his foot on the lowest step. With his eyes he kept searching behind de Vire. He burst into a laugh. "Mother of God, they must have stuck you with a really ugly one, if you must hide her!"

Geoffroi dropped his arms in surrender. "Yes," he said between his teeth. "Ugly as the queen of the devils."

Falco and Kallyna found themselves face to face. The eyes of the scarred man flashed with surprise for such a small instant that she didn't even notice.

"Oh no, no, no," he reproached Geoffroi, smoothing the air with his hands. "How can you say such a thing, my lord de Vire. She's very pretty instead, a real dove… that just flew from one end of the kingdom to the other."

Kallyna forced herself to lift her face, but she could not force herself to look at him. The door creaked open.

"At long last, by god!" Geoffroi hissed, shoving Marotta out of the way with fury.

Marotta didn't say a word, for this time Kallyna was so well escorted.

Geoffroi, like a good sheepdog barking at the wolf, was moving quickly away from her so that Falco would follow him.

"Come on, let's go see how those two renegades die."

Falco smiled, but he was still looking at Kallyna.

"Of course, my lord, of course. There's always so much to be learned from that sort of theater." He followed Geoffroi down the steps. Marotta slammed the door shut.

Kallyna locked herself in her room and sat by the window, waiting, her hands torturing one another in her lap. From the square she could hear the crowd buzzing like an angry swarm. Twice their voices grew louder, and she knew the two prisoners had been executed.

Now Dalibor would come back, she thought. She would brave the world to go meet him; he would protect her. As soon as the first groups of people passed down the street on their way back from the execution, she almost ran downstairs. Dalibor wasn't there, and neither was Geoffroi. There was only the same mob, angrier now and ready to lash out.

As she leant from the landing to see, a woman below pointed her finger up to her.

"The whore of the Normans!"

A boy bent down to pick up a stone, weighing it in his hands. Kallyna's eyes swept frantically the street in search of a known face. Even Falco would have been a welcome sight.

"Whore of the Normans!" the woman cried out again.

A stone hissed past Kallyna's head, thudding against the door. She stood paralyzed with fear. If Maso hadn't come up the stairs to pull her down behind the landing's low wall, the second stone would have hit her.

"Mistress, don't be afraid," Maso whispered. "I'll make them stop, you'll see."

"No, no," she said numbly. "I don't want them to hurt you. Go… leave me!"

Landolfo and Marotta came running from the stable. Landolfo was trying to make his voice heard above the ferocious uproar. Pushing Maso away, Kallyna ducked into the doorway and up to her room. Stones rained onto the threshold and the kitchen floor. Up in her room she could still hear the crowd calling out insults at her. Landolfo threatened to call the guards; Marotta screamed at the top of her lungs.

The room was in the dark. Kallyna didn't dare open the shutters or light a candle. Her legs felt weak with terror. Sitting still on the bed, she waited for the endless time it took the two innkeepers to drive the crowd away.

Finally the last insult died down and the street was quiet again. She fell onto the bed, sobbing savagely until the last flicker of light left the window. No one had come to see what had become of her. Dazed with crying, she stretched out on the blanket and slowly fell asleep.

Downstairs, Marotta and Landolfo sat at the kitchen table with one of Falco da Torre's soldiers. The man had put a purse full of money on the table, and was waiting. Landolfo shook his head, waved his hands, listened to his wife and then shook his head again, a little more feebly each time. Marotta talked and poked her finger at the ceiling, in the direction of Kallyna's room.

In the end Landolfo reached out to touch the money purse. He felt the thick coins between his fingers, and grabbed it. Marotta heaved a sigh of relief.

XIX

I T WASN'T SUNUP YET WHEN MAROTTA CAME to knock at the door of Kallyna's room. Kallyna had long been awake, dreading the day ahead. She still hoped against all sense that Dalibor would come, even though she knew he had left for Amalfi soon after the execution.

She opened the door. Marotta was with the soldier who had come to the inn the night before.

"Mistress?" she said. "This man wants to talk to you." She stepped out in a hurry.

The soldier bowed to Kallyna in a respectful, reassuring manner.

"Speak," Kallyna said sullenly.

"The lord d'Hancourt sends me to escort you to him," the soldier said. "He has found lodging for you elsewhere." She looked the man up and down, taken aback. "He sends word that he's sorry he couldn't come in person," the man quickly added.

Marotta, hidden behind him, kept sweeping the hallway.

Kallyna nodded. "All right. Let me get my things."

She was ready in no time, and almost ran out of the room. Marotta hastened to walk her to the door.

"Is everything paid for?" Kallyna asked.

Marotta waved her hands impatiently.

"All paid and set. Go with God."

Kallyna put her bundle across her forearm.

"Thank you."

Out in the street were three more men waiting on horseback, their faces hidden by their helmets. The one who had come to the room held the stirrup for her. While she mounted she saw that Maso was still asleep in the alley, all curled up on the ground by the cold brazier. The sun was coming up.

She didn't even ask the men where this lodging was that the lord d'Hancourt had found for her. She was too happy to be joining him. He must have arranged everything the night before, she thought, thanking him in her mind.

Then she saw that the four soldiers were headed toward the main gate. She pulled in the reins. In an instant the men drew close all around her. "We're going out," she wondered. "You didn't tell me we were leaving Salerno!"

The man set his jaws. His eyes had the same color as his helmet, the same dull glint. "I thought I had, my lady. We're going to Amalfi."

She didn't understand. Dalibor had told her she mustn't go to Amalfi yet. "Why to Amalfi?" she asked, panicking.

The soldier shook his head. "No questions. Just come along."

She clutched the reins to her chest. "I'm not coming along. I demand to be taken to the lord d'Hancourt."

The man tore the reins from her hands and drew his sword. Then he spurred his horse ahead of her and kept her reins. She shut her eyes, so she wouldn't see Salerno becoming smaller and smaller behind her. Once again the lord d'Hancourt had been quite careless, she thought. He should have left two guards posted at the door of the inn; or perhaps he should have locked her in a jail cell and thrown away the key.

The road to Amalfi was a ribbon of dizziness tied around plummeting cliffs and steep gorges. The mountainsides were covered with olive groves that had the sheen of silver leaf, and terraced vineyards stepping all the way down to the sea. On the coast clustered towns as white as doves, the roofs of the houses covered with gleaming blue and yellow tiles. Maiori and Minori, then Atrani, then Scala and Ravello; with the names alone a goldsmith could have made a necklace.

For many hours Kallyna rode on surrounded by endless beauty that seemed to pierce her. Her frightened thoughts were like children who wouldn't stop asking questions. The men didn't stop to eat, to drink. She knew to whom that blind obedience belonged.

They reached Amalfi before sunset. Mansour was right, she thought, this was as close to paradise as she'd ever been. A thick nest of domed houses gathered above a narrow strip of sand. From a distance she could see the cathedral, a mountain of precious marbles built to celebrate the glory of the oldest Maritime Republic, the one who rivaled Venice herself.

The harbor was thick with galleys filled with rare merchandises like floating treasure houses, and with the huge *dromon*, warships guided by a new invention called the compass, that only Amalfi possessed and jealously guarded. Beyond the main gate were narrow quiet streets perfumed with orange trees and jasmine. They rode past the great arched buildings of the shipyard, past the mansions of ship owners and spice merchants. So different was Amalfi from Salerno, untouched by war; truly an enclave for princes.

The horses stopped in front of a palace that dominated the city. Above the bronze doors guarded by half a dozen armed men was sculpted the pointed cap that was the symbol of the Doge. The man took Kallyna down the saddle and through the inner courtyard. The palace was so quiet it seemed empty, but only because it was so vast, and surrounded by a belt of gardens and orchards.

Two old women appeared at the gate. The soldier pushed Kallyna toward them. One of the two motioned to her companion, a hag with a mouthful of bad teeth and almost bald under her black veil.

"Aziza," the woman scolded, "can't you see that this poor little thing doesn't know which way to go? Help her in, she must be tired out of her wits."

"All right, all right," Aziza grumbled, taking Kallyna by the hand. "But did they have to keep me waiting all day long for her?"

Kallyna followed the woman up a vast, magnificently carved marble staircase. She kept tugging at her hand.

"Tell me where I am," she said, "I want to know where I am. I want to know if the lord d'Hancourt is here."

The old crone walked speedily ahead of her.

"Listen, my lamb. Better not to mention names. You mustn't worry. You're in a very safe place."

"A jail is a very safe place. Where are you taking me?" Her strained voice echoed across the colonnade set around a tiled pool and rustling with palm trees.

Aziza turned around and put her finger on her lips.

"My lamb, if you don't behave yourself I'll have to call Black Osman."

The name was enough to silence Kallyna for the time being. She was shown into a room gleaming with mosaics, whose floor was entirely covered with thick oriental carpets. A young girl was waiting for her by a low table laden with food. Kallyna glanced at the full trays and hated herself for being so hungry.

Aziza took her bundle.

"You won't need this now," she said.

Kallyna pulled back at the flaps of her homespun Calabrian blanket with fury.

"You'll have to skin me alive before I wear anything that's not in that bundle," she replied in her teeth.

Aziza stepped back, scowling.

"All right, all right." Then she headed out of the room. "What a wild one I've got on my hands this time!" she grumbled to herself.

The young girl sitting by the table motioned Kallyna to eat.

"Can you tell me where I am?" Kallyna whispered. "Please. Can you tell me what they want from me?"

The girl looked at her shyly with her soft round face.

"Please help me," Kallyna begged her.

The girl still said nothing. Finally she opened her mouth to show her: her tongue was cut. She again motioned Kallyna to eat, but now Kallyna was too horrified to even look at the food.

Aziza was back. "Not hungry, uh?" she said with an air of displeasure. "My lamb, you and I won't get along at all if you keep being so stubborn." She told the mute girl to take away the table. Then she took Kallyna by the hand. "Come with me now."

"Where am I, where are you taking me!" Kallyna kept on asking, her voice raised angrily.

Aziza tried to shush her. "This is going to be much harder than I thought," she said in despair. "Girls these days are impossible."

Past the colonnade was a smaller white palace as wonderfully dressed in latticework as to resemble the finest lace. By its door of carved rosewood stood a brawny guard wearing a formidable black mustache that looked like a flourish of Arabic script painted on his dark face.

The white palace had all the unmistakable trappings of a harem: the opulent softness of silk divans, the sound of ivory-handled lutes, a cloying scent of perfume. A sullen company of women inhabited it, kept animals of pleasure in a royal menagerie.

Terrified, Kallyna saw their eyes in which there would never be compassion or friendship, but only a merciless assessment of the virtues and shortcomings of the new rival. She watched them comb their hair, choose dresses, bicker and gossip. She tried to find in her heart compassion for those stunted, replaceable creatures whose only yardstick of themselves and of the world was the lust of a man. But the thought of becoming one of them left scars of loathing in her soul.

She searched the room desperately for a dark nook. Below a tiny grated window was a fountain rippling down from a niche of pink stone. She went to sit by it. She needed the piece of sky beyond the window, and maybe the sound of the water would trick her into believing that she was away from that place, free.

❋   ❋   ❋

At twilight the following day Dalibor and Geoffroi left Atrani, where they had been sent to witness the election of Amalfi's new Doge. They rode down to Amalfi under a crescent of red moon that looked like the handle of a new copper pitcher. The houses of the city were of an almost phosphorescent whiteness in the soft spring evening. The first shadows were welling up among the orange groves.

"Is it that ring?" Geoffroi asked.

Dalibor wrung his hands around his leather wrist guards, nervously.

"Yes. She told me I would see it only on the hand of the woman she wanted me to marry."

Geoffroi looked pensive.

"One could almost say they've conspired behind your back, sweet lord. The first time you got off the hook the easy way…"

Dalibor made a face.

"Don't talk like that. I've been told the dead have ears. I wasn't crazy about Marie des Louvelles, but I didn't dance for joy when she died, either, may she rest in peace."

"All right," Geoffroi said. "But to be honest, given a choice between Marie des Louvelles and your little witch?"

Dalibor directed his horse past a jutting boulder and didn't reply.

"She's the daughter of a fisherman," he said after a while, uncomfortably.

Geoffroi's voice became loud with passion.

"So? Do you know who *my* father is? You don't and neither do I, and still we've saved each other's lives a dozen times between us."

He jabbed his finger. "Do something about her. The alternative is marrying out of convenience, like you almost did three years ago, to some blue-blooded nag who will breed you the prescribed number of blue-blooded heirs, while you jump forever after from one mistress to the next like a grasshopper in heat. Or perhaps you intend to make *her* your mistress?"

266

Daunted, Dalibor was silent for a while, then changed the subject.

"George of Antioch has offered me the command of a warship. He says we might sail against Pisa soon."

"Don't count me in," Geoffroi said. "I get seasick and I can't stand the food."

Dalibor chuckled.

"Not to mention you can't swim?"

They rode into the streets of Amalfi and headed up toward Prince Guglielmo's palace.

"How does it feel?" Geoffroi asked.

"How does what feel?"

"Well, damn it, to be in love."

Dalibor smiled wide. "Like you're... brand new, ready to start the world from scratch. You should try it sometimes."

"Who says I haven't," Geoffroi bragged, touchy.

"You don't seem particularly angry," Dalibor said. "After all I did breach your favorite commandment."

Geoffroi shrugged. "I knew you would. I knew it from the start. You have breached *all* my favorite commandments... and I have always let you do it because I was too damn scared to do it myself."

They had reached the palace. The guards opened the gate and took their horses. While they walked toward the prince's quarters they could hear the long, plaintive notes of a *saz* wafting from some inner garden. Soldiers were stationed atop the walls, like ebony statues against the turquoise sky.

"You look really worried," Geoffroi said.

"I won't *sleep* until Mansour comes back to take care of her."

"Listen," Geoffroi said, "there is one thing I must tell you. Falco saw her, that day at the Bear's Inn."

Dalibor stopped abruptly. Geoffroi started to wave his hands. "We couldn't help it, there was nothing we could do!"

Dalibor's face had become grim. He strode on with the hurry of a man whose house is on fire. The guards at the door of Falco's room stopped him.

"Well arrived, my lord d'Hancourt. The lord Falco is waiting for you in the Latticed Room."

"The Latticed Room!" Dalibor shouted. "Seat of Mercy, this is his last night."

One of the guards reached out to stop de Vire. "He wants to see the lord d'Hancourt alone," he said.

"I'm sure he does," Dalibor spat out, and was already headed toward the harem.

"Wait!" Geoffroi called him. But now he was alone in the wake of Dalibor's footsteps pounding the floor.

※　　　　　※　　　　　※

Aziza had led her to a room no larger than a jail cell, where light and shadow played subtly, deceptively, on the pearl-colored walls. High above was a balcony covered by latticed screens, to conceal those who had come. Aziza had threatened to have the guards undress her if Kallyna didn't do it herself. Then she had taken away the lilac dress, and Kallyna had entered the room naked.

A single oil lamp hung from the ceiling. She craned her neck, trying to see beyond the screens, to guess where the hidden entrance was. She felt as if she were in the pit of an old tower where bats cried unseen in the dark, ready to wake up and lunge with their sharp little claws.

Aziza had told her that she would stay in that room for a long time, until her eyelids would droop with sleep in the heavy, dim silence. But Kallyna wanted to be fully awake, so she could spit in Guglielmo d'Hauteville's face.

※　　　　　※　　　　　※

Falco paced the landing in front of the small door, swinging a key on a chain. When Dalibor's head emerged from the spiral staircase, the key seemed to dangle in front of him like a noose.

"No need to hurry, my lord d'Hancourt," the scarred man said. "The prince is patient. He has agreed to let us take a look at the new girl before he does."

Dalibor put his dagger to Falco's throat.

"Speak now, while I let you. Who's in there?"

Falco stood very still.

"Don't you want to see for yourself? Here's the key…"

"No," Dalibor said. "I want to hear it from your own mouth, like a heretic's confession, so I can prod you to the stake myself."

Falco didn't blink.

"You know perfectly well who's in there. Your little embroideress from Tropea. The first time she… escaped from the window, was it? and Guglielmo didn't speak to me for a week. I never understood why you put up such an extraordinary charade. You were ready to risk your life for a peasant girl, just like in an old-fashioned romance."

Dalibor's shoulders rose and fell.

"I don't expect you to understand anything about it. All you do with people is sell them to the highest bidder. Let her out."

Falco smiled.

"Not so easy, my lord. First I must learn why she came here. You're not going to tell me it's because she missed your lovemaking?" His forehead creased a bit. "I know she was with that Arab pimp of yours, but how do I know they're not both in the same conspiracy as you are? Come to think of it, perhaps I'd better not send her to Guglielmo's bed. She might hide a vial of poison in that lovely long hair of hers."

For a while Dalibor was unable to speak. He could hear the hysteria in Falco's voice.

"Well," he said then, "at least now I *know* you are insane. Good. This time not even Guglielmo will believe you, and he's nothing but a bear dancing on your leash."

Falco smiled again, pleasantly. "Oh no, my lord. He believes me. He believes everything I tell him. And this time I can make him dance to a tune that will cost you your head… and hers."

He nodded toward the small door. "You and I know how suspicious he can be when even the smallest thing doesn't follow his wishes... and he's had his eyes on you for quite a long time. Suppose he wants to keep her. I'm sure you will *again* do something stupid to take her from him. So the scales tip, and you are once and for all a branded traitor."

He wrinkled his nose. "It's a tangle, I know. But sometimes he's slow at seeing things as they are. Personally, I never had any doubts about you."

"She has nothing to do with any of this," Dalibor hissed. "You don't take her and use her as if she were a dog without a master!"

"She's not worth a minute of this trouble, either," Falco countered. "There are scores of prettier girls. But I am a good servant of the Crown. If my prince asks me for something, I don't keep it from him. I leave that to you, my lord d'Hancourt. You never cared much about loyalty."

"Loyalty! To me that never meant licking the boots of any of the Hautevilles. She is with me. Touch her and it will be as if you had robbed me in broad daylight."

Falco's mouth rippled. His voice was brimming with sweetness.

"So she *is* with you. You've said so yourself. Did she come then to bring you money so you can bribe your spies, for instance Geoffroi de Vire?"

Dalibor's face had become ugly. His dagger quivered closer at Falco's throat.

"That would be even better," Falco said. "You kill me and you're dead."

Drunk with defeat, Dalibor had to lower his dagger and sheath it. After a moment he took the key from Falco's hands and opened the small door.

At the sudden noise above her, Kallyna started from head to toe. She curled up on herself, arms and knees drawn against her body. The open door let in a fan of light, which the latticework filtered and distorted.

Behind the screen Dalibor cursed fiercely under his breath. Then he called her.

"Kallyna!"

The name clanged inside the narrow walls like the tolling of a bell. She couldn't see him. She only knew where he must be, and kept her face raised toward that point.

"My lord!"

He rattled the latticed screen savagely.

"I'm here. Don't be afraid."

Kallyna's throat was too tight with sobs for her to answer. The door slammed shut, and the lamp went out in the draft. She remained alone at the bottom of the dark room.

※　　　　※　　　　※

Prince Guglielmo was sitting in the large, beautiful inner courtyard, under thickly interlaced Moorish arches. The elegant space around him was punctuated by the green fans of young palm trees potted in bronze jars. With his eyes half closed he was listening to two musicians weaving notes from their lutes like long strings of pearls.

The night seemed to waft in as soft perfume from the tall white walls. Beside the prince sat Richard of Selby. One step behind stood Geoffroi de Vire, who kept his hands clasped nervously behind his back. Geoffroi kept glancing at the door, as if expecting to see Dalibor being dragged through it on a noose. When the door did open, it was Dalibor who led the way, and at a good pace.

"My lord Guglielmo," Dalibor saluted the prince, out of breath as if he had crossed the entire palace at a run. Falco motioned the two musicians to leave.

Alarmed, Guglielmo sat up in his marble chair.

"Wait, wait!" he cried out. "What's all this now?"

Falco leaned back against a pillar, arms crossed.

"It's an official hearing, my lord," he sneered. "The lord d'Hancourt has… some sort of a petition to make."

"He does?" Guglielmo said in surprise. "Well then, the crown, bring me the crown, come on, come on," he ordered.

Selby rushed out to find it. Geoffroi fidgeted even more nervously, utterly confused.

"Please tell me it's nothing serious, my friends," Guglielmo pleaded.

"I'm afraid it is," Dalibor said quietly, putting his hand to his sword. Guglielmo's eyes followed that gesture with a scowl. "Oh God," he whined. "And it was such a lovely night!"

Selby was back with the heavy crown. In his hurry he carried it as unceremoniously as a parcel. Guglielmo grabbed it and pressed it down on his head. Then he stood up.

"Speak then, and do remember that you are before the justice of Roger, by the grace of God King of Sicily, Calabria, Lucania, Campania and Puglia."

Falco kept his eyes fixed on Dalibor's face, with an insolent half-smile. Now Dalibor would whine a little before the prince, remind him his father's titles, beg for mercy and succeed only in making a fool of himself.

"My lord," Dalibor began, "I'm being wronged greatly before your eyes. I'm being called a traitor and a spy, and I'm being unjustly robbed of your benevolence, which I have never dared to abuse. I demand reparation."

Geoffroi couldn't keep himself from clapping his hands with a muffled sound of triumph. Dalibor had jumped over all formalities as if over a heap of dead bodies and he had charged in a rumble of hooves like the perfect soldier he was. Falco's smile died on his lips.

Guglielmo sat rigidly, trying to look solemn, like a caricature of Roger.

"What you say saddens us," he intoned, aping the plural of kings and popes. "But we cannot deny the accusations made against you, my lord d'Hancourt. In fact, we have long been waiting for you to prove them false before us."

Dalibor drew his breath in. "That is why I am here, my lord. I want to give you proof. I ask to stand trial by the Judgment of God."

Astonished, Guglielmo slumped in his chair. Falco took a step forward. "What sort of judgment?" he asked in his teeth.

"The kind reserved to knights of my rank," Dalibor answered. "Ordeal by combat."

Falco's eyes bulged out. "You must be out of your mind to challenge a prince of the Crown!"

Dalibor looked at him calmly. "Not a prince of the Crown, my lord Falco. You, who have slandered me with your lies. You like to make great claims of loyalty to the Crown. So be the Crown's champion, and let God settle this matter once and forever."

Guglielmo was in a sweat. He looked anxiously at Falco, waiting to see what he would do.

Falco bowed his head. "Nice trick, d'Hancourt."

Guglielmo looked from one man to the other, bewildered and forlorn.

"Then this Judgment... it will have to be done," he moaned. "Where, when?"

"Here, my lord, now," Dalibor said. "We will summon the archbishop and set the terms with him."

Guglielmo looked almost pitiful in his confusion. He seemed to be desperately looking for a way to save both his lover and his dignity. Eventually he realized that he must sacrifice the first in order to keep the second. He raised his hand with a gesture that resembled more that of a beggar asking for alms than that of a ruler asserting his power.

"The Judgment... my lord d'Hancourt... is granted," he said in a whisper.

Geoffroi de Vire came up to Dalibor and threw his arms around him.

"Jesus, I could just kiss you," he blurted out.

Dalibor fended him off and addressed the prince again. "Before we send for the archbishop there is one term of the Judgment that I must settle with you alone. In the harem there is a young woman by the name of Kallyna d'Àrgira. You know that she was brought here against her will and my own. If I am victor in the ordeal, she must be freed and treated with the same respect you would show to myself."

Guglielmo seized on those words the way a drowning man would reach for the last rope tossed by rescuers. He took Dalibor's arm, smiling.

"My lord d'Hancourt... no, my *friend* d'Hancourt ... If you and Falco are arguing over the girl, we can solve the matter in a much more civilized way. We didn't know she was yours, but now that we do, of course we'll set her free. We set her free this very instant, then Falco makes his apologies to you, and we forget everything without any shedding of blood. What do you say... huh?"

His words managed to enrage not only Dalibor but Falco as well. Falco turned to him in cold fury.

"This isn't a matter of skirts, Guglielmo! In God's name, don't you understand? You should be thankful for this opportunity to reveal a traitor who's been plotting behind your back for months under the cover of his friendship with the Hauteville."

"He has?" Guglielmo asked. "How?" His face showed how desperately he wanted to believe Falco.

"Remember what happened when they tried to assassinate you here in your own home," Falco said. "Only the people of your personal escort knew that you were staying in Amalfi: myself, de Vire and d'Hancourt. For the sake of protection everybody else had been told you were still in Aversa with your father."

"Yes… yes, well, you're right," Guglielmo mumbled, falling from his pretentious loftiness to a stuttering anger.

"And the ambush on the road to Aversa," Falco went on, "where almost four hundred of our best knights died, and where Charles Antigny was taken prisoner while our "good friend" d'Hancourt escaped without a scratch… miraculously, the only captain who survived."

He paused, looking into Guglielmo's eyes. Then suddenly he grasped Guglielmo's hands.

"I do love you, my lord," he said with a hard, passionate sincerity that startled everyone. His face had lost the strained mask it always wore. "I do love you, Guglielmo," he repeated. "That's why I'm trying to make you understand, to keep you safe."

Guglielmo bent his face toward Falco's without a word. His head trembled in a faint, terrified assent. Then slowly Falco let go of Guglielmo's hands and turned his face, struggling to regain his composure. He pointed a finger at Dalibor, but now his voice sounded tired, almost toneless. "Here is your traitor. Let me crush him for you."

At the end of his patience, Dalibor stormed forward. "Enough words. Send for the archbishop now."

"With the greatest pleasure," Falco obliged him. He walked to the door, then turned and addressed the prince.

"If you don't mind a piece of advice, my lord Guglielmo, have the girl brought here so she can watch her lover die. Aziza tells me she's hard to manage... I'm sure a sight like that will teach her something." He bowed and closed the door behind him.

Selby went to call the archbishop. Dalibor and Geoffroi left as well. Guglielmo remained alone under the crown, holding onto the arms of his tall marble chair. He closed his eyes and laid his head against it, with a small noise like a sob.

XX

T HE DOOR OF THE LATTICED ROOM was opened cautiously by the outstretched arm of someone who didn't want to come too close. The hand held Kallyna's dress.

"Little witch?" Geoffroi called softly, unseen. She didn't answer, her throat still raw with crying.

"You can come out safely now," Geoffroi insisted patiently.

"All right," she finally replied. The dress was tossed into the room. She put it on and came out.

Geoffroi was standing in the hallway, with his back to the door, one leg swung over the other. He was humming to himself. When he saw her, he grinned to her from ear to ear.

"Great news, little witch. The lord d'Hancourt has asked for the Judgment of God."

"He has asked for what?"

He was walking ahead of her in a hurry. She almost had to run to keep up.

"Lord," he was muttering, "I feel like jumping for joy. What a most absolutely *elegant* way to get rid of the bastard. Why didn't I think of that?"

The revelation of what he had told her became a terrifying truth when they entered the chapel, on the lower floor of the palace. Hands clasped before his bent face with the most absolute concentration, Dalibor was kneeling in front of the altar, with his sword lying on the floor before him like an offering.

She stopped at some distance, lest she distract him, and even Geoffroi tried to smother the sound of his boots. At the light of the candles, Dalibor's hair reminded her of the skeins of gold yarn she used to braid for the finest fabrics.

After some moments Geoffroi softly cleared his throat. Dalibor turned around, saw Kallyna with him, and opened his arms to her. She didn't lift her mouth to his, as they were in a church. His own embrace was sweet as a brother's.

"I meet Falco in an hour" he said simply. "I wish I had done it earlier. I wish I could have spared you all this. But it's good that I do it, because I'm right."

She kissed his hands.

He turned to Geoffroi. "Do you have everything at hand?"

Geoffroi nodded. "The archbishop is on his way. We'll wait for you in the armory."

As she left the chapel with Geoffroi he saw that he was looking at her with a look of reassurance and tenderness; but her heart was pitching like a foundering ship inside her.

It was a night for a wedding, not a duel, she thought as she watched the servants light more candles in the courtyard. Amalfi resembled a flock of white sheep sleeping close together on the side of the mountain. The moon was about to set. The sea made no sound except a soft purring, so faint it seemed to come from a dream.

She walked in Geoffroi's shadow in a silent panic. Geoffroi's calm, almost nonchalant manners sought to encourage her; but they were like a distant fire whose warmth couldn't reach her.

They went into the armory. Suits of mail hung from wooden frames, like scaly bodies without heads or limbs. Maces were bundled in one large basket, lances in a taller one. The walls dripped with iron molded into every point, blade and spike imaginable.

Kallyna thought of the harem, where everything was soft and pleasant just as everything here was hard and unyielding. Men and women had split the world into two opposite realms, like a halved apple that nothing could bring back together. The thought of that chasm filled her with despair.

Geoffroi was running his hands on the weapons with a sensual pleasure, much as he would have touched the body of a woman, smiling his approval at each one of them. He went to sit next to Kallyna, dangling his long arms between his knees.

"It would be good if you stopped moping," he advised her gruffly. "Falco's good with the sword, but my lord is better. Even if my lord dies," he added perversely, "you don't have to worry. I'll get you out of this place one way or another…. Maybe I'll keep you for myself as a souvenir of him."

She raised her face to him wildly, as if ready to sink her nails into his eyes. He burst out laughing. Then got up and left, still laughing. When he came back he was holding Dalibor's sword on both hands like a platter, talking affectionately to it.

"Here, beauty. Let's see what sort of kisses you can blow tonight." He unsheathed it and brought it under the light. "This is steel, you know," he said proudly. "Ten times better than iron… and ten times more expensive. Those Arabs come up with a new invention every day."

Kallyna twisted her hands together. "How long must we wait?"

Geoffroi gave the sword a series of quick strokes with a whetstone, then again examined the edge at the light.

"Not much now."

"You seem so sure of everything," she whispered. "I know I should be too…"

"Must, not should," he said sternly. "Or else you're on the side of the enemy."

Frightened by the harshness in his voice, she didn't speak.

Geoffroi looked at her again, gently.

"I'm only passing on to you what other men have seen fit to teach me," he said. He shook his head. "It's amazing what sort of wisdom we invent to fool ourselves."

He stood up and went to see if Dalibor was coming, leaving the sword next to her. She reached out with her fingertips to touch it. It was so cold, she thought.

❋   ❋   ❋

"Watch every blow from the left, you know he's left-handed. Now, I never did like certain upswings of yours, either. Don't lift too high, or your chest will stand like that of a pheasant ready for the spit."

Geoffroi spoke slowly, soberly, as he helped Dalibor put on his chain mail. He made him raise his arms so he could slip the suit on him, then pulled it down and smoothed the cowl around Dalibor's face.

Dalibor looked at Kallyna with a grin.

"Little witch… are you conjuring up a good-luck spell for me?"

She shook her head, trying hard to smile back.

"You don't need any, lord."

The chain mail encased him from head to knee with its great weight of iron. She didn't think he could even move in it, yet he wore it as comfortably as he did his own skin. She wondered in what way that hard husk he kept so close to his body touched also his soul.

While de Vire was out she had taken off the ribbon from her braid and she had tied it around the sheath of the sword. Dalibor saw the ribbon, and nudged Geoffroi.

"Wouldn't she make the perfect squire?"

Geoffroi, still puttering around the chain mail to check its seams, answered with a grunt of approval addressed both at the seams and at his words. Then he went out again, to call a servant for some light.

Dalibor drew Kallyna into his arms. "Look me in the eyes," he said. "Not just now, but out there too. Let me see you, so I'll remember what I'm doing and do it well."

She could hardly bear to meet his gaze, but she forced her soul into it like a piece of raw clay into the kiln.

"And if I have to die after all—"

"You will not die," she stopped him. "You must still make me a child."

The clean marble flagstones of the courtyard seemed to be waiting for blood, like an expanse of snow for the footprints of birds. Guglielmo sat next to the archbishop, looking as if he were choking on tears. He had already handed over the entire judgment to the archbishop, wanting nothing to do with it. He hardly even looked at Falco anymore.

Geoffroi embraced Dalibor, then went to stand with Kallyna in a corner of the courtyard, as far from Guglielmo as they could. Guglielmo only glanced at the two of them, a glance cluttered with unreadable emotions.

The archbishop raised his arm toward the two adversaries who faced one another in the middle of the courtyard.

"Here begins this Judgment of God, of which I shall be true and rightful witness," he proclaimed. The swords rang out of their sheaths.

Almost unconsciously Kallyna grabbed hold of Geoffroi's hand. Geoffroi crushed her fingers into his own. Mercifully, the pain stopped her from giving sound to the words that kept twisting around in her mind: she could not watch, she would not watch.

Dalibor and Falco stood a few paces apart, motionless. Then Dalibor kissed the blade of his sword and stooped down, ready. Falco began to circle around him like a bird of prey, never taking his eyes off him; then quickly, unexpectedly, he dealt the first blow.

Instantly Kallyna shut her eyes. Her whole body shook in the wake of that dreadful sound.

Geoffroi bent toward her. "I tell you to watch," he whispered savagely. "There is a price to pay for the love of a man like that!" Stiff as a corpse, Kallyna forced herself to open her eyes.

Dalibor sidestepped another blow and retreated. Then he grasped his sword in both hands and stopped a hailstorm of rash, indiscriminate thrusts with the same number of clean and precise counter-thrusts that rustled close to Falco's face like fans. Geoffroi gave a grunt of delight. Kallyna was forced to pull her hand from his, or he would have crushed it.

The combat had prematurely turned into a frenzied, reckless clash. The two aimed at one another with naked fury, at times forsaking the simplest rules of defense and merely lunging at each other, driven only by their hatred. Dalibor groaned at every blow as if to lend strength to his arms with his voice.

Moving so close to the side of the courtyard that the archbishop suddenly sat up startled, Falco struck a blow against one of the pillars, missing Dalibor's face by a matter of inches and sending plaster flying into his eyes. Blinded for an instant, Dalibor swung around helplessly, then jumped to safety. Both he and Falco crouched away from one another for a moment, gasping for breath and drenched with sweat.

At that moment Kallyna realized that the judgment was going to last for a length of time as endless as a deathwatch. Dalibor and Falco would first wear themselves and each other to the bone; only then would the man with the last spark of strength left deal the final blow. This was the sort of terrible patience Malva d'Hancourt had warned her about, the patience to stand still and watch the man she loved more than any other thing in the world dance closer to the edge of the pit.

Dalibor's sword hissed in the air a little lower, a little clumsier each time. Falco's strength was dwindling at the same pace. The sound of the swords was a music of iron shredding the night to pieces. Then suddenly Falco swooped down onto Dalibor and forced him to parry the closest, most dangerous blow yet. As Dalibor tried to duck away, Falco's sword painted a strip of red on the side of his neck. Shrunk against Geoffroi's side, Kallyna tried to smother a cry that seemed to rend all of her.

But at that same moment Dalibor, bent over and gasping for breath, looked across at her from where he was standing. The feel of blood set his eyes ablaze with wrath, the wrath she knew. Instantly he bounced back to his feet; then, with the last spark of strength that fate awaited, he drove Falco all the way back to the wall. When Falco's shoulders were about to touch the wall, one last blow struck the sword out of Falco's hand and sent it skittering on the floor like a pebble on water.

Kallyna was nestling so close to Geoffroi that she could almost feel the beating of his heart. She looked at Falco standing perfectly still against the wall.

He'll let him live, she thought. *He's had his victory now.*

There was too much anger in Dalibor's soul, and the memory of all the pain Falco had brought into his life. He stepped back a bit and planted his feet apart. Falco seemed made of stone.

Mansour would have recognized the way the hand gripped the hilt, the curve of the wrist, the angle of the elbow. High in the air Dalibor's sword described a perfect circle; at some point along that circle Falco's head came off his neck. It fell down and it rolled toward Kallyna's feet. If she hadn't jumped back it would have stopped against her silk slippers like an apple from the tree. Geoffroi saw that she was retching, and turned her face away.

Guglielmo had jumped from his chair with the look of a man in agony. Richard of Selby and the archbishop had to restrain him from lunging at Dalibor with his dagger. He sobbed hysterically. Selby called the servants. Struggling and weeping, kicking like a wounded beast, Guglielmo had to be carried bodily from the courtyard. The archbishop did not stay to declare Dalibor acquitted. Running his hand on his sweaty face, he begged Selby to be taken home.

Dalibor closed his eyes and smiled faintly, as if after a long, pleasantly exhausting night of lovemaking. He came up to Kallyna, put his arms around her and kissed her hair. He touched her face, dazed.

"Please get me out of here," she whispered.

He picked her up so she wouldn't have to step on Falco's severed remains and carried her out of the courtyard, up the stairs, to the door of a room he knew. The palace around them was in an uproar; servants were rushing everywhere. Deaf to everything, Dalibor kicked the door open and then shut behind him. He put Kallyna down, tore back the hood of mail from his face, then fell onto the bed.

The room was surrounded by a balcony of carved stone spilling over with jasmine. Underneath it was Amalfi asleep. The night outside was deep and still. Away on the horizon, between the two different darknesses of sea and sky, the lamps of the night-fishing boats grouped together like the skyline of another city made of tiny dots of light.

For a while Kallyna hovered quietly around him. She pulled off his boots, slipped off his leather gloves and poured him a cup of wine. While he drank she wiped the blood off his neck with a corner of the bedspread.

"I don't like the way you rub yourself on Geoffroi," he said then. "From now on I am the only man on God's earth who can lay a finger on you."

She smiled.

He saw her, and his voice grew full of anger. "Why that smile? Aren't you afraid of me?"

"More than of my own father," she lied.

He nodded, satisfied with her answer, and handed her the empty cup. After some time his breathing slackened down into its regular rising and falling. He pulled her roughly to him.

"You haven't even congratulated me yet," he scolded. "Don't you like to see how strong I am, by god."

She straightened herself up.

"Congratulate you? I should kiss your hands."

But as she was about to do that he took hold of her braid to stop her.

"No," he said. "Don't listen to me when I speak out of nothing but pride. I should know better by now."

He made her lie down beside him.

"This room used to be mine… I brought women here, women who meant nothing to me and for that I hated myself… Seems like a hundred years ago."

He sighed deeply, tired. "Tomorrow I'll go to Roger… leave forever this whining brat who dares to call himself his son. I want to start everything new. I want to show you my home. And If I ever have to leave my home, I'll put a cordon of soldiers around it. Only the Almighty will be able to find you in there."

They lay together in the silence. As if dreading his old loneliness, Dalibor held her against him harshly, mailed still. In the dark he was nothing but a great shadow against the blind eyes of the stars. She didn't know what he was thinking, but that didn't frighten her. Nothing frightened her anymore.

He settled his head on the pillow and fell peacefully asleep. She curled up in his arms. After a while their breath and that of the sea became one.

※　　　　　　※　　　　　　※

She couldn't tell if it was a dream, but it if was, she had never dreamed a more delicious one.

In the faint light of dawn she felt him come closer to her, his body taut and eager against hers still limp with sleep. She sighed, stirring a little, but didn't open her eyes, giving in again to the heaviness that seemed to hold her down on the bed like a silky net. There was a brief feeling of cold as his hand lifted her dress and moved up her skin with a light, almost stealthy motion.

His breath seemed to catch for an instant. Everything was a blur in which nothing was real except the pleasure he was drawing from her. Then as she turned toward him he took her gently, barely resting his weight. She couldn't even be sure he had called her name before he moved away and sleep enveloped her again.

When she woke up it was full daylight. The first thing she saw was his mocking smile while he was trying to wipe the smudge of blood he'd left on her cheek. He had taken off his chain mail and changed into comfortable traveling clothes.

"Lord what a sleeper," he mumbled. "A squadron of Turks could have you in shifts without waking you up."

She laughed. "What makes you think that I was asleep and that I didn't like it. The Turks, I mean."

He lay on top of her, but she fended him off halfheartedly. "I'm hungry. What time is it?"

He kept tugging impatiently at the strings of her dress. "Does it matter? It's time for someone to bring breakfast."

She still tried to stop him. "Then we should get up."

"When I say so," he whispered huskily.

Someone knocked at the door, and he had to stand up to go open, while she tried to smooth over her horribly crumpled dress. The mute girl from the women's quarters brought in a full tray and set it down on a table.

Dalibor smiled to her. "*Shukran* Thank you, Leila."

Kallyna craned her neck toward the tray. "Aren't you going to eat?"

He went out on the balcony. "Later, maybe."

Kallyna looked at him as he stood watching Amalfi underneath him, with his hands on his hips. The sunlight made his shirt look gauzy around the strong lines of his body. It moved her to see him dressed like that, without his shell of iron mail. In her mind she prayed that she would see him every morning like that.

"When do we leave?" she asked, helping herself to some apricots and a slice of *halwa* cake.

"As soon as Geoffroi comes up."

"What about the prince?"

Dalibor shrugged, but without contempt. "The guards say he's locked himself into his room with Falco's body and refuses to see anyone. Sincerely, I wish him a better companion, the next time he chooses one."

Kallyna licked her fingers clean and joined him on the balcony. Down in the harbor a galley was getting ready to set sail. Amalfi had awakened like a beehive to one more day of peaceful liveliness.

She took Dalibor's arm. "You look like the lord of the place. I wish you were. A city like this would be lucky to have you for its master."

He pulled her to him, searching her face. "And you? Are you lucky?"

Her head bent softly back in his hands.

"Oh, lord. If I had words to tell you…"

There was no need for words. Geoffroi, coming into the room, had to wait patiently for their kiss to end. Kallyna saw him, and left Dalibor's arms.

"I'm as glad to see the two of you as I am to see the sun," Geoffroi greeted them. He put his hand on Dalibor's shoulders. "All's ready. We have good horses and an escort of five men. And I'm so damn happy this morning that I won't even ask you where we're going." He threw his arms up. "Just take me anywhere!"

Kallyna looked at Dalibor, who was picking up his sword.

"I wonder if the lord de Vire could tell me where that bundle is that I had with me?" she asked.

"I'll buy you all the clothes you want on our way out," Dalibor said. "Let's just get out of this place."

She looked at him pleadingly. "No, lord, it's not the clothes I want. There's a silver buckle in that bundle… I'd be very sad if I lost it."

Dalibor smiled. "Ah, yes. It must be still in the women's quarter." He turned to Geoffroi and took a bow. "Well, didn't you hear what she asked? Won't you please take care of this matter, *sweet* lord?"

Geoffroi swung his big paw at him, but Dalibor was quick to dodge it. Laughing loudly, de Vire left to look for the bundle.

Dalibor took Kallyna back into his arms. "I told you there's always time for what I want."

Then he stopped, no longer looking at her. His eyes were now riveted to a distant spot beyond the white houses cascading down the mountainside. The look of amazement in his eyes made Kallyna's blood run cold. There was nothing more frightening than the surprise of a man accustomed to all kinds of surprises.

From behind the northern watchtower a fleet of war had appeared, sails struck, oars lashing the water into a white froth. A din of horns, bells and shouts broke out from all over Amalfi, as the city sounded the alarm at one voice. Suddenly the beach swarmed with black dots like an anthill in danger.

"Ships from Pisa," Dalibor gasped. "It must be at least twenty of them!"

The ships kept pushing toward the harbor with unstoppable speed. The galley that they had seen setting sail and that now was barely out in the open, stood caught in their path. From the prow of a Pisan ship a smoking trail of Greek fire arched high in the air. It hit the mast under the flag of Amalfi, showering death onto the deck below. The galley swerved and lurched. Kallyna didn't see it sink only because Dalibor had pulled her away from the balcony and had started to run with her toward the main gate of the palace.

There he found Geoffroi and the five men of their escort. With their heads raised, they were listening to the noise and the cries on the other side of the walls. Dalibor helped Kallyna onto her horse.

"The Pisans are landing," he told Geoffroi. "They'll be up at the gates in no time."

In Geoffroi's eyes was mirrored the same terrified surprise. "Lord God, what do we do?"

Dalibor motioned the soldiers to open the gate. "I don't know. But it's going to be a slaughter, may God call me a liar."

Rashly, Geoffroi made as if to spur his horse through the open gate. "Then let's take the coast road before it's too late," he said.

"Wait!" Dalibor roared. "We're not going anywhere without Guglielmo. Stay here with her, and don't budge until we come back."

Geoffroi looked at the street, where people milled about in a mindless rush. "Look, we'll only waste time," he said. "Guglielmo will come out on his own with Richard."

Dalibor tore himself away from him. "Damn it, Geoffroi, sometimes I almost think you're either a coward or an idiot! Don't you understand that if we leave Guglielmo to the Pisans the ransom they'll ask will be Naples? Six years of war for nothing!"

Chastened, Geoffroi fell silent.

Dalibor was already running toward the prince's quarters. The palace now resounded with cries and footsteps. He could hear the women in the harem shriek in terror above the shouts of the guards. Richard of Selby joined him at a run, sword in hand.

"He's locked himself in," he panted. "The guards won't let me through."

"We'll break the door down," Dalibor said without stopping. "We'll kill the guards, if we have to."

The guards looked like they were standing on live coals. "Please, my lords," begged one of them, "do talk the prince out, or it will be his ruin."

Dalibor made the man move aside. He and Richard put their shoulders against the door and pushed. The door held. The two guards joined in; they all tried again until at last the door gave.

Guglielmo was hiding behind Falco's open coffin. Selby knelt down before him.

"Forgive us, lord, but you are in great danger. The city is being attacked, the Pisans will soon be inside the walls."

"The main gate is still well defended," Dalibor said. "We must reach it before they do."

"But the palace... the women..." Guglielmo babbled.

"Your life, lord!" Dalibor shouted. "Nothing's worth more than that!"

The boy seemed unable to move. He kept clutching the coffin as if it were a lifesaver. Dalibor took him by the arm and forced him to walk out.

"Don't you lay hands on me, d'Hancourt!" Guglielmo seethed. "Don't you touch me or I swear to God I'll hang you for this!"

Dalibor kept dragging him along.

"You may do that," he said. "Once I'll have you standing safely in front of your father, you do just that."

Back at the main gate, Kallyna strained to see if they were coming. Beyond the walls of the palace the sounds of a nightmare reached her closer and closer. Ships sank, the water teemed with bodies. The Greek fire, erupting in black clouds and burning everywhere on the sea, carried a reek of sulfur and charred flesh. The dreaded crossbowmen of Pisa had come ashore.

Finally Dalibor came back, still hauling Guglielmo by the arm. Distraught and terrified, the prince had lapsed into a wordless obedience, and mounted his horse without offering resistance. Surrounded by the soldiers of the escort, the group rode out of the palace's gate. Instantly the crowd in the street stopped them, wild with panic. People clamored around Guglielmo, demanding protection. Not even the soldiers' drawn swords could drive them away.

A woman in tears fell on her knees in front of the prince's horse.

"O lord of our lives, O gracious lord, save my children!" she begged. They were stranded in a living quicksand of desperate terror.

Dalibor tried to make himself heard above the noise.

"Go to the buildings of the shipyard," he shouted. "To the shipyard, it's safe in there."

But the crowd only pressed closer in a frenzy. Dalibor seized a man by the arm and spoke to him alone.

"Get inside the palace. There are weapons, and good strong walls. Lock these people in, hand out the weapons."

The man understood. He and others started to rally the crowd and lead it into the palace's courtyard. Now at last they could put their horses to a canter, breaking dam after dam of people blocking the narrow streets. One of the city gates had already been breached; houses were burning.

Kallyna felt as if she were teetering on the edge of the world. She tried to keep her eyes on Dalibor as if on a beacon while the horses rumbled down toward the main gate. From where they were, they could see that the gate was the core of the worst fighting. The Pisans were trying to force their way in and the soldiers of Amalfi were savagely defending it.

Dalibor reined in and made a quick count of the enemies. "We'll have to charge through," he told the others. "Now, while the rest of them are still coming up from the beach." Geoffroi had to agree.

Dalibor helped Kallyna from her saddle onto his own and fastened her hands around his waist.

"Hold on," he said. "There's no other way out." He drew his sword and dug his spurs into the horse's flanks.

They hurtled down toward the gate like boulders from a mountaintop. With her eyes shut, Kallyna felt the hooves of the horse trampling flesh underneath. No one would ever know whether it had belonged to friend or foe. Dalibor struck down a Pisan who had grabbed hold of his stirrup, and Geoffroi's arm was scratched by the blade of a lance swung high. But they had galloped clear of the gate, and they still didn't know how. Ahead of them now was the coast road, still empty and still safe.

It was then that Kallyna saw the lone crossbowman hiding on top of the curtain wall. The next thing she saw were two soldiers of their escort tumbling off their mounts, pierced through by the three-foot-long arrows.

Dalibor was forced to ease up his horse to avoid crashing against those of the two dead. Turning around to check on Guglielmo who lagged behind, he didn't see the Pisan overhead reload his crossbow and take aim at him.

Kallyna did; as the man crouched down for the shot she stretched out behind Dalibor and threw up her arm as if to catch the arrow. The iron spit ran into her shoulder instead of into Dalibor's neck.

Dalibor felt her body sag against his. He let go of the reins and freed one arm to hold her steady behind him. Geoffroi gave a cry of horror, making Dalibor turn to look. All Dalibor could see was the long black shape of the arrow sticking out of her. She heard him call her, but from what seemed like a very great distance. She had no breath to answer him. She slumped against his back, held only by his arm.

No one could tell how much further down the coast road they galloped, while the carnage raged behind them. When they were well past the last watchtower and could no longer be seen, Geoffroi had to put his horse in front of Dalibor's to make him stop. Dalibor couldn't be persuaded to dismount and look at Kallyna dead. He kept fighting Geoffroi while Geoffroi shouted and cursed. Finally Geoffroi ordered Richard to stay with Guglielmo out of the road, and led the horses to a grove of olive trees. He forced Dalibor to come down and to let go of her.

"Why not me?" Dalibor wondered in a stupor. "Why not me instead?"

"Sweet friend," Geoffroi said wildly, "you'd be dead, and she's only wounded."

"What difference is there?" Dalibor wanted to know.

Geoffroi sat on a rock holding Kallyna in his arms. He laid her head on his arm and ripped the sleeve around the shaft of the arrow.

"Come on, it's nothing serious," he said. "The arrow didn't even go through. We'll pull the damn thing out." When Dalibor put his hand on the arrow, he stopped him. "Your hands are shaking. Let me do it, or you'll ruin her."

Dalibor nodded.

"Oh God," he fretted. "She's bleeding so much."

"I tell you it's all right," Geoffroi countered, rolling up his sleeve. "Thank heaven she's not going to feel a thing… if that can make *you* feel any better. Hold her now."

He took hold of the arrow and moved it gently back and forth to loosen it from the flesh, to see how deep inside it was. Then he pulled it out in one move. The soft lilac cloth on her back was soaked black with blood.

Dalibor took off his shirt and pressed on the wound until the bleeding seemed to stop; then he wrapped his shirt around her shoulder.

Geoffroi checked the arrowhead to make sure it was whole.

"The wound's not deep," he said. "She'll be like new in a couple of weeks."

"Let's hope to God," Dalibor whispered. He cradled her in his arms, caressing her hair away from her face.

"What now, sweet lord?" Geoffroi asked then with a sigh.

"My place is with Guglielmo..." Dalibor said. "I must take him to Roger." He looked up. "Take her to Salerno, to the School of Medicine. And keep in mind that if she dies I'll cut your throat and the physician's, too."

Geoffroi mounted his horse, pulled Kallyna up in front of him on the saddle. He set her against his body and Dalibor helped him tie her to him with his double belt.

"I'll catch up with you later, then," he said.

Dalibor gave Kallyna a last brief caress. "I wish I'd never met her," he said, almost to himself. "She makes me feel like I'm not whole all the time."

Geoffroi took the reins and rode away. Dalibor watched him for as long as he could. Then he returned to Guglielmo and set out in the opposite direction.

For hours Geoffroi cursed the feeling of moist warmth passing from her wound to his chest. He cursed war, love, life, and his horse that wouldn't run fast enough. In his mind he could see what was happening in Amalfi. The Pisans had slashed their way through to the Doge's palace, looking for Guglielmo. They had killed everyone inside, and herded the women off to the ships. They had burst into the prince's room, found Falco's body and thrown it out the window, into the blue tiled pool reddened with blood. They had sacked the palace down to the last silk cushion and ebony chair, then they had set it on fire. Geoffroi thought that if Kallyna had still been in the harem a few hours earlier, they would have never seen her again; and he decided that if Dalibor never thought about that, he would never make him think about that.

When he was under the walls of Salerno, Geoffroi stopped his horse and glanced over his shoulders. In his mind he could see all of white Amalfi going up in a cloud of black smoke. Then he rode toward the School of Medicine.

XXI

THE EVENING SUN GLOWED THROUGH HUGE WINDOWS like the reflection of a fire burning noiselessly outside. Every stained-glass figure carried with it a second universe of shadows, like men and their souls.

Kallyna had regained consciousness some time before. The pain now was stronger than anything she had ever felt, a torturing haze through which she could barely see or hear. Not even the surprise of being still alive could help her out of that throbbing stupor. She searched the face of the man who was carrying her, hoping it was Dalibor. It was Geoffroi, who strode on calling loudly and impatiently for a doctor.

He walked past the garden where the medicinal herbs were grown, past storerooms where scalpels, forceps and cupping glasses were kept. In the library, bindings secured by locks guarded the treasures of books of medicine, biology, philosophy. He peeked into the Hall of Anatomy, where teachers and students crowded around a corpse being dissected. Finally he crossed the long hallway between two wings of cells for the sick.

Finally, seeing a light in one of the rooms, he walked in. The room gleamed with countless ceramic *alberelli* pots neatly labeled and lined up on shelf upon shelf. On one side were opium, henbane and belladonna, on the opposite side myrrh, valerian and aconite. One shelf was reserved to mortars of every size, another to jars full of leeches. On the walls were hung drawings of the human body and sheets of herbal recipes. A woman was sitting at a desk, weighing on scales the ingredients for an infusion. Geoffroi's calls forced to interrupt her painstaking chore.

"Skirts of Saint Anne, is there anybody at all who can show me to a physician in this bloody maze of a place?" he shouted.

The woman turned around. Good-looking and plump, her every gesture seemed to emanate a self-assured cheerfulness, an earthy and pleasant energy. She wore a long man's robe, dusty with the handling of medicinal powders, and her brown hair was cut in bobs like that of a boy.

"My good lord," she chided with knitted eyebrows, "you must be one of the few lucky people who were never in a hospital, or else you'd show a bit more respect for Doctor Quiet."

Baffled, Geoffroi looked around for this doctor, to whom she must be a maid.

The woman motioned him to put Kallyna down. "On that cot there, yes."

Geoffroi didn't want to waste his time with a maid. "Look," he said, annoyed. "I need a physician. Where the hell can I find one?"

The woman looked at Kallyna's makeshift bandage all streaked with red.

"I'm a physician," she said. "Now, won't you please put her down? I must undo these bandages and get to work. She's fainted again... she must be in great pain."

Geoffroi's mouth hung open. "You... a physician?"

The woman prodded him toward the cot and pushed his arms down so he would let go of Kallyna. Her keen grey eyes sparkled with delight at his bewilderment.

"Come on, now." she said amiably, "Don't tell me you didn't know our School is also open to women. I've done my five years of studies, passed all my examinations, and completed my year of practice, just like any male doctor you will find in this… maze of a place, as you call it."

More flabbergasted than before, Geoffroi could only stand aside while she quickly threw the soiled bandages into a hamper. She added surprise to surprise by washing her hands in a basin with soap and water; in field hospitals he had never seen anything resembling that medical procedure.

"At any rate," she went on, "my name is Rebecca Saba. I would like to know yours, and, if you don't mind of course, I would like also to know what happened to this young woman."

Geoffroi began to pace around the room, sniffing at the herbal smells that filled it.

"I'm the lord de Vire. We come from Amalfi, we were attacked by the Pisans there. She got a little present to remember them by."

He looked at Kallyna lying on the cot. "Damn plucky thing to do," he muttered to himself. "Now on top of everything else he owes her his life, too."

He picked up a vial of laudanum, then put it back on the wrong shelf. He eyed the woman with unregenerate mistrust.

"Look, ma'am, I don't want to sound impolite, but…are you sure you can handle this? The lord d'Hancourt has promised to cut my throat if she dies, and he does keep his promises, you know."

"Really," Rebecca mused in tones of good-natured mockery. "Now I understand why you were making so much noise before." She looked at him with a bright smile. "Please don't worry. She's in good hands."

Geoffroi hunched his neck in resignation, getting out of her way.

Rebecca prepared a cauterizing iron and laid it on Kallyna's shoulder with a swift, secure motion. She didn't even wrinkle her nose at the smoke from the burning flesh; but Geoffroi, who had smelled that smoke countless times before, now found it suddenly revolting.

Kallyna was tossing on the cot, as if struggling to come to. He looked at her, then he turned to Rebecca.

"Glad to hear that, ma'am," he said, "because I have this hunch she's going to be the next lady d'Hancourt."

Rebecca was feeling Kallyna's pulse.

"I will take the very best care of her," she reassured him. "Tell the lord d'Hancourt that he has nothing to worry about."

De Vire put Kallyna's bundle on the desk, along with a purse full of money. "For your fee," he said. "I have to go now. Tell her that we'll be back as soon as we can, either of us." He glanced at Kallyna one last time. "Please don't let anything happen to her," he said with a strangely bashful voice, and left.

The room in which Rebecca had put Kallyna was her own study, comfortable and full of sunshine. She had assigned her a nurse by the name of Costanza, who slept in that room and brought her meals. In time, Costanza would also find a place for all the books that cluttered the study, from huge illuminated folios to dog-eared drawing sheets tied together with string. On one of the shelves piled high with notebooks stood a silver menorah. From the windows Kallyna could see the garden with its long, neatly kept rows of herbs shaded by fruit trees, and the fountain and the sundial. High above it rose the great mass of the old Lombard castle.

The School of Medicine was an oasis of serenity in the noisy core of the city. She had learned from Rebecca that it was also the only place in all of Europe where for the first time ever illness was being confronted in a methodical struggle. But being back on her own made Kallyna sad and listless, and the pain from the wound was a constant companion. Rebecca had told her that Geoffroi had promised to return. The woman's company was affectionate and reassuring; but at night Kallyna needed drugs to sleep.

With her medicines, Rebecca brought also news, which was mostly bad. As if the war with Naples weren't enough, the Germans had now crossed the borders of the kingdom and were advancing into Campania, killing and looting. The news made Kallyna feel like a bird without wings. She begged Rebecca to be allowed to get out of bed and start walking again. Rebecca forbade her, as she was still much too weak.

Easter Sunday approached. The wound healed normally, if far too slowly for her. Rebecca spent many an hour in the study, reading and jotting down notes. The rest of the time she spent teaching in the nearby Hall of Biology, visiting the sick or preparing medicinal infusions. To Kallyna she was a constant source of admiration. She was in awe of Rebecca's knowledge, even more so after she learned why Rebecca had chosen to pursue it.

"I gave birth four times," Rebecca told her. "The first time it was twin boys. They and all the others died, some after a few days, some after a few years. My husband and I used to be happy... When the last baby died, so did our happiness. I argued constantly that he must not get me pregnant anymore... I just dreaded the thought. Then I asked him to let me come to the School. I wanted to learn what it was that had taken those five little lives, besides what he calls "the will of God."

"He wasn't the only one who opposed me. My parents raised me in the strictest Jewish faith. They too thought it blasphemous that a woman should challenge God's patience. I ended up having to leave my parents, having to leave my husband, and having to come to the School entirely on my own. So you see, you don't have to pick my story as an example of how women should make their choices. And if you honestly believe in the will of God, be satisfied with it. It's a pleasant delusion, certainly more comfortable than doubt."

By the time Holy Thursday came, Kallyna's wound pricked and stung horribly, but at least it was a sign of healing. She had resigned herself to a lonely Easter. That evening she lay in bed remembering Easters past, back home where everything seemed so simple even though it had never been that.

At that time of twilight, mass was being celebrated in Tropea as all over the kingdom. At the end of it the priest walked down the altar steps carrying a gilded basin full of water. Twelve among the poorest of the town sat in two rows in the middle of the church. As Christ had done with the twelve apostles, the priest would wash their feet, bending in humility before them while his robes billowed on the church's floor.

The women baked great loaves of bread in memory of the Last Supper, and the priest blessed them and broke them, handing out the pieces to the faithful. Kallyna could still see Vasili carrying home that morsel of bread in his big callused hands. Once he had been poor enough to sit among the twelve.

Her quiet daydreaming was brusquely interrupted by Rebecca's voice just outside the open door of the study. She heard her and a fellow physician engaged in a lively discussion about the course of a certain illness. Unable to win the argument, Rebecca finally stormed into the room and shut the door behind her.

That noise, although neither unexpected nor loud, shook Kallyna from head to toe like a slap. From her shoulder an excruciating pain shot to her neck and jaws, fastening them together like a vise.

Rebecca muttered a few last comments on the stubbornness of her colleague, then sat down on Kallyna's bed.

"Is something wrong?" she asked.

Kallyna tried to answer. Another terrible spasm locked the muscles around her mouth.

Rebecca frowned.

"Lie still," she said. "I'll send in Costanza."

She left the room and made her way to the Library, up on the third floor. She searched nervously among the books lined on the carved shelves in their bindings of gilded leather. She ran her fingers on the titles in Arabic, Hebrew, Latin, Greek. At last she found the title she was looking for, the *Aphorisms* of Hippocrates. Quickly she turned the great pages thick with ink, then stopped and put her hand under a line of Greek writing.

"A spasm occurring around the jaws a few days after a wound is fatal," she read. "Those who are attacked by this illness either die within four days or, if they recover, are cured forever. Such is the nature of tetanus."

❋   ❋   ❋

By evening on Good Friday the *Sepolcri* were ready. Every crucifix was wrapped in cradles of black veils. The candles seemed to play among the long ribbons like naughty children at a funeral. Great vases of new wheat were grouped together in a pale-green carpet in the middle of the nave, the wheat from which the Easter cakes would be made.

Rebecca had told her. Kallyna's mind remained painfully lucid, enough to anticipate in terror the next convulsion of the lockjaw surging through her body. At first she had cried and begged desperately for help. She could not die alone, she pleaded. Dalibor could not come back and find just a piece of damp earth. She was without comfort, weeping and beating her fists on the wall. Rebecca was forced to drug her into a blank-eyed drowsiness.

Out in the streets every light was out. A dark murmuring crowd surged through them, its slow, halting pace marked by the roll of a lone drum. The image of Mary, clad in a black mantle, staggered on the shoulders of the men who carried her. She was looking for Jesus, asking for him at every door. Nobody could tell her where he was, and so the crowd went on with her, moaning with her, seething in the darkness like ghosts.

At the doors of the cathedral the eerie procession stopped. The doors were shut. On top of the stairs the bishop was waiting. When Mary begged him to be led to Jesus, the bishop unveiled a statue of the dead Christ.

"Come, Mary, take Thy son!" the bishop cried out. The doors of the cathedral swung open and the drum gave a long thundering roll. In a tide of sobs, Mary mounted the steps and was swallowed by darkness inside the cathedral.

Kallyna's face was awash with tears. Rebecca kept her face hidden in her hands.

Holy Saturday dawned in tense, silent wait. Every bell in the kingdom was mute; their happy sound must not be heard on that day of bereavement. Only the wooden rattles cackled in the empty churches. But under Mary's black robes peeked already the blue mantle of triumph edged with gold.

All day long, neglecting her other duties, Rebecca sat by Kallyna's bed. She left only once, to go talk to her elders, her revered teachers. Their answer was one: Kallyna's life was about to end. Her anger at that death was great, she who had seen so many deaths. She went to walk alone in the garden, trying to clear her mind.

Perhaps her parents and her husband were right, she thought. She seemed to have gained nothing by all her prying into nature's secrets. But her soul fiercely rebelled at the thought. She wanted to tear to pieces all books of medicine and every rule they contained. In the garden the trees nodded and the sundial cast a shadow like a blunted ax. After some time she clenched her fists and went back to her study in a hurry, hoping she wouldn't be too late.

It was night now, and she had to work by candlelight. First she prepared a potent sedative mixture and made Kallyna drink it. Then, when it had worked its effect, she slashed the wound open with her scalpel and drained it thoroughly, scooping out every particle of infected tissue with a controlled, determined fury. Finally she cauterized the wound again, bandaged it, and sat down to wait, dozing off with her arms on her desk.

About an hour before midnight Costanza woke her up to tell her that a man had come looking for Kallyna. From the end of the hallway Rebecca could hear his spurs breaching the silence of the great building. Immediately she stepped out of the study and closed the door.

Dalibor was smiling, impatient to go in.

"My lady, I want to thank you from my heart for everything you did," he greeted her in a hurry, moving toward the door.

Rebecca barred his way.

"My lord d'Hancourt, I'm sorry."

Dalibor frowned.

"Why are you sorry? What's wrong?"

Rebecca tried to assuage the look of threat in his eyes with a smile. For a moment she thought he would really kill her as he had promised.

"She has lockjaw," she forced herself to say at last.

Dalibor seemed to crumple. He had dreaded that word so often himself in the wake of battles, when the smallest piece of metal that came his way could carry the disease.

Quietly Rebecca repeated the confession of her defeat. "My lord, I'm sorry."

Dalibor got hold of the doorknob and burst into the room. He stopped by Kallyna's bed.

"Is she dead?" he whispered.

"No. Indeed, she may yet survive," Rebecca said. "Lockjaw, as you certainly know, either kills within four days or disappears forever."

Dalibor bent down to listen to Kallyna's harsh, labored breathing. "And what day is this?"

Rebecca sighed.

"The fourth."

He dragged a stool by the bed. For a long time he sat there, with his face in his hands. He was glad that she was in her drugged sleep, that the grief was all his own. The weight of his pain was crushing.

"She just can't leave me like this," he said. "I thought I'd have more time…" He shook his head. "I've done everything wrong. I've given her nothing but pain, from the very first day… and now I've killed her. If she thinks I don't care enough, I will go mad. O sweet, sweet God. I never even asked her how old she is." Rebecca checked Kallyna's pulse and didn't speak. Then she took some beeswax and put it in Kallyna's ears; it was almost midnight, soon the Resurrection would ring out all over the city.

It was a warm, starry night. The silence had grown deeper all over the city. The deacons stole up the bell towers to untie the bells' ropes. From the cathedral the voices of the faithful sounded like the distant murmur of a river.

Sitting by the bed, Dalibor kept whispering to himself. In such a short time he had to resign himself to losing her; but he didn't even know where to start.

Regrets crowded his mind, like noisy petitioners brawling to be heard. "I could have done so many things… I could have burned my whip before setting foot in Tropea. I could have comforted her when she was scared, I could have made a baby with her."

Suddenly he stood up and looked at Rebecca.

"My lady, where can I find a priest?"

"The chapel's on the other side of the garden," she answered. "There's always someone there."

"Thank you," Dalibor said. "The least I can do for her is send her to God as my wife."

"If she lives," Rebecca interrupted him.

"If she lives," he promised, "no wife will be loved by a man more than she will."

The old priest had to be dragged to Kallyna's bed, after Dalibor had barely given him time to grab his prayer book.

"But it's not proper," the priest kept complaining, "not at all proper. There are precise rules and ways…"

"If I must get down on my knees before you, Padre, I will," Dalibor begged him. "Do understand. There is no time for the notification to the bishop."

Rebecca came forward.

"Please, Padre. If this young woman could speak she would give you her full consent. I'm sure God won't mind for this once."

"Donna Rebecca, baptisms can be administered *in extremis*," the priest countered. "Weddings are a different story… not quite as simple as my lord imagines."

Dalibor spoke to him again with urgency.

"I beg you, listen to me. Tomorrow I will do all that's needed. It will be proper, I promise you."

The priest looked at him, then at Rebecca, and finally nodded. "We need another witness."

"I'll call Costanza," Rebecca said. As Costanza rushed in, Dalibor looked for the signet ring Kallyna wore around her neck and slipped it off the chain. Rebecca took Kallyna's hand and tidied up her hair on the pillow.

"*In nomine Patris, et Filii, et Spiritus Sancti,*" the priest began.

A thunder of bells broke out from every church. Midnight had struck, the wait was over. Kallyna's face was serene. Dalibor stood beside her straight and shy as any bridegroom.

"Do you take this woman to be your wife before God and all men?"

The bells rang and rang wildly. The shouts of the faithful in the streets rose loudly as if at the end of a war. Flickers of light blossomed everywhere, kindled from one candle to another.

"I do," Dalibor said, in a clear unwavering voice.

The cathedral's door sprang open. Surrounded by a blaze of light, the bishop walked to the threshold holding in his hands a sheet full of rose petals.

"*Christos anesti!*" he announced with the old Greek words. "Christ is risen!" And at one voice the faithful roared the response, "*Aleithos anesti!* Truly He is risen!"

Kallyna moaned softly in her sleep. The priest addressed her with the benedictions of the bride "May she be faithful as Ruth, joyous as Sarah. May she be virtuous and fruitful."

He saw Dalibor dropping his head with a motion of anguish, and quickly turned the page of his prayer book.

"Do you take this man to be your husband before God and all men?" he asked then to her who couldn't speak.

Rebecca held Kallyna's hand tighter in her own and answered for her.

"I do."

"*Ego conjungo vos in matrimonio, in nomine Patris, et Filii, et Spiritus Sancti.* Amen."

Dalibor put the signet ring on Kallyna's finger and kissed her forehead. It had been brief, like the time they had left. The old man left with Costanza. He asked Rebecca to stay with him a little longer.

They sat together, while the bells died out and the night thinned into the long hours before dawn. Rebecca checked the incision, then bandaged it again. She had told him that she had reopened and drained the wound, but without leading him to believe that that would save Kallyna's life.

Dalibor sat all night nestling Kallyna in her arms. He prayed and cursed and wept and then was silent again. Finally toward dawn he begged her to go get some sleep. Rebecca obeyed reluctantly, reminding him first to call her at the slightest change.

Beyond the garden a chalky white light was creeping toward the sundial. All of Salerno was now soundly and contentedly asleep. Easter Sunday would be a day of noisy rejoicing. Lent ended, food would be plentiful even in the poorest house. In the market vendors piled up the round Easter loaves with eggs nestling in the crust like gems set in golden rings. Winter was conquered, death defeated. Nature received the congratulations of those she nourished, like a new mother receives the good wishes of her guests. It was a feast of abundance and love.

Alone as he had never been in his life, Dalibor waited for sunrise; quietly now, without any strength left. He made up his mind that when he went to the bishop he would pay to cancel every wedding ceremony scheduled for all of the following day. He would force upon the entire city the burden of his pain, foul the day for everybody to remember.

The thought of the future terrified him. For a moment he had been granted a chance of redemption, a glimpse of deliverance. Now he had nothing to look forward to but a lifetime of his own loathed and inescapable occupation — war. Friends could betray him any day, and lovers any night; the only person who wanted him just as he was would not be there anymore. By the age of forty he would lash his children and curse the name of God like an old drunkard.

The sun came up. In Tropea the *Confronta* was being made ready. Deep in her difficult sleep Kallyna found herself once more surrounded by the crowd gathered in Piazza Portercole.

Vasili had found a high place for her so she could see, because she was still no taller than his elbow. On his shoulders he carried Arni, even younger than she. He had bought each of them an Easter bun, and they were nibbling it delightedly. At one end of the square stood the statue of Mary, still wearing her black mantle of mourning; at the opposite corner, hidden from Mary's eyes, was Jesus wearing a great banner fringed with gold.

It was a magnificent April morning. May idled around the corner like a boy sent to deliver a love note. Neia had been able to bring her first roses to bloom, and their scent was like that of a new bride.

Vasili took Kallyna under his arm. "Look!"

From the back door of the church a third statue had crept out, carried by the strongest of the town's young men. It was Saint John, the messenger. Michele craned his neck from under the wooden pedestal, looking at Sila with a flashing smile of pride, and Sila blushed in her young girl's love.

Saint John went over to Mary and gave her the news that her son was alive; but she could not believe him, and the messenger had to return to Jesus. Three times he shuttled back and forth at a run, as the young men strained under the heavy statue.

If a confrontation like that had really taken place on some dusty road of Galilee, the bystanders would have behaved just like the crowd in Piazza Portercole. They called out passionately to the three images, urging John to try again, Mary to believe, Jesus to show himself. The children pointed Christ out to the Virgin, to show her where he was hiding.

Kallyna clapped her hands with impatience. The scarlet cloak of the messenger ran like a flame back and forth, faster each time.

"Father, why won't she believe him?"

Finally, in a hush of anticipation, Jesus and John walked together toward Mary. She took a few uncertain steps and faced her living son. Christ's banner waved in the morning sunlight. All her bewildered anguish was swept away by the joy of the recognition. Amidst shouts of triumph she ran toward Jesus, as her mourning robe fell revealing a shimmering cloak of pale-blue silk studded with gold stars. The crowd seemed to burst with jubilation.

Happy, Kallyna brushed the cake crumbs off her pretty new dress. Suddenly someone shouted. The crowd around her parted in confusion. A man on horseback, whose face she couldn't see, came charging down the square. She grasped Vasili's sleeve, screaming in terror.

Knocking down the statues, the man plunged toward her, scooped her up and carried her away, no one knew where.

XXII

I N THE AFTERNOON DALIBOR WENT TO THE HOUSE of the bishop and had the wedding registered in the canonical books. Then he made his way to the street where they had told him the coffin-makers had their shops.

Salerno was deserted. The market was closed, the churches empty. No one seemed to be out except beggars and stray dogs. From a window he heard the voices of men and women seated around their festive meal and happily singing. A young man hurried homeward carrying a gift for his beloved.

He wandered aimlessly for a number of hours, fighting the tears that kept coming back to his eyes. The clear sunlight seemed to pierce him through. He found the street he had been looking for; the coffins were lined up by the closed doors of the shops. He stopped and looked in horror at the parade of black boxes leaning against the wall like grim, broken-down whores. Then he turned around and hurried away.

He ended up in the cathedral, at the grave of his parents. He sat watching their images for a long while. His thoughts were like the candle stubs left in the rack by the altar. They gave a dim, smoky light that made even the face of

God look like that of a leper. His foot scratched the marble floor where he would have her buried. Then he entrusted her to his mother and left.

While he returned to the School of Medicine he started to think about what he would do now. He would look for Mansour first, then go back with him to Naples, where the rest of the army was. Frightened by the advance of the Germans, the city seemed finally willing to submit to Roger's rule and protection. When that war ended, he would take the warship George of Antioch had offered him and sail off to some other war somewhere. At least he belonged to a profession that was always in demand.

Rebecca had gone back to Kallyna's bedside during that time. She told him that her fever had abated, and that there had been no convulsions in several hours. She sounded hopeful, but his unremitting desperation was beyond her reach.

The evening came with the subtle sadness of the holiday too long awaited and too quickly passed. By now Dalibor was so numb that he no longer spoke a word. He contented himself with snuggling close to Kallyna's bed like a chilled beggar at the warmth of a bonfire. Rebecca couldn't bear to look at him, at anybody reduced to such helplessness. When a fellow doctor called her from the Hall of Anatomy, she was almost relieved to leave.

It grew dark. Dalibor was still trying to make up his mind. All he knew was that he didn't want to be there at her last breath; but he could not find it in his heart to leave her. At last he stood up. He looked at her one last time, kissed her mouth and went to the door. On the threshold he sighed. An instant later he realized that the sigh hadn't come out of his lips. He turned around and saw that Kallyna had opened her eyes.

He stood riveted to the spot, in the dark of the doorway. Kallyna stretched her arms out of the blanket. As she did that the signet ring shone above her like a small star. She frowned, wondering why it was on her finger. She turned her head toward the door, searching with her eyes the tall shadow that seemed made out of stone.

Dalibor stepped out of the dark.

"Why don't they ring the bells now, the fools," he whispered.

Kallyna held her arms out toward him. Slowly, dazed, he lay down next to her on the bed.

"You came!" she said. "I can't die now, can I?"

He was fighting for breath, unable to speak. On his face was the mark of a fear that had been harrowing and deep. Somewhere in his soul it had left a scar just like the ones he carried on his body.

"Don't you ever play another trick like that on me," he gasped, and as he kissed her he cursed her, frantic. "Damn you, damn you. Don't ever do that again to me, Kallyna d'Hancourt."

She pulled away from him, as if trying to catch the echo of those last two words. Then she twisted her mouth.

"I'm dreaming again."

"No, no, no," he shouted, laughing and rocking her in his arms, pressing her to him like a man who'd been granted a pardon from the gallows. He took her hand, showed her the ring.

"Look, wife, look!"

Emptied of whatever little strength she had regained, she went limp in his arms, too weak to say a word.

Rebecca rushed into the room, alarmed by the loud voices. Dalibor lifted his mouth from Kallyna's and looked at her wildly.

"She doesn't die, Donna Rebecca," he said breathlessly. "Not this time, not today."

Rebecca put her hands in her lap and shook her head, smiling. "Such a sweet way you have of making a prognosis, my lord. And I do take it for a true and definitive one, too." She went to the bed and embraced Kallyna. "How do you feel?"

Between Kallyna's open arms life seemed to be rushing back in triumph. "If I could even move one step I would dance, Donna Rebecca."

Rebecca felt her pulse, her neck and jaws. "Dear God," she murmured. "I don't think I've ever been so happy to see one of my patients cheat the odds," she said with a pensive smile.

She hugged her again. "Welcome back," she whispered. "Welcome back." Then she looked up at Dalibor. "I imagine you will want to stay here until she's fully healed. I'll have a room made ready for you right away."

Dalibor was quick to frown. "A bed, you mean. In *this* room."

Rebecca stood up, grinning. "My lord, Kallyna will need her own good time to recover, her own good rest. I'm afraid your honeymoon will have to be delayed a bit."

Dalibor flashed her a scowling glance, grumbling under his breath. The moment Rebecca was out of the room he moved toward the bed. But Kallyna raised her hand, smiling bravely.

"I'll be up and about sooner than you think..." she ventured.

He stopped and squinted at her. "So much the worse for you, wife. It all adds up to your debts, and those I always collect to the last penny," he said.

She was laughing and sobbing, quietly

"Husband, what will we do?"

"We will live, wife. We will make love, we will eat and we will drink and we will go hunting... and if we don't know what to do, we will sit around asking ourselves what are we going to do."

✻   ✻   ✻

Time had finally found a peaceful rhythm, like a river returning to its bed after a flood. May that year was so warm it made them wish they could spend it all on the deck of a ship. They talked together, under their breath even when there was no need. There was so much to tell.

Nothing that happened outside their room mattered much. Dalibor had become a deserter, and he knew it well. His sword, untended, rusted in its sheath. He had no news of the war, and sought none. Had the Germans taken Salerno, he would have let them ride all the way to the front door before he took notice.

"This is the most dangerous thing I've ever done," he told her, "and the happiest I've ever been. If my father were alive he would wise me up with his belt."

At night Kallyna fell asleep to the sound of his voice. He smiled, got up and left, to sleep soundly in his own bed. One day he came back from the market with an armful of dresses for her, silk, brocade, furs. He looked everywhere for a wedding present, and found a sewing basket all threaded with ivory and gold. He yelled at her if she didn't eat everything on her plate, if she tried to walk too much too soon. When at last Rebecca allowed him to move Kallyna's bed into his room, he was no more her husband than he had been all through the past days.

"Are you going to sleep with me every night, husband?"

"Every sweet god-given night, wife."

"That's not true. You'll be away months, and years, making war."

"Then I will leave you my children to keep you company."

"But Rebecca says we must wait."

"We will. Nine months at least."

And every time he took her he never ceased to wonder.

"How can it be... You feel so small sometimes, small as a child, but you give me the strength of two men. Let me sink to the core of you. Let me sink deep, and good. Don't let go of me."

On the feast day of Saint George he went to the barracks in Piazza Portanova to get some soldiers for his escort. He found the place packed with people. The soldiers wobbled drunkenly in the arms of the prostitutes who had flocked there in droves to celebrate some wonderful occasion. He plowed through to the sergeant's booth and asked him what the rejoicing was all about.

The sergeant lifted a sloshing cup of wine.

"A miracle, my lord," he answered tipsily. "A miracle from Saint George, the patron saint of soldiers!"

Dalibor put his hand on the man's chest, ordering him to explain himself. The man's face was all one smile.

"Naples has surrendered. King Roger entered the city this morning. It's over, my lord, the war is over!"

Without a word, Dalibor raced out and leaped onto the saddle. Kallyna head him coming at a run.

311

"Get up, wife," he shouted from the hallway. "We're going away." He gathered up her clothes all in a heap and started bundling them into the blanket.

"Where are we going?" Kallyna asked. "What's happened?" He put his arms around her, out of breath. "Roger's in Naples. The war is over. This war, at least."

He left her and started packing again. "You can ride now, can't you? It's only a three-day journey."

She pulled the clothes from his hands and went on packing herself. "If I'm with you I can do anything."

"Then I'll call Costanza to help you, and I'll go talk to Rebecca." He nuzzled her hair. "God, I love how you smell of warm bedsheets... You know where we go from Naples, wife? Straight to my home in Monreale. No more roaming."

She hung from his neck. "God bless you forever, husband."

They were ready in minutes. At the door of the School of Medicine they thanked Rebecca and kissed her goodbye with all their gratitude and affection. Rebecca looked at Kallyna with a strange melancholy on her face.

"I guess I will never know what saved you in the end," she said. Then she smiled, reconciled to her destiny that was like charting a few islands of certainty in a vast ocean of chance.

"If there is a God who will listen," she said, "I pray that he keep you. I have a feeling you two will last... unlike so many others. *Mazel tov,* from my heart." She stood watching them as they rode away. Kallyna turned to wave at her one last time; she thought that Rebecca looked so very lonely.

Dalibor had wrapped her in his cloak and seated her snugly in his saddle; sideways, so she could sleep leaning against him during the journey. Salerno was so lively that guards were posted by the market stalls. People ran everywhere in the streets celebrating the end of the war. The shops were a riot of merchandise, the bargaining a battle of words.

Dalibor swept his arm around him. "Anything you want is yours. Just say, 'I want this, and I want that, and I want that over there.'"

"Really," she challenged him, laughing.

"Really," he countered. "Which reminds me that I must buy you a couple of servants. We'll stop by the slave market before we leave." He turned his horse, headed for that corner of the marketplace.

Kallyna put her hands on the reins as if to stop him. "Husband... do I really need slaves?" She smiled. "After all, how long does it take me to get dressed in the morning? I don't have to work much harder than that these days."

He was waiting for a cart to move out of his way. "What do you mean, do you need any slaves. There's a house of twenty rooms to take care of in Monreale."

The cart wouldn't budge. He waved his hands at the driver, busy by the door of a pawnshop.

Kallyna twisted her wedding ring around her fingers.

"Husband, I know, but... my mother and my sister were taken away as slaves... It would be like having them scrub floors in my very home, and I—"

She felt him jerk the reins up with a sudden gesture of anger.

"You must learn one thing from the beginning, Kallyna," he said without looking at her. "You are not a fisherman's daughter anymore. You are the duchess d'Hancourt, and the duchess d'Hancourt does not work. You can weave and sew and embroider if you want... if you're so afraid that you'll get bored in my house. But you will not scrub floors, and that is as true as the Godhead."

She breathed in. Her voice was low and pained.

"Husband," she whispered, "now you're speaking to me as if I were a slave myself."

"You and this damned talking back of yours!" he shouted. "Just do as I say, for a change. And start calling me 'my lord,' like every other wife."

Kallyna forced herself to be silent. Behind her he now felt as hard as a shield.

They reached the slave market; he stopped the horse. There was a black-skinned woman tied to a pole, being inspected by a customer. She wore curious bracelets of leather and beads around her ankles. Kallyna never knew what the woman looked like; she could not bear to look at her face. She loathed that ritual as much as Vasili had.

Dalibor watched and nodded with a strained attention. At the highest bid the auctioneer swung his cowbell, and the woman was bought off. Her dusty feet followed the hooves of a horse out of the marketplace. When the second item was brought to the pole, some of the bystanders wondered contemptuously what price that poor creature could possibly fetch.

"Which one of you good people is willing to do a charitable deed and purchase this young boy fallen on hard times?" the auctioneer announced. "He's offering himself for sale of his own will, and he's an excellent bargain. Just put some food in his belly and he'll work like a donkey."

Dalibor spurred the horse.

"No use wasting time here," he muttered.

As he turned the horse around, Kallyna glanced in the direction of the pole.

"Maso!" she cried out in surprise.

"Who are you calling?" Dalibor asked.

"That boy, my lord. He was with me at the Bear's Inn… Maybe he knows whether Mansour ever came back to Salerno."

"Then I want to talk to him," Dalibor said.

"The knight of the white eagle has offered nine ducats," the auctioneer declared. "Who gives me ten? Nice round number, ten ducats."

Kallyna had never seen Maso so ragged and dirty. He was skin and bones; he must be starving to death. She didn't want to provoke Dalibor's anger again, but the sight of the boy was making her eyes sting.

"My lord," she ventured, "while I was alone in this city that boy helped me whenever he could. You told me to name what I wanted to buy… I want to buy him his freedom."

Dalibor shook his head to himself. Then he took out his money purse and held it in front of her face. "I guess I must be more careful about what I say to my wife," he said, but his voice wasn't harsh.

The auctioneer was about to swing his cowbell again.

"Ten ducats!" Kallyna shouted, waving the money purse at him. "I offer ten ducats!"

The man's face was all contentment. "The kind-hearted young lady just bought herself an errand boy!"

Kallyna slipped down the saddle and made her way to the pole. Maso was staring at her without much curiosity, a rope tied around his neck. Kallyna put the ten coins into the auctioneer's hand, then helped Maso take off the rope.

"Get this thing off your neck," she said, throwing it away. She led him to where Dalibor was waiting.

From the saddle, Dalibor looked down at her.

"Well now, are you happy? Excellent bargain indeed," he commented, cocking back his head.

Kallyna didn't look at him. "Ten ducats is what you would pay for a pair of slippers, my lord," she said evenly.

Maso wiped his nose. "Mistress, am I going to your house now?" he asked.

"No, Maso, my house is much too far from here."

She glanced up at Dalibor. "With my lord d'Hancourt's permission, I'm going to find a place where they can take care of you. I'll ask around, someone here should know."

A young woman who was nursing a baby overheard her. She pulled at Kallyna's sleeve. "There's the monastery of San Giovanni," she said, "just outside the main gate. They take in orphans for an honest sum."

Kallyna glanced again at Dalibor, waiting for his answer.

"All right, all right," he said, then motioned her to get back in the saddle.

There was money left in the purse he had given her; she pressed it into Maso's hands.

Suddenly Maso smiled. He took her hand and kissed it.

"I would have liked to go with you, mistress," he said. "When you want to go out of the inn again, you can still call me."

"Ask him about Mansour," Dalibor said impatiently.

"Maso, do you remember that… my father, do you remember my father who was with me at the Bear's Inn?" Maso motioned yes. "Do you know if he's come back?"

"He came looking for you at the inn," Maso answered. "A few days ago. I told him you had left, and he seemed very sad to hear it. Then they took him to jail."

"To jail!" Dalibor shouted. "Who took him to jail?"

Maso hunched his shoulders.

"I don't know… Some soldiers came and took him away."

Dalibor cursed between his teeth.

"The jail in Piazza Portanova?" he asked. Maso nodded. "Then that's where we're going."

Then he looked at Maso's haggard face, and his voice softened.

"You just earned your ten ducats, you know."

The young woman with the baby took Maso under her arm, smiling to him kindly.

"I'm going to take you to Padre Bernardus," she said. "He's old and a little deaf, but he'll let you eat all the buns you want if you save a couple for his pigeons."

Maso followed the woman, his head turned back to look at Kallyna. Then he disappeared in the marketplace crowd.

The jailhouse in Piazza Portanova was an old, ugly building the color of rust. The six soldiers that Dalibor had chosen for his escort were waiting for him in the courtyard, playing a game of *morra* by the executioner's block. He called them to stay with Kallyna, then went in right away. Kallyna thought that she would not want to be in the shoes of the jailer.

The man was reduced to silence and to obedience as soon as Dalibor mentioned his name and his rank. He handed Dalibor the keys and got out of his way, bowing low. The cell was pitch-dark and stank. Mansour blinked painfully at the light from the door, covering his eyes with his hands. His clothes were in rags, and he had been flogged; the red welts on his back were unmistakable.

Dalibor clasped him gently in his arms. "Look where I have to find you, my dearest of friends," he said, with a tone of remorse. "But thank God I find you alive."

At the sound of his voice, Mansour's face wrinkled into a smile of joy.

"God must have been deafened by my prayers, my lord," he said serenely, "because now He blinds me in His turn." His eyes wandered for a few moments, unseeing; then they slowly opened up.

"You are alone," he worried.

"She's outside. And I will spend the rest of my life thanking you for bringing her to me."

He looked at Mansour's ragged clothes and battered body, shaking his head. "No need to ask you how they've treated you…"

"No need, my lord," Mansour answered.

"I think I know who I should thank for this last favor," Dalibor said.

"So do I," Mansour said. "I keep wondering why they did not kill me. Surely Falco da Torre did not mean to keep me locked in a jail cell forever."

"He didn't have the *time* to kill you, my dear Mansour" Dalibor said. "I didn't give him any. Remember all that hacking of sheep's heads you made me do in every damned butcher shop back home? It finally paid off."

Mansour's face lit up with delighted pride. "What a most comforting piece of news," he said. "I knew there was a reason why I was bought into the house of the d'Hancourts."

As they reached the front door, Mansour saw Kallyna out in the courtyard, and stopped.

"Your mother, God bless her soul, was very fond of her. Before she died she made me swear that I would guard her with my life, as I would guard you. And she rewrote her will… My instructions were that if you had died I was to split everything equally with her."

Dalibor smiled. "I thought so. But I'm alive, you see, and so she gets nothing…" He nudged him in the ribs. "Only a piece of paper that says she's my wife."

Mansour took him by the arm. "*Mashallah* !" he rejoiced. "Now that great woman can truly rest in peace." He looked again at Kallyna. "You know, my lord, she is brave," he mused. "True, sometimes she behaves more like a baby in arms than a duchess d'Hancourt, but still she is fearless enough to survive every war… including the ones you two will wage between yourselves, in the fateful manner of all married couples."

Startled by those last words, Dalibor looked him askance.

"You don't read minds now too, do you?"

"Why, I—" Mansour began. Then he knit his eyebrows. "Already?"

When Kallyna saw Mansour, she jumped down the saddle and ran to him. She was too happy to see him to remember that that wasn't the proper, sober greeting for her husband's servant.

Equally happy to see her, Mansour bowed his head.

"My lady d'Hancourt," he intoned, with a good-natured tone of mock importance.

Stung, Kallyna stepped away from him. Dalibor had ordered her to call him 'my lord,' and now Mansour too treated her so coldly… She struggled not to let either man see the tears that were welling up in her eyes.

She nodded toward Dalibor's horse.

"Shall I ride with you like before, my lord?" she asked in a whisper.

Dalibor crushed her to him and pressed his mouth on hers.

"I'm not your my lord," he grumbled. "I'm your husband."

She looked up at him, warily.

"Then it's not the same thing?"

Dalibor made a face.

"To imbeciles, yes," he said, trying to sound pedantic. "You and I, wife, have always known better."

She beamed; she had to tell him how pleased she was to hear him say that, pleased to death.

He helped her mount.

"Find a horse for my friend, and some clothes," he ordered the soldiers. When the soldiers found them, they took the road to Naples.

❈ ❈ ❈

On the mountains of Cava dei Tirreni the air had the coolness of new, ripe green. There was a rippling of small streams and waterfalls around the shady path. The horses went at a comfortable pace. Kallyna dozed off from time to time in Dalibor's arms. His voice and Mansour's lulled her with their familiar, beloved sound.

The hunt in those woodlands must be good. With their eyes and ears the two men seemed to follow imaginary quarries, dreamily. Ahead of them Mount Vesuvius gathered around its summit a blanket of clouds, like a giant at bedtime. That night Kallyna dreamt that she was making a baby, and the dream made her happy.

"Red in the morning, sailor take warning," said Mansour when they set out the following day, watching a sky that seemed to drip watered blood. They were approaching the Sarno river, headed for the ferrymen's hamlet.

While they rode, Mansour couldn't resist narrating the tale of Kallyna falling into another river. Dalibor laughed and she protested that it was funny only because she hadn't drowned. When they came to the ferrymen's huts there was not a living soul in sight. The rafts were lined up along the riverbank with the oars nearby. It looked as if they hadn't been used in days.

Dalibor signaled silence. He dismounted and cautiously crept up to the door of one of the huts, sword in hand. He stopped to listen; then he kicked the door down and put his head in. The place was empty, untouched. In the light rain every leaf seemed to rustle suspiciously around them.

He lowered his sword. "I guess this means we won't have to pay toll," he said nervously. He waved to the soldiers. "Start with the horses. Keep your eyes open."

The soldiers didn't look happy at the prospect of the extra work; but they obeyed silently, out of habit. Dalibor looked impatient to get the crossing done. There was worry in the curtness of his orders. Once the horses were ferried across, the soldiers came back to help the travelers onto the rafts. Dalibor handed them Kallyna first. He glanced again at the deserted hamlet, ready to follow her.

The Germans sprang out like monstrous black cats and raced toward the riverbank without a noise, a call. Their single, precise target was Dalibor, whose captain's insignia designated him as the rich prey they sought for ransom. Mansour leapt from the raft and drew his dagger; but when the soldiers did the same, Dalibor pushed them back on.

"No!" he shouted. "Take her to the other side first!"

Kallyna threw herself toward him with a scream of outrage. The soldiers forced her back onto the raft and started to work the oar with a hurry born of panic. She screamed until the opposite bank, where the soldiers left her while she still held onto them to go back. She fell down on her knees, bent over the wet grass that her hands grasped and tore up with a motion of agony. Behind her were all their mounts; without them Dalibor and the others had remained entirely defenseless.

Caught from all sides, Dalibor and Mansour defended themselves as best they could. Their swords clanged with an ominously hollow sound against the shafts of the terrible German halberds. The Germans wanted Dalibor alive. It didn't matter to them if he was blinded or maimed or bleeding from a hundred wounds, as long as he could still breathe for a week or two. The moment his ransom would be paid, he would be left to die.

After leaving Kallyna on the opposite bank, the soldiers were now hurrying to join the others. One of them never touched the ground. A mace flew through the air, cracking against his head. The soldier sank into the river, and the current carried a swirl of blood like wine spilled in a washtub. Kallyna's distant cries were the only human sound opposed to the din of the fighting. The soldiers jumped ashore and hacked their way through to Dalibor and Mansour, who were entirely surrounded.

She could see Dalibor defending himself truly with the strength of two men, with the maddening awareness of her alone on the other side of the river. He retreated more and more toward the edge of water, while Mansour and the soldiers covered him. Finally he was left facing a single adversary, who pursued him with a ferocious determination. Waist-deep in water, they kept lunging at one another. A more desperate blow from Dalibor's sword sent the German face down in the mud of the riverbank. Dalibor dived and started to swim.

Kallyna had crawled to the water's edge, stretching her arms out to him. She cried and called him over and over. The German dove after him and with a few strokes was right behind him, trying to grab hold of his leg. The two swords beat in the current like gleaming oars.

With her whole body she reached out for Dalibor as he splashed out of the water, helping him to his feet. The German, still floundering after him, snatched at her ankle, making her scream in terror. One of the oars had been left lying on the grass behind her. While the German scrambled up the bank, Dalibor dropped his sword, picked up the heavy paddle and swung it edgewise against the small of his back. The man fell forward; he started with an odd jerking motion, as if trying to stand, then became a still black lump.

Soaking wet, Dalibor and Kallyna held onto each other in a breathless embrace. Beyond the river the Germans were losing ground. Their quarry lost, the fight had become unprofitable. They let Mansour and the soldiers drive them back toward the edge of the woods. Then one of them shouted to the others in his unknown tongue, ordering the retreat. One by one they disappeared from sight, leaving behind too many dead for an unsuccessful ambush.

Mansour and the surviving soldiers ferried the stream. Dalibor mounted his horse, took Kallyna with him and started to ride ahead without a word.

❈　　　❈　　　❈

Toward noon the sea of Naples appeared, a sea of corals that had quenched the boiling lava of Mount Vesuvius and had received the bodies of Roman slaves fed to the moray eels.

They rode past Pompeii buried in its cradle of black ashes, past ruined flights of columns that had been the palaces of emperors and had become storerooms and stables. From the vast plain the sides of the great volcano rose up with a smoothly sweeping thrust. They rode along its slopes wondering in their minds, like everyone else who had ever stood in its shadow, whether the ancient fury was still brewing inside.

Silent with disquiet, Kallyna clung tightly to Dalibor. Yes, she thought, perhaps the war was over. Yet she knew well, like him, that in the times they lived in no war was ever really over. The road skirted empty beaches where no fisherman had returned. Here and there bloated corpses rolled in the slow dark waves. Along the way bands of scavengers hunted for dead to rob of weapons and clothes. Bones picked clean by the dogs didn't look as though they had belonged to oxen or donkeys.

In their room at the inn Kallyna stayed awake for a long time. She watched Dalibor sleep beside her, as if trying to convince herself that he was really there. It was as if having him near made her even wilder with worry, and her dread of being separated from him even deeper. But in the middle of the night Dalibor woke up and scattered all her nightmares with a single move of his hands, as he had disposed of the German at the river.

The following day dawned clear. All along the road was a stretch of beaches bordered by thick groves of umbrella pines.

"Husband, which dress do you think I should wear when we go to see Roger?"

"Makes not a bit of difference to me, wife."

"But I want to look pretty, really pretty."

"You waste time asking me. You know which way you look pretty to my eyes."

"Well then, if you don't tell me I'm going to look pretty that way for everybody!"

At last, at the end of the perfect crescent of its bay, there was Naples, bristling with towers   against the soft beauty of the hills. As they rode through Porta Nola, noise surrounded them from all sides, a liveliness like that of a bustling marketplace. If they had expected to find Naples in a chastened silence only because she had lost a war, they had been wrong. Naples is never silent; in fact, the more she is in pain the more she cries out.

They made their patient way through its crowded streets. Women sat in clusters by their front doors, immovable as dowager queens around a tray of sweets; pickpockets scampered away under the very eyes of the guards; children ran everywhere in noisy swarms; the air echoed with the whimsical chants of peddlers.

"Who wants my octopus? Boiled in sea water, tender as mother's teat!"

"They made love to the sunshine, these cherries!"

And beyond the dark tangle of alleys, beyond draperies patched out of laundry hung to dry, the sea murmured on, impartial as always.

They reached the Marina, packed with ships and fishing boats. Dalibor pointed at Castel dell'Ovo, high and isolated on the blue waters of the bay like a man-made island tethered only by a stone causeway.

"That's where we're going," he said. "Roger's been dreaming of waking up in that castle for I don't know how long."

Kallyna looked at the high walls and smiled. She could just see Roger yawning happily at one of the windows and breathing in the tang of the sea in that lovely May morning.

Two Neapolitan sailors in new uniforms let them through at the gate. Richard of Selby was coming down the stairs to meet them.

"Well arrived, my lord d'Hancourt," he greeted Dalibor pleasantly.

Dalibor dismounted, then held the stirrup for Kallyna.

"Well found, Richard." He nodded toward her. "Say hello to my wife."

Selby's eyes shifted to her with a look of surprise, the surprise Dalibor had expected, and not only from him. But young Richard was a faultless courtier; he bowed his head to her with the practiced grace of a pageboy.

"My lady, welcome. Your rooms are ready. I've put you all up on the same floor, I thought you would like that."

"Yes, thank you," Dalibor said. "Would you mind telling Roger that I'm here?"

Selby ushered them into the castle, waving a couple of servants along. "I'll be glad to oblige you."

"We'll look for Geoffroi in the meantime" Dalibor said. As they passed the chapel they saw a nurse go by with a newborn baby in her arms. Kallyna tugged at Dalibor's sleeve. "It's a baptism," she whispered. "Can we go watch?"

Dalibor rolled his eyes. "All right," he surrendered then. "I might as well get used to this sort of things now."

They followed the nurse to the chapel and sat in the last pew, away from the small group of relatives and guests. Under his breath Dalibor made fun of the baby's father, who looked disconcerted at the way his offspring kept shrieking inconsolably. Kallyna craned her neck to catch a glimpse of the baby, who was shaking his tiny fists inside a basket lined with white lace. At last the little heathen fell silent, while the priest began his prayers.

Then in a far corner of the chapel she noticed a man whose attitude of complete despair couldn't help but draw her attention. He was alone, on his knees and stooped low over the ledge of a bench. All that was left of his right arm was a stump that the empty shirtsleeve barely covered. He looked as if he was sobbing, but his shoulders were still, and that stillness seemed worse than tears.

She turned to Dalibor. "He looks familiar," she whispered.

"Really," Dalibor said. "He's just a cripple."

She looked again. A horrible suspicion was dawning in her mind. Then she put her hand on his and that gesture seemed to transmit her suspicion to him like a poison.

Dalibor shut his eyes. "O merciful God," he stammered.

They rose and stole up to the corner where the man was. Dalibor stopped behind him, unable to say the man's name or touch him. Finally he made him turn around.

Geoffroi's eyes shone with tears he didn't know how to shed, and with a naked, astonished humiliation. Dalibor staggered back, and Kallyna had to hold onto his arm.

"You know," Geoffroi said, "up to now I'd never set foot into a church because I wanted to..."

"When... how did it happen?" Dalibor asked.

Geoffroi lifted his left hand to the stump, as if trying to hide it. "Do you remember that small cut I got in Amalfi? No, of course you don't remember. I didn't notice it myself, at first... A small cut a boy might get while playing leapfrog..." His voice was full of horror and revulsion. "It got bad. It got black, swollen. They had to amputate..." He hung his head and was silent.

"A cut..." Dalibor murmured, dazed. He pulled Geoffroi to his feet and clasped him in his arms.

Geoffroi stood back, keeping him at a distance.

"I'm glad to see you both alive and well," he muttered. "The little witch especially... She looks like a rose." He started to walk away.

"Wait!" Dalibor called. "Please wait."

Geoffroi shook his head, still holding them both away from him.

"No," he said. "It doesn't matter. You are supposed to say things, but I don't want to hear. You're a good friend, and it's nobody's fault, as always."

He turned around and walked out.

XXIII

R ICHARD OF SELBY came to tell them that King Roger was ready to see them.

They had been waiting by the window of their room. They could hear the waves of the bay breaking with a soft sound against the sides of the castle, and the voices of fishermen and sailors in the ships passing below.

At the last minute Kallyna hid the lush spread of her hair under a long pink veil. Dalibor didn't like that self-effacing choice, although he knew it mirrored the sadness Geoffroi had put into their hearts; but the silver buckle was at her belt. He helped her set the veil around her head with a silver band. He kissed her on the cheek and walked out with her.

The room where Roger was waiting was graced with two rows of columns, all that remained of the villa of the last emperor of Rome, a boy of fourteen exiled by barbarian invaders. Roger had just finished putting his seal on a great sheaf of parchments, and he was now observing the columns with a look of curiosity. When the two guests walked in, he waved them in without averting his eyes.

"Do you know how this came to be called Castel dell'Ovo?" he asked. "Somewhere inside it a magician of old put a cage with an egg in it." He stood up, running his fingers on the blond marble. "They say that when the egg breaks the castle will be destroyed, and Naples with it." He grinned. "I hope the darn thing's still in one piece, wherever it might be."

Dalibor came in, holding Kallyna by the hand. This time Roger heard them; he turned around. It was known throughout the kingdom that he had a passion for handsome garments. For that day of triumph he was wearing a *dalmatica*, the garb of Byzantine rulers.

He was a man of forty-one at the apex of an exceptional life. In a time when a single individual could bend empires to his will, Roger seemed like the incarnation of majesty itself. Even his enemies called him "the man whose sleeping is the waking of others." And to see him smile out of genuine pleasure was a sight of grace.

"My dearest Dalibor! I didn't know it was you. Please sit here with me." He held out his hands to both, but he was looking only at Kallyna. She kept her head bent in a deep curtsy.

"*Mon Seigneur*," Dalibor said, and his heart was beating as fast as if he had been standing in front of his father. "I have brought you my bride."

Roger drew himself up.

"Really! Every woman I know will go into mourning."

He tried again to catch a glimpse of Kallyna's face behind the gauzy screen of the veil.

"But it's worth it... I think."

She raised immediately her face. Roger's eyes seemed to open a little wider for an instant. Then he frowned.

"Haven't we met before, my lady? You're the princess Alliata... no, no, Nicole de Crécy, am I right?"

Dalibor quietly intervened.

"*Mon Seigneur*, she's the lady d'Hancourt."

"Of course," Roger said. "Perfect choice, just like your father." He gathered the ample folds of his blue robe and sat with them by the huge windows opened onto the bay.

"Allow me to congratulate you on your victory, *Mon Seigneur*," Dalibor said, visibly more at ease. "This is truly a great day for all of us."

Roger looked at the city beneath him with a look of satisfaction.

"Aye," he said softly. "And by the grace of God she's finally mine, just like my wife was on our wedding night."

He was silent for a long moment, alone with his pride and haunted by the memory of his dead queen. He had so loved her that after more than ten years he refused to remarry, against the wishes of his entire court. Then he blinked.

"It would seem that the people of Naples have finally come to their senses," Dalibor said. "I cannot tell you how happy I am about this change of hearts."

"Indeed, dear friend," Roger replied. "This time, however, I intend to *keep* them thinking sensibly, whether they like it or not."

He nodded toward the parchment rolls cluttering his desk.

"You see these? They cost me — forgive the pun — a king's ransom. Tax exemptions, liberty charters, relinquishment of harbor duties... all to their advantage. But if a single word of discontent reaches my ears, I'll have their heads on a pole."

He waved his hands with a motion of annoyance.

"What's wrong with them, anyway? Can't they recognize a good king when they see one? They know they have as much to gain from me as I from them." Dalibor nodded. "They will find out soon enough, sire. But I am worried about the Germans. They are all over Campania."

Roger laid his hand on the smooth marble top. "Let them come. This side of the Straits of Messina, if they can. In a few months' time I will have my lands back once and for all. And the pope, who won't recognize me as king? I still don't know how or where, but I'll bring him over to my side, as I did with all my enemies. Purring like a cat in love, he'll be," he promised with a grin.

Then he stopped, looking at Kallyna with an air of dismay. "Good Lord," he sighed, "I'm getting old.... boring a woman to death."

Kallyna shook her head. "If you say so, sire," she ventured. "But I assure you, you do that more pleasantly than any man."

Roger burst into a delighted laughter. Dalibor saw that she was blushing crimson, and he gently took her hand to make her understand that she had committed no unpardonable sin.

"Listen to me, young man" Roger said then. "George of Antioch has been keeping that warship for you. Take it and enjoy your honeymoon in Monreale or wherever you wish. I will not bother you and your sweet wife with my wars for a good long time, and that's a king's promise. What do you say?"

Dalibor smiled. "I say I like your promises, *Mon Seigneur*. I was going to ask you for a leave of six months."

"Make it nine," Roger winked. He offered his arm to Kallyna to escort her to the door. There he knocked to call the footman.

"Oh, wait," he said. "I can't let you two go without a wedding present." He stood thinking for a moment, touching his beard. "Dalibor, are you familiar with those two large estates I keep near Monreale? Mondello and... help me with the name... Aspra, yes." He turned to Kallyna. "They're all one big almond grove. Marvelous to see when they bloom. How would you like them?"

"Sire, I—"

"I knew she would," Roger said.

He put his arm around her shoulders; his voice became sedate. "It's something I wanted to do for your husband when he saved Guglielmo's life in Amalfi. Vassals like him and his father are rare," he added, looking at Dalibor with gratitude and trust. "Four times my barons have rebelled against me, but not once have I doubted the loyalty of a d'Hancourt."

The footman opened the door. Kallyna bowed to the king and stepped out.

Still in the room, Roger drew Dalibor aside and spoke to him in a voice she couldn't hear.

"I know everything that happened in Amalfi," he whispered. "Guglielmo's ears are still stinging with the scolding I gave him. Nothing like that will ever happen again, not as long as I'm alive."

Astonished, Dalibor couldn't help frowning.

"Then you do know who my wife is?"

Roger nodded, smiling.

"As you said so well, she's the lady d'Hancourt, and that is all I care to know. Go know, and God bless you. You are a very lucky man."

Dalibor joined Kallyna out in the hallway. His eyes were fixed in those of Roger with a look of worship. They bowed their goodbye to him and walked away.

"And don't forget that I want to be godfather to your firstborn!" Roger called out after them.

❈   ❈   ❈

Night came slowly, almost reluctantly after such a day of triumph. Now another celebration had begun. Long garlands of torches were lit along the beach facing the castle. A procession of boats festooned with lamps rowed slowly around the massive slopes of its walls. Musicians and singers filled the warm twilight with their voices.

Sitting on the bed, Dalibor and Kallyna listened to the songs in a silence filled with pain. The thought of Geoffroi could not let them enjoy a time that should have been nothing but happiness. Finally he turned to her and touched her cheek. "I must go see him," he said.

"Please, yes," Kallyna begged him.

"You go to sleep, I might be late." He waited to see her lie down before leaving. Kallyna got back up as soon as he closed the door.

He looked first in the chapel; Geoffroi wasn't there. He went back up to the second floor and to Geoffroi's room. He put his ear to the door. When he heard strange broken noises inside, he beat his fist on the wall. At last he forced himself to knock.

Geoffroi kept him waiting for a long time. When he finally emerged from the darkness of the room, he was keeping his eyes half-closed and the door ajar, as if Dalibor were someone he couldn't trust.

"It's you," he muttered. "What do you want?"

"I want to talk to you," Dalibor said angrily. "You could at least open the door."

Geoffroi let him in without bothering to light a candle. They groped their way to a bench and sat there in the dark.

After a long silence Dalibor said, "Don't you think you've sulked enough? It's not a pleasure to see you like this."

Geoffroi laughed a hard, low laugh. "Whereas I am having a great time?"

"Damn it I think you are!" Dalibor blurted out. "I think you've just discovered a new pastime, ruining other people's peace of mind."

Geoffroi shrugged. "Your peace of mind and other people's peace of mind is no concern of mine. I've got my own scabs to scratch."

Dalibor shifted his weight, making the bench creak under him. "Fine. Just fine. It wasn't women who came between us, it wasn't war... It had to be this."

Geoffroi said nothing. After another long pause he asked, "What did Kallyna say? Do I disgust her?"

"Imbecile," Dalibor growled.

"Well, maybe not her," Geoffroi said. "She's good... She works healing on those around her. I guess in the end that's the only virtue worth having." He smiled a bitter little smile. "But so many other women I *will* disgust. It's a funny feeling... like I've been castrated. Do you know what I mean? Of course you do. All our damn lives you and I have been taught nothing else. Seems we were never trained for anything but handling a sword... And we can go around saying we don't like it, but we're wrapped in it up to our necks just the same."

In the darkness, because they could not see each other, they seemed to be talking each to himself.

"I've been thinking about becoming a monk," Geoffroi said then.

Dalibor made a noise of derision. "Dear Jesus. I thought you'd lost an arm, not your head. You, giving up the world?"

"Well, what else is there for me?" Geoffroi rebutted. "I've been going to a monastery these past days, just to be away from everything. But the things they told me are like wine... They will taste right only after a long time."

"Listen," Dalibor said eagerly, "why don't you learn instead how to use your left arm? Why don't I start teaching you tomorrow?"

Geoffroi answered with a tone of contempt that wounded him in his very soul.

"Why not, sweet lord. And will you also handle my reins, my lance and my shield? Ah, friend, never mind. Even a child would understand... I can hear them now... 'There goes Onearm de Vire, who can't hold his breeches up when he goes to piss.'"

Again silence fell between them, stubbornly. Through the closed and shuttered windows they could hear only the faintest strains of music coming from the celebration on the beach.

Then Geoffroi put his hand on Dalibor's shoulder.

"Look, forget about me. You would have anyway, now that you have her. As they say, it's another page of the book. I'll find something I can do."

Dalibor nodded. "The sooner the better. And no, I would not have forgotten you as easily as you hope," he grumbled. In the dark, Geoffroi smiled.

"To begin with," Dalibor said, "I won't be handling my own sword for a good while, either. Roger has given me a leave, and two new estates in Sicily. I plan to do nothing but watch the grass grow for at least six months. Don't you think we could both do that? Then we'll start worrying about the rest."

"Which lands are they?" Geoffroi asked.

"Near home. Mondello and Aspra."

"Good lands. I used to know a girl from Aspra—" He broke off. "Congratulations," he said. "When are you leaving?"

"I don't know yet," Dalibor said. "But when I do, I want you to come with us. Kallyna wants you to come with us. If you don't care about me, do it for her sake."

Geoffroi didn't answer, and Dalibor didn't force him to. After a while Geoffroi stood up.

"You'd better go back to her," he said.

"I'll go when I feel like," Dalibor replied. "Do you make me the sort of husband who's under his wife's thumb?"

Geoffroi's voice lightened into a tone of dispassionate surprise.

"So you finally did it." He sighed. "I might as well tell you the truth, then. You are the first man I have ever envied."

Impulsively, Dalibor threw his arms around him.

Geoffroi didn't return the embrace. "You make me feel like a father," he muttered. "Either because you've grown younger, or else because I've grown ten years older in a week." He pushed Dalibor away. "Now please," he begged, "please get out of here."

Dalibor left. As he walked into his room, he saw that Kallyna was still awake. He blew the candle out and lay next to her on the bed.

"I've lost him," he whispered, and his voice cracked. "He won't come with us. He might never come back."

She curled up against him without speaking. Tears gathered in her throat.

"He used to be like thunder to me," he said. "Something whose strength is taken entirely for granted, something that just could not be destroyed. I should have known better... There's nothing I can teach him."

✳   ✳   ✳

Mansour came to wake them up before dawn. Together they rode down to the Marina. With them were the maid and the valet Dalibor had hired; there would be no slaves in their house, he had told her.

In the dim light the ship rocked on the water, her stern features of war emerging from the night. Like on a Viking *drakkar*, shields hung all along the gunwale, and the figurehead was a crested dragon thrusting forward with the dawn in its teeth. The iron tail jutted out for ramming. Spears were bundled in tall sheaves, arrows in shorter ones. In a corner was the huge blackened cauldron where the Greek fire was boiled.

Kallyna drew her cloak around her. She stood watching Naples asleep behind her. The past two weeks had been all a celebration of peace. Now, again there was an unknown journey before her. She smiled thinly, touching Dalibor's hand.

"So this is where it ends, husband?"

His face was turned toward the sea and toward the future.

"This is where it begins, wife."

The first light of day was spreading behind the white cliffs of Posillipo. Fishermen were pulling up their full nets. The helmsman took his eyes off the last stars visible in the sky and welcomed the passengers aboard. Dalibor made a round of inspection of the ship, took formal possession, then ordered to weigh anchor. At the turning of the capstan the ship slipped away from the wharf, and the sea began its soft wash against the hull.

From the prow, Dalibor and Kallyna watched the coast, waiting for the sun to rise. He nudged her, nodding toward Mansour. His hands grasping the ropes, Mansour was listening to the familiar, long-lost sound of the sea with an air of rapture.

"I'll put him in charge of navigation," Dalibor whispered to her. "I'm sure he will love it. Besides, I know absolutely nothing about ships."

He lifted his arm toward the island of Capri, black and rosy on the horizon.

"It's true," he said, "it does have the shape of a sleeping girl." He sighed, becoming pensive. "This country of yours!" he said. "I've always thought that it's like a beautiful woman, too lovely for comfort. She's bound to attract the lust of all sorts of strangers... We Normans were only luckier than the others."

When it was broad daylight and the sun grew hot, the sailors stretched a canopy over the deck and brought a couple of benches. Kallyna poured Dalibor a cup of wine; then she picked up her sewing basket and started to thread a needle.

"What are you making?" he asked.

She spread out a great square of red silk.

"A banner for the mast, with the coat of arms of the d'Hancourts. Do you like it?"

He nodded, crossing his arms on his chest.

"Very much. I hope it's finished by the time we call at Tropea, so the whole town can see who's coming."

She looked up with a happy smile.

"We're stopping there? I wanted to ask you, but I wasn't sure I could do that."

He gave her a playful frown. "You still don't seem to understand how much you *can* do," he said. "I must stop at Tropea so I can buy from your uncle's landlord the farm, the vineyard and the spring."

"Why would you do such a thing?" she wondered. "Do you intend to become a farmer now, my lord d'Hancourt?"

He pinched her arm. "Who says I'm buying it for *my* side of the family? The farm is for your uncle and aunt, and for Arni. I want them all to enjoy it for many years to come."

She put down her needle and looked at him, shaking lightly her head.

"Oh husband." She took his hand. "Husband, you're the best half of the world."

Mansour stopped by to mention that one of the spars was cracked and must be mended right away.

"My friend," Dalibor said, "Take as many sailors as you need and make them work as hard as you wish."

Mansour bowed gravely his head. "We shall also need a new astrolabe."

Dalibor nodded with equal gravity. "Whatever that is, it is granted."

Mansour smiled and left.

Morning merged into noon. It was so wonderfully warm that Kallyna could hardly keep her eyes on her stitches. Her eyelids drooped with the most delicious drowsiness; she leaned back, daydreaming. Then suddenly she asked, "Did you ever regret marrying me?"

Dalibor tried to smother a growl. "That I will answer tonight. And I promise you, wife, it will be an answer you won't forget."

She muffled her mouth with the red silk cloth to keep from laughing too loud. After a moment she took up her work again. "I'm not used to all this," she said. "I don't know how to handle power... I'm afraid of doing the wrong thing, saying the wrong word..."

"I've been trying to learn that myself all my years," he said quietly. "I have handled power badly more than once…" He stopped, then looked the other way. "I don't need to remind you what was the worst time ever."

In the silence that followed they could hear the soothing sound of the waves against the side of the ship, and the long creaking of the mast. Kallyna's hands become idle again on the red silk.

"I remember that once we were sitting in the garden making nets," she said then slowly, "and Arni asked my father, *"Father, if someone offered you power, would you take it?"* And my father shrugged and said, *"If you ask me Vasili d'Àrgira, I don't think I would. But there's more than one side,"* he said. He picked up the knife that he'd been using to cut the loose ends of the nets, and he showed it to Arni. *"Power is like this knife,"* he said. *"You can use it to slit a man's throat, to erase the face of God painted on the wall of a church. Or you can use it to cut up and share bread, to carve the name of a bride on a wedding chest. If a man is a good man, a truly good one in his soul, he will always know how to use the knife."*

She bowed her head; her eyes welled up at the memory. Dalibor took her in his arms.

"I believe he was just such a man," he said.

Suddenly Kallyna had to steady herself against him. A wave of dizziness blurred everything around her. She had felt like that all morning. "Good Lord," she grumbled. "Born and raised on boats, and all of a sudden I'm seasick."

He took a step backwards and turned her around. He bent his face toward her and peered at her. "Seasick?" he gasped. "That's not what it is! Seasick!" he shouted, laughing as she had never see him laugh before. He rocked her in his arms, her and the precious new life that was inside her. Then she understood; she closed her eyes and held onto him, stunned with joy.

Underneath them the sea wrapped white garlands of foam around the ship. From a distance the land rose in a mist as light as a bridal veil. Men were seeds, she thought, battling the wind to ensure survival, and women were roots, deep in the earth that never changes. Life was a dandelion, a thirsty thing that kept stubbornly blooming at the start of each new, short and magnificent summer.

PART FOUR

T HE STONES ARE PATIENT. Those of Athens must be even more so, for they are very old and they have seen so much. In a warm autumn night of the year 1147 the city seemed to be burning from the top of the Acropolis down to the Piraeus, and the noise kept the moon awake.

The Norman fleet had conquered the islands of Corfu and Zakintos, had sacked Corinth and Thebes, and had now invaded the ancient queen of the Mediterranean with unexpected fury. Down in the harbor the ships had been swallowing plunder like hungry whales day and night — gold, silver, priceless marbles and bronzes.

But the most special care was reserved for the most treasured prize of the Empire of Byzantium, the silk mill. A squadron of soldiers was busy stripping it of all it contained. One by one they hoisted on carts the looms that were worth nearly their weight in gold because of their excellence and size. They drove them away along with thick skeins of Chinese silk shimmering like frozen brooks in the torchlight.

From the doors of the mill the men and women who had worked the looms watched them roll away. Soon they would join them, bound for Palermo, where they would weave in the *Tiraz* no longer for the glory of Byzantium but for that of King Roger d'Hauteville.

Dalibor turned around in his saddle to see why his sergeant wasn't joining him. Then he cantered back to the mill alone. He left the horse at the entrance and ran up the stairs. Flames flickered outside the broken windows; the stairs were littered with torn mosaic pieces and shattered glass. On the first floor he spotted the sergeant.

"My lord, we've found about twenty women," the man said with a tone of urgency. "Some have children with them."

Dalibor didn't answer, but by instinct he lowered his sword.

The sergeant pointed out a door for him. Shrieks and yells and noise filled the room. The women were heaped together like a litter of blind puppies. They kept the children pressed against their bodies as if wanting to force them back into their flesh, where no one could hurt them.

The soldiers were trying to separate them from the youngsters, who screamed and cried; they had been able to pull nine or ten out of the group, but the women lunged desperately back toward the children. As Dalibor was coming in, a soldier dragged a pregnant woman away from the others and kicked her. Dalibor threw himself onto the man, grabbed him hard by the scruff of the neck and shoved him against the wall.

"What in the name of hell is going on here?" he demanded to know. "Are you my men or a pack of mad dogs?"

The soldier started to wave his hands in defense of himself. "They won't let go of their brats, my lord... They scream and bray and make every damn thing harder for us."

"Then let them keep their children," Dalibor shouted. "What difference do a dozen little ones make, you imbecile?"

One woman, her head twisted backwards, was screaming louder than all the others.

"Vasili!" she called. "Vasili!"

The way she cried out that name, the anguish she put into every syllable as if her soul were being torn from her, made Dalibor start. Suddenly the little boy she was calling, perhaps eight years old, sprang out of his hiding place. Instead of running to his mother he lunged at Dalibor with all the strength in his small fist. Dalibor grabbed the boy by the arm. The woman turned to him imploringly, and he winced: she looked like Kallyna, only grown old before her time.

Dalibor handed his sword to the sergeant. He stared at her, then at the boy who kept struggling against him. The boy stared back with a look of challenge, undaunted. Dalibor walked over to the woman and forced her to stand still in front of him.

"Look at me," he said. "Don't be afraid. Look at me."

The woman tossed in his grip, crazed with fear. "Vasili!" she called again. "Don't touch him, don't you touch my Vasili!"

"Are you Sila d'Àrgira?" Dalibor asked.

The woman seemed to recoil, as if hit by a slap. She looked at him with pain and astonishment. "My name is *You there*. Nobody's called me anything else for eleven years." Her eyes glared under her disheveled hair. "What do you want from me?"

Dalibor took her face in his hands, searching her features. "It cannot be," he whispered. "I must be wrong…"

"Please give me back my son," the woman begged.

Dalibor led the boy into her arms. "Here. No one's going to hurt him."

As he was turning around to leave, the woman ran after him and grabbed his sleeve.

"Wait. I am Sila d'Àrgira. Who are you?"

Dalibor's face opened slowly into a smile of wonder. He took her gently in his arms, trying to make her stop shaking.

"Don't cry," he said, "don't cry. We'll have time."

Once the women were allowed to have their children back, they stood up quietly, opposing no more resistance, and left the mill without having to be threatened or pushed.

❋ ❋ ❋

The place Kallyna loved most in her house in Monreale was the loggia surrounding the garden. The olives on the trees below were ripe, and she could hear the songs of the pickers along with the cries of seagulls. She leant against one of the carved arches overhung with geraniums, surrendering to the sweetness of the sunny December noon. She looked at the letter she had been reading, and smiled.

"Beloved wife. Although it was not my intention to address you in such a conventional manner, I must explain that the worthy person helping me to write this letter is a man of the cloth, so that I am forced to dispense with further marital niceties. You will be pleased to know that I am in good health and that the war in Greece is over. We have secured the Ionian Islands to the rule of our lord Roger, and we have challenged the might of Byzantium to its very heart. So laden are our ships that the hulls sink to the third line of oars—"

She looked up. An elderly nurse was coming up from the garden, with two young boys scampering around her ample skirts. The woman trudged on gamely, pretending to be running away, while the boys chased her wielding wooden swords.

"Come on, come on, let the Byzantines have it!" the boys cried, and not in a playful way.

Puffing and giggling, the old woman came up to Kallyna.

"Bless my heart, the little lords are as healthy as colts... With what little food they eat!"

Kallyna pressed the children to her.

"My treasures, I have wonderful news. Father's coming home!"

Nine-year-old Ruggero, looking already like a man with his handsome serious face, wanted to know when.

"Soon, my love, soon," she answered. "Are you happy?"

The boy beamed.

"Oh yes! I have to show him how well I can leap the black mare over the pond. I've been trying for more than a week."

But younger Goffredo began to pout, stricken by one of the many woeful afterthoughts of his five years of age. "Mother, do you think he'll bring me the present I asked for?"

Kallyna put her hand under his chin. "And what did you ask for?"

Goffredo hesitated, making a grim face. "A yellow parrot. But I know he won't bring it to me, I know."

Kallyna laughed. "A yellow parrot! Why I don't even know if they have parrots in Greece." She picked him up. "We'll just have to wait and see, all right?"

Goffredo bobbed his head. "All right."

She handed him over to the nurse. "Rosa, did you send for Padre Iacopo?"

"Yes, mistress," said the nurse. "He should be here any minute."

Goffredo began to whine. "Mother, I don't want Padre Iacopo to come to our house," he protested. "I'm scared of him… He told me he has only one arm because a dragon came to snap the other one off and ate it!"

Kallyna kissed him on the cheek. "No, love, that was just a story. You know he likes to make up stories like that. If you keep being such a wise child nothing bad can ever happen to you, nothing."

Goffredo twisted his mouth, unconvinced. The nurse walked with the two boys back into the house.

"You're so silly," Ruggero chided his younger brother. "Still believing in dragons like a baby."

Kallyna followed them with her eyes. Then she returned to her letter.

"I long to be reunited with you and with our children. You know well already how hard it can be for us all, but do pluck up courage. This time I am bringing you a gift that should be quite impossible for you to guess. I shall say only that it's a most extraordinary one, and that it will make you extra-ordinarily happy…."

Again she raised her head with a puzzled look, trying to imagine what that amazing gift could possibly be. Then she folded the letter in two and gave up. She heard the bell ring at the gate, and hastened down the brick steps hedged with cypress trees. Behind the wrought-iron curls of the gate she saw Padre Iacopo's brown robe. She lifted a key from the many that hung from her belt and opened it.

"*Pax vobiscum,* Donna Kallyna."

"I hope I haven't bothered you, Padre."

"You know you never bother me," the monk said, smiling. "I was coming here anyway, for that prayer book I'm making. I didn't know whether you wanted your name on the first page or on the Nativity page."

Kallyna grinned.

"With two children alive, one dead, and a fourth on the way, I think the Nativity page would be more appropriate... with all due respect to the Holy Mother, of course."

Padre Iacopo burst into a loud, healthy laugh. Even at a glance one could see that he was a most singular monk. The habit never seemed to fit him, too short and too tight, with the right sleeve cut in half. He had been wearing it for eight years, yet on him it still looked like a suit of mail.

"How's everything at the monastery?" Kallyna asked as she walked with him back to the loggia.

"As usual," he replied, "and thank God for that. The harvest will be good this year, I should be able to set something aside for my orphans."

He turned to her.

"You should just see them, Donna Kallyna... They're such a bunch of helpful rascals! If I ask for a paintbrush or a pot of ink, they fight with each other to fetch it."

"What you do for them is a true blessing," Kallyna said. "But then you've always been a generous man."

Padre Iacopo eyed her sideways.

"Well... as the Gospel says, I don't let my left hand know what my right one is doing."

She wrinkled her nose. "God, what a way of joking you have."

They sat together on a marble bench. Kallyna handed him the letter.

"This is why I called you. Dalibor's coming back. Seems that the war in Greece has been a good venture."

The monk took the sheet of paper, held it at a distance from his eyes and read while moving his lips in his grizzled beard. Kallyna lay back against the wall and reached for the small silken blanket she had been embroidering. It would be wonderful if it was a girl this time, she thought.

Padre Iacopo nodded.

"Uh. Whoever wrote this letter surely larded it with plenty of misspellings."

He looked up. "I'm very, very glad he's coming home. In war the hard part is coming home." He laughed. "But he certainly knows how to keep you in suspense with this big present of his, doesn't he?"

She shook her head, sighing. "Quite. I can't make anything of it... I guess I'll have to wait and see, just like Goffredo and his yellow parrot."

After a moment she looked at him with an air of quiet curiosity. "Please don't take it wrong, but every time I see you I can't help noticing how little you seem to miss the outside world. While you were teaching to your boys Roger took North Africa, and while you were making the Book of Psalms for the cathedral they launched another Crusade. Now you're painting me a prayer book, and we have stormed the Byzantines in their own home... yet I've never heard you say a word about all this. It's a comfort to see you so distant from our squabbles, so at peace."

Padre Iacopo's eyes wandered in the distance. "My peace is still young, Donna Kallyna. But it's growing up. I've seen what hell is like... real hell, not the one I make up to scare my flock."

She noticed how many wrinkles had blossomed on his face. He spoke in a low, gentle voice.

"All my life I'd lived by a mentality of rank, of major and minor lords all set on a ladder according to each one's power... And then all of a sudden there I was, with no rank and no power at all..." He paused. The sound of a loom came faintly from inside the house, and a smell of fresh hay from the garden.

"I began to think of God as the ultimate overlord," he went on, "the one who would protect me from the others. If I don't seem interested in the world it's only because I can't afford to be... because there were too many things in the world that I loved."

There was a moment of silence that passed between them like a brief winter hiding the scars of the earth under a blanket of snow. Then Padre Iacopo clapped his hand on his knee.

"Enough with this nagging. Where are those two little devils of yours? I have an account to settle with Ruggero. The last time he came to church he shoved a dead lizard down my collar."

Kallyna suppressed a laugh. She looked at him quietly.

"Was I ever... one of the things you loved?" she asked evenly.

He held back, taken by surprise. "Funny how much time keeps going by all the time..." he mused. "Yes, I have loved you. But in a very different way than Dalibor's. I'm a man of very simple needs. I've always thought you'd be completely wasted on me."

Kallyna didn't reply. After a while she stood up. "I'll call Rosa for some wine. Or would you like something else? A week ago we made some rose-petal jam... Mansour's wife gave me this exotic recipe of hers, I couldn't resist it."

Padre Iacopo twisted his mouth, but he was smiling.

"*Which* wife? That heathen never seems to have enough. Every time I go to his house there are more shoes at his door than at the door of a mosque!"

Kallyna couldn't keep herself from chuckling.

"Ah, but he can afford it. And he can afford to treat them all equally, as the Qu'ran prescribes. He's quite wealthy now. His ship visits every port, for spices, for cotton and oranges. He says he wants to open a store in Acri... which will probably mean wife number four."

She knocked on the balcony's shutters to call the nurse.

"The ways of the world, truly," she marveled quietly. "If you had asked me, I would have said you would end up the family man and Mansour the hermit."

Rosa peeked out.

"Please bring us some wine and something to eat," Kallyna told her. "And some jars of the new jam from the pantry." Then she went back to Padre Iacopo, who was leaning from the stone railing.

"And how is everything here at the house of the d'Hancourts?" he asked.

Kallyna snapped a yellow leaf from a geranium.

"Everything is going to be right as soon as Dalibor comes home... But I can't complain. God knows I'm busy enough, what with the olive harvest, and the well that went dry in Aspra, and the overseers who want to talk to me all at the same time… Any caretaker would have his hands full, even one without morning sickness."

She let the geranium leaf fall from her hands. Beyond the garden, on the mule path, a peasant was pushing his loaded donkey.

"You know," she said, "you're one of the few people who still call us d'Hancourt. Our name has become Italian… Now we are the Accorti."

Padre Iacopo shook his head.

"Small loss, like Hauteville turning into Altavilla. Nothing that this land has changed was ever much of a loss to us. A hundred years ago, before we came here, we were nothing but cattle thieves and mercenaries. I don't remember ever seeing a library in our villages in Normandy… or a harem, but that's another story."

Rosa came in bringing a full tray and left it on the bench.

Kallyna poured wine in a cup and opened one of the four large jars of jam.

"Some weeks ago I was in Palermo. There are some girls in the Tiraz that I've taken under my wing because they're very talented. Someone there told me that times like ours will probably never come back. They said this is *La Bella Monarchia*, the Good Kingdom. I think they're quite right," she said, "and Roger's still sound as a bell, he'll reign for another hundred years."

Padre Iacopo nodded in full agreement. He scooped some rose-petal jam on a biscuit and let out a sound of pleasure. "Donna Kallyna, this is delicious!"

"I'm glad you like it. Then please take all four jars with you when you leave, more if you want. I'm sure your orphans will appreciate it a lot more than my two spoiled princelings."

"You call them spoiled? Out all day rolling around with the sons of fishermen and peasants!"

"And believe me, Padre, they learn more from their playmates than from all the teachers and tutors we find for them."

"Including me, of course," Padre Iacopo said. She bit her lip; but he just looked at her and laughed. "It's quite all right" he said. "Their father went to the same school, and if I'm not mistaken, it did him a world of good."

Kallyna took the small blanket on her knees and looked for the needle she had left stuck in the cloth. "Sometimes I feel sorry for them, you know, having to grow up without grandparents."

Padre Iacopo smiled in his beard, looking at her hands that smoothed the fine pink silk. "You and Dalibor are the best of parents."

She bent her head to one side. "Still, we ask so much of them, like all parents…" Another small season of silence passed between them.

She looked at the house around her, remembering all the many good years she had spent in it. The stones had a texture almost like bread crust, and in its many creases the honeysuckle grew. The wooden rafters of the roof looked each as different from the other as the fingers of a hand.

She laid her head against the pillar. It was warm, and it was peaceful. Where the stone was too rough, the cheek of a flower softened it, and where the light was too naked the wood cupped the shadow in its secret holds. All those years with Dalibor had been like that, staying together and taking from each other what each alone could never have; in that terrible year, too, when the baby had died two days after he was born and they had buttressed each other through their grief.

Everything fell in place around her. The world felt whole, and she was a very lucky woman.

❋   ❋   ❋

The sowers in the fields at the sides of the road raised their heads and waved at the small group as it rode toward the harbor. Ruggero had wanted to go in front with the armed escort. He looked as if he were daydreaming, leading the men to some bold adventure perhaps, because he sat all upright in the saddle with a martial air. Little Goffredo had preferred to stay close to his mother, and he dozed off in the arms of the servant who shared his horse. Monreale behind them was red and golden as an apple, a skyline of bellowers and crescent-topped domes. By now the ship would be mooring. Yesterday the fleet had returned to Palermo, there had been triumph and rejoicing in the capital; but Kallyna wanted no other celebration than to see Dalibor walk once again into her arms.

"There!" she cried out.

The great sail with the Hauteville banner rested securely in the harbor, tall above the colored wings of the fishing boats. She wished she could put her horse to a gallop and outstrip everyone else, but the baby inside her wouldn't let her. Goffredo woke up with a start of anticipation.

"Come on, come on," Kallyna said impatiently.

A boat had already come ashore from the ship, and a small crowd had gathered around it. The men took off their caps and welcomed my lord, talking all at once. Ruggero jumped off his saddle and dashed through to his father. Then he flew briefly in the air as Dalibor tossed him high above his head. Dalibor was trying to embrace all three of them at once, and he was laughing.

"Too many of you, too many! I ought to have eight arms like an octopus!" But then he put the boys down and hugged only Kallyna. "Wife! And what's happened to you, wife? You've grown all over like bread dough. Great fat wife of mine."

"Please, not so tight," she gasped. "Let me look at you, how are you?"

He tried to put his face in her throat, but she squirmed out of his reach. The women around them started to titter.

"I'm all right all over, except for sweat making me itch sometimes," he lowered his voice, "and a few other itches and horribly impure thoughts, about laying my hands on you and—" He glanced down; Goffredo was staring at him with his big blue eyes.

"And little Malva?" Dalibor asked, putting his hand on Kallyna's stomach. "How has she been?"

"She's been a very good girl so far," she answered. "But pretty soon she should start kicking."

Goffredo tugged at his father's sword with a glowering look. "Who's little Malva?" he demanded to know.

Dalibor picked him up with one arm. "Your sister, God willing. Hey, why that long face?"

"I didn't ask for a sister!" Goffredo protested, outraged. "I asked for a yellow parrot!"

Dalibor ruffled the boy's blond hair, putting him down. "You rascal... Go look in that boat over there." Goffredo was off at a run.

He turned to Kallyna. "You don't want to know what *your* present is? I thought I'd have you standing on live coals with curiosity by now."

Kallyna shook her head. "I know all about my present. It's this tall and it needs a bath." She frowned, putting her hand on his head. "What did you do to your hair?"

Dalibor shrugged. "I'm starting to lose it. I thought I'd crop it."

A second boat was rowing from the ship. Dalibor pointed at it with a proud smile. "Wife, take a look at that."

A cry of joy rose from the boat that was already ashore. Goffredo had found the wicker cage and was jumping up and down. He splashed in the surf, shouting. He fell against Kallyna's skirts, breathless.

"Look, Mother, look!" He held up the cage, showing the small yellow parrot inside it. "It's just like the one I wanted!"

Kallyna was still watching the rowboat. "Who's that woman?" she asked, screening her eyes against the sun. "And that little boy...?"

Dalibor poked a finger at her. "Go see for yourself." Then he saw her losing all her color, her eyes shrinking to a look of utter amazement, and he stopped her. "No, wait. I forgot that in your condition the last thing you needed was this sort of surprises."

"Dear God," she whispered, with her hand on her mouth. "Oh dear, dear God."

Sila looked dazed, awkward in the fine gown that had replaced her ragged dress. Vasili goaded the rowers on with a commanding gesture, as if impatient to be restored to the freedom he had never known but seemed to have always considered his birthright. He was so self-assured that Goffredo, with the precise intuition of his age, instantly recognized him as his peer.

Dalibor followed Kallyna with a look of concern as she walked to the boat. Leaning over, Vasili kissed her on the cheek as unaffectedly as if he had only been away from his aunt for a few days. Kallyna started to weep, looking at him in awe.

He resembled no one but his mother. Whoever his father was, Sila seemed to have managed without him when she had made that boy. She had poured all of her into her son, as if to create a living replica of herself. He must have been loved of a love so savage and complete as no other child ever was; and he was a beautiful, proud child.

Dalibor gently led Sila into Kallyna's arms. Sila was quite calm. She watched Kallyna with a sort of curious sympathy.

"It's all right, sister," she whispered. "Please don't cry."

Kallyna spoke at one voice with her.

"I'm not crying," she sobbed, "I'm not crying…. Oh God, I love you so much. And Mother?" she asked. "And Michele?"

"Mother died a few days after they took us," Sila said. "It was much better like that," she added with serene conviction. "Michele was sold off. I'm sure he's alive, wherever he may be."

The small crowd around them pressed closer, whispering. Dalibor watched with a look of worry the way Kallyna kept putting her hand to her lap. Finally he ordered his men to start moving toward home. Ruggero and Goffredo were confused, jealous; but when they got home Ruggero reached out to take Vasili's arm in the gesture of welcome he had seen his father use with his guests.

It was a noisy, happy afternoon. Kallyna had no peace, and wanted none, until everything had been said about the past and a thousand plans had been made about the future. Dalibor had to force her three times to sit down and be still for a while.

"We'll start all over again, Sila," she kept saying. "You'll have the best there is. We'll make up for everything, for everything."

It was night already when at last the house grew quiet and she joined Dalibor in their bedroom, drained with excitement and joy. Dalibor came out of the tub, wrapped himself in a sheet and glanced at her, sunk in a chair as if no strength were left in her body.

"That boy is going to steal my heart," she said. "He looks like a little prince. Isn't he beautiful?" Suddenly she started to cry again, her face turned away.

Dalibor didn't speak. He rubbed himself dry and got into bed. Kallyna kept puttering around the room, picking up the sheet from the floor, bolting the windows. She knew he was waiting, but she wanted time.

"Your nosepiece seems properly bent," she said, nodding toward the helmet he had tossed on a chair.

"Oh, that. Thank God for Norman helmets. I never figured out why others don't have a nosepiece. Maybe that's why we Norman males are prettier than most."

Kallyna still wouldn't join him. "It took me all these years," she finally whispered painfully to herself. "All these years to convince myself that they were really lost... Now it's as though everything were happening all over again."

Dalibor stretched under the blanket. His voice was tired, but gentle.

"Nothing ever happens all over again. Sleep now, and start thinking about it some other day. Better yet, don't think about it at all."

"Perhaps," she said, sitting on the bed. Then she turned toward him. "Dalibor, I don't know who she is, and she doesn't know who I am. It's as if I've taken into my house a perfect stranger."

"She heals quite well," he replied. "In the time it took us to return from Greece she was another woman already. Why, up to a minute ago *she* was the one who comforted you!"

Kallyna was silent for a while, twisting her hands together. Then she shook her head.

"You don't understand. I feel... guilty toward her. How can I explain it?" she fretted. "I feel it should have happened to me. I just can't get rid of this thing, it poisons everything else."

He smiled, looking at her from the pillow. "You don't seem to know what you're saying, wife. If it had happened to you, you would have never survived. Some birds can learn to live in a cage, others die of heartbreak just at the thought of a cage."

Kallyna stopped torturing her hands and raised her head, as if a great weight had been lifted from her shoulders.

"Yes," she murmured. "Yes, you're right. You said the right thing…. Oh husband, thank you. You don't know what you just did for me… Now and all my life, you don't know what you did for me!"

Dalibor took her arm and pulled her down beside him. "It's going to be all right. She might marry soon. I'm sure you already have a few prospective suitors in mind?"

"No, but now that you brought it up, I'm sure I'll find a few… It would be nice, wouldn't it? And we must go to Tropea soon, we must see Arni and his wife and little Neia who will be seven years old next month…."

She slid between the sheets and looked at him with an air of happy surprise, as if seeing him for the first time.

"What are you doing in my bed?" she chuckled. "It's been such a long time, I'd finally gotten used to the extra room."

He put his hand on her shoulder and pushed her down.

"Be quiet now," he grumbled. "Do you *know* how long you've kept me waiting this time?"

❋   ❋   ❋

"So tell me, husband, how are Greek women?"

"There she goes, always the same question. How are French women, how are Sicilian women, how are African women, how are Greek women."

He looked at the ceiling, his expression so perfectly blank that, as usual, she could make nothing of it.

"And how would I know, wife?"

"You too always give me the same answer," she said, frowning.

He hacked at the air with his big hands.

"Lord, this woman's out of control. Listen, wife, you will *never* know the truth, and shall I tell you why? Because either way we would both be sorry. If I told you that yes, I do go to bed with other women while I'm away, you would blind me with your nails in my sleep. And if I told you that no, that I keep myself as chaste as some Sir Galahad of old, you would convince me most thoroughly that I've become impotent. Holy Mother," he concluded, feigning despair.

She pounded his chest with her fist, laughing.

"Damn you, husband, you're always right."

The night had grown deeper. It was the time when the silence belonged all to them. Dalibor drew Kallyna closer to him.

"What did you do while you were waiting for me?" he asked.

"A world of things. The most important thing I did was wait for you."

Her words touched him, but he preferred to turn to gentle irony. "You think small."

She shrugged. "I don't care."

As she lay against him, she felt a sudden ripple, like a shiver coursing through her. Dalibor felt it too, and put his hand on her body. "There she is!" he whispered. "She just moved... and some kick it was. I don't know how I'm going to survive with three women in this house," he mused.

✳   ✳   ✳

The following day Kallyna sent a messenger to Tropea to let Arni know about Sila's return. Together with the message, the man carried a piece of paper she had given him at the last minute.

It was an inscription she wanted to have carved on Vasili's tombstone, a message she had long wanted to send to her father across the years that had grown between them. She had sought the right words, changing them and then putting them back together. Now, with Sila found back, the time was right.

But no one seemed to understand. No one could have, because her words expressed a thought that was centuries ahead of its time, like Vasili had been a man centuries ahead of his time. When the carvers were finished with the stone and set it back into the floor, the brief ribbon of words merged smoothly with the dappled light of the chapel.

"If work confers nobility upon man, Vasili d'Àrgira is most noble."

AUTHOR'S AFTERWORD

I WAS BORN IN THE SOUTHERN ITALIAN REGION OF CALABRIA, and I lived in Southern Italy for thirty years, half of my life. I know its people, studied its history, witnessed the customs and traditions, traveled the roads and visited the towns. All that I describe in the novel comes from personal research and personal knowledge. By the latter I mean also the split between lords and commoners that was the most distinctive feature of the feudal age.

My mother's mother was the Marchesa di Montecorvino, who still used her family crest and title. The nobility was officially abolished in Italy in the 1930s, but the Old South is slow. My father's father was a peasant, who after a lifetime of hard work was able to buy the lands he had worked on and leave them to us. The inscription Kallyna puts on Vasili's tomb is paraphrased from the one carved on my grandfather's tombstone: "If work confers nobility upon man, Giuseppe Idà is most noble"

The same religious plays are still staged at Christmas, Easter, and other occasions. The Easter ritual of the *Vattienti* was abolished in the 1800s, but it has come back in a less gruesome form. When Tresa curses, "May the black soul of Mohamet drag them all to ruin," I hear the same words spoken — but only playfully — by my aunts and grandmothers. They loved to frighten us unruly youngsters with threats of *Mahammetta mu ti raha,* as if Mohammed were a bogeyman still haunting the collective memory of the Calabrese, who suffered for centuries the raids of pirates from the northern coast of Africa.

Yet the same devout old women who used that oath still used to go to church wrapped in their black shawls that left free only a small portion of the face, like the women of North Africa. Italy, which in the course of her history has seen over half a dozen foreign dominations, is a true melting pot of cultures. The presence of several languages in the novel also reflects this. In the times of the Norman domination, in the Southern half of the Peninsula at least six languages were spoken: Greek, Latin, Arabic, Hebrew, Italian and French. To these must be added countless regional dialects, such as Calabrese and Sicilian.

All these cultures merged together between the 11th and the 13th century to form what is called "the first Italian Renaissance." The historical background of the novel is still a part of everyday life. Many for instance are named Altavilla, the Hauteville of the original Norman French. Today's Altavilla are the descendants of the Twelve Brothers of Normandy who came to Italy around 1016 C.E. and stayed to found what would later be called the Kingdom of the Two Sicilies, destined to endure whole in its original boundaries for over eight hundred years.

Tropea was my family's favorite summer resort. We discovered it long before it became "the gem of the Tyrrhenian Sea" that today attracts tourists from all over Europe. Every year we would rent from Signor Fazzari his 17th-century palazzo, which had something like twenty rooms, high ceilings covered with faded frescoes and antique furniture. We always had the most wonderful summers. My playmates were the sons of the local fishermen, who still go out after the swordfish in their *ontri* with the tall mast for the lookout and the catwalk for the spearman.

My father and I were tireless explorers, always seeking out someone who could find for us the keys to a castle or a cathedral closed to the public for centuries. The Normans were great builders, who dotted all of Southern Italy with fortresses, watchtowers and churches. In my hometown of Arena, during the reign of Roger d'Hauteville my paternal ancestors built for the local lords Culchebret the only acqueduct built in ancient times in Italy between the Lombard one in Salerno and the Roman one in Agrigento. The Idà family is still known as "Pilieri"; in French, the Normans' mother tongue, *pilier* means a pillar or pylon.

The castle of Aieta, because of its panoramic location has been transformed into a luxury hotel. On the ground floor is a fashionable discotheque called, of course, *I Normanni*. On its door is a neon sign representing three fierce-looking knights in Viking helmets. I've always wondered what they think of the music.